NOVA

BOOK 1 IN THE TIME
BENDER SERIES

BY

ISABELLE CHAMPION

For my mother, who inspired my love
for storytelling

Dear reader,

It's hard to assign a specific genre to this book. But with its dystopian themes, I feel the need to put a disclaimer out there: the story is told from the point of view of the corruption itself. So much so that instead of being described as 'morally grey', Nova was once described as 'light black'. Therefore, let it be known I don't encourage stabbing, maiming, killing or throwing people off of buildings. Despite her lack of morals I hope you fall hopelessly in love with Nova's dark humoured, sassy personality and follow her on her journey of self-discovery.

More importantly, I feel I should put a trigger warning here. There is some mention of sensitive topics such as rape, violence and suicide.

So now that we've met, I'll shut the hell up and let you escape into a world of time travel, assassins, reincarnation and romance. I'll see you on the other side...

PROLOGUE

So turns out I'm pretty awesome. Like superhero – god worthy kind of awesome. I'm guessing you've heard of reincarnation? You die, you get reborn blah blah blah life after death, whatever. Boring.

Well, I've been reincarnated more times than I can count. Sure, I don't remember every single detail of all my lives so that's kind of a let-down. But the fact I have hundreds of lives where I look exactly the same, have certain recurring themes, and can actually go travel to any life I choose, is pretty mind-blowing to most people.

I don't know which person upstairs screwed up by bringing me into existence or giving me this power but I'm not complaining.

It's complicated and I'm probably not as good at explaining it as Vix was but I know the basics so brace yourself for a headache.

It's easy to think of it as a timeline. I live all my lives on this one continuous timeline, the end of it being the present. This is *the* Timeline. The timeline I come from. Now - there are other timelines - all parallel to mine. Some are shorter, some longer but the ends of each timeline are different presents - some seconds, minutes or years in difference.

I have the ability to visit any of these timelines presents providing I have a life during one of those moments and I'm not dead. Although I've organised the parallel timelines in a way that meant all the ones I'd visited before and hadn't bent with my own - stayed far away - in the bin as I liked to think.

So yes it's confusing. I have multiple lives (208 if we're talking numbers) and there are multiple timelines (infinite amounts) - like parallel universes almost, but all usually remain the same as the past of my own timeline... providing us Time Bender's don't come along and mess with it.

Anyway, I can follow my Totem into a timeline with the present of the exact time I need and I essentially possess my past self. (What's a Totem you might ask? I'll get to that later). Bending time (or a timeline) is a whole other confusing topic and they don't teach it at school... well, not that I'd know because I've been doing this since I was 10 and I was basically the first to discover changing the future by going into past lives.

Look it's confusing which is why I'm trying to explain it before we get into the really juicy part. Your mind is either open to the "power" or it's not. For example, it should be impossible to make changes in the past that cause the future to change, right? Because cause comes before effect, not effect before cause. Stay with me. Have you ever watched *'Back to the Future'*? Let's say you travel to the past and meet your granddad when he was five, but for some reason you cause his death (dark). That would mean one of your parents would never exist, right? So you wouldn't exist... Which would mean you wouldn't have existed to kill him... so it would never have happened.

Alas, that's because you aren't a Time Bender. Sorry. Apparently, only these weird ass people who have past versions of themselves scattered around different timeline's can slip between the loopholes of time travel and make changes.

Well, it's a good thing there's only a few of us who can do it that we're currently aware of because it'd be pretty disastrous if one of us stepped out of line... ahem like I did but this is the story before that.

CHAPTER 1

There are three main rules to Time Bending: Stay on your previous life's path, be there no more than two days, and under no circumstances do anything too drastic. Yes, that means no blowing up people. Also, and I know I said three, but there's one more crucial rule: know that time frame inside out.

This was a quick job. A simple find, kill, and get paid. The job wouldn't be easy but there was a reason I was hired for it.

I knew how it worked. I'd been in the business long enough to know you could never make it simple without following the rules and still getting paid enough to maintain your reputation.

Trust your Totem and stick to the rules. Make it back alive. I'd done it a bunch of times before with no problem... Apologies, here I am going off on one and you probably have no idea what a Totem is. Not that I'd blame anyone for not knowing because I don't even get the science behind it - but this is what I do know:

Your Totem was what kept you attached to the present. It was your only way of finding your way out of your past life and the only thing that gave me the courage to continue diving into the past and changing it every time without feeling guilty. Well, most of the time. The word Totem came from the Native Americans. They were animal guides of some kind. But seriously don't ask me anything about how this shit works. I was never good at science and I definitely did not come up with a fancy-ass name like *Totem*.

My Totem was a blue light: the blue light surrounding the doorframe of the White Room in the present time. It was the blue light of a glittering jewel pinned to the hair of a woman whose name I'll never discover in the year 1921. It was the blue light of a flame flickering in the depths of a fire in the year 1844. It was the blue light of a television screen in 1979. It was every blue light in any random moment of my 208 lives and I only had to remember the light to go back in time. Either that or my Totem would just whisk me away to wherever I wanted to go - any date, any time of day I knew one of my past selves would be living in.

Thinking about it, I had a serious amount of lives. I like to think of myself as an ancient soul - moulded by experience. I'd had all kinds of adventurous lives. I'd fallen in love with women, men, and life itself. I'd been around since the Saxons, maybe even before that... hell - I'd probably never stop counting lives. There was still so much to be discovered about Time Bending and what it meant.

This day was no different - just another insignificant (but significant enough to need killing) person. I caught the blue light in a flicker and started to draw myself toward it. Gradually, as though I'd been cured of blindness I could see my surroundings. A woman glided past me like a delicate and colourful butterfly, the same blue sapphire catching the light and twinkling in her hair. She laughed and held onto her companions arm as they exited the building.

New York in the 1920s: one of the most popular speakeasies - where some of the wealthiest gangsters gathered. It was said the owner was a cousin of Al Capone but nobody had ever met the owner and I was pretty sure no one really wanted too - they valued their lives too much. Not even I had and I'd gone back into this lifetime more times than I could count - for fun... and for business. Maybe more fun - the cocktails packed a pretty serious punch.

My mission that particular day was to find the owner and kill him before morning. I didn't know the details on why this had to happen or how it affected my client so far in the future but I didn't ask questions. I didn't care to know anyway. It was probably one of the reasons I was employed to kill so often. I don't want to come off as arrogant but I was the best. Better than all other six Time Benders combined with all their lives. I didn't ask questions and lacked any conscience. People like that apparently.

As I entered the well-hidden speakeasy in a warehouse not far from the city I felt a sense of familiarity. The room looked like it was straight out of a casino from Las Vegas. There were the usual circular tables containing beautiful women dressed head to toe in their finest jewellery - their lips were pressed between cigarettes that men held for them like spoons. The smoke rose and misted between the faces of a colourful sea of people who all did their best to put on a facade of glam and fortune. I was literally living in The Great Gatsby.

Fake laughter echoed through the room but there was no question as to if they were having fun. These people wouldn't be here if it weren't for the promise of alcohol and company - relying on those around them for a good night.

Welcome to the roaring twenties.

I glanced around the room, taking note of where people stood, realising the last time I had been here it hadn't changed much. There were still the two identical twins wearing green, latched to the same gangster I'd never bothered learning the name of. On the table closest to the stage, there was a group of strangers exchanging names that I had heard every time. One male dressed in a bright blue suit took a sip of champagne and raised his eyes to meet my own.

His name was Charles and every time I had arrived into this life we had exchanged eye contact and every time I couldn't bring myself to stop from looking at him at just the right moment. He was the one person I could remember everything about in this lifetime and usually I tried not to. Although for the sake of how Daisy's life ended in the next week I had to introduce myself for what seemed like the hundredth time.

"Pardon doll, but I think you dropped this." He swooped in beside me and I had to refrain from rolling my eyes and sticking a finger down my throat. Every time he would hand me a coin he had taken from his pocket - an excuse to talk to me.

Sure enough, when I held out my hand he placed a silver coin into my gloved palm, his other hand caressed my thumb.

"Does the pretty lady have a name?" He flashed me a smile, the dimple in his right cheek calling me closer and his eyes glowing cheekily, dangerously.

"Daisy," I said, handing the coin back toward him. "This isn't mine."

Charles' eyes creased and he flashed another white smile. "Well, keep it," he said, wrapping my knuckles around the coin. "I hope to see you around, Daisy."

I nodded my head with a small smile before turning my body away from him. Charles started to back away with a similar look he had when eyeing up a motorcar he wanted and I felt my stomach flip. Being the person I was today I wouldn't look twice at him but I couldn't ignore the history Daisy had with him and the connection he had to her death. It gave me a sense of thrill and danger anytime I was near him, which was exhilarating but annoying all the same.

I took a step back and pulled the sleeve of my gloves higher. Maintaining eye contact I winked cheekily. Daisy had a reputation here and I needed to maintain it if things weren't going to change too much for her. Rule number one: stick to your old life's past.

I turned my back on him, feeling his eyes follow my hips as I walked toward the bar. A weight was lifted off my shoulders as I saw Williams already pouring me a glass.

"What a sight for sore eyes," I said, reaching over the bar and kissing the elderly man's cheeks.

Every time I'd been here he had never failed to give me hope, he was something of a Totem himself.

"Ms Monroe, it's been a whole week since I saw you!" he exclaimed, his familiar New York accent warming my chest.

"Miss me?"

"Always." He slid the drink toward me and I folded my arms on the surface of the bar counting down in my mind until Charles' hand landed on my shoulder.

Except it didn't come. I paused for a moment, wondering if I had miscounted. It was common to be a second or two late but after a minute you could start worrying.

After tapping my foot impatiently, I realised he wasn't coming and I felt a surge of irritation. What was I expecting to happen, for things to be simple every time in this life? Who gave a crap? *Just get on with the mission.*

Annoyed, I swivelled to face his direction only bumping into his chest when he came up behind me. I let out a shriek and he chuckled. Quickly I looked around the room to see if everything was rolling smoothly and sure enough nothing was out of time. I was the one who'd miscounted - a simple mistake and one the others wouldn't take lightly. I figured I'd keep that out of the mission's summary later, for the sake of my reputation.

Charles and I spoke for a moment, keeping to the script before he finally dismissed himself and I turned back to Williams. Daisy would see Charles again tomorrow and then she'd be on her rightful path to death. Boring.

"Hey, Williams?" I whipped my head around and gave him a warm smile. His aged eyes twinkled as he cleaned a glass. "I don't suppose you know the owner and could introduce me?"

The old man gave a small smile. "No Ms."

"You don't know who your boss is?" I exclaimed, running a gloved finger around the rim of my glass, I leant forward raising a perfectly arched eyebrow.

"And you don't know who the owner is by now?" Williams gave a short chuckle and slid a drink towards a couple standing by. I turned to face them flashing a quick smile, the man's eyes widened and his face flushed red as he brought a hand to adjust his glasses and timidly smiled at me. The woman didn't notice but instead watched a younger male behind her husband with a hungry look.

I rolled my eyes and took a sip, not much had changed from the twenties up to the present day.

"I can't possibly get to know everybody here," I replied, giving a small smirk and taking the last sip, feeling the alcohol rush to my head. "There's not enough time in the world," I continued, winking subtly and taking a step away from the bar.

I grinned. "I'll see you soon darling."

Williams nodded his head laughing. "Have a good night Daisy."

I walked back into the rush of the crowd and climbed the stairs. I leaned against the golden railing and cast my eyes across the room, my eyes catching on Charles who had cornered another stunning girl.

"Oh, for god's sake," I muttered under my breath, jumping at the feel of a hand on my wrist. I looked down at a red-gloved hand and followed my eyes up the arm to find a dancer I had seen performing on the stage regularly.

She wore a tight red dress that hugged her figure perfectly, I couldn't help but appreciate her beauty. Her smile held a kind of naivety and innocence within it as though she hadn't been exposed to the harshness of anything. Or perhaps she had been exposed to awful things and paid no attention to them - she was an open book in other words. I could see right through her deep blue eyes.

Her blonde hair was short and gelled up onto her head to match the other dancers and she had a small gap between her two front teeth, which gave her a quirky look. I'd never spoken to her before but I'd seen her every time I'd travelled back to this time.

"Your hair is absolutely stunning." Her voice screamed New Jersey and her smile practically sparkled like a disco ball. I looked back at her hand which was still on my arm and snatched it away uncomfortably. I'd never liked people touching me and she gave me the impression of trouble.

"What colour is that? It's almost silver," she asked, taking a finger and wrapping it around one of my curls.

My hair was pretty unusual. It wasn't in any way close to grey but rather a silvery-white. As a young girl in all of my lives, my hair was always a faded white until it seemed to fade into some kind of striking silver. I'm sure I would have been self-conscious of it but gradually it became fashionable and I didn't have to pay to have my hair dyed such a unique colour, which so many people did in the present.

The girl still had my hair curled between her fingers so I smiled tightly and leant back slightly. She seemed to follow me though, so I took a sudden step back landing into a firm chest.

"Mags, stop annoying the lovely lady," a gruff voice said behind me.

I swivelled around to face a burly man carrying himself in some kind of bearlike manner. His eyes lingered uncomfortably on my breasts for longer than I deemed necessary and instantly I felt my face flush with anger.

"Watch where you're walking," I snapped, brushing a strand of hair from my face and looking past the man.

"Yeah Mitch, you almost gave the poor girl a heart attack." Mags stepped in, narrowing her eyes slightly. Mitch took a step past me and clenched his fists as he watched Mags and I couldn't help but want to throw his ass down the stairs.

"Excuse my wife," he grunted and turned his back on her to face me.

"Don't excuse her, she was being perfectly polite until you came along," I snapped, not breaking my deathly eye contact.

Mags looked away suddenly before jumping into a bubble of excitement and turning to hug another woman.

Mitch let out a bark of laughter before taking a step toward me. Sandwiched between him and the bannister I held my ground and tilted my head to face him.

"I like you," he mumbled huskily, breathing into my face until I caught a whiff of stale tobacco. I refrained myself from slapping him and instead smiled sweetly.

"See you around." I ducked quickly under his arm and made it out, without pressing my heels into his face. Lucky for him.

Noticing a few familiar faces, I smiled, making small talk and glancing towards the clock. The night was nearly over and I didn't want to risk spending another day here until I completed the job.

I glanced around the room quickly until I caught sight of my Totem. Its familiarity gave me the boost of confidence I needed and so I continued to talk to people, subtly questioning where the owner could be and if they had met him before.

"I heard he was an American spy in the World War."

"That's just a rumour, he's actually a close cousin of Al Capone - runs this place for him."

"And here I was thinking he was an immigrant serial killer," gasped a woman laughing

"You never know these days Betty," her husband said, glancing around the room wearily.

Nobody seemed to know who the owner was and it was probably for the best. Owning a speakeasy this popular with no well-known owner was what made it run for so long. I'd just about given up on the mission when a glass of champagne was almost spilt over me.

"Oh, hi there," chirped a voice I thought I had escaped. Mags took a sip of her golden champagne, letting a waterfall of bubbles cascade to the floor.

"Hi," I mumbled, smiling and taking a drink from a passing waiter. I chugged it down in one and looked at Mags who had a grin plastered to her face.

"Sorry about my husband, he's a bit of a brute really. He gave me this you know!" She pulled back her glove to reveal a purple bruise around her wrist and I instantly felt my blood boil. "Such an animal."

Stick to the rules, Nova. Need I remind myself of them? No. Blowing. Up.

"Why are you with him?" I asked, staring at the bruise with wide eyes before her glove concealed it.

She cleared her throat and took another sip of her drink. "That's not really any of your business is it?"

Well, I tried. It wasn't my fault if she didn't want my help or advice. Her loss.

It was silent for a moment and I quickly scanned the room. My eyes landed on a dark-haired gentleman standing at the bottom of the stairs alone, black hair gelled back. He turned his head to face me and I paused momentarily, wondering how I hadn't noticed him before.

I didn't look long before gazing up to the glass chandelier in the centre of the room and admired its beauty. If you paid closer attention to it you could see the reflection of people fluttering in and out like a changing tide of faces, all painted with smiles and laughing, all talking to people about their lives, how much they earned in their different businesses, about the new movie they'd seen on the weekend and exchanging compliments of how wonderfully perfect everyone looked, how they were thankful for alcohol because they couldn't live without it and how great America was. How great life was.

It was all a joke, stepping into this time was like a bubble of fun but inside it was full of lies and materialistic people with their hedonistic lives.

I smirked. It sounded exactly like home and boy did I love it. I loved not knowing who everyone truly was. The mystery was somehow beautiful and the way we all came together as one intrigued me.

Mags cleared her throat and turned her forehead forward with a questioning look,

Shoot, what had she said?

"Pardon?"

"What's your name?" Mags repeated, I wondered how she didn't already know who I was. I held a higher reputation than most here and I was here most the time, - well Daisy was.

"Daisy Monroe."

"Oh! You're Daisy? I've so wanted to meet you."

That's more like it. Now, now - I'm not some self-righteous prick (though it depends who you ask). I just wanted to make sure Daisy remained a well-known name. She deserved that much.

"Oh no! Please, I mean you're an amazing dancer." I returned the compliment and smiled at her as she giggled and took a small sip from her glass.

"Thank you, thank you, Ms Monroe - that means a lot."

"Please, call me Daisy."

I glanced at the clock and chewed on my lip nervously, people were starting to leave the speakeasy and realised

I'd completely tuned out of whatever the red dancer was talking about.

"Pardon me Mags, I don't suppose you know the owner?"

Mags let out a long, high-pitched giggle. "I would have thought you would know by now, you're here all the time, aren't you?"

"Yes-"

"My husband's the owner," Mags cut in with a string of giggles following shortly.

Well crap.

The big walrus guy who smelt like he hadn't had a shower for a month, stank of tobacco and abused his wife owned this successful place I'd been to so many times?

You had to be having a laugh.

Mags' eyes trailed over the room before finally landing on Mitch who was talking to a group of gentlemen at a table. He had a thick cigar hanging out of his mouth and I instantly cringed at what I had to do.

Mags gave a short wave, gesturing for him to come over, which he ignored for a minute. We watched patiently as he eventually bid his farewells to the men and swaggered his way over here. He didn't focus his attention on his wife but rather looked me in the eye.

"Darling, this is Daisy! The one who-"

"And so we meet again." Mitch took hold of my hand and brought it to his lips. I sucked in a breath and smiled, refusing to take the chance to jam my fist into his mouth and knock out a tooth. There was no way he was getting off easy tonight without some damage. Obviously.

"Darling, she's a loyal customer you know."

"I wouldn't know. I'm hardly here," he said, inhaling his cigarette and blowing it in the direction of Mags' face. *Doesn't he know those things kill?* I supposed someone else could tell him... well it was a bit late for that talk anyway since I was going to kill him.

"What can I say, this place is wonderful. It's so nice to finally meet the owner," I said, smiling coyly and accepted a drink he held out for me. I raised it and took a sip, continuing to look him in the eyes. At least I didn't like him. That made it easier to kill the man.

"Sweetheart, I think it's time you get back on stage for a final dance, don't you?" Mitch said. I really wished he would look her in the eye for once. It was disrespectful and irked me beyond belief.

Mags made a high-pitched sound in her throat as though she could predict why he was telling her to leave and instantly I felt bad.

Just get the job done and get the hell out of here.

Mags flicked her gaze between Mitch and me with wide and innocent eyes before she turned her head to the ground and walked back to the stage like a dog with its tail between its legs.

Now get on with it.

I had somehow convinced Mitch to show me the view from the roof that I'd secretly already been to several times. Thankfully he agreed with an animalistic hungry look in his eyes.

I leant my elbows against the side of the wall taking small sips of my drink and was admiring the view of flickering lights of the city and streetlights below when I saw my Totem flickering off in the distance.

That made things a lot simpler.

"I'm glad I found you."

Oh please, as if you were looking specifically for me instead of a good night with a stranger because you weren't happy enough with your beautiful wife.

His arms circled around my shoulder and he put his head beside my own. His hands were dangerously close to my neck and I tensed. He took it as a sign of me somehow enjoying his touch and so placed his hands lower dipping round to the front of my body.

Quickly, I twisted round to face him, finding his body closer than I would have liked.

This was a bad, bad idea.

"What about your wife, Mags?" I backed away and cringed when he leant even closer. His breath was rank. He ran a rough hand over my cheek, trailing a finger behind my neck and up to my hair. He pulled out the pins until my silver hair fell out in loose waves, his hand grasped it as he leant in to kiss me.

"Who's Mags?" He chuckled and I joined in with loud fake laughter to avoid his lips. This was not one of my proudest moments, oh just end me. I'd never felt so low -

so embarrassed. In fact, nobody was ever going to hear about this. Ever. I could already hear the others laughing if I told them about what happened here.

His hands suddenly yanked back my hair causing my neck to fall back painfully and then his tongue ran up the side of my neck like I was a rack of BBQ ribs.

I was going to kill him. Painfully.

This was actually the most disgusting experience of my life - of every single one of my lives. When I didn't respond he pulled away with a frustrated and confused look.

"What? I thought this is why you wanted to get away from the party." His tone was cold and instantly I knew this wasn't going to go well. I didn't have an opportunity to kill him with no weapon and I couldn't just strangle him. I was a badass fighter but he was big.

"I think I need to thank you for setting up this wonderful place."

I deserved an Oscar.

He still looked puzzled and so I coiled a finger around his tie pulling him closer and holding my breath as I kissed him. I really deserved an Oscar. "Please," I begged. I really, really deserved that Oscar now.

It seemed to work as he lifted me until I was sitting on the balcony wall. OK, this was perfect positioning for me to throw him off - it was like he was asking for it.

Just as I was about to launch into full-on ninja mode the bastard placed his grubby hands on my waist.

"Somebody's desperate." I winced.

He growled in response before he slammed his lips on mine - and I mean quite literally slammed, he could have knocked a tooth out. "You're just so-" he started to mumble before I shoved him off of me.

Oh man, bad idea Nova.

His eyes seemed to glow with violence and for a moment I thought I'd seriously messed up before I saved it by undoing his belt slowly, taking it off and feeling him breathe into my neck.

I felt like... *ugh.*

He made a deep noise in his chest before suddenly stuffing his face in my neck and biting.

Uh ouch? By this point, he managed to shuffle his trousers off like a dancing walrus.

"Open your legs," he ordered. Oh hell to the no. This idiot had the hormones of a dog. He didn't wait for a response before his hands had forced my legs open and his hand reached under my dress. The hairs on my body stood up as he whispered huskily. "Now who's desperate."

Not me asshole.

My heel came forward, jabbing him into the knee with enough strength that he fell. I caught him with the belt, quickly wrapping it around his neck and tightening the straps. He struggled and elbowed me in the side. I buckled gasping for breath as he grabbed the belt again.

"Bitch," he sneered. "Who sent you?"

"Santa Claus," I wheezed, quickly slipping off my heel and throwing it at him, he dodged it and ran forward. I tripped him and rolled as he landed with a thud. "You've been a naughty boy."

Quickly I sat on him and turned us so he was on the floor. I wrapped my arms around his throat and wished that every time I came into this life Daisy had some muscle... or a gun... a gun would be nice.

His hand came round catching me by surprise as he yanked my hair back, I screamed as he threw me into the side of the wall.

The hair? Oh, you are so dead.

I stumbled up against the side of the balcony wall and watched as he charged toward me. My back cracked from the force of his body crushing me against the wall and for a moment I was stunned by the pain. Red dots danced in front of my eyes. He took advantage of my pause and immediately wrapped his hands around my neck. All I could see were his angry eyes and smell his disgusting breath as I struggled to get away from him.

My head was hanging off the side of the building and he was so focused on me that if I could stun him momentarily I'd be able to throw us both off the building. He wouldn't be expecting me to sacrifice my own life but by hell - if it meant I could escape this awful male's grasp then sure. I'd take the repercussions.

Oh thank god, I thought when I saw my glass was still on the ledge beside my face. Speedily, I made a grab for it and crashed it against his head with all the force I could muster.

He let out a cry and instantly I tipped him over the building, catching myself and dangling off the side of the wall. When I heard the scream and a crash I pulled myself off the side of the ledge and stood up, stretching and dusting myself. I took a look down at my torn dress, and tore it slightly more, exposing my chest where bruises were forming.

Cue the waterworks. I let out a perfectly crafted scream and waited for the people to come running – for them to listen to my story about almost being raped and then how he fell off the side of the building. It probably wouldn't change a great deal in the remaining time of Daisy's life but at least she had an excuse for not remembering anything.

Once done I followed the blue light which beckoned me forward as though I were a moth trapped in its glare. I followed it until I returned back to myself with no problem.

Nova was back. Miss me?

"Nova, can you hear me?"

I felt my finger twitch until I could finally open my eyes, at first seeing nothing but blue until everything focused and I could see a familiar face just as every time I came back to the present.

"Ugh man - hi Vix," I mumbled, gradually sitting up. I took off the cord, which recorded my heart rate and all that jazz, as well as the IV, which supplied my body with all it needed whilst I was gone.

"You were in there longer than expected. What happened?" Vix asked, watching as I stood with eager eyes.

I sent him a look. He knew whatever I did in the past was confidential on behalf of my clients but I had to still log it into the system so everything that changed was recorded.

For them, nothing might have changed, which was why I got my clients to pay me before I did the job. Otherwise, they wouldn't remember asking me to do the job because they wouldn't remember why they'd want a person who's already dead, dead. Get it? Well, I struggled to understand. If the problem the client wanted to get rid of were erased from existence before it became a problem then how would I still have the money? I didn't know. Somehow, we Time Benders were just freaks of nature and could break the rules of time and existence surrounding money and people.

Some would ask me what they'd asked me to do and I'd willingly tell them - that's why I had such a reputation. There was no point in doing any of it if not for the money and fame.

I'd never go into the past to do anything for myself though. I wouldn't go and bring my parents back to life or save anybody's lives or kill them years in advance of when they were supposed to die. It would be messy.

Don't get me wrong, I want a lot of things to be different but in ways, it felt like cheating when you did things for yourself.

And the job I just completed seemed to go well; nothing too major was ever going to change since Mitch was going to die relatively soon after. It was what would have happened in between his death and my appearance, which would have changed. My client had told me he would make a decision that hundreds of years later would affect my client. I didn't know how it would, nor did I care.

I tended not to get so involved in what the client's motives were - as long as they sounded fine to me and I got paid more for killing then it was all good.

I was essentially an assassin I guessed... that sounded pretty cool so I'd accept the title. However, it was rare I'd get offered to kill people since it was the most dangerous for the timeline. But that didn't mean I knew the numbers of how many people I'd killed - I'd lost track. I'm sure some log could tell you though.

Most of the time I gave messages to people in the past, which somehow influence the wealth of my clients in the long run. Again, I didn't ask questions. I just did what I was paid to do.

"The others are training," Vix said, turning off the monitor and handing me a drink. I took a long sip of the cool liquid and followed him out the door, the blue lights turned off once we'd left.

I stared at the back of Vix's dark black, slightly greyed hair. "Still? I would have thought they'd been getting ready for tonight." I tied up my silver hair into a quick ponytail and stepped into the pod - a sort of transport that basically looked like a see-through elevator and took you anywhere in the building.

Myself and the other six lived here most of the time. It was essentially a skyscraper in the centre of the city glittering away and we each had our own levels, the bottom one - deep underground was where we trained. Other levels were held for various things: swimming pools, indoor cinemas, control rooms that kept track of everything we did in the past - which was where I need to go now.

I was thankful we each had our own floors to ourselves - mine being the very top with the best view. Not to mention the various places we held parties to host our clients. Not everyone could say they shared ownership of a skyscraper they lived in.

It was a good time to be alive.

CHAPTER 2

Time: Present
Location: Prospect

I was right. As soon as the others looked up from their logs that held all the records they were howling with laughter.

The six were like the siblings you never really asked for but were occasionally grateful for in the moments where you needed to borrow their stuff.

We had Cedrix who stared at his log with a faint smile. He had the least lives with only 8 but he was built like a truck - a big blue truck. He spent most of his time training here (for what I don't know). He was rarely asked by anybody to go back into the past. This might have something to do with the fact he looked like huge boulder-covered in blue tattoos, and had face enhancements, which made him look like a bull. He might not be your first option. Plus he didn't speak.

Then there was Aeron, the clown of the group with striking purple hair, although he was constantly changing it. He had a useful 50 lives, which was good for a select amount of clients... if you wanted something from 500 years ago. Even if he wasn't used much in missions he was great company.

Then there was Landon. Not as great a fighter as us at the age of 54 so he played the role of a messenger for whatever one of his 55 lives needed interrupting. Landon tended to keep to himself but was strict on the rules - seeing as he created them with Vix. He was a tad grumpy but a father figure to Halo.

Now... Halo. Sweet Halo whom I would absolutely love to blow up. But that went against the rules... obviously. Halo had manufactured her body in any way possible to gain the most artificial body with the biggest boobs I'd ever seen. It was probably how she took out her enemies: by poking them in the eye. In fact, every time I'd seen her in the past she looked completely different. But still, there were obvious signs of her Mexican heritage with her rich brown curls and plump red lips. In fact, despite her manufactured body, her face was beautiful. However, it still didn't excuse the fact she was a bitch, quite literally the everyday wealthy and corrupt citizen of Prospect.

That's where we lived. The wonderful, lavish city Prospect: built on the graves of the forever changing past. But don't look at me. I was just as guilty as everyone else: the fame, the money - it was addictive.

Then there was Ace with his 103 lives, the guy who would quite literally do anything for fame and sex. He was trouble, and irritating but good looking. He was one of those guys who didn't need to change how he looked because with his beautifully sculptured body, boy band worthy style you didn't need to. As you could imagine, women usually employed him. Compared to myself who got employed by old men who had tried and failed at making themselves look younger. Joy.

And lastly, there was Fynn, slightly older than the rest of us in his mid-30s but quite possibly one of my favourite of the six. He had 145 lives, which wasn't nearly as many as I had, but he was the closest, and for that, we could relate the most. Still, those lives didn't matter much when you were mixed race. The further back the better and I'm talking ancient for him. Clients don't want anything from before the 18th century and unfortunately for Fynn, his only life after the 18th century was 1925 and then jumped to 2044. Yikes. But hey I've got to give him some credit since apparently before slavery was a thing he was bathing in wealth, and a couple thousand years back from that he was worshipped by ancient civilisations. I could understand why. Fynn was the most genuine person in this world of non-genuine people and an amazing fighter. He was my training buddy (much to Ace's displeasure).

Anyway, back to them all laughing at me: "You pushed this dude off of a building in only his underwear?" Aeron was in fits of laughter, hitting the ground with his fists as tears streamed down his face.

"I just can't get over how much detail you put in the record, couldn't you have just said you killed him?" Fynn was also in hysterics but was at least trying to control his laughter.

I scowled in response. "You weren't supposed to read it-"

"Oh but I'm glad we did," Aeron laughed taking deep breaths and puffing out his cheeks as he tried to hold it in.

"And you call me the slut of the group." Halo rolled her eyes and wrapped a towel around her neck.

"Nova's not a slut, she has class. Something most girls don't have nowadays," Ace said, running his eyes appreciatively over me as I took off my jumper.

I rolled my eyes at him. "As if you look for class, you'd sleep with anything with a pulse."

"Or without," Aeron laughed.

Ace ignored Aeron's comment and instead walked over to put his target away. "True Nova, but if I could choose, it would always be you."

I raised an eyebrow. "You can choose, you just choose to sleep around because I don't like you."

Ace swivelled to face me with an arrogant look in his eyes. "You just aren't sure about your feelings yet."

Fynn took a long sip from his bottle and wrapped a brown arm slick with sweat over my shoulders. "Can you just kill him?" I mumbled hugging him from the side.

"Why do you need me to kill him? I'm sure you could just strip him naked and push him off-" I jabbed him in the side and ducked under his arm making a run for the door that Landon held open for me, shaking his head as he watched us act like children.

The others piled into the now cramped pod and Ace wiggled his way through so he could be next to me. I rolled my eyes as he placed an arm by my head.

"You smell like sweat," I grumbled and held my jumper to my face.

"Most girls find it sexy."

"I'm not *most girls*." I rolled my eyes.

"True. You're a killer," Halo grumbled from the front.

I resisted the urge to smack her over the head and defend myself but she wasn't worth the effort and I'd just make myself sound more psycho.

"Nova's the one keeping us all in business whilst you make yourself pretty." Fynn took to my defence and I couldn't help the smug smile that took over my face. "So don't say such horrible things. She does what she has to, it's not like she enjoys it."

I didn't feel much of anything towards killing but sure - I'd take Fynn's attempt at making me seem more human.

The pod suddenly came to an abrupt stop and Cedrix clambered off giving us a faint grunt. The pod rolled into action going further up the building and pausing on Landon's level, then Aeron's, followed by Halo until it was just Fynn, Ace and I.

Fynn sent me a sympathetic look as it came to a stop at his apartment and I sighed in defeat. Being left alone with Ace and his flirting was my least favourite but also the most exciting part of the day. It was confusing.

"See you at the party."

31

"What floor?" Ace asked, catching the door before it slid shut, Fynn turned around and I caught a glimpse of his apartment full of a pure bright white. "35."

We nodded our heads until the door slid shut. *Refrain from even looking at him Nova. As soon as you make eye contact you're done for.* I turned and faced the glass, where night had settled and white light filled up the pristine city. We climbed the building, rising taller than most surrounding skyscrapers.

When we got to his level I waited but he didn't move, I let out a long sigh. "Ace, I'm tired. Can we not do this right now?"

"Nova, I really need to talk to you about something."

I rolled my eyes. "I'm so tired and I have to do some research-" There was a beeping sound in my earpiece and I sighed irritated. "And I'm not done for the night apparently." I held a finger to my lips and Ace closed his eyes for a split second before reopening the doors and stepping out with his head hung low.

"Nova speaking."

"I have a job I need doing. Was Fynn in Germany in 1943 to 45?"

I scowled. Of course, he had another job. "He died in 1941 in the war. But it's your lucky day. I was an English spy. What dates do you need and location?"

"Excellent. 1944." He began detailing the mission and I agreed reluctantly. The details were easy to understand but he wanted me to save a Jewish family from a concentration camp. The number of things I could change in WW2 and the butterfly effect I might cause secretly terrified me. It would be extremely difficult especially without causing trouble, and a whole family? Saving people who were meant to die was sometimes more dangerous than killing people. It could change too much, but then again I'd done risky missions like this in the past and it had worked out. Plus it was good money. I guessed my last mission had put some money into his pockets if he was asking for another job on the same day.

I made my way back down the levels and into the White Room and asked Vix to check if the money had been transferred. His mouth opened wide and he nodded his head quickly, adjusting his glasses. Now all I had to do was go back into my former body, save a family (probably my most moral mission) and intertwine it with my current timeline so I could take the money with me. I know. Confusing. But it meant I would still get paid and the money wouldn't cease to exist.

CHAPTER 3

Time: 13th February 1944
Location: Some quiet town in Berlin, Germany

Soon enough I was back in my 24-year-old body, Lucy. It was four years after my daughter had died and I'd made the decision to take up the offer of becoming a British Spy working in Germany.

The date was 13th February and I woke up in bed with a German soldier and another woman draped over me. Oof. I remembered this life almost like the back of my hand. I moved around the two expertly, sliding out between them and finding my clothes thrown haphazardly around the room. I knew where to find the note instantly as it was such an important moment of my job working as a spy. He'd foolishly kept a note with written down orders taken from his commanding officer in his pant pocket that had fallen onto the floor.

The room was plain, white sheets and a light blue wall with stains and cracks across. I turned to face the two of them, scowling at the man and focusing on the female with a curious gaze. *What had she been up to?*

My job as a spy during the war did not include sleeping with soldiers for information - let me make that abundantly clear. Lucy was a strong-willed woman perfectly capable of doing her job without the sleeping around. I was too. It just so happened that during last nights much needed pleasure and relaxation with my female friend, she'd invited someone I hadn't even known was a Nazi.

From what I remembered she'd been working on helping Jews escape so I hadn't expected the man to be a Nazi. Maybe she was the one doing it for information - perhaps she was helping my past self - perhaps she knew what I had been. Still, looking at her sleeping - or rather lying still and pretending, I narrowed my eyes. I found it difficult to trust coincidences. But what did it matter now?

I left the room quietly, my heart a steady beat and my steps fluid. I had visited this moment a couple of times - never for a mission though. Just to gather intel about my life here.

I could remember this morning quite clearly. Lucy had checked herself, making sure she hadn't said anything secretive last night, let alone left anything out in the open like the idiotic soldier and his folded note. I remembered the moment I'd read it and realised it had been a Nazi - I ran out of the house and threw up onto the side of the street.

I reached the payphone further down the road and as I brought the receiver to my ear I paused, looking at the wooden shelf of the booth where a wooden sculpture of a bird stared me down. It was strange to see a bird from this angle; its eyes pointed outwards and its beak staring right through my chest, peeling through layers of clothing and skin to see what truly lay beneath.

Throughout the coded message my eyes kept drifting towards the toy with a feeling of unease. It hadn't been here before. Had I somehow managed to create a tiny butterfly effect somewhere in the past that led to it being here? I could just have forgotten...

Thinking about it was making my head hurt with unease so I promptly made my way into a small German town where I found who I was looking for. We wouldn't stay together long but we had become good partners and I knew we would never get caught as spies.

When I got a glimpse of his blonde hair I grinned and made my way towards him, embracing him tightly and causing him to stumble backwards into his car.

"What's that for?" Robert mumbled in English, a strong American accent that contrasted to my British one. I pulled away and looked at him closely. He was my dearest friend in this life - and just friends might I add - he was gay, which if you can remember being gay any time before the 21st century was rough going. I'd also fallen in love with women in some of my lives, as any Time Bender who had as many lives as I have would. Although it wasn't a struggle for me as much as it was for Aeron. It was his recurring theme in all his lives that he struggled with being a homosexual - and I mean *struggled*. Try being gay in a strict Catholic family in 1500. At least the future now embraced it just as they embraced crazy lifestyles, fashion and… changing the past by wiping generations for money.

But anyway, this wasn't about Aeron or the future that was much more tolerant. I was talking about Robert. I remembered attending his funeral in 1977 as a thirteen-year-old girl who'd been next-door neighbours to him when he was sixty-three before he died from lung cancer. He'd tell me stories of his friend Lucy who died thirteen years ago and how I had the same silver hair as she did. I think he knew in some kind of unexplainable way.

"You look well." I smiled.

He opened the car door for me and instantly we were off, leaving the town and the payphone at the bar where I'd sent a coded message to my boss.

"Where to today Luce?"

"To save some lives," I replied, closing my eyes and trying to remember the quick research I'd done before arriving in this body ten minutes ago. In a cool manner, I opened my eyes and began giving directions.

They would either be inside the concentration camp split up or on the journey there and that's if he was even right about the specific date and time they were going to Sachsenhausen. I held my breath and prayed to God they were still being transported North of Berlin and hadn't arrived.

When I saw smoke from a train rise above a frosty hill I grasped onto the edge of my seat and told Robert to speed up.

"What are you planning on doing?" Robert asked, suddenly panicked as we travelled far behind the moving train, coming off-road and making our way through a line of trees.

"I'll figure it out," I grinned. "It's only the children I'm supposed to save."

"Who are they?"

"Important."

"And everyone else?" he asked, keeping his eyes on the train and speeding up. I blinked my eyes and watched myself in the mirror swallowing tightly. "If I have the opportunity I'll take it." It was a lie. I couldn't. Could you imagine saving a train of German prisoners, Jews, completely innocent people whose fates were to die? It would change history too much. But I wish I could. I wish I could use my power for good. Actual good...

"Uh, Lucy - 3 o'clock." My head twisted to the side where another car had emerged from the tree line. They weren't German soldiers? *Or were they? What was this?*

A head poked out from the driver's window and I caught a mess of dark hair hidden under a black hat. It became abundantly clear they weren't with us when the man began shooting at our car. I let out an irritated growl. "Speed up."

The engine roared and I produced a gun from the back of the car and held it to the window, ducking my head as a bullet shot through the windscreen. Someone wasn't fast enough however and Robert let out a shout as the bullet skimmed his arm, he gritted his teeth in agony.

"Bastard," I hissed under my breath, shooting at the car and windows. The man seemed to be driving with no one else in the car. Soldiers didn't accompany him, which was strange. Or maybe he was only shooting at us because he thought we were the bad guys. They too could have been attempting a rescue mission. *Did that used to happen?* I should really brush up on my history.

Robert hissed in pain and I ducked below the window watching as he steered with one arm.

"Plan?" he asked.

I faltered, searching my brain for an answer before sighing. "When do I ever have a plan?" I mumbled and Robert let out a strained chuckle through clenched teeth.

I watched ahead as the car began to trail behind the train and a head poked out to see where we were behind them. I pulled the trigger narrowly missing as the person deflected the bullet in extreme reflex. For a moment I was shocked I had missed a shot so perfect it could have been handed to me by the Gods with arrows pointed at the male's dark mess of hair.

"Are they German?"

"I couldn't say," I replied, reloading the gun and shuddering at the sound of glass shattering from another shot.

"Lucy, we're going to be found if we continue with this."

"No," I replied, aiming and sending the shot, finally catching the male shooter's hand, he dropped the gun.

"Good shot. But we still aren't going to make it."

"Why are they chasing the train?" I asked and my eyebrows pulled together in confusion.

Over the roar of the engine and the shots I was still firing I heard a frustrated voice scream. "Stop shooting for fucks sake!"

Robert and I looked at each other with raised eyebrows. "Are they with us?" We rolled over red snow.

"They shot at us first," I replied, my narrowed eyes watching them diagonally ahead, now on the train tracks keeping to the same speed as the train.

"Let's see what they do."

"At this rate, we're going to arrive at the camp," I replied hastily. But watched as the man in the car stuck out another gun and pointed it at my own gun. We shot at the same time, only I missed and he'd punctured our tire.

"Damn it," I hissed, as the car rolled and skidded in the snow, there was another shot and then the other tire went.

I hit the dashboard with my fist as the car finally stopped and Robert rested his head against the wheel with clenched teeth.

The car continued to follow the train shortly, before pulling off to the right, so they were just there to stop us? Bastards. I climbed out of the car, coming face to face with a Raven.

A surge of anger bubbled and I aimed the gun at the bird shooting it directly between its eyes.

"Woah, woah!" I heard Robert exclaim from behind me but I was still staring at the bird, its beady eyes looked into mine briefly and my mouth dropped open in shock. I had hit that bird. So why wasn't it dead? My heartbeat increased as I watched it cock its head to the side and caw before taking off in a flight towards their car.

"How did they know?"

"I don't know," I replied, looking up at the black Raven flying away. I climbed back into the car and turned to attend to his arm with stitches now the mission was a failure. My aim hadn't been off... the enemy was just a better shot.

Typical that I failed the one mission that wasn't to do something horribly corrupt and awful. I failed at being good - only *I* could fail at doing something good.

Robert and I made it back to the town as I pretended to inform my boss of the failed mission, which wasn't really a mission sent from him but Robert needn't know that. Once that was all cleared up, Robert and I went our separate ways to our next stops. I followed my Totem home.

I awoke with a headache - a bad one.

"How was it?" Vix asked.

"A failure."

Vix raised his eyebrows surprised, as I hadn't failed a mission since I was fifteen, which was 4 years ago. I made a lot of mistakes when I was younger. However, this was out of the ordinary for me.

"I'll return the money to him and let him know," Vix said, continuing to type before handing me a log.

I filled it out in detail, explaining what must have been changed in the past. Something had happened, perhaps in my last mission, a butterfly effect from killing Mitch that somehow led to those men following the train. Not to mention the sculptured bird. Who had put it there? Had one of us Time Benders gone back to change events?

I was incredibly confused.

As I was climbing the floors to meet Gia, my makeup artist, I rested my head against the window of the pod. I really did not feel like having a party tonight. My client could be there and if he saw me he'd know I hadn't completed the mission because nothing would have changed. Not to mention how embarrassed I was.

The pod slowed down and I felt my heart drop as I turned to the doors and Ace walked in urgently. I groaned. "I'm so tired and I need to get ready. Gia will be here soon to do my makeup and-"

"I'm being taken in," Ace interrupted and I felt my body turn cold. I turned to face him sharply.

"When?" I whispered.

Ace looked sharply to the camera in the corner of the pod and turned to face the doors instead. When they slid open I followed him wearily into my apartment.

As soon as we entered, the curtains covering the windows slid open to reveal the city. I walked over to the bar and grabbed us a drink. When I turned to face Ace he wasn't anywhere.

"Ace?" I called - two glasses in my hands. His head poked into the room and I realised he was standing on the balcony.

"When?" I repeated the question, he grabbed the drink and chugged it down. Then he placed both hands on the glass balcony, giving a forlorn look across the skyscrapers surrounding us. Lights twinkled across the city and a blanket of darkness and artificial stars covered the city. I rarely ever saw Prospect in the day, as it was usual for me to sleep in the day unless I was working.

I leant against the balcony and faced him.

"A week, maybe two," he sneered and when he turned to face me I could see how distressed he looked. He ran a shaky hand through his black hair and leant back.

"Don't tell the others, I only told you because you've been taken in before."

I nodded my head. "What happened?" I asked cautiously. When I was taken in it was to stop me from going back into past lives because I'd made a minor mistake. It was a kind of prison they called a 'retreat' where you were made to 'reflect' in. I was there for only a week as I'd had fans stand outside protesting for me. I didn't doubt that he would also have hundreds of teenage girls fighting for him.

"I lost my Totem. I'm on this new drug Vix fixed me on but they want to make sure I don't go back," he laughed coldly. "I can't go back without my Totem anyway and I don't see how chemicals are going to get it back."

I placed a hand on his shoulder, watching him thoughtfully. It was some kind of unspoken thing between us about our Totems. We never really speak about what each of ours is. It was like that with a lot of things we'd discovered.

"What- what's your Totem?" I whispered, almost as though I thought the whole world might be listening to our 'I'll show you mine if you show me yours'.

He gazed down at me and my throat tightened. "The moon," he mumbled, his tongue flicking against his lips. In a haze of emotions, I leant into him until our chests were pressed against each other. His eyes widened and he looked down breathing in sharply.

"What's yours?" he whispered I felt our bodies drawn in a way I couldn't explain. Like an effect of telling a secret: an exhilarating rush of excitement.

"It's a blue light."

His hand came up and cupped my cheek, holy crap were we going to kiss? Sixteen-year-old me was screaming but nineteen-year-old me had a reputation to uphold: hard to get.

"What's your recurring theme?" I blurted out and suddenly his hand was by his side and he'd turned his back on me.

When he turned back around his lips were pursed and he shook his head. "I don't know. I haven't been able to figure out what my recurring theme is."

How was that possible? We all had a recurring theme. That's what made us so unusual. It's what made fate seem real and thus justified our actions. It was the only thing we couldn't change.

He laughed bitterly. "I guess that makes me even less of a Time Bender. No recurring theme and no Totem. I'm basically human."

I opened my mouth to ask him more but he sent me a forced, almost cold smile, which warned me not to push further. So I didn't. But I should have. I should have pressed him for answers because it couldn't be true. He must be lying. But why lie about it? What was so terrible about his recurring theme that he was afraid to tell me?

CHAPTER 4

Time: Present
Location: Prospect

The pod doors opened and Gia walked through with hair straighteners in one hand and a suitcase of colourful crap in the other.

"Oh, Ace!" she exclaimed as she waddled her way over to us in the tightest dress imaginable. Ace shot her a charming smile and held her hand to his lips.

"You look stunning Gia."

If you called Prospect fashion stunning then you were certainly correct. Her dress was a neon green, and her hair a vibrant purple fluffed out on top of her hair. Gia's eyelashes were also something and I wondered how she could even see through them they were so long - like large spiders attached to her eyelids. Gia had a different look every day but this one was certainly one of my least favourites. It was like looking into a sci-fi film with aliens - except they were still human.

"Nova darling, I was thinking about that silver dress the other day - I have the perfect shoes for you to go with it. Please wear it for me?" Gia asked as she took both Ace and me by the hand and into my bedroom. The lights turned on as she stumbled on her heels into the walk-in closet.

"Shouldn't you go to your own stylist?" I asked Ace over my shoulder.

Gia groaned. "Oh god, don't even get me started on how annoying Juno has been all week!" She produced a silver dress practically transparent and I sighed.

"She's hot though," Ace smirked as he looked at my dress and back at me with a suggestive look.

Gia smirked. "Well aren't you lucky then because she was chatting the whole way here about her plans with you-"

"Can we not." I rolled my eyes at Gia and Ace's gossip. "Can you leave?" I glared at Ace and pressed a panel so the bathroom door closed behind me. Then I pressed another button to turn on the shower.

"There's no need to be jealous, Nova," Ace smirked and I felt my stomach dip. "As if I could forget what just happened between us," he called from my bedroom. Gia gasped and I felt my face grow hot with anger.

"We never did anything!" I snarled loudly from inside the shower. Already I felt a sense of dread settle onto my shoulders. Gia would spread that like wildfire and before I knew it I would have nothing but reporters trying to find a way into the building and screaming fans 'shipping' us again.

Soon enough I was in the short sparkly dress that left very little to the imagination. But compared to past lives, there was no need to feel self-conscious. There would be more than one person who came to the party wearing barely anything but shoes. At some point along the line, being in your birthday suit became fashionable - it was a shame I hadn't been around to see how that came about...

Don't look at me like that. I still had some decency from my last lives.

At the entrance to level 35, the music was blaring and reporters were scattered in a staggered line. I made my way over to them as part of the routine. They took my picture more times than I could count and began asking questions.

"Nova! Tell us what's been happening between you and Ace?" I flashed a smile and tucked a silver strand of my hair behind my ear.

"Don't you guys ever get bored about asking the same questions?" The group of reporters and myself all laughed. Another faceless person snapped a picture and shouted amongst the commotion of reporters. "What are you going to do with the growing threat of the rebellion?"

My eyebrows raised in response. I'd heard about them, a rebellious group outside the city who fought against Prospect. But they weren't anything out of control.

"Yeah! And the Raven!"

I felt a chill cross over my spine but I plastered a smile over my face and raised an eyebrow in question.

"Perhaps I've gotten too caught up in past news." They all laughed. "Who is calling themselves a Raven?" I rolled my eyes.

"There are rumours of another Time Bender with more lives than you. 210."

I rolled my eyes again. There were always rumours. I moved on thinking nothing of it and gave an uninterested shrug. If it didn't worry me then they had nothing to worry about. It's what they wanted to see. They didn't want to see a concerned Time Bender. But 210 lives? Even if it was 2 more than me it still made my brow twitch. Rumours. That's all they ever were.

"Nova!" shrieked Aeron. His purple hair had been curled into a flick on top of his head and he wore a jacket lined with gold that reached his knees. He looked like a pope - a very colourful one.

"Looking great." I smiled tightly, accepting the pink drink he held in front of me.

"Is this-"

"You betcha. Drink up." He winked, and took a sip until a bubbly smile appeared in his face. I also took a sip of the mysterious drink and immediately felt my face lift into a grin.

I was sure I looked like a madman.

But hey it tasted good and you didn't get this kind of drink in the 1920s.

Now, *this* was a party. Not some popular speakeasy with some asshole named Mitch running it. Here in

Prospect you could drink what you wanted, dance with strangers and have a great night just for the sake of it.

Which was precisely what I was doing up until someone tapped me on the shoulder. I swivelled to face a guard - one of the presidents to be precise. *Of course* she wanted me to go back and do something for her. If it weren't the president asking me something I wouldn't have bothered following him since I'd just gotten off two jobs.

I sent the guy I'd been dancing with an apologetic look and followed the Guard to a secluded area on the huge terrace overlooking the city.

The president sat on a bench looking across the city with a faint green look on her face. She looked stressed, needless to say. Not how she should be spending her time at a party. She was as corrupt as every other individual here. Her hair had been dyed a light silver and I felt myself smile.

Nova, you trendsetter.

"Ms President." I bowed my head slightly and took a step forward. She smiled wearily at me.

"Nova, are you having fun?" she asked as though she'd organised the party. There was a certain slyness in the woman's voice. I'd never really gotten on well with those kinds of people in Prospect, or anybody who ran the place. They didn't like us Time Benders - they feared us even when we were on the same side as them.

Keep your enemy's close and all.

She didn't wait for me to respond before getting to the point. "I presume you've heard about the growing threat of the Rebellion?" She scowled at the ground.

Or kill your enemies.

"Yes, I have Ms President."

"I need a favour from you."

Oh hell no, if she wanted me to go back in time and erase the Rebellion it wasn't going to happen. Not a chance. *I wanted to sleep first.*

"With all due respect-"

"I'm not asking you to go back in time, I need you and the other Time Benders to kill a certain individual in the present."

I swore if she asked me to go looking for some twat who called himself the Raven I was going to jump off the side of the building.

"There's a threat." *Oh here we go.* "Another Time Bender. We can't have them going back into the past and doing anything harmful to us now can we? Or else they might take away your precious life here." I squirmed uncomfortably. She had a point. If there was a Time Bender with the Rebellion then they had a huge advantage, and they probably cared less about rules than I did.

"Alright, so what do you want me to do?"

"Kill him if necessary. I understand you've developed a way of following people into the past?"

"It's... a theory," I replied cautiously. A theory and a huge risk Vix was only just starting to study - none of us had ever tried it.

"Well find a way to follow him when he goes into the past," she said shortly. *What... she literally just said I didn't need to go into the past.*

"How do you know this isn't just a rumour?"

"Because I've had people studying your logs." *OK what the hell?* "And I understand you found a wooden sculpture of a bird in your previous mission, which hadn't been there before - not to mention the randomness of being ambushed on your mission?" So it was a little weird? Why the hell was she going through private information? That kind of stuff could only be shared between Time Benders.

"How do you know that?" I took a step forward intimidatingly and a guard caught my arm.

"Well nobody had visited before the 1940s since you went there a few hours before. Therefore I have reason to assume this is all strong evidence of another Time Bender. One rumoured to be called the Raven. Tell me it's not suspicious. He knew who you were in that life and how to screw it over." She smiled as she finally had me wrapped around her finger.

"This is all a little far fetched don't you think? It's not really strong enough evidence of anything and I very well could have changed something in 1921."

She raised an eyebrow. "Sure. Killing some low life bootlegger ended in having a wooden bird resembling a Raven on a phone booth in Germany."

"I never said it looked like a Raven... Ma'am, I don't mean any offence but-"

"Well, who was shooting you then?"

"I don't know. It's over now so-"

"Nova dear, my people have done their research and even if it was all just a slight meaningless change and the Germans happened to see you following that train - this other Time Bender still needs to be brought down."

I stared at her with my mouth wide open. She smiled bored. "So, bring back his head within the week please."

A tad bit morbid but OK your majesty.

"Bitch," I murmured under my breath when I turned away.

"What?" she asked, genuinely not hearing what I'd said.

I turned my head back around. "Nothing."

That pretty much ruined the rest of the party for both the others and myself. I began rounding them up into the pod to take them to one of the meeting rooms.

They clambered in with annoyed expressions from their night being interrupted so early and sat on the chairs, waiting patiently for Vix to arrive so I could begin telling them our mission. When he arrived he was dressed in sleep attire and had a scowl on his face, similar to the one Landon had from also being woken up.

"Our precious majesty," I said sarcastically, "wants us to kill another Time Bender who's working for the Rebellion."

Some shouts and groans followed shortly as I told them what the president just informed me.

"Well she can shove her request up my-" Aeron started to shout before Fynn interrupted him.

"What do we get out of this?"

Everyone agreed, suddenly turning to me as though I knew the answer.

"Uh well, I guess we get to exist? Guys if you don't want to kill him fine - I will. If there's a chance he has more lives than me he's going down. This dude is going to erase all of us the next time he goes into the past, which by the way he's already done according to her." They held expressions of confusion.

"She has access to all of our records and logs."

"Even I don't!" Vix exclaimed angrily, I held my arm out to him and looked at the others expectantly.

"And Mr Tweety Bird-"

"I thought he was called the Raven?" Halo spoke up.

"Whatever," I snapped. "The *bird* or whatever has already been messing up my past lives and watch out - he likes to leave souvenirs and tries to kill you. In 1944 I found this wooden toy bird on a payphone, then got into a car chase with some twat trying to kill me and stop me achieving my mission."

"Well, that's just rude," Aeron mumbled.

"I know!" I exclaimed. Finally somebody saw what I saw: a threat.

Halo sighed. "A wooden toy and someone chasing you don't necessarily mean it was this Raven person. And why call themselves the Raven?" Everyone turned to watch me expectantly.

I snapped. "Can everyone stop staring at me like I have the answer to all your problems?"

"OK," grunted Cedrix and we all turned to face the boulder. He smashed his fist onto the table leaving a slight crack in the glass, we all groaned.

Well, at least we had someone willing to help.

"How do we find him?" Landon asked. *Yeah... thanks for presenting a logical question I don't actually know the answer to.*

"Well, we can find him when he goes into the past... if we work out how to do that first..." I slowly turned my head towards Vix with my puppy dog eyes.

He pursed his lips and nodded. "I'll do my best to help. I have some theories that need testing as long as you're all willing to help."

I looked around the room expectantly before Halo let out a long sigh. "Alright." *Nobody asked you – okay - sorry she could help.*

Aeron jumped up from the chair with his fist in the air and yelled out. "Woo! Let's get this shi-"

Fynn grabbed his long pope coat by the gold hem and yanked him back down until he fell into the wheelie chair.

"Yeah, I'm in too." Fynn sounded less enthusiastic. I'd never really thought he enjoyed this life, he'd much rather be with his wife and daughter than with us lot partying and earning money by doing... not so good things.

Everyone turned to face Ace who was staring intently through the glass table. His face had turned a chalk white and I coughed awkwardly.

"Don't worry Ace, I don't expect you to."

"Why the hell not?" Fynn asked, narrowing his eyes. "He's a part of the team. He doesn't just get to sit back whilst we do the dirty work."

Ace's lip turned down into a sneer and he continued to look at the glass, I sighed loudly.

"Come on Ace mate, it'll be fun," Aeron prodded, elbowing Ace's side.

"Oh come on, you're the one who loves existing the most." Halo rolled her eyes, crossing her arms in front of her chest watching him expectantly.

Just as everybody was about to burst into a discussion I interrupted. "He can't."

"Why not?" Landon watched on curiously. Ace's head snapped up suddenly with wide eyes, he was about to shake his head when I continued.

"Ace lost his Totem, he's being taken in."

Silence.

Ace stared at me in shock - like he thought I would have understood - and I did. But he couldn't just keep it a secret before disappearing for a while. Besides, it wasn't like it was his fault he'd lost it, and the others deserved to know.

"Well *shit*," Aeron suddenly said, shortly followed by silence. I swallowed the lump in my throat and looked away from Ace. It was lucky he liked me because if it were anybody else he would have seriously done some damage to them.

"Watch your language..." Fynn mumbled, looking down at the glass and tapping his foot.

It seemed nobody knew what to say.

Apart from Ace - he apparently had a lot to say.

"What the hell Nova," he growled standing up abruptly, it seemed like the whole room came alive as everyone stood up, ready to defend me and keep him where he stood.

Landon had a hand against Ace's chest pressing him back whilst Aeron and Fynn stood either side of me. Halo even stood, feet in a wide stance and flicking her gaze between the two of us.

Cedrix, however, continued to sit with his feet on the table. "Ha!" Cedrix grunted watching the encounter as though he were at the movies.

Vix was the only one not shouting over one another and instead leant against the wall rubbing his temples.

Suddenly he shouted out. "Stop! All of you!"

The room suddenly crawled in on itself and we all took a step away from one another, silently crawling back into our chairs. We all respected Vix.

"Ace, I understand why you didn't want to tell the others, that's why I didn't. I respect your decision. But now it's out, there's nothing you can do. We'll get you fixed up when you're taken in."

Vix understood why he didn't want to leave and probably wanted to help him rather than him being taken away. However some things were out of his control and it was his job to inform authorities if a Time Bender was at risk of doing damage to himself, or to existence.

"When are you leaving?" Halo finally asked.

"Whenever they decide to pop out of nowhere," Ace grumbled. He refused to look at me and I felt a flicker of regret - quickly I suffocated it. It was for the best. I'd done him a favour.

"Don't worry mate, you'll get your Totem back... somehow," Aeron contributed, not so helpfully.

"Nova's been there before, she survived so it can't be that bad," Landon added reassuringly, Ace looked up with a fierce glare.

And I thought because he liked me he would be easy on me.

"Back to the mission," Vix interrupted and we all turned to face him with serious expressions.

"I want you all in the lab tomorrow - 6am sharp." There were groans of protest. "There's a way I think you'll be able to follow other Time Benders and I'd like to test it. I'll see you then," he said.

We all stood with sour expressions, tomorrow was going to be a long day if Vix had more than one theory. It usually took him hours just to try one theory. And no doubt I'd be doing all the hard work since I had the most lives.

As we all clambered into the pod and it set off I noticed Ace watching me. I didn't look at him but said goodnight to everyone else as they got off.

When it was just Ace and myself I finally looked at him. "Ace-" I began to say but I stumbled on what I was going to say next. I'd never really been used to saying sorry and honestly, what was I even apologising for? I'd done the right thing by telling them.

"I should have at least been the one to tell them," he said.

"You were never going to do that."

"That doesn't make it okay for you to Nova," he said tiredly. I bit the inside of my cheek. Then his tone went cold. "I told you because I thought you'd understand. Clearly not."

He left the pod and I watched through the glass as he slammed his fist into the wall and turned to face me with a tired but nonetheless scary glare.

He'd get over it in the morning…

CHAPTER 5

I was right. Ace got over it pretty quick but he was still a little moody with me... OK, he was very moody around me. And being moody didn't help with trying to get his Totem back by a strange technique Vix called meditating... I know. Apparently punching and blowing things up wasn't going to get it back. Crazy.

Actually, you know what was crazy. I hadn't eaten at all since that morning because I'd been doing what Vix said all day: Running tests and 'meditating'. I could already tell there was going to be some peer pressure for me to do all the hard stuff.

Needless to say, I was right. I arrived back at the White Room last. And by last, I meant the only people taking part were Vix and Fynn. Who knew where the other four were?

"Where are the others?" I asked as I resumed my position on my pod and lay on my back. I turned my head away from the blue light beckoning me to step into the past.

There was a loud yelp followed by the sound of a grunt. "Did you just pinch me?" Ace appeared in the blue-lit doorway, gripping Aeron's ear.

60

"No," Aeron snapped back. He jammed an elbow into Ace's stomach. He didn't flinch.

"Look who I found." Ace let go of the purple clown and shoved him forward.

"I was going to come," he grumbled and feebly waved his hand whilst shuffling his feet towards his pod. "I don't see why we all have to be here. Nova has the most amount of lives so out of everyone she has the highest chance of catching a glimpse of his Totem."

"What if he has more lives than her?" Ace asked. I felt a bubble of anger build up inside me. I chose to ignore it. If he had more lives than me then I'd know.

Vix pinched between his eyes. "None of that matters unless we can find a way to locate him, and the only way we can do that is in the past-"

"Providing he's real," Fynn pointed out.

"Yeah well, how do we find him?" I asked with crossed arms.

"Don't look at me, I don't actually know how it truly works for you. But judging by research... start with looking for his Totem on the timeline."

"And how are we supposed to know what his Totem is?" I replied in a not so kind tone.

"Fair point," Ace said from across the room and looked at me with a scornful stare.

"Are you all idiots?" Aeron suddenly laughed, looking at us incredulously. We returned curious expressions, prompting him to continue. "Seriously?" He paused for a moment, not believing we didn't see what he saw.

"Spit it out," I said as I placed my hands on my hips and watched him expectantly.

"Raven...?"

We stared at him in surprise, dumbfounded either by what he'd said or that Aeron had said something smart. I then remembered the Raven I'd failed to kill, I'd purposely written it off as bad aim but now I was almost positive. I had found a wooden Raven that wasn't there before, was ambushed to stop me changing the future and shot an immortal bird. You couldn't destroy Totems, which would make... the man who called himself the Raven, have the Totem of a Raven. Did you get all that?

"Jesus," Fynn said under his breath.

"That's Christ to you," Aeron replied with a chuffed smile stretched across his face. "So now I've done my service to the group can I go back to my personal business?"

Ace narrowed his eyes. "I didn't know hiding in the VR room to avoid us was personal business."

Vix spun around in his chair and rested his hands on a control panel. "What's the point in you guys having a VR room when you could just go to any of your lives?" Vix questioned.

Ace scowled and fired back. "What's the point in going back to your lives if you can't do what you want?"

Fynn and I looked at one another and shared the same look of *here we go again.*

"To earn money." Vix narrowed his eyes. "You should be more grateful-"

"OK!" I exclaimed and took out a small metal case that rested below my monitor. I fumbled to open it and dipped my fingers into the black gel.

"We ready?" I held up my black covered fingers. Aeron made a grumbling sound and lay down, also opening his case. Fynn had already dipped his fingers in it.

"Bye buddy, hope you find your dad!" I heard Aeron quote a line from an old movie before there was the sound of a grunt and Ace's fist hitting his stomach.

Vix quickly wheeled over to each of us, handing earplugs so we could concentrate. He gave us a thumbs up and we began to smear the black gel over our eyes.

I don't really understand why we did it and who and why they'd invented it but it was useful for us to concentrate on seeing all the different timelines we'd bent with our own.

That probably didn't make any sense to you but it's okay. You don't need to understand how it works unless you have the ability, which only a few people do… in this lifetime at least.

At the time I also didn't see how it was supposed to help us find the Raven but according to Vix meditating or doing whatever this was helped to 'open our minds' - as if our minds couldn't already connect us to a body we lived in hundreds of years ago. I thought our minds were pretty open already.

But not open enough.

A blindfold didn't work the same. This gel prevented you from opening your eyes, and it separated you from reality or in a Time Benders case - from the present.

(This isn't an ad I swear - but go ahead and picture it as one of those dramatic perfume adverts).

Anyway, the trick is not to let your thoughts float around aimlessly. You close them off; bury them deep until you become your subconscious. Concentrate not with your eyes (well because you can't open them) - rather concentrate with your mind, and focus on black. Feel it, sink into it, surround yourself with it. Wrap yourself in the silky strands of darkness, and let it slip between your body - your mind. Then open your thoughts.

What do you see?

The timelines. Everything, every moment, every memory of every life, every path you could have taken in front of you. All parallel beside one brighter timeline: *The* timeline - my timeline.

And there she was: my Totem right in front of me, a grasp away waiting. She waited for my signal - for me to choose a timeline, a moment. Some timelines were shorter than others - all with different presents that were minutes or years away from another timeline. But all stretched far, far back to my first life. I couldn't see before then simply because it was so far away.

Occasionally my Totem chose a timeline with a different life to me - it would lead me into the life and somehow it was always the one I desired. I turned away from my Totem and watched for something else. I concentrated deeper and waited. Waited for the flap of wings, a loud shrill cry or something.

But nothing came.

Eventually, my mind began battling itself, my thoughts wanting to resurface, I was tired and my Totem was fading. I knew as soon as the blue light began to fade even more I'd lose it forever.

So I brought myself back to reality. I grasped the darkness - wrapped my hands around and tugged, pulled on its tendrils and felt it slip between my fingers, slipping away teasingly. My thoughts resurfaced. The timeline vanished and I was aware of my body.

I gasped and made a soft groan. Vix had his hand on my arm within a split second, shaking me into reality. The earplugs were taken out and I could hear him.

"Nova."

"Nova." Another voice.

"Nova." And another.

"Hi, bitch."

I swiped my hand across my eyes, wiped away the gel and blinked vigorously. Aeron bent over me with a grin that stretched across his face. I jumped and accidentally bumped my head against his.

"You were there for a while," Fynn exclaimed from across the room.

I blinked confused and began looking around the room. Fynn stretched his arms out and had a towel wrapped around his neck. Ace sat directly opposite me crossed legged - meditating or something.

"Did you find him?" Vix asked urgently.

"No. How long has it been?"

Aeron's face dropped into a concerned grimace. "Nova... it's been a month."

"What?" I shrieked. I sat up suddenly and swung my legs over the side of the pod and jumped. My legs crumbled underneath me and I crashed to the floor. Aeron let out a fit of giggles and he too fell to his knees, laughing with tears in the corner of his hazel eyes.

"It's only been two days." Fynn rolled his eyes.

Only? Did he just call two days only?

"What..." I replied hazily, accepting Fynn's hand and he hauled me to my feet. Fynn wrapped me into his brown arms and I felt myself relax.

He rubbed a soothing hand across my back. "I know, even 22 hours takes me out. I can't imagine two whole days."

"I only managed 6 hours. Oh well! Guess I'm no help," Aeron exclaimed and shrugged helplessly.

"It didn't really feel like two days," I mumbled. Fynn helped me sit back down.

Vix groaned and placed his head in both his hands. He swivelled to face me and scooted over on his chair.

"Get some rest and get back here as soon as you're ready-"

"Are you sure that's a good idea?" Fynn interrupted. He placed a hand on my shoulder. "Look at her. She needs a day before going back."

Vix flicked his gaze between Fynn and me before sighing. "Okay. But I need you to train after you have a nap. Remember the meeting with all the clients is in two weeks and by then we'll need to have a plan to bring forth to your clients and the leaders."

So much for 'resting' then. I may as well have just vanished back to the timeline. At least then I'd be doing something productive. He also referred to it as a meeting when in actual reality it was more of a formal, posh as hell party. The closest I could compare it to be was like a red carpet but for politics and we were the main attraction.

"The Rebellion or whatever they call themselves made a statement yesterday night. The rumours about another Time Bender are true and you're expected to give a speech that will be broadcasted at the event to the city on a news station."

Ugh - no rest for the wicked.

"Why me?" I groaned, resting my hands behind me.

"Because you're the one with the most amount of lives," Fynn said.

"Unless you count the Raven," Aeron added. I flashed a glare at him and planted both my feet onto the cool ground. Once I'd gained my balance I began walking to the door.

"So who is this Raven? And are we positive that it's his or her's Totem?"

Aeron nodded. "Well. Seeing as you were ambushed in 1944 the same day you shot an immortal raven and found a wooden bird. Yes, it's definitely a raven."

"We also know it's a male then," I said.

"Maybe he's hot." Aeron escorted me to the elevator as we left the others to continue 'mediating'.

I nodded my head, watching him through the glass doors as they shut. When I soared into the air, a bright light suddenly lit up the elevator and I watched the city as I skyrocketed to my level.

As we slid around the building I noticed on the other side - way below me were crowds of brightly coloured people like a concerned mob of ants. I found myself rolling my eyes. The rebellion wasn't a threat. Prospect held too much power and we could easily eliminate them if need be.

CHAPTER 6

I slept for what seemed like only half an hour when in reality it was the whole day. I woke up to the sun setting and a persistent voice.

"Super-Nova!" It squealed with a high pitch.

I wondered hazily out of my bedroom and into the kitchen and the lights immediately turned on. I looked over to where the elevator sat patiently. Inside were Fynn and his daughter, a young girl, with the same curly brown hair and brown skin.

I slid open the doors to reveal not only the two of them but also his wife, Mia with a large pregnant belly and her dyed red hair curled around her tanned shoulders. She looked normal - and by normal I meant anything but the average Prospect citizen. No dramatic clothing statements and no facial enhancements or bright tattoos. That's why Fynn loved her so much I presumed. Not only because she was wonderful but also because she reminded him of the past we'd gotten so far from.

"Hey, there superstar." I held open my arms to Star and she eagerly jumped into them as I hauled her up on my hip and swung her about.

"You're getting big," I commented. She let out a high-pitched giggle and wrapped a finger around one of my silver strands.

"Star wants her hair to be just like yours." Mia stepped forward and kissed me in the cheek.

"You look amazing," I told her. "But no - you don't need your hair to look like this. It's become basic." I rolled my eyes.

"Guess you set a trend," Mia laughed and followed me to the sofa. Fynn went and grabbed us a bottle of something delicious.

"How come I don't set trends?" he called from the kitchen.

"It means you're unique," Mia called back. Star giggled again and jumped from my lap onto her mother who let out a groan.

"Careful sweetie - don't hurt the baby."

"How long?" I asked.

"Any day now hopefully. We're eager to meet her," she began to say before trailing off. Her words set in and I let out a loud shriek.

"A girl? Oh my gosh, I'm so excited for you!"

Fynn handed me a glass and rolled his eyes. "How come you didn't tell me?" I accused him.

"We've just been... busy - I don't know," he fired back.

"Huh," I grunted, narrowed my eyes at him and took a long sip - I needed it.

"Sorry, I thought he'd told you." Mia smiled wearily and placed a hand on her stomach.

"Apparently not. No worries I'll just be extra hard on him during training."

Mia grimaced. "Don't hurt him too badly, last time he was a wreck-"

"Okay! We get it," Fynn interrupted with a roll of his eyes. "Nova can fight."

"Nova's the best in all the universe," Star interrupted, grinning brightly at me.

Fynn narrowed his eyes and ruffled her brown curls. "Hey now you. What about Daddy?"

"Meh." She shrugged. "You too."

I let out a bark of laughter and reached across to pat his arm. "Maybe one day you'll defeat the unbeatable Super-Nova."

"Or maybe the Raven will," he teased and I rolled my eyes. *As if.*

"What's a Raven?" Star asked instantly and I felt my heart drop, she would never see a real-life Raven, only ever in pictures.

"It's a type of bird," Fynn explained.

"Commonly associated with sadness. And death," I continued, finding myself snort.

Whoever this guy was he must have had a lot of sadness in his past lives - if you believed in that.

But then again, why wouldn't you believe in it if time travel were actually possible…?

"That's sad. Poor Raven," Star pouted her bottom lip.

"Not poor Raven - stupid Raven," I mumbled under my breath. He'd unknowingly given us a pretty big clue on how to find him in the past. Now, all we had to do was take it in turns to wait for him to show up.

Easy. Hopefully.

"Honey, why don't you go put on something to watch?" Mia whispered into Star's ear. She eagerly jumped up as though she were no longer sad for this Raven and made her way over to find something to watch. I watched the curly-haired beauty from across the room and smiled. She had a beautiful mixture of her parents in her: Their dark skin, Fynn's amber eyes and Mia's face shape.

Now don't get ahead of yourself. Just because I had a soft spot for Fynn's family - it didn't mean anything. Everyone else could evaporate into dust and I'd stretch my arms out at the extra room - but these people meant more to me. I wasn't a complete sociopath... I liked to think of myself as morally grey - don't laugh. Fine, we'll go with *light black.*

"So what are you guys doing about this?" Mia finally asked.

Fynn opened his mouth to speak but slammed it shut when I flashed a fierce glare in his direction.

"Yeah... that's confidential. Sorry babe," Fynn replied. He wrapped an arm around her shoulders and kissed the crown of her head.

"Oh sorry, I understand." She took a small sip and let silence engulf us.

It was an awkward silence frankly. I didn't really have anything to say to her since nothing was going on in my life that wasn't confidential.

I didn't particularly know why they'd decided to come to see me considering they only ever got to spend a couple hours a week with each other. It was a wonder she was even able to come here with everything that was going on.

"So... have you decided on a name?" I finally asked. Phew.

Mia immediately perked up and grabbed her husband's hand. "Well, almost. I want to call her Moon since Star and Moon," she giggled.

Hell no. You couldn't call your daughter Moon after calling your other daughter Star. "What does Fynn want to call her?"

"Emily."

My body turned rigid and I swivelled to face him. My eyes went wide and my mouth dropped open. He looked up at me through his dark lashes and grimaced.

"It just seems too out-dated," Mia continued. "I understand that out-dated is your guys' thing, but you can't keep living in the past. Life must go on."

Emily was a special, sort of intense name for both Fynn and I. We'd known her before we took her from existence.

A client had ordered Fynn to kill a man in the year 2075. What he hadn't told us was that the man had a daughter, named Emily.

Long story short - Fynn couldn't do it and brought me into the mission without telling me it would end an entire generation. I could only go into the year 2065 before the girl was born because I'd die before 2075 from an incurable disease. And I killed him. Without knowing I'd been the one to wipe out an entire generation of people.

I came across Fynn's logs a month later and read about a girl named Emily on a mission he'd gotten me to do. And it all made sense. Then I was taken in - specifically because of Fynn.

"Why would you do that?" I mumbled angrily.

"I - I... Sorry."

"Yes," I replied hotly. "Go with Moon."

After that, the conversation pretty much died and we found excuses in talking about Star and how well she was coming along in school. Then they decided it was late and left.

Once I saw the pod float away I angrily hit the glass with my fist and poured myself a glass of wine. I hated wine.

But then again no amount of the new fun alcoholic drinks could take away the simplicity of a bottle of wine and I needed something simple.

So much had changed over the years. I remembered when the light bulb was first invented, albeit I barely remembered anything past the 19th century. Mainly because I hadn't been to those lives since... well since I lived them and recorded that I had a life there.

There was no reason to go back other than that... I mean who wanted to catch the plague nowadays anyway? Or crap into a bush? Or - *oh god...* not brush your teeth ever. And I really didn't fancy somehow being accused of a witch before I was supposed to die in that life.

Then that would mess up all my other lives from an early stage and it would just annoy me to the max.

Too much could go wrong and I had no way of knowing what I was supposed to do in those lives. They were so far back I had no memory of them at all.

It was too big a risk for even me.

Besides... what was I doing anyway? Oh yeah. Drinking.

At some point in the night, I stood up from lying flat on my back staring at the LED lighted ceiling and floated over to bed wondering when the sky had become artificial too.

I woke up in the early hours of the morning with the taste of blood. Stumbling over to the bathroom and flicking the lights on I groaned.

It took a moment for my eyes to adjust to the sudden white light and when they did I felt my heart drop.

My face was smeared in blood from a slow nosebleed. Thankfully it wasn't still bleeding but I did look like I'd just gone on a murder spree. And *trust me* I knew what that looked like well.

I immediately began scrubbing the blood off of me and into the sink. I watched the red blood mix with the cool water and swirl around the basin before sinking into the drain.

I peeled off the clothes I'd fallen asleep in and threw them into a pile. I stumbled back into the bedroom and gasped when I saw a figure standing by the windows.

I covered my underwear with my arms and crouched down, grabbing a blanket with my foot and quickly hid under it.

"What the hell? How did you get in here?" I shrieked, flicking my eyes between my blood-stained bed and the figure by the window. A crazy obsessed fan?

The person stepped out of the shadows and into some of the light the bathroom provided. I gasped a second time.

An elderly man stood there dressed in a fancy tux, holding a glass of champagne in his hands. But it was no man from the present. It was Williams, live and in the flesh standing in my bedroom, the champagne glass held towards me whilst I crouched down naked.

And that was pretty much all I remembered from the so-called dream after I woke up, still on the floor naked and wrapped in a blanket - a killer headache and blood-stained bed sheets.

It was a catalyst night that set off a whole series of future problems.

CHAPTER 7

Time: Present
Location: Prospect

I'd been kicking Fynn's ass for an hour before someone finally stepped in to give him a break.

It felt good: letting out all that bottled up anger I'd saved for a rainy day. The bloody lip, bruised jaw and quickly approaching black eye somehow made me feel ten times better.

For once I was looking forward to Gia dressing me up in a couple of weeks like a Barbie doll and strutting my way into the 'meeting'. Perhaps I'd get to know some new clients by breaking down boundaries and addressing this Raven person finally.

"Oof!" Landon grunted as I flipped him onto his back and held the tip of my blade to his throat.

"Hell, Nova are you trying to kill me?" he wheezed.

I dropped the blade and held out my hand. "I wouldn't be helping you up if I was trying."

"He just got out of the infirmary," Halo sneered. He brushed past me, handed Landon a water bottle and helped him over to a bench.

"Then he shouldn't be fighting against me," I sneered back, feeling a familiar sense of wicked triumph watching Landon rock back and forth in pain. "We all know-"

I was cut off by a fierce battle cry as Aeron came charging from behind me in an attempt to catch me off guard.

In one swift movement, I ducked below his arm and swivelled to jab my elbow into his side. Now he was the one caught off guard and backed away winded.

"Oh - come... on!" He gasped for breath, curling into his stomach and falling onto his knees. "How did you see me coming?"

"Your reflection in Landon's glasses," I took a swig of water and watched his mouth drop open, "and the battle cry kind of gave it away."

Aeron stomped his foot to the ground and looked me dead in the eyes. "One day Nova."

Uh-huh OK purple boy.

The sound of the pod slid open and we all turned our heads to an angsty looking Ace.

"Why are you here?" I used a towel to wipe the sweat off my forehead.

"Vix let me okay?" he snapped with a glare.

Alright moody. No need to get your panties in a twist.

Ace made his way over to one of the dummies on the far end of the hall and our eyes followed him until he began repeatedly punching the doll. Cedrix glanced at Ace from his own dummy and made his way over to us.

"You." He bounced from foot to foot and gestured for me to step back onto the mat.

"Bonus round." Aeron cupped his hands over his mouth and shouted before wincing and grabbing his rib with a sharp glare in my direction.

"Can't I just-" I began to say before Cedrix charged into me. In one fluid motion, I was flying through the air and landed into a rack of weights like a sack of potatoes.

"Oh crap!" I heard Halo exclaim. "That's got to hurt."

Actually no - OK - yeah it had really hurt. But I bounced right back up, two feet planted on to the ground. I sprung into action like a flying badass/ninja/assassin squirrel.

Cedrix was busy laughing with Aeron on how I flew through the air and so didn't hear me as I silently sprang on him, jumping until my foot made contact with his face.

I imagined his face being slapped to the side in slow motion and I smiled smugly.

Although my satisfaction didn't last long before he swiped my legs from underneath me and I landed on my back.

We went back and forth delivering strong jabs. I used his slowness to my advantage and he used my significant weakness to his strength - well, it wasn't that I was weak... it was just he was significantly stronger than me.

There was a reason people called him a Boulder, and today I was getting the tour of how his name came to be.

"Ugh!" he cried when he delivered a painful blow to my cheekbone. He pulled away sharply and waved his fist about in pain. That's right. My cheekbones were as sharp as a blade. *Feel the pain asshole.*

"Watch it, buddy. Don't ruin my face." I panted, leant back and brought my leg up to kick into his stomach but he grabbed in a swift motion and brought me back down onto the mat. I heard the crunch of my back before the flare of pain. There was a chorus of "Oohs!" from my fellow peers.

"You're doing great sweetie!" Aeron shouted. I wearily tilted my head in his direction and flipped him off. "Be nice," he called timidly.

There was no 'nice' in the Nova vocabulary. Try 'beating the absolute crap out of this guy and showing him how I'm way better than him'.

"That's quite enough." Landon stepped onto the mat and guided Cedrix away from me.

"Hey..." I panted. "I wasn't finished with him." Landon raised an eyebrow and offered his hand to me. "Watch your back," I said to Cedrix, noticing a familiar metallic taste in my mouth.

"Watch yours," Cedrix grunted with a chuffed smile on his face.

Show off.

"Chill Nova, we know you could take him if you weren't being worked to the bones," Landon reassured me

81

and helped me over to a bench with the others. I smiled tightly and nodded my head.

But still. I should have done better than *that*.

Aeron grinned. "Alright then... who's actually looking forward to this year's so-called meeting?"

"What?" Halo asked suddenly, her eyes fluttering away from Cedrix and then to me. "Oh yeah, I can't wait. Last year was so fun," she said with a bright, slightly less miserable smile.

"It isn't really a meeting though," Landon said with a strained chuckle. He used his t-shirt to clean his glasses before placing them back on his nose.

"It's been nine years and I still don't understand the significance of it," I murmured to Landon. He and I had been here the longest and so the excitement of the event seemed to have faded. We also knew best that it wasn't a meeting. It was just an event to remind us Time Benders weren't the ones in power.

Landon offered for me to sit down but I knew if I sat down I never would have wanted to get up again. Fynn finally emerged from the target practice room with his knuckles wrapped up in a white bandage. I felt a surge of energy and satisfaction swell up in me.

"How's the pinky finger?" I raised my eyebrows and smiled proudly.

"Painful. This one works though." He flipped me off with a triumphant grin.

"I could break all those fingers right now." I glared and his grin wavered into a grimace.

"Sure Super-Nova."

"Try me," I continued with a tilt of my lips.

"Alright, we all know you can fight," Aeron said, still holding on to his side. "Can you guys check to see if when she elbowed me my kidney went straight through me?" He twisted around and held up his shirt.

"She isn't that good." Halo rolled her eyes.

"Bull. Did you not just witness what she did to me? Cedrix is just a Boulder," Fynn exclaimed leaning back against the wall. "I think it's safe to say she's better than me and that's saying a lot."

Cocky much but I still held my head up triumphantly pleased with the compliment.

"Yeah but she's no assassin." Halo pulled a face and I snorted, *seriously?*

"Then what do you think our job is Halo?" I fired back. "Oh wait. You aren't an assassin because you don't kill anyone. Have you ever murdered someone?"

"You sound proud." She turned her lip up.

"I am," I fired back. It sounded slightly morbid when I said it like that – well it sounded morbid any way I said it.

"Then I'm worried about your health."

"I'm not worried about yours, I already know you're just a whack job." Ugh, that was a quick and cringe-worthy comeback. Usually I was better than that. Cedrix must have knocked a few thousand-brain cells out of me.

"What did you just call me?" *Don't make me repeat it. The unbearable cringe-*

"A whack job." *And I said it.*

"Okay guys. Let's have no more fighting today." Landon interrupted. "Nova was doing pretty well before Cedrix showed up and I don't doubt that she'll continue to do well."

"We'll see how long that lasts." Halo jumped up, her boobs following her and practically slapping her in her face. As if she could even reach her arms past her chest to hit me anyway.

Apparently she'd found a way because suddenly her red nail had sliced through my cheekbone and her fist had wrapped itself around my hair.

"Hey now! This isn't fighting, this is just catty," I shouted over her yelling in an attempt to get her off my scalp before she ripped it off entirely.

Finally she let go, but not without taking a chunk of my hair. I felt my vision turn red as I stared at the silver strands in her hand and instantly wanted to send her to her next life where I'd kill her again and again and again... and you get the picture.

Heck, I could have if my own cockiness hadn't made an appearance.

I'd been doing pretty well, delivering swift and hard hits to her face (not that she could feel any of it with the amount of plastic in her body) but then I felt someone yank me off her and throw me onto my back.

Ace looked over me, his hands pinning me to the mat and legs either side of me. I looked down wearily and struggled underneath him.

"That's not fair," I panted and tried to bash my head against his but my neck didn't stretch that far. A shame considering how good it would have felt. Maybe it would have bashed his Totem back into his head.

"Figured it was my turn," he murmured, his tongue flicked against his bottom lip and I followed the movement with a clenched jaw. This would have been the moment he looked down at us and made a suggestive comment but instead he stood up and offered me a hand.

There was no way I was going to fool for that.

I reached my hand out towards his and just as we were about to meet I swiped my leg behind his knees and caused him to tumble down. I'd planned on rolling out just in time to jump up and fight him but as he fell he grabbed hold of my waist, turning me with him until I was a tangled heap on top of him.

Now he would make a suggestive comment. Ace opened his mouth with a faint smirk but was interrupted when a voice echoed throughout the room: "I believe I've found a way to follow Totems. Can you all come up for some testing?" Vix ordered.

There was a series of groans as we began making our way towards the pod to go up a level.

"What was that?" Fynn murmured.

"What was what?" I asked, taking long gulps of water and following the others.

"You and Ace."

"You're actually delusional." I rolled my eyes and clambered into the pod where we all panted heavily.

"Did Cedrix hear?" Aeron asked and we all looked towards the man punching his dummy vigorously with his headphones in.

Ace didn't wait for a reply before throwing a water bottle towards him; it sailed through the air and smacked Cedrix directly in the head. He looked up puzzled then eagerly leapt his way over to us in long strides.

The doors closed before he had a chance to climb in and we looked through the glass as his face turned into a scow. The others laughed loudly.

"Tough luck big guy." Ace shrugged and waved a hand as we began to move.

CHAPTER 8

Time: 1ˢᵗ August 1979
Location: United States of America, California

Vix was a genius: an actual genius who never ceased to impress me. His theory seemed to work, we found a way to follow each other's Totems into the past. Now if we saw the Raven whilst meditating, we would actually be able to follow him instead of watching in despair as he floated away. It took a crap ton of attention and you had to know what you were looking for or else other Totems were barely noticeable. But they were there.

I was attempting to find Halo's moth and when I caught a glimpse of it I followed it until I appeared in my 1979 body.

Wow, it had been a while Nicki. This was the life after my 1940s life and was about 4 years after my neighbour (Robert from the last mission) had died. I'd only ever visited this life once, mainly because you weren't much use in a seventeen-year-olds body with the strictest dad. Even then it was just to take notes on what the life was so I could read my logs if I ever had a mission in that life.

I'd visited all my lives when I first discovered the ability with Vix and Landon. After visiting all 208 lives my memories seemed to refresh. I'd remember tiny details... like where all that information was in my 1940 mission or the fact there wasn't meant to be a wooden bird on the payphone. I seemed to remember less about any life before the 1800s though. I couldn't even name a life before then without needing to scroll through the logs.

Everything came into focus and I held onto the bedpost staring around at my old pink bedroom covered up in various posters of old bands. I quickly realised I had no idea how to find Halo.

Quickly, I searched for my calendar finding it on the back of my door as I'd left it.

There were 5 months left till I died. 19th December 1979. She had the day marked as her first day of Christmas holidays on their annual trip to Colorado to ski. Little did she know, she'd marked the very day she would die.

I yanked open a drawer and pulled out my diary and read yesterday's entry. Christopher (my old boyfriend) had taken me to the movies to watch Alien. I shuddered, instantly remembering the first time I'd seen it.

Today was a day spent at home, I remembered correctly that I stayed in bed and attempted not to remember the freakish film.

It'd have to change - sorry Nicki no time to catch up on sleep. I had to find Halo.

I sat crossed-legged on the floor and calmed my breathing, this meditating crap was boring but it needed to be done if I were to find Halo.

I saw the moth, floating in front of me teasingly. I stood following my mind, which in turn followed the moth. Gradually I weaved my way through my old home and clambered into my dad's car, he was in the backyard playing catch with my half brother Michael so he wouldn't notice.

Nicki didn't know how to drive but thankfully I did.

Now a lot of stuff could go wrong, so I kept to the speed limit and followed the god damn moth. I'd been driving for a good hour until I arrived outside a public swimming pool.

Here? She was here?

The moth floated persistently until I stepped out of the car and walked over to the metal fence. I peered through, watching children as they splashed into the pool and teenagers who were jumping off a diving board and blasting music.

I entered and scanned the area for the moth. It was flying over towards a brown skinned figure sunbathing. I stood over Halo, covering her with my shadow.

She opened her eyes and scowled. "Took you long enough, can we go back now?"

"I was an hour away." I crossed my arms in front of my chest irritably, Halo looked nothing like how she did in her future. For one, her chest was flatter and she now had frizzy brown hair and looked about ten years older.

"Can I help you?" she suddenly said her voice hinting she had a Mexican accent and she looked at me puzzled.

You had to be kidding me. Halo just left me here?

"Oh no, don't worry."

She just freaking left? I travelled an hour for her just to go back?

"I'm just kidding." A hysterical giggle erupted from Halo and I turned sharply to her.

"That sure as hell wasn't funny," I sneered. "I've got to drive Nicki back now, she can't drive."

"Well, that's stupid," Halo tutted. She grabbed a magazine and looked distastefully at the fashion.

"Well at least we know we can follow each other's Totems. Come on, let's get her back and go home."

The hour back with Halo was a pain in the ass and I ended up getting an earful from my dad. His quickly receding hairline and red forehead kept me entertained, although I felt bad for leaving Nicki with such a hassle. I was thankful I didn't have that obstacle in the future. It would be a burden.

Eventually, I snuck Halo into my room and I followed her moth back to the present. Halo promised to sneak out before Nicki realised she was there.

Somehow, despite leaving way after me Halo woke up just moments after me.

Vix was there to greet us, relief on his face to see us back in one piece. The others were dotted around the room, eyes closed and each attached to monitors.

"You're the first ones awake," Vix said and lent me a hand to sit up. I took it shakily and began rolling my head side to side in an attempt to relax my muscles.

"Can we find a way to bring our Totems in? I'm not going to be able to get back with the Raven when he dies... unless he changes sides of course."

Vix nodded his head. "Yeah we'll try that next. You just have to force your Totem with you."

"How are you feeling?" Ace opened one eye from across me. He was sat crossed-legged on the floor in an attempt to search for his Totem.

I replied with a wince. "A little tired."

"I was talking to Halo." He crossed his arms and turned his head towards Halo. *Someone's a little snarky still.* Halo shrugged and swung her legs off the side.

"I feel fine."

"You're supposed to keep your eyes closed," Vix scolded, narrowing his eyes at Ace.

"It's not working," Ace snapped. He jumped abruptly to his feet and poured himself a glass of water.

"Well maybe if you-"

"Ughhhh!" Came a long groan from the other side of the room, Fynn clutched his head and rolled onto his side.

Aeron who was across the room shouted out, suddenly bolting upright with a loud shout slamming his head on the light above him, we all jumped towards them.

"What? What happened?" Vix asked urgently, examining their heart rates and flashing a light in Fynn's eyes. Ouch.

Aeron stumbled to the floor and crumbled into a heap. "Can someone turn off the lights?"

"The others aren't back yet," Halo said, lending him a hand. I stood in the centre of the room wondering what the hell was going on, Fynn was clutching his head, his face growing red with suppressed pain.

"Holy shit. What happened to you?" Ace contributed. Aeron self-consciously ran a hand through his purple hair and sat up straight.

"Well, Fynn took his time finding me." Aeron took generous sips of water and he brought his knees to his chest.

"Wow, make me seem like the twat why don't you." Fynn shrugged Vix away from him with a groan and lay back down.

"What life did you go to?"

"1790, how was I supposed to know he was a slave?" Aeron grumbled under his breath. "I thought they were freed by then..."

I rolled my eyes, and *that* was why we did our homework - reading each other's logs. Or just brush up on history in general because he was about 60 years too early.

"It's not that difficult to remember. Half of my lives are useless because I'm always a slave you idiot." Fynn had an arm covering both his eyes and went to rub his temples softly. Time Bending had always given him a headache. It had apparently gotten significantly worse the more he did it, especially going further back than the 19th century.

I cringed. How could Aeron have made that mistake?

"But then I'd only have like one life with you and you'd know it easily! We were supposed to surprise you," Aeron exclaimed in an attempt to defend himself. Fynn didn't look too impressed by him.

"I have other lives further back where it's fine," Fynn retorted.

"Oh? So what happened to half your lives being in slavery-?"

"Okay shut up," I snapped. "Aeron, you're just useless, do your studying." I looked at Fynn and felt my heart clench at the way his eyes were glazed over like he might be sick. "Fynn are you okay?"

He grimaced. "I haven't – haven't been to any lives like that since the first time."

That was a dark year. Fynn's second year here had consisted of visiting former lives and filling out logs. The emotional strain of those lives sent him into a long depression. I could kill Aeron for not using his brain and making Fynn go back to that time - it was unnecessary.

Aeron bit his lip nervously and wrung his hands together. "I'm sorry."

Fynn waved his hand. "It's fine. It was supposed to be a surprise anyway. I'll get you back in training."

Aeron's face paled and he turned to Vix. "Well I guess I should just quit now. Who wants to volunteer doing this full-time?"

"Not me." Fynn sat up gradually and I handed him a glass of water. "Thanks," he mumbled.

"How did you get back without Aeron's Totem?"

"Managed to use my own, thank god," Fynn replied, rubbing his eyes again. Well, at least we knew it was possible to use our own Totems now.

Ace meanwhile was helping himself to a drink and standing over Cedrix who lay peacefully snoring. "Is Cedrix asleep?" Halo asked, also appearing next to Ace.

"You out of everyone should know he can sleep easily." Ace raised an eyebrow at her offering his drink to me.

"What's that supposed to mean Ace?" Halo sneered.

"It means I know you've been sleeping with another Time Bender. And *that's* against the rules."

My eyes widened and I wondered if he thought I could still hear him or whether he thought I was too focused on Landon - waiting for him to arrive back.

She was sleeping with a team member, was he being serious?

Halo made a low growl in her throat and my ears perked up curiously.

"Whatever... you... too much... on... Nova..." What? What was she saying? I couldn't hear over the persistent beeping.

"Nova?" I looked up at Fynn who was watching me expectantly. "You alright?" he repeated. I nodded my head in reply.

"Is Landon back yet?" Fynn began to say before there was an even louder beeping sound. We froze startled by the noise and looked around intently.

Vix jumped to his feet, flying across from us to where Landon lay - the surface beneath him glowing red and continuing to beep.

"Get me the-" Vix began screaming, but Ace was already holding a metallic rod to Vix. He snatched it quickly.

Landon's shirt was ripped down the middle and Vix had shoved the rod into his chest until a popping noise was made, followed by a long hiss. The beep paused for a moment before beginning again, filling the entire room.

The rest of us stood around helpless as we began to watch Landon's body convulse and jolt. He was in some kind of mental paralysis - stuck between the past and the present.

"Landon!" Vix began calling, gently pinching his arms and legs, trying to bring him back down to reality.

"Can someone stop that beeping?" Aeron whined, his hands were pressed to his ears and eyes were screwed shut. I sneered - *weak*. A flicker of shame washed over me. Maybe he had some kind of trauma to do with loud noises. I scoffed, *what did I care?*

Fynn managed to sort the settings out on Landon's monitor until it was just a faint beeping we could all cope with. "Everyone out!" Vix shouted loudly standing over Landon distressed.

Everyone left the room panicked. Halo was weeping softly. I backed out of the room last, staring at Landon's body as it went slack and his eyes opened and stared right through me.

Vix came out after fifteen minutes of us all staring at the door shocked. "He's stabilised."

Halo was the first to rush back into the room and over to the table where he lay, his head hung to his side and his mouth was opened slightly. He looked dead.

As everyone crowded around Landon's body that was now hooked to various items of equipment I stood back with Vix.

"What is it?" I asked quietly.

"What I feared."

And that was enough for me to realise we had lost Landon.

CHAPTER 9

Time: Present
Location: Prospect

Halo didn't leave Landon's side for two weeks. She stayed, holding his hand refilling IVs, brushing his hair, washing his face. She even shaved him at one point.

When Vix tried to explain to her what was wrong with him she started shouting over his words refusing to listen - let alone believe any of it, so then I attempted to talk to her.

It began with me arriving on Landon's level where he had been moved to, I found Halo right where I had expected her to be: right by his side. I'd never seen her look so vulnerable... stripped from her makeup, hair tied up and bags under her eyes. She looked like the past: crumpled, damaged and vulnerable.

"You look like shit." I crossed my arms and leant against the doorframe. Her face turned to me blotched and tear-stained. Instantly I felt bad. She was clearly hurting and me bullying her wasn't going to do any good.

"You should get some sleep," I said but it came out harsher than I had intended. This wasn't like me at all - to come up here and offer kindness. Well, I wish I could say it was out of kindness but really I thought she needed to get a move on and stop slacking.

"You aren't helping so just leave us alone." She wiped her face with the back of her hand and leant over Landon again.

"Believe it or not but we're trying to help." I narrowed my eyes at her and flicked my ponytail over a shoulder tilting my head up. "What does Cedrix think?"

Her breath caught and then she shuddered. "Cedrix has the brain of a cow, why are you asking?"

My face lifted into a condescending smile. "I think you should cut it off before it becomes a problem. Don't you think?"

Her mouth dropped open in surprise and she cleared her throat. "Thanks for the help Nova-"

I stood up straight and cut her off with a sigh. "Okay relax. That might have been mean. But I really did come here to help. How's it going?"

"Vix wants to kill him," she mumbled with a sniff. She rose and stood between Landon and me protectively.

"There's a difference between killing and pulling the cord on someone already gone." I crossed my arms.

"We don't know that-"

"There's no sign of his Totem which means he's lost it, which means there's no way for him to get back."

"Then I'll go get him and he can follow mine back."

"It has to be his own Totem for this. Besides you wouldn't be able to find him, his body could even be dead in that life-"

"But his mind isn't."

"Then don't you think he'd rather be at peace?" I replied stepping closer. Halo flinched and gripped Landon's hand, watching his face closely.

"I can't believe you're on Vix's side, you've both known Landon the longest," she grumbled. And there it was. One of the many reasons Halo hated me. I belonged here, she was the new kid and she was jealous of my knowledge, my lives, my relationship with Landon and Vix she'd never have. As if being ten and staying up till the early hours of the morning listening to grown-ups talk and prod me with different stuff was fun.

"We have been bending time a lot. It was always bound to affect us."

"So why aren't you the one like this?" she snapped.

I thought back to the nosebleeds and seeing William from 1921 in my room, then swallowed the thought. "I'm younger. I don't know." I growled in frustration. "But now we know, Vix can find a way to help us when we start showing signs."

"He didn't show signs-"

"Yes, Halo. Yes, he did," I replied with my eyes closed. I was starting to get annoyed by her persistence. "You can't just sit here grooming him and waiting for him to wake up. He's *brain dead*, you can't go back from that."

"Then we'll find a way to fix him."

"No!" I snapped finally. "No we won't. There is no point in wasting time trying to find a way to fix him when there's a chance we'll all be erased by the Raven."

And there she was, the real Nova. The one you only saw in person: the uncaring bitch.

Halo looked slightly taken aback by my outburst as I continued. "You don't have to come tonight. Let the people who actually care about what will happen to us all if there's an uncontrollable Time Bender out there handle it," I said calmly, walking to the door before stopping and turning to her. "The longer you delay the inevitable the more he'll be suffering, he's trapped in his own mind, not just the past. Try to imagine how that feels."

She didn't look at me, just picked up a wet cloth and patted his forehead. I clenched my eyes shut, irritated. Then I closed the door shut and made my way down to the White Room.

I meditated for only a couple hours and there was still nothing. No Raven. Vix was busy plotting a timetable of when each of us had to meditate. My number was up three times as many as everybody else and for an hour longer than everyone else.

How long was he expecting this to take? The Raven had to show up in at least one of our timelines at least once.

So where were they?

"You've got a busy night tonight," Vix mumbled with his hand on his chin as he analysed the screen in front of him.

"What's the plan then?" Aeron asked.

"Get ready. We'll make our way to the Dome and meet with the news interviewer, then you can go to the meeting downstairs."

"We've never had to do an interview before," Ace mumbled moodily. I sighed at the sound of his voice. *He was still here*. He hadn't been taken in yet, much to the disappointment of Fynn and I.

"We've also never been doubted by the entire city," Fynn replied to Ace's comment with a roll of his eyes.

"They have no reason to doubt us," Ace fired back.

"That's the attitude buddy," I sneered. "One of us has lost their Totem, another one is basically dead, another is *grooming* the dead person. And the rest of us can't find the Raven."

It was silent for a moment as everyone looked at the ground. Ace raised his head and glared at me. "Thanks for the optimistic input, Nova."

"So…" Aeron interrupted the stare down between Ace and I. "How much are we allowed to say about the Raven tonight?"

"You don't have to worry about that. I know the Director personally so I asked for questions to direct only to Nova." My ears perked up at the mention of my name and instantly my heart dropped. Why was it always me that had all the responsibilities? Typical.

"I want you to say a direct message to the Raven and the Rebellion. He'll be watching as well as some of the city, people have actually been paying attention to the news, and they've been hyping up the fact you're all doing an interview."

"Interviews are stupid." Ace rolled his eyes.

"You know what you have to do Nova?" Vix rubbed his eyes tiredly.

"Mhm yeah, I've got it." *Nope, I really didn't.*

"When asked about the Raven you...?"

I...

I...

"I look at the camera and be like 'Oh hi Mr Tweety Bird, you've pissed us off and I'm coming for you?' Oooo suspenseful music."

Vix let out a long sigh and looked up. "Something along those lines. Don't tell him you're going to find him. Tell him he has a chance to turn himself into the Time Benders where he belongs."

"Another male Time Bender is much appreciated," Aeron smiled to himself.

"The Presenter will do the rest," Vix continued.

"Another one? Are four boys and only two girls not good enough for you?" Fynn asked.

"Yeah but you're married," Aeron replied. "And straight," he added quickly.

Ace clasped Aeron's shoulder, causing him to jump. "Well how about you do some meditating and you can meet him before Nova kills him?"

Aeron slammed his mouth shut and mumbled some excuse about leaving the oven on when we all knew he had a deathly fear of cooking as well as fearing this mission.

I crossed my arms frustrated. "Is that all Vix?"

"Yeah, go have fun and stick to your schedule," he said without looking up from his screen. "Oh wait-" he said suddenly, looking up with a sombre expression. "If on the off chance they ask where Halo and Landon are, say they're working on the Raven situation... and under any circumstances don't say we haven't found him yet."

I nodded my head firmly before the door slid open. "You coming Ace?" I watched him cautiously as he stared at the wall.

"Huh?"

"Coming?"

"Sure."

CHAPTER 10

Time: Present
Location: Prospect

"Could they not have been more careful with your precious face?" Gia shrieked as she smeared my face with makeup in an attempt to cover up the bruises and cuts plaguing my face.

"Pff, you should've seen what I did to them."

"I did. I'm glad I'm not having to fix their-" she scowled at the makeup brush, "mess."

My hairstylists were eagerly yanking at my hair with excited expressions. "So soft," they moaned as they wrapped the silver strands around the curling wand.

When they weren't complimenting my features, they liked to gossip. I didn't mind since it was refreshing to separate myself from the past and who I was now. It was these moments I genuinely enjoyed: engulfing myself in the life of fame. The future was something to look forward to - providing you lived in Prospect. I doubted the Raven cared for dressing fancy and smiling for the cameras.

"I know. I was sure as hell lucky to fill in for Mona, he was *something*," giggled one of the girls working on my hair, the male next to her sighed dreamily.

"What's it like Nova?" One of them asked.

"Hm?"

What's it like going into the past to kill people for money from corrupt businessmen? Oh it's great.

"What's being famous like?"

"Alright," I replied with a shrug.

"Just alright?" they exclaimed, pausing from what they were doing to look at me in shock.

"It's great in moments like this, but I never get to enjoy it without having something to do."

They all nodded their heads sympathetically - as if they understood. "Maybe you should have just become an actress." Gia pursed her deep purple lips and coated my eyes in a dark eyeshadow.

"Eh-"

"Or a singer! Can you sing?"

"You don't want me to sing."

"I've heard her," Gia contributed, turning her lip up at the mention of me singing. "It's a good thing she never pursued a singing career."

Normally I'd be offended if somebody criticised something about me - or embarrassed. But at least I could agree with her on that.

"I don't know why you'd ever want another career! You can visit the past and change the future. Do anything you want!" exclaimed the girl who jammed a pin into my head to fasten my curls into a bun. This hairstyle was clearly new to her, nobody wore their hair like this nowadays but maybe I could bring the classic style back.

I watched the girl's reflection in the mirror. She made it sound like Time Bending was a choice. It wasn't really. I was made this way, born this way. I was an anomaly in the creation of humans.

"I can't do anything I want." I rolled my eyes and shook off the uneasy feeling creeping up my spine. They all tilted their heads to the left with solemn expressions.

"Ah..."

"If Time Benders didn't stick to their own past lives then it could change even the minor details. Sure, we're pretty lenient with what jobs we do for people, but a lot of research goes into them on their end." At least that's what I'd been told to help me sleep at night. "Think what would happen if I killed someone who was supposed to have a family. It would wipe out and an entire generation - it could be you. Never to exist." Their faces went from solemn to terrified.

Maybe I shouldn't have used the 'K' word. These people knew I was an assassin and were barely fazed by the other side of my job but I'd been told not to talk about my killing habits plenty of times by Vix. Apparently telling stories of how I once took off someone's head using hedge trimmers made people uncomfortable.

"But that won't happen to us will it?" The male exclaimed and sprayed my hair with hairspray.

"Hopefully not, this Raven asshole is going down."

That was another thing I probably shouldn't have told them but since I was about to announce it to the entire city, Vix could probably let it slide.

Standing in front of the full-length mirror I felt myself smile, the dress hugged my body perfectly, a long slit up to my hip where Vix's assistant had insisted I wore a knife strapped to my thigh just to add a little more badass and sexy-ness to the look.

I needed to look strong and like I was protecting the city. But if I was being completely honest, I would have always worn it if not on the leg that was showing then it would be hidden.

I was an assassin before being famous and not everyone liked me.

I smoothed my palms over the black velvet and tilted my head to the side. That was definitely the best part of the night. Having my hair like this, a small connection to the past where I'd pin my hair up into a bun. Back in the 18th century, it was for practical use but now it made me feel less like everyone else... until every young girl would want to wear her hair like this.

I was standing at the bottom of the stairs about to enter the stage in record time, my bright red lipstick was newly applied and I was listening to the latest news broadcast that led on to us.

I stood in front of our little line; Ace was behind me, and behind him was Fynn, Aeron and Cedrix. One of the Producers had deliberately put us in this order. I was always going to be first and then Ace was always going to be next to me since we played up to the beautiful couple everyone wished we were.

I knew exactly what to do when we were out there: you please the news channel and you please the public. Always give them what they want. Our clients might have been the ones paying us but the public were the one keeping us in business.

I was so focused on Ace being pressed against my back I hadn't heard our cue to go on so Ace placed a hand on my lower back and guided me onto the stage. *Thanks a lot Ace, you just fuelled about five thousand teenage girls watching.*

There was one thing that hadn't changed a great deal in the last hundred years, and it was the news.

The stage was small, the majority of it glass with one small red sofa big enough for three people, and two stools were placed behind it. I was glad they'd gotten news Halo and Landon wouldn't be attending.

The interviewer stood shaking out hands before gesturing to the seats and sitting in an armchair. She had a pixie cut, wore a smart black suit with sharp edges. She looked like the new futuristic businesswoman.

I sat closest to her on the sofa, with Cedrix behind me on a stool and Ace pressed against me on the sofa. Aeron stood holding out a hand for Fynn to sit on the sofa before pulling a 180 and cheekily sitting next to Ace before Fynn could, we all laughed.

It was moments like this in which I loved Aeron, he wasn't as serious as I was to the public, and he kept us looking like ordinary people. That was exactly what everyone wanted; they didn't want to feel indifferent to us biologically, they wanted to relate. Aeron was relatable. I was… an assassin - a celebrity assassin at that.

It was likely that everyone was watching as we rarely did interviews… like ever.

"It's so great for you to join us, even if it is just the five of you we understand you're very busy." She smiled kindly.

Fynn was first to speak, his perfectly white teeth almost as blinding as the lights directed on us. "We're really sorry about that, Halo and Landon were unable to make it tonight. We decided it was best for us not to all come and instead keep the city guarded at all times. I'm sure you can understand."

The interviewer blushed and nodded her head before her attention drifted to Ace's arm as he placed it behind my shoulders. I smiled sinking into him and placed a hand on his thigh as though he hadn't been ignoring me for the past two weeks.

"You guys have a busy night tonight I understand?" She smiled.

Ace began running his finger in circles on the side of my shoulder and goosebumps pricked up on my arms. "Yes," Ace began. "We have an annual meeting with the leaders of Prospect, it's all very formal," he laughed and another round of goosebumps appeared as his smooth voice melted into my ears. The bastard was enjoying this.

"Well, we won't keep you too long," she chuckled and turned her attention to one of the cameras. "Join us back here after a break where we'll be asking some rapid questions about Time Bending, relationships and more serious topics."

There was the sound of the bell and instantly the crew began moving busily around.

"Hi, it's great to meet you." I finally addressed the interviewer whilst there wasn't a camera on.

"You too, I'm Lola."

"Nova." I reached across shaking her hand.

"You look so much more beautiful in person," she gushed. "And tall."

"She does," Ace agreed, reaching across to shake her hand. I leant away from him uncomfortably and he smiled knowingly at me.

"Thank you," I replied to her compliment, smiling gracefully.

The break was over and we were back to being live with wide smiles.

"Right so the first question from one of our viewers *IshipNace101: what's your favourite life?*"

I didn't break the smile from my face as Ace recognised the username and brought his lips to my ear. "You wouldn't want to disappoint the fans."

I rolled my eyes giving him a nudge, trying to shake off the pleasant shudder from having his peppermint breath fan my face. I tried to focus on the others as they answered the question until it was finally my turn.

Good question, easy to answer. "Oh easy, I love the 1920s, I'm always there. In fact, I love anything from the 19th century and onwards."

"Why's that?" Of course, she was going to ask me more. I thought this was rapid-fire. Nonetheless, I bathed in the attention.

"Well, anything before the 19th century is a nightmare. Besides business doesn't bring me there anyway so I haven't visited any life before the 19th century. The risks are way higher and life is just genuinely crappy - no TV or anything," I joked, gaining a few laughs from the others.

Now, remember that for later... I specifically hated anything before the 19th century.

"Right next question."

"Let's do it." Aeron cracked his knuckles besides Ace.

There were a few questions - all ones we'd answered before, normal easy ones like what our favourite hobby outside Time Bending was, and other ones about Time Bending we had to give brief careful answers to.

"Right okay, I've purposely saved these questions from viewers till last but it's all the people are asking."

111

Here we go.

"You all spend a lot of time together…" We all nodded our heads slowly with cautious smiles of 'oh shit here it comes'. "Do any of you get closer than...?" She clenched her teeth and smiled awkwardly, unable to finish the question. I laughed softly, placing my hands on my lap.

"I think…" I chose my words carefully, taking my time to think about it and imagining all kinds of viewers leaning closer to their screens - the whole city holding their breath. "There is a lot we don't share about Time Bending, it's a very confusing and complicated topic in which rules have to be in place. There's also a lot of personal and biological - some might say magical rules and restrictions which means it's simply against our nature."

Lola sat forwards watching me intensely as I opened up slightly. "We're all incredibly close to each other." Ace wrapped his arm back around my shoulders. "We're family - bonded through past and present."

I had to force my eyes ahead instead of turning and looking to see Cedrix's reaction to the word *family*.

Aeron made a large movement off to the left dramatically crossing his legs before stretching his arms. "Relationships are forbidden," he said bluntly, shrugging and we all laughed as the tension left the room, but I caught a glimpse of Ace wiggling his eyebrows. I jutted my elbow into his side.

"But we like to break the rules sometimes," Ace added. This time his arm dropped from my shoulders and gripped my waist. I barely blinked an eyelid. The gesture may have been unnecessary but he was right to give the fans what they wanted, even if it was talking about breaking rules; rules that were also about not wiping out everything as we knew it.

"Well, there you have it," Lola said to the camera with a small laugh before her face turned serious. "Now that we've gotten the fun stuff out of the way, it's time to address the elephant in the room."

I crossed my legs, and all of us sat forward keeping jokes aside. "Onto more pressing matters."

She turned to a cue card beyond the camera. "The Rebellion is a growing threat to our everyday lives and children. They are growing stronger by the day and we have been growing more and more fearful in our homes."

Ace sat forward, his arm coming from around my shoulders to rest on his knees. "Lola, let me interrupt you here. You have absolutely nothing to fear." *What the fuck Ace?* But I kept the encouraging smile going. *I was supposed to say that...*

"We're happy to say the Rebellion is being carefully dealt with and we can assure you things will not get out of control."

Lola sat forward in surprise. "And the Raven?"

I quickly cut in before Ace could say anything else. "This Raven," I looked into the camera, "is no threat. They stand against the seven of us defending you - our home and city." I felt a surge of confidence when I could see the

113

others nodding their heads and so looked back at the camera.

"Raven. We are offering you to turn yourself in, you have the chance to train alongside us and be an official Time Bender…" People started moving around offstage with confused faces. "Whether you have more or fewer lives than me…" They started speaking over me. "If you fail to do this, you will face…" I paused, looking at my friend's faces and then around the room.

"What is it?" Lola asked.

A producer sent a confused look toward us. "We're offline. Something's interrupted the broadcast and-"

"Sir…" A small woman entered, a screen in her hand. The Producer looked at it and grabbed the remote, turning one of the large screens in our direction so we could see.

What I assumed was the Rebellions logo flashed onto the screen before a slightly fuzzy face appeared. They clearly had crap cameras in the Rebellion. Although it definitely made a dramatic first appearance. It was a woman, surprisingly young, probably in her early thirties. She looked kind, deep brown hair - almost black, and warm brown eyes. She was looking to someone off-camera who most likely signalled for her to begin.

"Hello, citizens of Prospect." Her voice was slightly crackled but everyone could hear. "My name is Cleo, leader of what you call the Rebellion and I'm here in direct response to Time Bender Nova. From my brother, the Raven: Catch me if you can." Her lips formed a confident smile and she began to open her mouth before the screen turned static as the people surrounding us regained control.

It seemed the Rebellion was coming for my 'dramatic entrance' crown.

CHAPTER 11

Time: Present
Location: Prospect

Immediately after the incident, several guards rushed us from the building and into a white car.

"Nova?" Fynn lent me a hand. I nodded and lay across the seats, resting my head on his lap.

He scrambled into his pocket and found a pair of earphones to put in my ears. We had no blindfold and so made the best out of a tricky situation and Ace began taking off his blazer. As my eyes fell shut I saw my friend's anxious expressions for the last time.

Ace's eyes were intense, his lips in a straight line as he fumbled with his jacket. Aeron had a hand over his mouth in concentration, watching me with an expression so serious it almost didn't look like him. Cedrix - well for once Cedrix actually looked interested in what was going on and sat on the edge of the seat behind us.

I leant my head back into Fynn's lap, his brown eyes soothing me with the sheer calm in his expression. I clenched my jaw, as the blazer settled over my eyes until I could see nothing.

"Can you hurry?" I heard Ace say and felt the car pick up. Thankfully new technology made the car run so smooth that I could barely tell we were moving. The only thing I could feel was Fynn's hands moving up and down my arm in an attempt to help me.

It only took a minute before I was completely absorbed in darkness. Time had stopped and I was no longer in the present or the past. Nothing existed at that moment but the timeline and the Raven whose rich black feathers almost blended into the darkness. Its wings were outstretched as if floating through the air but getting nowhere. I paused and watched my Totem patiently waiting in the distance but this Raven asshole stayed put - probably watching my Totem to see if I went anywhere.

I don't have all day, asshole.

He failed to do anything and I had no idea if I'd been here for a minute or an entire week but then it didn't matter because suddenly I could feel my body falling - whether it was falling in the present or something was wrong I had to force myself back. Except I couldn't, my body felt like I was falling but I could still see my Totem in front of me and a Raven hovering tauntingly over me. And then suddenly it soared into the air - or well, darkness. I reached upwards in an attempt to grab hold of my Totem to follow the Raven but my hands only wrapped around silky strands of darkness.

Suddenly I wasn't falling anymore. I was standing upright - black glass surrounding me - reflecting my

117

image. I stepped forward and greeted the darkness in front of me, my face morphed slightly - like looking into a window at night.

And then as if a finger was comfortingly stroking my face I was drawn forwards and I could see past my reflection.

And there it was - my Totem: a blue firefly outside of a glass-paned window.

"Oh my!" shrieked a voice. There was an attempt to hold me up as I slumped to the floor.

"Wha- what..." I murmured, leaning my head onto the woman's lap and staring out into the night sky where a blue firefly flickered in front of me.

And that was all.

I was hot, sticky and my eyes would flutter open every now and then to the sound of concerned voices and then shouting. I finally fell into a deep sleep only to awake several times during the night restless and muttering things that made no sense to the people tending me.

By the time I awoke, rested and aware, it finally set in that I definitely wasn't in Kansas anymore.

I was lying in a four-poster king-sized bed with silky sheets and feathered cushions propping me up. The room was adequately sized with a dressing table and mirror in the corner of the room with a chest of drawers next to it. Candles covered every corner of the room and there was a window seat on my right with an arched window that overlooked trees and hills for miles. On the opposite side of the room was a fireplace with intricate designs.

I didn't remember this life... at all. I couldn't tell what year it was but the stonewalls, furnishing and the white nightgown I was wearing would suggest it was pre 20th century.

Feeling myself begin to panic, I scrambled under the duvet until I got to the side of the bed. I swung my legs onto the wooden floor and paused when I heard voices outside the wooden doors.

"I want to see my daughter!" An English voice grunted. Good. The location suggested England, which wasn't unusual for me. I was used to having different lives in Europe and occasionally America. So I could be in England but let's face it... the British were everywhere back in the day so there was no telling just yet.

"My Lord, I've been told by-"

"She is my daughter. I will see her if I want to." The door swung open and a man most likely in his late fifties maybe early sixties stood before me, dressed in... old clothes. Like robes and white wig kind of old.

What the hell was this year?

"Ah, Marion you're awake! What's all this nonsense of a fever?" He glared at who I could presume was my nurse. My name was Marion. "Here you are standing before me as though there were nothing ever wrong with you."

My eyes widened in shock, I was confused - very confused. I only held some recollection of being called

Marion but I had no idea what this life was about, which was bad. Really bad, I couldn't conform to rule 1 if I didn't know what life this was.

"Uh."

"Richard!" There was a shrill voice from the doorway, my father's face dropped into a deep scowl and he pivoted to face the doorway where a woman appeared.

She was stunningly attractive, and surprisingly young compared to my father but then again was anything that had happened so far *not* a surprise? Her hair was a curly brown and piled into a bun on her head and she wore a tight corset accompanied by a deep blue navy dress.

"Hello?"

"My god, lie down child." The woman came rushing forward with her arms held out as though I were going to fall. "I told you that you shouldn't have sprung such a thing on her! After what happened to Nugget."

"Nugget?" I questioned.

Both their mouths dropped open in shock. "Tell me child, don't you remember what happened yesterday?"

It'd been a hell of a lot longer than yesterday for me. Trust me.

"No."

The woman looked towards my father in shock who glanced at me with an open mouth and then suddenly he snapped. His face went from white to an instant red and he lunged towards me. "Stop fooling with me girl! This is not like you!" he yelled and instantly the woman stood between us, shielding me with her body.

"Leave Richard!"

"You have no right to tell me what to do! You hold no role here other than whoring around with my servants!"

So I assumed they weren't married... For a foolish moment, I had hoped this woman had been my mother but that was impossible. In all my lives my mother died - it was my recurring theme.

"You have two months and then you will give up your name for the sake of this family!" he screamed, slamming the door shut behind him.

What? What? Wait what?

What kind of hellhole was this lifetime?

"Shh," the woman murmured sweetly, guiding me back into the bed and placing a cool hand on my forehead.

Oh hell no, I wanted the hell out of this life.

The woman stroked my hair and spoke in a soft voice. "It happened to me too you know."

I blinked dazed. "What did?"

"An arranged marriage. I was in love with the gardener's son but I married the man anyway to please your father and our parents. Don't stress, child. I fell for him in time. Albeit not as much as my first love but love nonetheless. You will learn to love him in time too." She smiled warmly. "Besides he's long dead now."

Okay, so that was a lot of information to digest. I'd pretty much stopped listening after she had indirectly told me I was to be married and that she was my aunt.

"Oh," was all I managed to get out. I could only hope she would spill more.

"On the plus side, he's far richer than us."

I strained my neck to face her. "Who is?"

She blinked in surprise. "Why... the Count of Eldermore you're to be married to." My face dropped - as did my mood. Not that I was feeling particularly cheery in the first place.

There was a loud caw from the window and we both jumped, turning quickly to see a Raven pecking its nose against the windowpane. It was the same unusually large bird from 1944 with eyes the colour of obsidian.

His Totem would lead me to where he was; I just needed to get out of this hellhole.

"I think I need some fresh air," I mumbled sitting back up and trying to get out of the bed. The woman had already crossed over to the window and flung it open whilst shooing away the Totem. I just wanted to get this over with.

"I meant outside, I think I need a walk."

The woman nodded her head in understanding. "Shall I send for Abigail to dress you?" she said, suddenly appearing at the foot of my bed with a bundle of clothing.

I'd forgotten the pain of getting dressed during these times. Beauty *literally* came with pain.

"Oh yes, please." I felt the material of the light blue dress under my fingertips and touched the corset that would accompany it.

It was as though at the click of my aunt's fingers the maid or nurse or whatever she was had appeared like she'd been waiting.

She flashed a grin of slightly dirty and crooked teeth and her rosy cheeks glowed at me. She was actually quite young, maybe a year or two older than me - Nova. Shoot, this is really confusing. I was definitely a few years younger than nineteen but not anything too unfamiliar. I felt lighter with my height and lack of muscle - my skin pristine and smooth, not covered in scars and calluses.

"How are you feeling?"

"Quite alright..."

"Lady Susanna said you wanted to go for a walk. Your father's men have gathered downstairs for you."

I'd rather they didn't. I sighed - the struggles of being a woman in... whatever year it was.

As though fate realised my struggle, a diary sat open on the chest of drawers across the room. I crossed the room in an instant, my head swirling at the sudden motion.

"Marion?"

"One moment," I called glancing over the last entry dated 16th June 1661. It was only a short entry with ink smudged and detailing the events of my horse dying and being told I was to marry in no more than two or so months.

Well that was lucky (that I found the diary). It meant the day was 17th June 1661... what happened in 1661? I lost track of all those lives and who the hell would want to come back this far anyway? The English Civil war had ended a decade ago. I was an estimated sixteen or seventeen years old, which meant some of my life had consisted of war. My father hobbled on his left foot, which would suggest a war injury, and he had the title of a Lord by either reward or heritage. Charles the second sat on the throne in 1660 so life was relatively peaceful - but maybe hesitant? Right? I should have paid more attention to my logs. I would have visited this life at least once and yet I have nothing on it.

It was only a guess. I'd lost track of all those lives and who the hell wanted to come back to 1661 anyway? The Raven apparently... I supposed it could have been worse. I could have been some whore or peasant with the plague.

Wait, wrong time-period. Or was it? It would probably hit within the next five years but I'd be long gone by then.

The sooner I found and killed him the better - hell to negotiations. He could be across the country and if he was then I was sure as hell screwed because I wouldn't be able to make it within a day.

I could only hope he was following my Totem in an attempt to kick my ass however unlikely it was. He had no idea what my Totem was.

I held onto the back of the bedpost as Abigail tightened the corset and helped me wiggle on a series of clothing.

It would have to go eventually.

There was no way I would be able to kill the Raven dressed like this - no matter how much I felt like a princess. Not to mention getting past whoever these *men* were.

CHAPTER 12

Time: 17ᵗʰ June 1661
Location: England?

Walking downstairs with tight shoes and a corset actually proved to be not as difficult as I imagined and soon I was out of that dreadful place.

Three men bowed their heads towards me with friendly faces. This was a screw-up. A really big screw-up I should have just found my Totem and gotten out of 1661 there and then.

Except a lot of people in the future were depending on me and I didn't want to seem weak. And I would. It'd be 1 point to the Rebellion and 100 for the Time Benders.

"Marion," one of the men said. A slightly scruffy brown bearded man stepped forward and lent me a hand onto the path.

"Good morning gentlemen." *Was that right? Who knew?*

The guy with the beard looked behind me and nodded his head to Abigail and then we were off through the stone gateway arch and away from the looming grey bricked building. There had been a weak attempt of adding some colour to the gloomy building by planting various flowers and plants around the courtyard, and what would be a beautiful tree if it didn't look so dead and grey.

The air was humid but there was a gentle breeze which I was thankful for or else I would surely faint in this dress, and that would be humiliating. I wasn't going to conform to the damsel in distress ideal of the past. I was Nova. No, I was Super-Nova and I was going to kick these men back to the civil war and then kill this stupid man-bird.

However, once we were a distance away from the building walls, the bearded man stopped and his slightly chunky friend turned to face me.

"We shall leave you for a moment's reflection." *What?*

And then they left! Just wandered off in the opposite direction and I was left in the middle of a clearing staring at trees. *What did they expect me to do?*

Well, that was easier than I would have thought. Once I saw their heads disappear under a mound I smiled giddily, picked up my blue skirt and bolted... which as you might have imagined was pretty difficult.

Almost instantly, I skidded down a slope of mud until my foot clashed with a mossy boulder and I tumbled the rest of the way down. Quickly, I clambered back up using the help of a branch (which looked way cooler in my head, might I add). It turned out wearing a puffy blue dress and corset didn't make you look like a badass ninja jumping from building to building like Batman... just some fairy godmother forgetting the controls to her wings.

127

Combined with blood dripping from my nose and into my mouth, my hair had flown out in every direction, I must have looked like I'd escaped an asylum... on dress-up day... or Halloween.

I looked to the sky trusting his Totem, hoping he was still here and close. When I caught the glimpse of black wings I took off, only taking me two minutes before I ended up in the direction I'd run from.

Typical. I swear I was usually better than this.

I heard the sound of voices. The two men began meandering their way towards me and I only had a moment of panic before I fell to the ground with a squeal.

Who knew what gave it away: the sound of the leaves I landed in, my bright blue dress, or the squeal. I know what you're thinking: *I thought she was an assassin?* Well in my defence I was completely out of my element.

"Marion?" Beardy shouted, also appearing through the trees. The men paused and the guy with the large beer belly pointed his finger in my direction.

I sprung up instantly, preparing to fight instead of run. That's what I usually did, but this dress made both options impossible.

I opted for running. I was fast so at least I'd be able to lose the large one. I think it took a while for them to comprehend what was happening before they suddenly came after me. I spared a look over my shoulder at the bigger guy and wheezed - shoot. Learn from my mistakes. Never underestimate *anyone*. He had *charged* his way through undergrowth and was closing in on me. My eyes widened and I flung myself forward, barrelling through trees.

I felt like Cinderella to be honest or some other kind of runaway princess. My cloak flew through the air; curly hair fell from its braid as I whipped past trees. A blue firefly flew beside me and a Raven cawed in the distance. I knew I was never going to get to the Raven in time. But I could be so close. I poured every ounce of my training into Marion's body - willing her legs to be stronger until it felt like I was flying through the forest.

The most responsible thing for me to do was follow my Totem out of there and hope to meet the Raven another time.

But looking back and not seeing either of the men I realised I could continue... that was of course until I ran into a branch. I know, please save me the *'Of course, how predictable'*. I was just having a really bad week. I swear I was usually a badass ninja. This whole getting sucked into 1661 had thrown me off my game big time.

Everything after running into the undergrowth because I'd heard voices seemed to be a blur (mainly because blood was dripping into my eye from a gash across my forehead). But the hand slamming onto my mouth and being dragged further into the undergrowth was as clear as day.

"Shh," an unfamiliar deep voice murmured into my ear. I did as he said. I knew better than crying out when the people I was running from were standing no more than 10 feet away.

But they weren't the guys I was running from, nope. These guys were dressed in red coats and held guns. These guys were the goddamn British army and clearly, some fugitive scum had his hand on my mouth.

And yet still, I didn't move. I obeyed and listened to the heavy breathing of the man. My head rested uncomfortably between his shoulder and neck and I could smell the scent of pine and smoke.

It felt like hours we were sat there, twigs poking in my cheek and blood coating my face and his hand. After a while, he took his hand away from my mouth and I hissed at him. "Who are you?"

"Who are *you*?" he repeated with a deep voice. I was ashamed to admit it made my stomach flip.

"I asked first. Were they looking for you?" We both froze as a figure emerged a few metres away from us. Beardy was running a hand through his scruffy beard.

I held my breath as he turned towards the bush we were hiding in. His eyes focused for a moment and I wondered if he'd realised - if he'd seen me. But then he turned around acting as though he hadn't? When the other man appeared he shook his head. "She must have been heading South, back to the estate."

"Why-"

"She's confused," Beardy replied sternly, leading him away from the bush. Before he became out of sight he turned his head back in our direction and I released my breath.

Thank you. I said silently.

"Okay, let's get out of here. Your elbow is digging into my side and you're bleeding a lot."

"Oh... sorry." I shuffled out of the branches, my head was pounding by now and I couldn't see very well. The man followed shortly and then turned to face me.

My heart quite literally stopped, he was here - flesh and blood. Standing no more than an arms distance away from me although his black hair was a lot longer and greasier actually. He looked at least ten years older and somehow more attractive. I'd never pictured him wearing a grey cloak and leather boots but it suited him.

I'd blame it on the fact I was bleeding from my forehead and being in my worst nightmare that I felt compelled to leap onto him.

"Ace," I sobbed embarrassingly, with my arms wrapped around his neck and his own arms presumably reaching for a weapon. Fortunately, before I had to work my way out of *that* one I blacked out.

I woke to the sound of running water and something stabbing my forehead. Ace was bent over, biting his lip like he always did when concentrating.

"For the love of God don't move," he mumbled. The voice threw me off and I realised this wasn't my Ace. This Ace hadn't lived nearly half of the lives Ace had. If anything, this could have been Ace's first.

Besides, Ace wasn't here to magically rescue me and nor were the other Time Benders. I needed to find my Totem *now*. Forget the Raven. I didn't care how close I could have been to him. I only had a few hours left for sure.

"This is my first time doing this, so sorry if it's not up to your standard." He smiled, dimples and all. My heart melted, this Ace wasn't a douche... couldn't he come back with me?

He wiped my forehead with his thumb, helped me sit up and then handed me a leather canister of water which turned out not to be water but some nasty tasting alcohol or something.

"It will help with the pain," he laughed, noticing my disgusted face. "I've been through worse pain." I rolled my eyes to which he raised an eyebrow. To him I looked like a runaway brat, prettily dressed with a pixie-like face.

"So what's your name?"

"No- Marion."

"Okay No-Marion then." He broke a branch with his hands and threw it into a small crackling fire. He was apparently not going to tell me his name.

"Yours?"

He looked hesitant for a moment and continued adding wood to the fire. "Tobias. So Marion, let me guess." He leant away from the fire and pulled out some bread from a bag.

"Family issues?"

"Wow, congratulations that was fast." I smiled, accepting a chunk of bread he held out for me and welcoming the stale tastelessness of it.

He cocked his head to the side. "The Montgomery house?"

So that's what it was called.

"Yes," I reply, eagerly chewing on the bread like a starved person. He hummed to himself and leant back on to his elbows. I watched him closely as his eyes fluttered shut. Although this Ace was older and a lot smellier, present Ace was only going to get more attractive.

"I can feel your eyes on me. What?" he grumbled and tilted his head towards me, his eyes falling open.

"Why were those men after you?"

"I'm a wanted criminal for a crime I didn't commit," he replied after a moment's pause.

"What crime?"

"Murder."

"Oh." Well, I really hope this was just a simple misunderstanding and he hadn't really killed someone.

"You can trust me," he said, gathering twigs into a pile to add to the roaring fire.

"I know," I said almost instantly, except I couldn't really trust this man. He was a stranger, he wasn't the same guy who'd been flirting with me the moment he joined the Time Benders. He wasn't my friend. He was just a kind stranger for all I knew. He could very well be a murderer - a wanted criminal.

But I was an assassin.

(Way cooler if you ask me).

"So where were you planning on going?"

I looked up into the deep green trees towering over us as though we were nothing more than ants amongst blades of grass, and I felt that way. I felt completely hopeless, hanging onto a small raft across wild, unfamiliar seas. I was out of my element and the Raven had beaten me completely and I hadn't even gotten a chance to fight him.

"Home," I replied. I caught my breath and allowed my eyes to close, to search for anything - a sign of a blue light in the future but his voice pulled me back to reality.

"I'm sure you're missed." His voice was soft, like the silky strands of darkness I missed so much. My time was up. It was time to go home - defeated but alive.

You've had your adventure, the freedom of a lifetime. But it wasn't enough. It was time to go home.

Gently my eyes fluttered shut - the thought of home a warm promise that I yearned for desperately. Then, it was like being sucked through time. Well, it was like that every time, but somehow this was different. I was in the balance of time except something was off. It wasn't balanced. Strands of loose time and darkness consumed me and when I opened my eyes I saw everything.

The beginning of my timeline to the present.

My first life was the beginning of time. I was among the first human species to develop - the first to climb that hill, the first to be engulfed in the purest water none had ever touched, and the first to walk there. It was real.

I had a lot more than 200 lives I began to realise, watching the numerous lives unfold before me, living them within only a second.

I'd met extraordinary people... I had *been* extraordinary people. I was everywhere, my timeline was endless and growing with every second and every breath I took. I could see everything and yet I could feel nothing.

I couldn't feel the sensation of being held in my mother's arms but I could remember the experience of taking my first steps. I could see but I couldn't live.

Then in a flash, I caught a glimpse of my father in this life and then a tall stranger, dark wavy hair, and then a man. The Count. It was over; I was onto the next life.

The extent of what I was seeing overwhelmed me to the point of breaking. Soon I was watching the terror of my lives - the horrors of human history and I was defeated.

Something inside me snapped - like the breaking off a rope that tied me to the present. The rope was my Totem and it had gone.

And now it was cold, the darkness didn't relax me and lull me in. It restricted my breathing. I suddenly felt how unfriendly and isolating it was and I felt like I was floating through space: A timeless space with no way home.

I'd lost my Totem.

CHAPTER 13

I was numb all over. So numb I couldn't comprehend what was happening to me as I was carried through the rain and dumped into a muddy puddle.

As I opened my eyes I was aware I was lying on a gravel path and my dress had been torn to shreds. I felt my throat tighten.

I was still here.

"Oh good, you're awake." Tobias looked over me - water running over his forehead, black strands of hair hanging in front of me. A sob rose to my chest and I smothered it with a growl of frustration.

"What are you doing?" I choked. "Where are you taking me?"

"I'm returning you home, a beautiful young virgin such as yourself would fetch me a handsome price with your father." His eyes were cold, his voice cruel and sharp. Someone had clearly turned sour.

I snarled in the back of my throat. "My father would gladly hand you over to those soldiers."

"Your father?" he scoffed. "Lord Montgomery won't believe a word that comes out of your mouth."

My head swam with hot frustration and I felt the need to kill him - how I usually felt - but I couldn't feel my arms and legs. My hair hung in wet strands and I felt the blood rush to my head when he picked me up again and dropped me over his shoulder like a rag doll. Had he drugged me?

I remember cursing him several times, staring at the puddles and listening to the sound of his feet squelching through mud, the sound of drops of rain as they fell onto leaves and then down the back of my neck.

When we came further away from the woods and onto the pathway leading up to the house I began screaming, hitting his back hysterically for whatever reason. I was mad, not specifically at him - well yes I was also mad because of him. But I was mad at the universe, for not being able to go home. I was mad at the Raven who had gotten me stuck here and I was tired. I was tired of fighting and Time Bending and I was close to giving up.

Except there was no way in hell I was going to let him walk me through those gates without putting up a fight. There would be no containing Nova.

I screamed foul words they'd probably never heard before. I pounded at his back with my fists with the little strength I had as he strolled up to the courtyard and dropped me on to the floor.

I lay face down in the gravel, my fists curled around the tiny wet stones and when I snapped my head up I flung the stones into his face. He let out a cry and clutched his eyes, whilst I made an attempt to run out of the gates I'd only just left that morning. However, he caught me around the waist and lifted me up, trapping my arms. He shoved me in front of him as he guided me up the double steps where servants stood with wide eyes, whispering to one another.

"Oh!" cried Abigail. Well, I thought it was Abigail. I couldn't see very well out of my wet hair and I didn't really want to see anything but his blood on my hands.

I must have looked insane to every eye peeking from every paned window as people stopped working. Those who were on their way to the stables paused in their tracks and gathered towards the screaming girl.

Soon I was forced from one brute to the other, screaming my head off and kicking my legs. As I was carried into the house I caught the glimpse of my father's furious expression as he stepped out onto the stairs and Tobias dropped to his knees breathing heavily.

"Don't trust him!" I began screaming over and over until the large oak doors slammed shut and the hall was engulfed in darkness.

I continued to fight whoever was holding me until one more door was thrown open and I was shoved inside. I stared at the shocked and solemn faces of Abigail and a servant, then they clicked the door shut behind me. The turning of a key proved I was now a prisoner in my own home.

Home. This wasn't my home.

This was a Time Benders worst nightmare. And what was worse was that I was here alone.

I ran to the bed and pulled the covers over my head to block out light from the candles. I didn't care that I was covered in mud and dripping wet. I held the feathered cushions to my ears and engulfed myself in darkness but that was all there was: cold unforgiving darkness with no comforting blue glow.

The protocol didn't work this far in the past, there was no way for Vix to track where I was and if they couldn't see my Totem this far back then I was stuck here forever. And with what happened to Landon...

The Raven has successfully trapped me in the past.

Instincts told me to jump from the window - my common sense told me in the state I was in I wouldn't nearly survive, then I began to think.

I could jump. I'd die and wake up back in my body. *Right?*

But was it worth the risk? Whenever I killed myself in a past life it could mess things up further down the timeline. It would disrupt the path and besides I wouldn't be able to find my way back to the present if I didn't have my Totem.

So that was out of the question.

Now what?

No Totem, no way back and no Raven. I needed to find a way back but first I needed a plan.

There was no use running away when I didn't know the land, anybody, or anything about this period. Either I sat back and waited for help from the future or I...

That's all I could think of. I would have suggested speaking to Tobias and hope Ace remembered this life. If he did remember this life then all he would remember was me as Marion acting peculiar and him betraying me. Surely he would remember me calling him Ace? That was all I had to rely on right now. Except even if he did, Ace in the future had also lost his Totem and what could they really do to help me get back? Nothing. I had to get back on my own.

So all I could and had to do was act like Marion and get her life on track, whatever that may have been: the *Count* probably.

It couldn't be that bad, I'd get to wear a pretty dress and cross my fingers that they'd find me before I had to sleep with him. Or rather - I had to find a way to find my Totem again before then.

Two options.

I'd meditate like Ace - and wait for them - just in case one of them did have a life here. Maybe there was a way they could pull me out from the future, who knew?

And now I was calm, I could sit back and listen to my lies: wait for the others to do the hard work.

It was then I remembered Landon and the feeling of cold realisation crept up my back. What if this was what had happened to Landon? He too could have lost his

Totem and had no way of getting back... And that combined with the effects of Time Bending I'd been getting. What if my current body had gone brain dead and they thought there was no hope for me? What if they didn't bother trying to find me? I was here, alive still.

It wasn't like I could do anything to stop them from killing me. But then again, I wasn't stuck in my mind. I was just stuck in the past.

They didn't know that though.

As the fear of my friends pulling the cord on me whilst I was still alive began to build, I tried to reassure myself. Fynn wouldn't let them, and Ace would probably be so stubborn that nobody would even be allowed to touch me whilst I was away. I was more important than Landon. That was the horrible truth.

So with very little options other than worrying and waiting, I meditated. Since Vix constantly ordered us to even when the slightest bad thing happened I figured this is what he'd prescribe me in this situation.

As it turned out meditating proved difficult when the door was unlocked and my father walked in, an expression of eerie calmness I knew was masking an absolute storm behind.

I stood from the bed and walked toward him. "Please forgive me, I was ill-minded to run away. It was the spur of-" my voice trailed off when he began unfastening his belt, breathing heavily.

"Please," I begged and the breath was sucked from my lungs as he proceeded to walk towards me. I'd experienced pain but that didn't mean I was going to be fine with just letting someone beat me with a belt and not retaliate. I could easily kill him with nothing but my hands but that might ruin my cover.

Get me?

"I'm not going to let what happened to your mother happen to you," he said in a stern voice and he stretched the belt. "Give me your hands," he ordered.

I half expected Abigail or my Aunt to come and save me but when he began whacking my wrists until the skin became raw and blood began dripping down my hands it became apparent this was normal.

I was angry. Extremely angry I couldn't smash his head against the wall and angry at how ugly the world had been.

Instead, I took the beating, apologised and agreed to marry the Count through clenched teeth.

"You are fine." He gripped my raw skin and squeezed. I bit the inside of my cheek as I felt hot tears blur my vision. *That hurt you asshole.*

"You are not ill. You are not insane." His expression softened and he released his grip on my wrist and wiped a tear away before it fell - acting as a comforting father - like he hadn't just beaten me with a belt.

"You look so much like her." He smiled and then opened the door to reveal Abigail who looked slightly pale. "Run her a bath will you? Dress her and get her down to dinner as soon as possible. We have guests."

"Father," I called, my voice wobbled. He paused in his tracks and faced me expectantly but I chickened out before I had a chance to ask him what happened with Tobias.

"I'm sorry."

He nodded his head and smiled tightly, before making his way down to the stone staircase.

Abigail led me to a small metal tub where warm water and a bar of soap waited expectantly.

"What happened to your corset?" She was surprised when she turned from lighting the last candle.

"It was suffocating me," I explained, waiting patiently for her to leave but instead she pulled the completely ruined dress off of me until I was left only in white undergarments.

Okay then...

She moved busily around me collecting the undergarments from the bottom of my feet and then waited for me to climb into the tub.

"Can't I have some privacy?"

She raised an eyebrow. "There are no locks on these doors sweetheart and you'll be sorely disappointed when you realise you aren't to be left alone until you're married."

Oh, wonderful.

I stepped into the tub, wincing as the hot water shocked me and the water became a grim shade of brown.

143

Abigail took a jug and began pouring water over my hair and scrubbing soap into it.

"That must have been an adventure," she said, pouring water over me and running her hands through my hair.

"It's been a pretty intense few days Abigail," I replied with my teeth clenched, using the bar of soap to clean my legs. It was nice to have a bath for a change, less so since the bath was covered in dirt from me.

"No – no I didn't mean it like that! Just... what changed?" she asked, her voice was comforting. I felt I could confide in her and I knew we were close at one time or another. But I couldn't tell her. She would never believe me and it was against the rules.

"I don't want to talk about it."

It was silent for a moment, only the sound of water splashing against the side of the tub and my curled up body. I closed my eyes and searched for anything. Allowing darkness and the heat of the bath to relax my muscles, I sank into the water covering my body and finding no Totem.

After I was bathed Abigail wrapped my wrists in a bandage and cleaned the cut on my forehead commenting on how well the stitching was. It angered me that Ace - Tobias had put my head back together so neatly. It had fooled me into trusting him but really I had no one to blame but myself. I'd been weak running away like that, injuring myself and then jumping into a stranger's arms. It was weak and pathetic. I should be ashamed of myself. I was no longer a ten-year-old.

I clenched my jaw. Anyone who had deceived me in the past did not get away so lightly. But I supposed I could try to find a way back to my timeline through him. "What happened to him?"

"The man who brought you here?" she asked, tightening the corset until all the breath had escaped from my lungs and my waist was even smaller than it had been in this teenage body.

I nodded my head and gasped as she tugged again. "On the road again, your father paid him well though." I internally groaned, so that was no longer an option - not that I wanted to talk to him anyway.

As my hair began to dry into loose curls she began pinning it up into the style I was wearing before I entered this time. I thought back to the sleek black dress I wore on the night interrupted by the Rebellion. I looked down on the light peach gown I now wore and flattened down the skirt with a soft expression. The person staring back in the mirror wasn't a stranger but she wasn't who I was in the future. This girl had the look of innocence and childhood I'd missed out on.

"Beautiful." Abigail smiled sweetly, her own face was bright and youthful, her brown hair pulled into a neat bun and wrinkles under her eyes that implied her days consisted of joy and laughter.

How could someone still smile when serving someone else, when being treated so poorly? And then I remembered I was always *this* person, I was always being served on. People like Gina, Vix and his assistant, the Rebellion. They all served me. And I served those above me, in every society throughout time there was a hierarchy and we learnt to smile and accept it because we've never known any better. Maybe it was why the Rebellion was rebelling.

Good, they could rebel all they want but nothing would change, history was proof of it.

Even better: I was at the top of the food chain.

CHAPTER 14

Time: 17th June 1661
Location: England (most definitely)

My father sat at the head of the table, on his left what I could assume was someone from the navy. Opposite him was another man and a woman slightly younger who I presumed was his wife. Beardy and his wickedly fast friend sat together on the soldier's side and I made my way over to the middle of the table next to the woman.

"Ah, Marion. So wonderful of you to join us," my father said, smiling and beginning to dig into the meal in front of us. Chicken with various vegetables was piled onto my plate and wine was poured into my glass.

I hated wine. I was more into the new alcohol that gave you crazy drugged effects. This wine was weak in comparison.

"I'd like to introduce you to a commander of the Royal Navy, Harrison." He smiled and nodded his head towards me. He was surprisingly young to be a commander, and I wondered why he was here, perhaps he was a family friend I'd never met?

"And of course, my dear friend Abraham and his wife." The man smiled at me whilst his wife didn't bother meeting my eyes. Instead, she took a sip of wine and sat up straight. I was aware she hadn't been given a name - she only belonged to him.

I smothered my scowl, thinking of how this whole patriarchal, misogynistic crap was going to be difficult.

"Hello," I said to them, attempting to sit up as straight as she was but it only made me uncomfortable.

"Gentlemen, I'll talk to you later," my father said to Beardy and his companions who had cleared their plates before I'd arrived. I met Beardy's eyes for a brief moment and he nodded his head. I cleared my throat and began cutting a carrot. Food fixed everything.

Once they left my father began a conversation with the men, laughing loudly as though he'd already forgotten about my fiasco. Even when Abraham mentioned the wedding he continued to smile and began boasting about how I was going to be married to a Count in two months and they were of course invited.

"Splendid." The Commander smiled kindly. "I suspect I'll be set to sail to the New World after the wedding."

They continued a pleasant conversation. No one bothered to ask about the stitches on my forehead though I could tell my father's only concern with the injury was whether the scar might tarnish my beauty. The atmosphere was ruined when my aunt stumbled into the room giggling to herself and adjusting her breasts.

"Sorry for the delay - oh never mind. You started without me." She laughed louder and pulled out the chair at the head of the table. The guests watched, their mouths half-open.

"Harrison!" she cried, surprised by his presence. He managed to smile politely though it looked like more of a look of desire. She was beautiful. I could hardly blame him, but a lot older.

"When I last saw you, you were no more than a boy! Now look at you!" she cried. "A man-"

My father's arm had gripped her forearm and he'd bent down to her level to whisper in her ear. Her expression revealed nothing as she politely excused herself and left the room with Harrison's eyes trailing after her, his tongue practically hanging out of his mouth.

The rest of the dinner had been ruined. My father was now in a sour mood and his guests were the ones trying to lift it, with no success.

"So how on earth did you gain those stitches?" Abraham asked politely, chuckling and scooping peas into his mouth. He chewed slowly, flitting his gaze between my father who glared angrily at the table and myself.

Should I tell him? Should I lie?

"It's rather embarrassing really." I decided to tell him, no matter how idiotic I felt saying the words. They didn't know I was an Assassin but I certainly did and the shame hit me like a ton of bricks. "I ran into a tree."

"A tree?" exclaimed Harrison. So posh.

"My! How did that happen?" the wife shrilled. She placed a hand on her heart and turned my way with an incredulous look.

"I wasn't looking," I replied cautiously. How else did she suspect I ran into a tree?

"I meant why were you running in the first place?" she answered.

Before I had to come up with an excuse my father replied. "One of the maids commented on her inactiveness and Marion decided to prove her wrong." He smiled. "Like a true Montgomery."

Okay then. It worked, they began talking about their own staff members, commenting on their unnecessary gossip - not taking into account they were gossiping themselves. It reminded me of my stylist team back in the present.

I missed it. I missed the flavoured food, the bright colours, the laughter, the clothes, the lights, and the attention. I missed my friends - hell by this point I was even starting to miss Halo.

There was something about being in an unfamiliar environment that made home seem all the more appealing.

I looked around the room: it was large, sophisticated and boastful. Expensive items covered almost every surface, angry flames reflected off of a grand marble fireplace. A servant stood by the door, head poised and dressed in a smart uniform. Occasionally I felt his eyes on me, the same look as most of the servants who watched my little fiasco earlier. I loved fuelling gossip - not much had changed in the last few hundred years.

When I was excused from the table I left the room in a hurry, finally able to breathe the moment the double doors were closed behind me. I found my entire body slump and I gently touched the stitches on my forehead, grimacing as I felt the return of a headache.

And this was where I could use some painkillers.

"Need a drink?" A voice asked from the centre of the room. This was the main entrance where there was a sitting area and a grand staircase that seemed to continue up the whole of the house.

It was the bearded man sitting on the sofa, staring at the flames in a fireplace. Apart from him, the room was empty and so I decided to sit with him, desperately trying to remember if he had a name.

He didn't say anything for a long time. We just sat staring at the flames in peaceful silence and it felt nice for once. Ever since I'd gotten here there had been news after more news.

"Your father wants me to keep an eye on you," he said after more minutes of silence.

"Oh," I managed to say.

"A couple days ago I would have laughed at him but now I'm thinking it's not such a bad idea." He took a long sip. "That was quite the stunt you pulled on us."

"I'm sorry you had to go through that and I'm also sorry for anything my father said or did to you," I replied quickly, genuinely feeling guilty. He was just doing his job, like everyone else in the world.

"I don't know what happened between the time Nugget died and you having a meltdown but I understand," he continued. "It's okay you know."

There was a brief silence and then he took a deep breath, turning towards me and placing a hand on my knee. The way a father comforted his daughter - without beating her first.

"It's not my business to ask who that man you were with was and where you were going. But I'm sorry you ended up back here."

"He was a stranger I met on the road. It's - ah I don't know - all the adrenaline had built up-"

"Adrenaline?" he interrupted.

Ugh, was I going to have to focus on every little thing?

I blushed. "I read about it - it's like a burst of energy and emotion I suppose."

He nodded his head slowly and then smiled. "You don't have to explain your actions to me." I patted his hand breathing a sigh of relief.

He ended up following me upstairs reluctantly under my father's orders and sat a little way down the corridor on a stool. I sat on the bed, touching the silky sheets and allowing my mind to shut off. Almost as soon I had slumped onto the bed Abigail came through the door, revealing the bearded man whose name I still didn't know.

He was sitting on a stool opposite the door picking his fingernails.

She helped me undress, handed me a satin nightgown and smiled sweetly. "Don't mind Harold, just got to get used to him sitting outside your bedroom now." So his name was Harold, good to know.

Once Abigail left the room and I heard the faint lock of the door I climbed into the sheets and sunk into the mattress. God it felt good. Just to lie down in absolute silence - alone for once. Even though someone was sitting just outside my door as a guard.

I meditated for an hour trying to keep my mind focused instead of falling asleep waiting. I analysed the timeline but I couldn't see straight. I could sense my timeline and all the others - but I couldn't *see* them.

I missed my Totem. I missed the comforting glow and the safety it provided.

At some point, I gave up and fell asleep, only to awake when I heard squeaking. For a moment I freaked out and grasped the candle on the bedside table before I realised it wasn't a mouse but rather the sound of a bed squeaking.

What the actual hell?

Was someone seriously-?

How late was it, Jesus?

Falling asleep to the sound of squeaking below my room proved difficult, and although my head was pounding and I was in desperate need of sleep. I decided to do some late-night reading of my diary just to get up to date - a poor idea.

Marion was pretty useless. She wrote in it probably once a month and had been for only a couple of years and it consisted mainly of horses. She was big on horses. Well - I was... it was hard to judge someone when you were that person.

Nugget was at least mentioned once in every page, she rode him every day apparently. He was her mother's and although she didn't remember her mother, she grasped on to what she had left of hers.

It was the perfect beginning for a Disney film.

January 3rd 1661 caught my eye, the first line being: *I overheard a heated argument about my mother with father and Aunt Susanna. From the fragmented...* blah blah... *my mother was insane, she had attempted to murder me.*

It explained a lot, it explained why my father was such an asshole and acted so weird around me. He was worried I would turn out like my mother, that my own health had been triggered by the news of marriage and the death of Nugget, hence why I tried to run away.

It wasn't really progress - or anything new to me. I already knew my mother had died, none of my mothers survived. It was the sick fate I couldn't escape from. Every Time Bender seemed to have a similar kind of fate of their own - we called it a recurring theme.

But we all had one thing in common: our inability to reproduce children. Well, we could have children - they just died quickly.

I continued to read, finding the issues in this family just kept piling up.

April 13th 1661 (only 2 months ago): *My suspicions are growing, I found a letter detailing a wedding with the Count of Eldermore and I doubt Aunt Susanna needs to be married a second time. Which leaves only me...*

April 16th 1661: The stable boy invited me to go on a walk to the lake with me but I refused. I had to prepare for the news of marriage and flaunting around with a mere boy would be foolish.

Thank Christ. So that kind of implied she went through with the marriage to the Count. Hell what if she was supposed to die before then? Then I'd just willingly hand myself over to be married when she wasn't even supposed to be alive?

There were too many questions and I doubted the number of unanswered questions would be reduced.

I just had to trust Fate - if there was such a thing.

Time Benders are always questioning Fate or whether things were only coincidences. Like the fact Ace was here in one of his first lives, was it a coincidence we met? Or Fate?

It was too complicated to think about. But if Fate existed then surely we wouldn't have to make sure we stick to plan.

155

I wished Fate were real. Then I could let everything roll and sit back. I wouldn't have to worry about every word I said. Or maybe it was Fate that we could change things in the past for something later in the future, some planned event I didn't even know about?

But surely fate was real if we couldn't have children - if there were the same recurring themes in each of our lives.

Anyway, there was a lot of juicy gossip here to sink my teeth into. Marion apparently had eyes all over this place but I wasn't surprised since she clearly had not seen much beyond the walls of the estate.

I'd definitely always had the sneaky assassin trait. Except I doubted Marion went around killing people for money. She was just sneaky... not immoral.

In fact, she sounded like the most innocent girl. Always did as Daddy told her, but she had strong political opinions that frankly bored me but cleaned up on my history. Though I was surprised she even knew anything about politics as a woman - respect.

At least I now had enough relevant information to at least know a little about Abigail whose favourite meal was apparently roasted rabbit but she never got it. Abigail's mother was the head of the staff going by the name of Cecilia and had a husband who worked in town as a blacksmith. See I was learning.

Then there was Harold and his quick companion Donald. He looked a lot like a Donald. They were my fathers 'guards' I guessed? But they were good friends to him and to myself.

By the sounds of it, my running away act was the most exciting thing to happen here since... my mother had tried to kill me I guessed?

Normal, mundane things.

CHAPTER 15

Time: 12th July 1661
Location: England, Montgomery estate

I wasn't making progress.

If anything, every time I meditated I came out angrier, a hell of a lot more tired and more attracted to the idea of throwing myself from the tallest window.

I was doing everything I knew I should be doing. Well, everything Vix had told Ace to do and yet nothing was working.

The only progress being made was learning people names and acting as though I were Marion.

I sounded ridiculous… I was Marion.

The only slip up that had happened so far was when Abigail steered me away from a man holding the reins of a horse. When I asked why she told me she was afraid I'd be upset because the horse looked like Nugget. I rolled my eyes in response and asked who cared.

It was a hot evening and the sun was just going down when Abigail snuck up behind me and placed two cold hands on my bare shoulders. I flinched at her touch and turned my body to face her with a laugh. I'd been sitting under the shade of a tree in the centre of the courtyard attempting to meditate. All whilst I tried not to think about Landon and what might happen to me.

"What are you up to?" she asked.

I shrugged helplessly. How was I supposed to reply to that? I paused and watched the stable boy who was leading a black horse in the direction of the stables. A group of women sat outside the house washing clothes in a large tub. As they chattered away water splashed against the sides and a few children played with the bubbles by the open gates. Harold was posted at those gates with his arms crossed, a hat blocking the sun from his face as he kept an eye on me.

"It's called meditating... I read it somewhere. It helps to clear your head," I replied. She looked at me blankly before grinning.

"Yes, well you're needed inside."

I nodded my head and hauled myself up using the trunk of the tree before staggering my way back into the house, sweating heavily from the humid conditions.

Inside was cooler and my pale skin always burnt so easily during summer leaving me to look like a tomato with silver leaves.

I leant against the thick door breathing deeply and fanning myself. The hall was fairly dark and the open windows allowed a light breeze to blow the thin curtains into the room, making it look as though ghosts were posted every metre away.

Urgent voices were heard followed by the sound of heels and heavy footsteps. Then a man and woman appeared by the doorway that led to the kitchen.

"So how many guests is that altogether Ma'am?" An old man with small circular glasses perched on the end of his nose asked, staring at a pile of papers.

"Marion!" cried the woman, stepping into a stream of sunlight by one window. "This is our beautiful bride, Marion Elizabeth Montgomery."

The woman was probably in her forties, with a round face and bubbly smile. She was the spitting image of Abigail, which meant she was probably her mother - Cecilia, the female head of staff. Of course, there was already a male head of staff but he was never seen.

"Hello." I stepped away from the door and stood next to the woman praying this wasn't going to be one of those situations where she knew everything about me and I knew nothing about her.

The man bowed his head towards me and shakily forced his glasses higher up his nose. Cecilia grinned brightly at me and then snapped her head toward the man.

She blinked, startled. "Pardon?"

"How many guests all together?"

"Roughly around one-hundred."

I almost choked, *what in the hell? How many people did I know? How big was this wedding?* I mean it was only the 17th century.

"I trust that... she'll look less... ill by the time of the wedding?" The man stumbled over his words, sizing me up and down with a concerned look.

"Oh, it's just the heat. I'm only dehydrated." I smiled meekly although he didn't look convinced.

"Splendid, expect me in a couple of weeks for more arrangements and the visitation of the Count."

Cecilia nodded her head smiling and we both watched Donald enter, holding the door open for the man and revealing a carriage waiting patiently.

I felt my stomach churn. *The Count was coming in a couple of weeks? Would I meet him?*

Well of course you'd meet him Nova.

But I didn't know what to do, I wasn't used to this. *How was I going to address the man I had to marry?*

"You look hot." Cecilia placed a cool hand on my bare shoulder and I sank into it.

"I'm just hungry." I rocked my neck from side to side with a sigh.

Cecilia smiled kindly at me. "Dinner won't be long. Your aunt has been wanting to talk to you, shall I walk you to her room?" I sighed internally, maybe she could tell me something about this Count of Eldermore.

She didn't wait for me to answer before she began walking up the staircase. I trailed behind her as we reached the first level. She walked me down a corridor identical to my own and I felt a draft that blew the hair from my face.

"Who was that man?" I asked.

"Oh, he was a friend of the Counts. We were discussing invitations, they'll be sent out now. I can only hope they'll arrive on time - this wedding is *very* short notice."

I chewed the inside of my cheek. "And so how many days until the Count visits?"

Cecilia waved a hand in front of her face. "Oh, he said a couple of weeks but I imagine they'll surprise us. That's what happened to the others." *Others?* "He'll want to see if you're fit."

My face dropped - as did my mouth. She continued absentmindedly. "Oh don't look so sad, no doubt with a young fertile body like yours you'll be able to bear him a child to continue the bloodline." My eyes were bulging.

"Although, I think it might be him who's the problem." She winked cheekily. "If the rumours are true you might be lucky."

"Rumours? What rumours?" I was ignored as Cecilia paused at a large oak door causing me to almost fall into her as she knocked politely.

"Come in," my aunt's voice called and the door clicked open. I stepped in to face my aunt who sat at a vanity table powdering her face.

"It's so humid," she moaned.

Her room was larger than mine. A canopy bed stood in the centre, rich dark wood and red sheets, and an easel sat in the centre of the room under a thick fur rug.

The door was shut behind me and I walked over to my aunt. "Oh sit down Marion." She gestured towards a cushioned seat beside the table.

"I'm supposed to give you a talk on how you should act around your husband-to-be." She examined her face in the mirror, stretching out her face to smooth a wrinkle.

"What talk?" I asked cautiously.

Please don't be a sex talk. Please for the love of God this life is already awful as it is - there was no need to make it worse.

"I don't think you need it. But I hope you've kept yourself pure for when you need to consummate the marriage," she continued and then turned her head to face me with a stern look. She looked a lot like my father at that moment. "You must be a virgin."

I nodded my head quickly. "Of course I am!" Lies... Well, maybe not for Marion. Marion was *definitely* a virgin.

"Listen closely, Marion." She took hold of my hand and placed it on her knee - *how could she breathe in that red gown?* "The Count is a very dangerous man surrounded by very dangerous people. You must do as he says or you won't only get yourself killed but you will also ruin this family. You would destroy the lives of everyone here." She was gripping onto my hand tight enough I was surprised the bone didn't turn to dust. "Do you understand?"

I nodded my head sheepishly with my eyes wide open. I could do that, for as long as I was here at least. It's not like I hadn't worked with bad people before. I was a bad person.

"Good, now help me with my corset," she sighed. I stood up and went to her back and saw it was already tightened.

"Are you sure?" I asked.

"I need my breasts to be falling out of my dress and my waist to be even smaller than yours is," she replied, gripping onto the table. I did as she said, listening to her speak whilst I attempted to pull it tighter without breaking the ribbon.

"I know the last thing you probably want is to marry this man. I understand - really Marion," she said, gasping for breath. "Tighter," she managed to say, though it came out more like a wheeze.

"But you must force him to consummate the marriage even if he doesn't want to.... with the rumours..." My stomach churned at the thought. Every time I heard that I instantly began picturing an old man in a wig touching me. I just had to 'Think of England' and put up with it. I'd consider it a job I decided. I'd been trained on how to use my body to my advantage before killing people.

"What are the rumours?" I asked.

My aunt only pursed her lips. "Just... give him a child please and then both our families' reputations will be reconciled." I looked at her in amazement. That was all she was going to say? What was our reputation? What was his?

"Now as soon as he arrives - whenever that may be. You stay in your room. Don't let anyone see you until I've come and prepared you."

Prepared me? *What the hell, I'm not some dish to be served.* I was not a chicken to be buttered.

Dinner lightened my mood thankfully, and it hadn't been completely silent like every other night I'd been here since I arrived. It seemed we were a close family, despite how dysfunctional we clearly were.

My father, however, dampened it with his agitated tapping on the table. He was concerned about the estate. He needed to impress the Count in his home if the wedding was ever going to happen.

Once dinner was over, Abigail followed me up the stairs chattering away. "I ran you a cool bath. It might help with your illness."

I nodded my head, holding onto the bannister for support. I felt like crap. My head was pounding and my muscles were uncomfortably tight.

Being released from the itchy clothes was a relief I welcomed each night though. I'd recently scrapped the corset, which probably raised questions from Abigail, but I was too tired to care.

And the water was wonderful. The windows were open and I could actually see the stars for once. Real stars, hundreds of them unaffected by light pollution. That was what I missed from the past - and the only thing I missed.

I sank into the cool water with my eyes closed, listening to Abigail's short breaths as she began massaging me, careful not to wet my hair. There was a knock on the door and Abigail ran over, slipping outside.

She popped her head back in after a moment. "I'll be right back, shall I get some oils whilst I'm gone?" I nodded my head smiling. "Be quiet when you come back in."

She clearly didn't think me asking her to be quiet was weird so I took this opportunity to shut out the sound of night wildlife and closed my eyes.

It was easier in the water. I could pretend the darkness was engulfing me and it felt a lot more real than it just being in my mind. Sometimes when I got really frustrated I started to wonder if my father was right. Maybe I was genuinely insane: I wasn't from the future - I had no power - no past lives. This was my only life and everything I believed wasn't real. I was just a poor insane girl who believed she had a special gift. Except now I couldn't use it. It would be easier if that were real. Then it wouldn't mean that I'd be stuck in the past. It wouldn't mean there was a rebellion. It would also mean I wasn't at risk of being killed by my friends.

I could vaguely feel Abigail's hands massaging into my neck and pouring most likely expensive oil onto her hands, massaging them into my skin. But it wasn't helping; it didn't lull me into it. I couldn't see my Totem and now I was too focused on her hands on my back. Although this time I wasn't angry, I was calm. I sighed out of relief as her hands found the spot causing me so much pain.

"Thank you," I said.

She poked her head round the side and smiled. "I'll go fetch your nightgown."

As I stepped out of the tub I became slightly cold. Goosebumps rose to my skin and I began drying myself with a cloth. There was a gush of wind that came in through the open window, blowing the candles out so I was dipped in darkness. I looked out the window, finding a balcony below me. I could jump. Quite easily, I could jump and escape, but what good would that do? I'd never be found and I'd change the timeline.

Not to mention the fact I was naked.

Maybe another day.

CHAPTER 16

I noticed the entire atmosphere of the estate had changed. Everything was spotless for once. The courtyard was beautiful and the flowers were neatly kept. But it was the servants that ran around panicked and my father's screams from downstairs that made my stomach churn.

Then, one day it stopped and nothing was heard. The busy footsteps came to a halt.

I dared not look out the window but my eyes had already drifted towards the thick curtains. I peered down to a black carriage, rimmed with gold.

I wanted to throw up. A flash of white hair opened the carriage door and as I peered further around to face the entrance I realised all the staff were lined up as my father walked down the stairs.

My door was swung open and my aunt and Abigail appeared with eerily calm expressions.

"Holy *shit*," I hissed. Both their eyebrows raised in shock.

"Pardon?" they replied surprised by my language.

I smiled sheepishly. "I'm just scared," I replied as they brought out a new dress: a beautiful deep yellow,

168

embroidered with gold flowers on a wide skirt with ruffles around the waist - an enchantress dipped in gold. Despite my protests, the corset was fitted until I couldn't speak anymore. They quickly fixed my silver curls into a neat bun, exposing my slender neck and they adjusted a simple necklace to my throat.

I was never really a nervous person. I tended to act confident and plaster a smile whenever I wasn't looking forward to something. Confidence was in my job description... with the additional killing on the side. However, walking down the flights of stairs and being led from the hallway to my father's office was the most nervous I'd ever been.

Maybe it was because I didn't know what was going to happen for once? In most of my lives, I knew them inside and out. Here I didn't know who the hell I was marrying. But at least it wasn't like I didn't know how to be a wife - I could remember being married before.

My aunt looped her arm into mine and the office doors were swung open.

My father sat at the head of the table, a glass of scotch in his hand. He was dressed in his favourite white wig and wearing the nicest outfit I think I'd ever seen him in. He looked relaxed - laughing even. *Damnit.* A part of me had been hoping the Count would hate this place.

Harold and Donald stood by the windows, their hands in front of them, also smiling as though the Count had said something mildly amusing.

Then the Count; he wasn't hard to spot and although his back was facing me I could feel the importance he radiated. His clothes also struck an impression of power with their gold embroidery. We looked like we were matching. Coincidence or intentional on my aunt's behalf I didn't know, but it made me squirm.

When he turned to face me, my heart sunk. He stood from his chair, his chest puffed and he stalked his way over to me. My aunt bowed first and he politely took her hand bringing it to her lips.

"My Lord," she smiled.

And then he turned me. He was maybe in his late thirties and wore a stupid white wig with dark facial hair.

The room must have practically heard my body sink with displeasure. His eyes were a dark grey and looked at me with only mild interest.

He looked… weak. By that I mean, he looked sensitive, slightly stuck up and as though he battled judgment in cruel manners.

When he took my hand and pressed his lips I flashed him with 'seductive' eyes. I'd been trained to deal with this kind of stuff - to use my body to my advantage and I could do it with him. It would be a challenge but I could definitely make him obedient.

"And this must be my beautiful fiancée?" His voice was posh to the point of annoyance but he said it in a bored tone.

"Yes my Lord." My father stood up. "This is my daughter, Marion."

"What a beautiful name." He released my hand and focused his eyes on my father, ignoring my glances all together. This was the most uninterested I'd ever seen a man be in my presence.

"Thank you," I managed from behind him. The room held their breaths as they watched him rotate back to face me, looking up and down before sighing. *Was this is?* They thought. *Is he interested? Will he reject her?*

That would be a first for me.

"How about a tour around the estate?" The Count suddenly shifted to my father once again, who grinned brightly and sighed out of relief.

"Of course."

I quickly turned to face the doors, closing my eyes and taking a deep breath. How the hell was I supposed to make him submissive when he didn't even look my way for two seconds without looking bored.

I reached for the door handle the same moment the doors swung open into me. "Crap," I shrieked, trying to grab hold of the person before I fell. We staggered for a moment and in an attempt to regain my balance I held on to the small table, which wobbled against my weight.

The man had reached forward in an attempt to catch me but it was too late, I'd awkwardly slumped onto the edge of the table sending a candle flying.

171

The room was silent as I quickly jumped to my feet and flattened my dress. My father's face was red with embarrassment... or anger and the crowded room held its breath.

The Count watched me for a moment before turning his attention to the man and suddenly his face broke out into a large grin. "My god Jack!" He clasped the man on the shoulder and I turned to face him with a glare. He was young, maybe a couple years older than me. Soft curls of rich dark brown - almost black hair was flattened to the back of his head and gathered into a loose leather band. He had high cheekbones and a sharp, angular face and his deep brown eyes had a playful yet determined twinkle that focused on me.

"This is my good friend Jack, he works for me now."

Jack looked at me with wide eyes and mouth open. Though I wasn't sure if it was because he found me attractive or because he'd just sent his bosses potential fiancée flying and had gotten away with it.

"Hello," he said, snapping his attention away from me, letting out a breath and smiling at my father, who returned it cautiously - like he'd seen the look Jack had given me and thought of it as a threat to my marriage.

He was handsome, and I certainly wouldn't mind him being a threat but alas he had just embarrassed me so maybe not.

Jack cleared his throat, "splendid building."

I turned to face my father and watched as his jaw tightened and the smile slipped from his face.

"Well let's be on our way," the Count said, strutting past me. My father dropped beside him and I followed weakly after them.

I was bored and embarrassed. I hadn't looked so badass when both my legs were in the air and I was stumbling around in a tight corset unable to breathe.

Listening to my father and the Count joke and boast in an awfully formal manner was tiring and these shoes were gripping my feet like tight claws. I was sure no one would notice if I just slipped them off and walked barefoot but I kept them on to avoid drawing attention to myself.

When we finally stepped outside I was instantly smacked by a blast of hot air. The breeze was light and did nothing to relieve me of my uncomfortable pain.

Jack was walking behind me and I was painfully aware of his eyes watching me - the same feeling you got when you were on a bus and could feel people watching you. So I looked back, matching my own gaze to his; only he didn't look away embarrassed. He held it until I was forced to look back at the Count.

What on earth was his problem? Would he somehow play an important role in Marion's life - her real lover? I cast a quick glance, appreciating his rugged - yet somehow boyish appearance and decided I would be most happy to play into Fate's plan if it involved him.

Once we stopped by the lake behind the estate the Count sighed breathlessly. "What a stunning place to live." He then proceeded to talk about how Eldermore had a lake twice the size of this and much larger land. I didn't know who he was trying to impress more, me or my father?

I attempted to admire the landscape, watching the sunset behind the trees across the cool green lake. There was a group of geese eagerly swimming towards us in the hopes of food. Screw that. Geese were evil. If they weren't already extinct they definitely could have taken over the world - attacking children with their spit until it gradually became *Planet of the Geese*.

I could barely breathe and sharp blades of grass were tickling my ankles. The heat of the sun on my neck was unbearable and although I was wearing a hat my eyes were still squinted and I wanted nothing more than to remove the itchy torture device.

"We'll leave you for a moment." My father bowed his head and began walking backwards with my aunt who shared a look of 'remember what I said' with me.

"Come along Jack," my aunt said, keeping her eyes focused on the Count carefully as he watched Jack turn his eyes away from me squinting curiously. Jack cleared his throat and adjusted the white scarf under his shirt.

We stood in silence for a moment, our eyes watching the sunset and the reflection of trees on the water, mirroring our surroundings perfectly.

"Apologies for being abrupt. But I assume you know of my past wives who were unable to give me a child." He was smiling with an underlying threat, but both covered what was underneath. Fear: Fear of being judged that was covered up by lies.

"Hopefully with my age and fertility God will provide." *Ugh kill me*, I was not religious at all - barely anyone in the future was. We relied on science. We believed in science. And the mere thought of trying for a baby made me sick. Had he ever considered he was the problem? I wouldn't be successful anyway.

He swallowed tightly, looking away from my gaze and back to the lake. I watched him, placing a hand on his forearm and watching as he became stiff by my touch.

"I suppose we should make it formal then." His lips were thin as he turned to face me allowing my arm to drop. I bowed my head with a smile when he reached into his pocket and produced a large sapphire ring. Well, I guessed he was rich.

He held my hand out and slid the ring onto my finger. It was official. I was engaged to the most uninterested man alive.

I began to lead the way back to the house, our arms interlinked as we strolled through the gates.

"Until later." He kissed my hand formally and turned away from me abruptly. Jesus, was he really the first man to find me unattractive?

I climbed the stairs slowly, thinking of how easy it would be to escape this marriage, but that would unnecessarily change the future. I reached the first floor and turned to climb the next set of stairs when two hands caught me by the shoulders and pulled me through a door and onto one of the balconies overlooking the stables.

It was Jack and he looked relieved. "I wasn't sure if I was grabbing you or someone else."

"Can I help you?" I asked curiously, as he took a step away from me.

"Well, providing you don't kill me first," he took a breath and continued, "Nova."

My mouth had pretty much dropped to the floor, but I was quick. Hell yes, I was going to kill him. I'd been waiting for this moment to come and it was finally here. I sprung into action, my leg swiping up despite the material of my dress preventing me from doing much and I caught his face.

He too was fast, grabbing my leg and turning in an attempt to get me to fall. It was predictable, so I twisted free and jumped, slamming my other leg into his stomach causing him to gasp. Before I could finish the job he reached into his pocket, a click was heard and a pistol was pressed to my head.

Jack grinned as I stilled. "Believe me. I'd like to kill you as much as you want to kill me, but you're my only way out of here."

"I suppose you didn't realise going this far back would be a lot harder," I replied cockily.

He huffed. "Well I don't see you safe and sound in your heated bed."

I panted. "Well then what makes you think I can help you?"

He stumbled on his words for a moment. "I just need you to tell me what you see."

"Why would I tell you that?" I snapped. He pushed the gun further into my head. "You might as well. We aren't going to get out of this life unless the other Time Benders find us and you're not going to last long anyway - not in your condition," he replied and I felt myself go cold.

"What do you mean?"

"Ah, so you Time Benders weren't smart enough to figure that out. How many times do you reckon you've fucked up the past?" he hissed.

"It's not fucking up the past you-"

"So killing and wiping out generations isn't fucking up the timeline. Are you shitting me?" He swore a lot, more so than Ace and Aeron combined together. Those three in a room together would be interesting.

"It's called being helpful."

"Maybe to your kind," he snapped. His voice was cold and I wouldn't be surprised if he shot me then and there. I was egging him on by this point.

"Hey don't shoot the messenger. I'm just doing my job-"

He growled. "Just tell me what you know."

"Tell me what *you* know," I mimicked.

"I reckon you've got a couple months before your illness takes over so how about we speed this up?"

"What illness?" I asked, half believing him but refusing to fully trust he knew anything about it. I wasn't ill, but every part of me was telling me I was. There was no natural or healthy part of going into your past lives every week.

"The one your friend Landon suffered from for months."

"How do you know?"

"Nope, my turn. What do you see?"

"Well right now I'm staring-"

"I'm not playing around Nova. We both want to get home and we can if we work together." He had a point.

I sighed. "My timeline is gone, along with all the others and my Totem has vanished."

I felt him lower his head to my ear. "What's a Totem?"

I barked out laughter. "Here you are playing games of chase in the past with me and you don't even know how Time Bending works."

He snarled, forcing my back into his chest and whispering into my ear. "We have your god damn cure. Although I don't know why we'd waste it on you. Now tell me what you know."

"Your Totem is the thing you follow. In every life, you've gone into, you've seen a Raven. Correct?"

I felt him nod. "I could follow you because I knew your Totem was the Raven. Mine's a blue light - we all have different ones."

"I know that - but why the hell do you call it a *Totem?*" he spat.

Perhaps I shouldn't have told him what my Totem was - but did it really matter? It was gone.

"I didn't come up with it." I rolled my eyes. "It's something to do with Native Americans."

"Okay, well how do we get them back?"

And wasn't that the million-dollar question.

"I don't know."

CHAPTER 17

Laughter rose from behind the doors and Jack took the gun away from my head. I felt my shoulders relax as I realised I didn't want to risk dying. Not when there was someone from home now. I wasn't alone.

Even if it was my enemy.

"Do you have a protocol?" he asked.

"Yes." I scowled. "But I'm not supposed to go this far back, my own pride told me I could find you in time."

"Well, you can tell them you found me first," he replied jokingly - but there was a hard - judgmental look in his eyes and his mouth was stretched into a tight line. I rolled my eyes in irritation.

"There's another Time Bender on this timeline, Ace. But he's an asshole in this life."

"Where did he go?" Jack asked urgently, taking hold of my shoulders and looking down on me.

"Well... I don't know," he sighed and his face dropped. I felt a slight stab of guilt but I shouldn't feel guilty - this was his fault.

"Meet me here at midnight," he said.

I shook my head. *I think not.* "It's too risky, I tried running away when I first got here. I'm not allowed to leave my room."

"Where is your bedroom?"

"Next floor - at the front of the house. Why?"

But he'd already disappeared into the house. I watched the back of his head with a sensation in my chest - a sort of hope?

I sat on my window seat staring out into the night, deep in thought as my aunt took my hair apart. She ran her fingers through my hair and I curled my legs up to my chest.

The door opened to reveal Abigail wheeling in a tray of food. "I'm not hungry."

"Well, you've got to eat," my aunt said, revealing a colourful dish. The cook had clearly gone out of his way to impress the Count. "Would you rather sit and eat with the men?"

Ugh 'The men'. I ate only because it smelt so good.

"So what did you think of him?" my aunt asked, brushing my hair for me. I shrugged, eating and looking at the stars, wishing every sky looked that way.

I could see in the reflection of the window the look Abigail and my Aunt shared. "The first meeting is always uncomfortably awkward. Besides once you're married you will barely see each other."

That was true.

"My lady." A knock on the door and then Cecilia entered with a bright smile on her face. My aunt leant away from the wall and placed the hairbrush next to me.

"Sweet dreams Marion." Abigail also followed my aunt and her mother out of the room and closed the door. I stood up from the window once I heard Harold lock the door shut.

I climbed under the covers of my bed, not sure how Jack was going to get to my room. Harold was outside and I'd been looking out the window. There wasn't much opportunity to scale the side of the wall a few flights and climb into my bedroom. And I didn't have long enough hair for him to climb up either.

To think a couple of weeks ago I followed him into this nightmare of a life to find him and negotiate until it turned into the intention of just killing him. Then I lost my Totem and my intentions turned to survival and my hatred towards him got personal because he'd clearly decided to go back before the 19th century (which I had coming for me since I told the whole city it was my least favourite period).

But now - now the Raven had a name and a face. He too was trapped here himself - like a hunter caught in his own trap. He was going on about this illness, which I chose to ignore since it was clearly a way for me to rely on him, but the dizziness? The fact I look like death and the hallucinations of Williams? It made sense, I couldn't argue with that.

Somehow, with my mind running at 200mph I fell asleep for once (the best sleep I'd had in years might I add) and a finger poking my cheek interrupted it.

I panicked and froze, keeping my eyes shut and then grabbing the finger, twisting it back until there was a sharp yelp. I swung my body onto whoever was trying to spoon me and wrapped my hands around their throat. As my eyes adjusted to the dark I realised the person I was strangling was the person I needed help to get the hell out of here.

I let go of him and climbed off of his waist with an awkward cough. He kept a blank-face when he said, "you snore." And then he proceeded to grab my pillows and stuff them behind his head, Jack sighed and closed his eyes.

My mouth fell open. "How in the hell did you get in here?"

"I opened the door?" he said, opening one eye. He kicked off his leather boots and climbed under the covers. I moved to the side, a good distance away from him and sat crossed legged watching him.

"I can feel you staring at me. Please stop, I want to sleep." *Did he just? What?* He just waltzed into my room, past Harold, unlocked my door and made himself comfortable in my bed?

"I think the hell not," I snapped, coming to my senses. But I didn't know what to do with him? Roll him off the bed? Pinch him?

"I've been travelling all day. I think I deserve some beauty sleep."

"God knows you need it," I snapped. That was a lie. He was incredibly attractive. What was it with all Time Benders looking unearthly gorgeous? "How did you get past Harold?"

He snorted. "Who the hell is Harold?"

"Oh I don't know, maybe the guy sat outside my bedroom. He just let you sneak in?" I hissed.

He began laughing and then sighed, chuckling slowly until he closed his eyes again.

"Well?"

He groaned. "Shut up or I'll find my own way back and kill you now."

Dumbfounded I stared at him sleeping, watching the freckle above his cheekbone move up and down with each breath. "At this rate, I don't care," I mumbled to myself huffing.

"What?" he murmured, lips parting slightly and he turned to his side to face me.

"You're drooling. Get out!" I shrieked, and then lowered my voice instantly. I grabbed the pillows from under his head so it landed on the mattress with a dull thud.

"Fine." He stood up and walked to the door. "There's no guard outside your door genius." He swung the door open and he was right. There wasn't anybody sitting outside as I'd expected.

Much to my despair, he didn't leave. Instead, he walked back into the room and sat on the chair facing my vanity table. He opened the diary I'd left on it and began flicking through the pages bored.

"So?" I asked.

"What?"

"Why are you here?"

He settled on a page, his eyes drifting over the words and smiling. "Dear Diary, today I forgot to feed Nugget." He smiled, adding his own words and thrusting his fist into the air as though he were a part of a theatrical performance. "How will I ever forgive myself?"

"You aren't funny."

He raised an eyebrow smirking and leant forward to examine the mirror, playing with his curly hair. "I look the same in this life as I do in real life. That's boring."

"This is real life still, you realise that right?"

"Well obviously. It's real, you can change things, interlink timelines. I know the drill. Why do you think we're so against you?"

"You say *you* like it's only me," I fired back.

"Well you're the one who kills. Correct? You're the assassin, the others just do odd jobs."

Not true, Fynn and Ace were both used to kill people. Sure, maybe not as much as me. I was trusted the most to kill people without screwing up too much.

"We don't just kill random people," I defended myself.

"I realised that since you're an assassin - not a serial killer." He rolled his eyes and then frowned. "Well I hope not, otherwise, an innocent pretty little boy like myself just walked straight into the monster's jaws. Ahhh!" He waved his hands in front of him and then laughed.

And he called *me* crazy? What did the Rebellion feed these people? *Crack?*

"Tell me. Do you wake up every day wondering whose life you're going to take away next? Then go celebrate in one of your elite parties and get paid by your sugar daddies-"

"What did you just say?" I growled, jumping to my feet, he watched me in the reflection of the mirror.

"I said-"

"What I do is immorally wrong, but I am by no means doing this for so-called *sugar daddies*," I spat the word. "Surely with how many lives you've had, you've realised there's a hierarchy." I was hot with rage, if I didn't calm down I would kill him and never get this 'cure' and I'd never find a way home. "You work your way to the top."

"And yet the poor stay poor and the rich get rich," he snapped, turning to face me and grabbing hold of my shoulder. I had no response, partly because I knew deep down it was right. I was the bad guy. But if being the bad guy meant my life didn't have to be crap I'd take it. So instead I slapped him.

He didn't react the way I'd wanted him to, instead he turned his head to face me with his eyebrows raised and a smile that only infuriated me more.

"Either we get to the point or you can leave and stay here forever," he said. My eyebrows raised in shock.

"Are you bipolar or something?" I said, following him with my eyes as he sat on the window seat, looking down into the courtyard.

"Were you the one in 1944 shooting at me?" I asked finally.

"Yup."

"You shot my friend."

"You tried to screw up the future."

"By saving innocents," I fired back.

"It's the same thing."

"Then what are you doing here?" I asked.

He looked at me silently before clamping his mouth shut. "I have a protocol."

What? He'd had one this whole time? Why the hell hadn't he already gotten his people to help him? Oh. His people couldn't help him from the future - unless there was a team of Time Benders there.

He grimaced. "They want me to kill myself."

Oh.

"If you die in this life and can't find your Totem before... whatever happens... you die for good."

"That's the point," he sighed. "The longer I'm here the more chance I have of messing things up. And that would

187

go against the whole purpose of us being here in the first place."

"Well, I'll put myself forward." I smiled brightly and placed two fists on my hips. "I volunteer for the grim task of killing you."

He snorted. "It's the protocol. I never said I wanted to die. Besides I'm not going to leave you here to mess things up, that just defeats the point in me dying."

"So what? You want to kill me and then kill yourself?" He didn't reply, but he looked conflicted. That at least brought some comfort to me. I continued. "I'm happy to die, it's not like it'll be forever. You'll be dealing with the next reincarnation of me in the next few years from the present. Hell, maybe we'll even be friends." I fought back a smug smile.

He glared at me. "You might be happy to die but I'm not. Not if there's a way out of here."

We were silent for a moment; each lost in our own thoughts. Each hoping either one of us would come up with a genius plan that didn't involve suicide.

I swallowed my pride and spoke up. "Meditation - that's the only way I can think of. But I don't know if my Totem is lost or dead."

He cocked his head to the side and stared at me through impossibly thick eyelashes. "Is it possible to get a new Totem?"

"I don't know."

"What if we tried it together?" he asked. I didn't understand what he meant.

"Like how you followed me here. We come from the same timeline, correct?"

"But-"

"Or we could just try piece it together-"

"Jack!" I snapped and he turned to face me startled. "Can we just slow down for a moment."

I needed time to think, to process what he was saying and see if it would work.

"The others could be searching for me," I finally said, having to clarify it for myself because by this point I was starting to have doubts.

"It's been a month now. Ace probably didn't remember you or they're busy debating killing you."

"I don't know." I was getting frustrated, my mind was jumbled and I couldn't think straight at all.

"Okay," he sighed. He acted like he understood - like he thought this was normal. No one had ever been stuck in the past before and by him going so far back, he heightened the chances of losing our Totems.

"We'll try tomorrow. We'll figure something out," he suggested and then stretched his arms over his head and yawned. "Meet here at the same time tomorrow night."

I narrowed my eyes. "Don't tell me what to do."

"Don't choke on your ego," he fired back with a lazy, close-lipped smile. By default my mouth hung open and my face twisted into an angry sneer that was wiped clean from my face as he leant forward and *flicked my nose.*

I blinked completely shocked. *Did he know who I was?* I was the best assassin in the world, I had over two-hundred lives, I was awesome and intimidating and powerful and he *just flicked my nose.* I snapped out of it with an angry growl but before I could punch him in the face he'd dipped away and slipped out of the door as silently as he'd arrived.

…

Asshole.

CHAPTER 18

I slept well into noon and only awoke when my aunt creaked open a window. The smell of sweet roses and horse manure wafted in through the window by a breeze that fanned my face causing me to sit up frowning – squinting at the bright light streaking in through the window.

That night I'd dreamt.

I dreamt of cocktails: of loud obnoxious laughter, fixed smiles and the faces of my friends. I dreamt of a crowd leaning so far forward I could feel their eyes on me like a stream of colourful ants crawling over my skin, suffocating me.

I sat at breakfast staring at the plate of food in front of me numbly. I wanted to get home. I didn't want to marry anyone. I wanted to feel better.

"Marion? Why aren't you eating?" My aunt asked from across the table. I poked the bland food gently and looked up with a smile.

"I'm not feeling myself. Might I go lie down?" I asked.

My father's head rose from the head of the table and he looked at me sternly. "Nonsense, eat. We don't want another one of those incidents again do we?"

I swallowed the lump in my throat and nodded my head stiffly. "Yes father."

And so I obeyed, I ate and then I was excused with the utmost politeness. I took the stairs two at a time, ignoring the light-headedness that had appeared recently. I was just about to storm through my bedroom door when I noticed Jack was leant against a wall, shielded by the shadows.

"What are you doing?" I hissed, twisting my head side to side to see if anyone was close.

"The Count requests your presence."

My heart dropped. "Now? My Father and Aunt didn't say anything at dinner-"

"Well, it isn't exactly formal," he said, taking my elbow and leading me down the corridor away from my room.

"Where are you taking me?" I asked, panting as we rose to the third flight of stairs.

"The Count's chambers."

My heart stopped. "What?" I breathed.

"Don't worry, I'll be there the whole time. I don't think anything happens."

"Think?" I hissed worriedly.

He shrugged. "He wants to make sure your loyalty lies with him," he chuckled to himself and god I wanted to slap him, kill him - either I didn't really mind.

192

I groaned frustrated. "I hate not knowing what's going to happen. Does he do anything to me?"

Jack closes his eyes for a moment. "No. You marry him and give birth to a stillborn but the Count never does anything bad - not by what I remember."

"So we've shared a life together?" I stopped suddenly and he turned back to face me with a grim smile.

"Why did you think I picked this life?"

"Because you love torturing me?"

"True." He smiled again and my stomach flipped. *God, could he smile again?* It really took your breath away.

I continued. "How do you remember all this anyway?"

He shrugged. "I just remember these kinds of things whenever something's about to happen. Why do no other Time Benders remember stuff from their past lives?"

"We do sometimes, but I can't remember anything this far back."

He shrugged absentmindedly and cheekily remarked. "Guess I'm just better than you guys."

I cocked my head to the side examining the side of his face. "Don't you ever want to change something if you remember so much? Surely there's someone you would save?"

Jack looked at me sternly. "No."

I rolled my eyes at his seriousness. "Okay let's not get back into one of those kinds of discussions. Let's just get out of here as quick as possible before I have to consummate any marriage."

He let out a bark of laughter. "We'll see. Hell, maybe I'll just take my sweet time figuring this out so you can suffer for all you've-" My elbow jabbed him in the side and he rolled his eyes. "I'm not as cruel as Prospect. I won't let anything happen to you." If he didn't look sincere then I would have considered genuinely killing the guy for real this time. However, he was being serious so I let it slide by hesitantly returning his smile.

If he weren't such a political, moral crusader who hated me he'd probably make a good friend. I doubted he saw me the same way though.

I was the villain in this story, remember.

When the door was opened by one of the Count's servants I could literally feel my heart trapped in my throat. I was panicking and fully aware I was wearing a simple blue dress and my hair was braided loosely into a side braid. This kind of wild hair was something I wasn't used to in the future.

Catching a glimpse of myself in the mirror I flattened the braid and muttered under my breath. "I look like freaking Elsa."

Jack stumbled and shook his head. I looked at him with a curious expression and he cleared his throat before replying. "I'm not used to hearing people make references from other times."

The Count appeared in front of us suddenly and clapped Jack on the shoulder looking at him longer than necessary before finally turning to me, kissing my hand politely. I painted on a smile and bowed my head.

"This is a very informal meeting - my apologies," he said, leading me further into the room. It was an impressive size, with sofas and a fireplace in the middle, the bed in a separate room and bathroom adjoined behind the fireplace. The balcony you could see from behind the estate was just through the doors and he led me through them. Jack followed much to my relief, but stopped just at the door, whilst we ventured to the end of the balcony.

"It's a gorgeous view," he said, clearing his throat. I nodded my head and scanned my eyes over the hills and trees stretched far and wide. You could see the lake from here and faint mist rose from it.

"It is," I agreed.

He looked at me with a slight awkwardness, as though he didn't really know why I was here.

"Might I ask why I am here my Lord?" I asked nervously.

His face twisted into a crooked smile. "I wanted to introduce myself without having an audience. Perhaps I wish to court you rather than simply marry you to benefit your family and myself. I fear I came off too harshly yesterday."

It sounded forced, and I didn't understand why it would be. But there was a part of me that felt he had to say this, to prove something to himself or someone.

"I look forward to our marriage," I said.

"As do I," he said, still smiling tightly. He faltered on what to say next before calling Jack over who bounded over with a bright smile on his face.

"Yes my Lord?"

"What do you think of my fiancée?" He smiled broadly, wrapping an arm around my waist and pulling me into his side with stiffness. Both Jack and my eyes grew wide.

"I think you're very lucky," Jack replied cautiously. Was this a trick? What was he supposed to say?

The Count's smile faltered. "She is certainly beautiful. My son will have a handsome face."

My stomach dropped and had to avoid the thought of ever having to provide him with an heir but Jack coughed awkwardly, of course. Marion gave birth to a stillborn. He was never going to get a living heir from me. No one would ever get a child from me, or at least one that had a long life ahead of them – it was what happened with Time Benders.

"I'll be glad to be by your side the whole time," Jack smiled graciously.

The Count's face blossomed into a smile. "Ah!" he cried, enveloping Jack into a hug. "I'm so grateful you're a part of the family now. I'm forever in your debt for saving me from those bandits."

Jack grinned proudly. "Damn straight."

The Count looked puzzled by the remark for a moment before suddenly directing his attention towards me. "Tough luck she's mine instead of yours."

I really didn't like being treated like a possession, and I didn't take Jack to be kind of a sexist jerk but he seemed to at least like me being treated this way.

Why did he hate me so much? Well - the reason he hated me so much may have had something to do with my career choice.

"Nah! I'm not interested."

Ouch. Did he have to twist the knife further in?

The Count's grin widened even more as he stared into Jack, completely ignoring me. "You excite me," he laughed shrilly.

Jack wasn't laughing, instead, he was staring at me thoughtfully. I raised my eyebrows glaring his way.

"Very well. Jack could you escort my fiancée to wherever she needs to be, presumably whatever female duties consist of."

I had to resist rolling my eyes. "I believe I'm meeting with Cecilia to discuss wedding arrangements."

"Wonderful," he cried, rolling his tongue and turning away from us back to the balcony.

Once the door shut I let the shiver out. "Let's get the hell out of here. Quick, just tell me what you were going to earlier."

Jack titled his head to the side. "I thought you needed to do wedding stuff?"

"I do. But I'm sure Marion can be a few minutes late," I replied. "What's the plan?"

"You realise you know more about Time Bending than I do..." he trailed off, watching my face concerned.

"What?" I asked quickly.

He reached into his pocket to produce a handkerchief and then pressed it to my nose. "Oh crap. Have you been feeling dizzy lately? Tired?"

"Sometimes..." I took the handkerchief away from him and dabbed my nose where it was bleeding.

"Okay, let's just test a theory. We can't be in there long though."

"What theory?" I asked, allowing him to guide me by my elbow down a corridor. "Where are we going?"

He unlocked a door and slid in quickly. I followed after him, waiting for him to lock the door. We were in a quaint plain and dark bedroom down the corridor from the Counts. There was a bed the same size of mine pressed against a wall and it seemed to swallow up the small size of the room.

"Your bedroom is a little nicer than mine," he said, closing the window and then going to a water basin sat on the windowsill. He wet some cloth and then walked over to me to clean the blood.

"Thank you," I said, letting him wipe the blood clean from my lips. I stilled as he tugged on my bottom lip and his eyes lowered.

"Uh, there's a little on your dress." He cleared his throat, looking away and handing me the cloth.

"It can wait," I said, my voice strained. "Let's just get out of here first. I'm done with this hellhole of a place."

He nodded his head quickly and sat on the bed cross-legged, I clambered on after him. Jack looked at me silently for a moment. "If this doesn't work then you still have to marry the Count. It's Fate."

I narrowed my eyes. "We can change fate! Well, the majority of it…" I looked at him incredulously. "But still we have the power to change fate."

His face went slack, as he breathed in sharply. I was waiting for him to go on his moral crusade on how we shouldn't mess with nature before he finally said something useful. "Genius. Holy crap." He scrambled up onto his knees surprised.

"We have the power," he repeated. "It's a power! Not everyone can do this! We have this gift – a power to bend time to shape the future. We are Time Benders," he rambled and I watched him as though he'd gone insane.

And he had clearly lost his mind.

He was a very dramatic and excitable person - I supposed most heroes in stories were.

"Do you understand?" He appeared in front of me, shaking my shoulders, his wide brown eyes looked mad.

"I don't," I replied blatantly.

"A power," he repeated himself, searching my eyes for understanding. He shook me again. "It's a power. We're special don't you see?"

Okay Superman - I know I just called you a hero but let's not get ahead of ourselves.

"Can I have some of whatever you've had?" I raised an eyebrow.

"There's a select people - sure there might be more. But this is a power is it not?" He let go of me and began pacing, a hand cupping his chin as he thought to himself. He turned to me suddenly. "A superhero doesn't just lose their power - you aren't really a hero but just pretend-" *thanks.* "Just think. It's not just something you train to do. You either have it or you don't. And it's always there. It's *magic*," he whispered excitedly.

I pursed my lips pissed off. "You've officially lost your mind. This is real life, not some comic book or sci-fi novel." I went to leave through the door but he stood blocking my way, hands clasped on my shoulders again.

"Nova. Please just have an open mind," he said strongly. "For once in your life. Just consider it."

I sighed and nodded my head, by this point I was willing to listen to any suggestion he had for me. He opened his mouth to explain and then closed it with an exasperated sigh.

"I don't know how to explain it."

"Well show me."

He stood thinking to himself for a moment, mind racing and eyes far off before he finally returned to the bed and took hold of both my hands. "I've never done this before."

"Well, what are you trying to do?" I asked.

"Interlink our minds."

I snatched my hands away. "Bad idea. You realise what that can do right?"

"No?"

"Judging by one of Vix's theories he thinks our minds would become interlinked. No secrets and it would be irreversible. You can't undo it. Our Totems become each other's. No. Your past becomes my past; I could go into any one of your lives even if I don't have a life there - well maybe not. I don't see how that would work, but it could be that I have access to your life. And I'm pretty sure you wouldn't like me around you-"

Jack grimaced. "Do you want to get out of here or not?"

I paused for a moment and shook my head. "Yes but I don't want you to - there could be bad side effects."

"What are the side effects?"

"How would I know? It's just a theory," I sighed irritated, he was getting on my nerves and there was no way in hell I'd let him see into my mind.

"So it hasn't been done before?"

"I don't think so-"

"Well, then we don't know if it's a bad thing. Nobody's ever lost their Totems in the past. Therefore anything we try will be the first time trying it," he explained with a wide smile.

"But we also don't know if it'll work," I fired back.

He sighed exasperatedly. "Fine. Suit yourself, marry the Count, go and get pregnant by-"

I jammed my fists into his stomach. "Go to hell. This is your fault-"

He caught my fist in his hand and instantly I was transported into darkness.

Fuck.

CHAPTER 19

Time: Does it exist here?
Location: Don't look at me

How did he do that? How could he just touch me and send me to the timeline? How in the hell had he reached into my mind without us even interlinking?

How does one even interlink?

"Holy shit." I heard a voice.

I wasn't in 1661 anymore. I wasn't *anywhere* and I couldn't see the timeline. I couldn't feel anything. I felt paralysed - no silky strands of darkness. I was stuck in the balance of time.

"Nova? Can you hear me?"

Yes you asshole, but I can't speak back. It's like I'm stuck in my mind or something.

"Nova?"

And then I was back - drawn into 1661 and Jack was looking over me with his mouth opened in shock.

"That was awesome!" he cried excitedly.

"What was that?" I scrambled up from the bed and pushed his shoulders away from my face. "What the hell did you do to me?"

"I don't know. You just punched me really hard and it really hurt and then bam your eyes like, I don't know - you were there one minute and gone the next."

"You didn't do it purposely?"

"It just happened, you hurt me, I got angry and bam there you go."

"We didn't just link minds though, right?"

"I don't know. What's my favourite food?"

"Uh... spaghetti?"

He gasped and I felt my heart drop, but then he broke into a large grin. "Nah, close but steak is a lot better."

I felt my body sag with relief. "Okay. We should go, let's try that again later. I want a go to see if I can do it," he rambled excitedly, leading me out of the room.

A lot had happened and yet nothing all at the same time. I'd finally sunk into the routine of Marion's life whilst also juggling Jack and mine's attempt at finding a way back to the future.

My health had escalated within the week and Jack had finally decided it was enough for me and only pulled me into our timeline when he felt a tug.

Oh yeah, that became a thing. 'Our timeline' seemed to appear overnight. Not the timeline we came from in the future - and it wasn't that we had linked minds either. This was different. I had no idea how to explain it and it was probably something Vix would get incredibly excited about and begin researching and experimenting.

But whilst we'd been taking it in turns to draw each other into that nothingness he'd suddenly started thrashing hold of my hands and drew me into what he was seeing. He'd caught the timeline, except it wasn't the one we'd come from originally - the one he thought it was.

At first, he'd been incredibly excited but then he noticed the details and I could feel his excitement sink until it became wonderment. Whilst it wasn't the timeline we were looking for - this one looked beautiful. A new timeline perhaps or the timeline we were currently in, I had no idea.

But it did nothing.

He was right though, what we had was a power. I wouldn't necessarily call it magic but whatever it was, we had no idea how to control it.

Our so-called powers were developing faster than our minds and we were struggling to keep up with it. Especially now my nosebleeds were happening more consistently.

Pathetically enough, I was more worried about a nosebleed happening during the wedding than I was worried about never returning to Prospect.

And that was another thing. The wedding was tomorrow and I was dreading it. Somehow I'd grown accustomed to the grey walls that trapped me in the past.

The people here were decent enough and I'd only just started acting relatively normal toward the people here.

But still, that didn't mean we didn't have serious problems.

And one of those problems was pacing back and forth in front of me.

"I should be the one pacing." I sighed, leaning my head against the headboard and sinking into the covers.

Jack came to a halt at the end of the bed and put his head in his hands. "Relax, the wedding goes smoothly from what I remember... well apart from the evening when your aunt-" He sniggered and shook his head. "Never mind." He turned his head to the floor.

I didn't bother asking questions. Soon enough, I'd see what happened after the wedding. It was still weird to me that he remembered my life here more than I did and that we shared a life together in the first place.

"Jack, what are the chances of me waking up in my body in Prospect after I kill myself?"

He froze for a moment and looked away. "You can't do that."

"I can't do that because there could be a chance I would survive and you would have failed your mission?" I asked, my tone flat. His shoulders tightened.

"Because I still need you here," he said and looked over at me with his eyes narrowed. I studied him for a moment. I was an excellent judge of character and could usually tell when people were lying.

"Do you think you can use me and then kill me before you have the chance to get back?" I smirked but he continued to hold my eye contact.

My smirk slipped as I tried to peel through his thoughts and couldn't determine his facial expression.

"You wouldn't be able to stop me though," I said sitting up. He turned to face me angrily. "Technically I'd be doing you a favour killing myself - you won't defeat me otherwise. Besides it's what you were supposed to do - you intended on killing me in this body correct? Because you thought I wouldn't be able to survive without my Totem?"

"You can't do that," he repeated. "Marion can't die yet. She's got a life ahead of her."

"What impact is she going to make within-"

"You don't know!" he shouted, slamming his fits onto the front of the bed. I watched him with wide eyes as his body moved up and down with frustrated breaths.

I narrowed my eyes. "No parallel timeline has to be identical to the others."

"That's what you think," he growled. "We have different beliefs - different opinions."

"I'm going to die either way," I rolled my eyes. "Whether I kill myself or whether this illness takes over."

"You will die - Marion won't." He looked back at me and scowled. "Besides, I lied anyway. The illness or whatever it is won't kill you in the next month. I don't even know if it will kill you, just drive you to insanity."

Well, that was a relief. Or was it? I was fine with dying - I was well acquainted with death. But what else had he lied about?

He seemed to read my mind and reluctantly assured me. "I wasn't lying about a cure. You aren't the only ones who know about Time Bending, we've been watching you."

I wondered why he was telling me this. Why he was revealing that they'd been spying on us.

I pursed my lips. "Let me get this straight. You knew my health wasn't in top-notch condition – it's why you waited so long before you went into this life - you were trying to get me to lose my Totem. You planned to trap me here."

His jaw clenched and his eyes flickered.

I continued. "You planned to trap me here and kill me so I wouldn't return to my body - but what really happened was that you trapped yourself too. And now you have no idea what you're doing?"

He growled. "I can't kill you because you clearly know more about this bullshit than I do."

"Yes. I get that. But why are you so focused on me sticking to Marion's life? This is a separate timeline. If we figure out how to get back I won't bend this timeline with our own - as long as you don't."

He blinked. "I haven't figured out how to do that just yet."

I scowled. He didn't know how to avoid Time Bending? "You're a goddamn hypocrite then. Any time you've gone back into the past you've bent the change with our own timeline, haven't you? You're just as bad as us-"

One second Jack was standing in front of the bed with his back turned to me and then next he was on the bed with me. His hands wrapped around my throat and his body pressed me into the soft mattress. "I am *nothing* like you," he snarled - a face of disgust and hatred blended together.

I fluttered my eyelashes down at his broad, calloused hands around my throat and winked. "Kinky," I wheezed.

If he was disgusted with me he didn't reveal it. Instead, he pressed himself further against my body and growled. "You are a *murderer*."

"Weren't you *just* planning on killing me?" I arched a brow.

He sneered. "One less evil person on the timeline - to save plenty of other people? Yes."

Despite the hands around my throat, probably strong enough to snap my neck, I still smirked. Unable to help myself I purred. "Try."

I moved too fast for him to even blink. One moment Jack was on top of me - the next we were both on the floor. The position was reversed and I had a dinner knife I'd kept under my bed to his throat.

He panted and struggled beneath me as I positioned my body in a way that paralysed him. I leant my mouth to his ear and hissed. "You aren't ever going to be able to kill me. So don't bother wasting that limited brain energy on contemplating how you'll use me to help you get home - and then slay me last minute." I pulled back and looked at him – he'd gone still under my body, his face no longer an angry glare.

Silence.

And then he grunted. "Okay well how about you get off of me?"

I continued to sit on him for a moment, looking down at our bodies and smirking. I looked back at his face, scowling when I realised he wasn't blushing or turned on in the slightest. I removed the knife from his throat with a bored sigh and climbed to my feet.

"How about we compromise?" he suggested, also rising to his feet. I stared at him bored and then he continued. "You can teach me all this Time Bending stuff - so I can figure out how *not* to bend time. And you can just do what I know happens in this life and make this timeline continue similar to the past in ours?"

I pursed my lips. "That's a lot to ask of me." And I got nothing out of it - well apart from a cure providing we made it out of this life alive.

He nodded his head. "I know I'm not the one who's being forced to marry an old fat guy and give him children. But if you could just... help me out a little with keeping to your old life's path. It's part of your rules too...

perhaps it's the only thing we agree on," he chuckled lowly.

I held my breath and spoke softly. "I know."

Cautiously and foolishly I placed a hand on his shoulder. "I'll help you - and you can help me," I rasped.

I didn't need his help in this life. Why was I helping him?

A cure my thoughts answered.

I swallowed the thought and watched the side of his face, his shoulder was warm under my hands and I realised just how much I'd been craving human contact. I wanted him to look at me - not even in a sexual way. You start to feel incredibly lonely when you're stuck in the past surrounded by people you don't remember and he was the only person from home... and yet we hated each other.

I say that we mutually hated each other when in reality I'd grown to like his brown eyes, his infuriating humour, love for history and the determination he had to get home.

Everything else I hated though.

"Thank you." He gritted his teeth and walked out of my touch, the space between our bodies grew cold.

I pursed my lips. "What do we do if we never find a way back?"

"We will." He stated it as if it were a matter of fact - that there was no chance we'd stay stuck here.

I wasn't sure whether to believe him - but I decided to - I decided to trust him.

CHAPTER 20

Time: 7th August 1661
Location: England, Montgomery Estate

Hell was I worrying. No matter how much I tried to focus on my steps, all I could think about was last night and Jack.

There were a large number of people here - all wearing their finest clothes and hats, no matter how bright and colourful they were I knew I stood out amongst them.

The dress was stunning; in all my lives I've been married in I'd never worn a dress this spectacular. It was white, with lace sleeves and an exposed neck, my hair was twisted up neatly and I wore a golden headpiece with metal flowers holding a long veil. It was my mother's and my father had given it to me, alongside the necklace she wore on their wedding day. He told me to pass it on to my next child, but I knew that wasn't going to happen.

One step in front of the other, my arm latched onto my father. The details of the location were blurry to me. I was too focused on my shaking hands as I reached the end of the aisle.

To my surprise, Jack was posted behind the Count, also dressed in a tailored outfit. He gave me a reassuring look, one that told me I just had to get today over with and we'd be on our way. Bounding over meadows hand in hand into the future.

Probably not the latter.

I tried to avoid looking at the Count as much as possible. Instead, I hid under the lace veil and looked at our joint hands after my father had handed me off like any other business transaction. Once the vows were over a sigh seemed to engulf the room. It was done. Our families were joined and now they could relax.

When the Count lifted the veil over my head and set his eyes on me I felt myself go numb. If anything, I think he felt the same as me, he'd spoken the vows as if they were just part of his daily routine. This was a feeling I was used to and I welcomed it. It was a feeling assassins needed - separate their feelings away from the job. I didn't know why he felt it though.

I took myself away from the situation. When he kissed me, my lips kissed back but it wasn't me who was kissing. I could feel nothing. I could only see his eyes and his surprisingly soft lips as they pressed coldly against mine.

"Countess," he smiled tightly.

And that was that. I walked out of there numb, my arm linked with my husbands, whose name I didn't actually know and I didn't care for it either. Numb.

I was on autopilot for the rest of the day, exchanging commentaries with strangers and accepting wedding gifts.

I was acting as the ideal wife: clinging on to my husband, only speaking when spoken to.

Partway through the day, I caught a glimpse of Jack. I'd have expected him to look confused but a look of understanding reassured me. It told me he was impressed - maybe even scared by my act. It made me wonder if he doubted how honest I was with him.

By the time evening swung in the numbness had faded and I could now detach myself from his side, have a few drinks and dance back at the garden of the house. A party was being thrown and I was in dire need of a drink.

A long table had been set up in which myself and the Count sat in the middle alongside my family and his companions. Jack - much to my relief - sat opposite me and sent reassuring smiles towards me every now and then.

Once my aunt stood up to make a speech I realised this was the moment Jack had mentioned to me. She was incredibly drunk and no matter how much my father tried to pull her down she continued crying hysterically on how she remembered her own wedding. She then stuck her hand in the mashed potato and wiped it on the ladies pretty dress next to her.

We all seemed to sink into our chairs for the rest of the meal until the music started to pick up and people began dancing joyfully, bouncing up and down happily.

I was high off the feeling of being drunk and when I caught a glimpse of Abigail tucked away with the other servants I strode towards her and pulled her into the ring of dancers. This far into the night people were having too much fun to notice and those who did look at her disapprovingly I shot down with glares.

"I'm going to miss you." She smiled, hugging me midway through the dance before she backed away quickly, as though realising she'd just hugged me out of nowhere.

"What?" I laughed, and then as it settled in I pursed my lips. Having different classes was such a weird thing now that I thought about it. "Another dance, please?"

Her face turned bright red likely as she reminisced the first dance she'd stumbled her way through. This was not the kind of music she was used to I realised with a coat of shame.

"I'm sorry," I said slightly out of breath. "I'll let you get back to whatever fun you want."

Her face brightened as she curtsied quickly and slowly I began to feel myself smile as she melted through the crowd and began giggling with another group of servants.

I blinked, suddenly realising Marion had very little friends herself. Still - being the bride attracted plenty enough attention and soon I was back to twirling to upbeat music. Somehow my feet remembered how to dance to this 17th-century music and soon I was swung between people laughing hysterically.

Jack even stepped in at one point to dance alongside me, swinging me around and twirling me whilst the Count watched clapping his hands and laughing with friends, but there was still nervous energy surrounding him.

Honestly, at some point in the night, I had forgotten this was my wedding with the Count since he was ignoring me.

"If you keep drinking at that rate you're never going to make it to your wedding night," a girl in a group of young ladies commented to me and they all giggled.

"That's kind of the point," I replied, looking at her own rosy cheeks and fighting the urge to roll my eyes at them. Alcohol didn't seem to have the same effects on Time Benders as it did on regular people. It's probably why drinking in the future was a whole lot more fun than drinking this.

I began smiling at guests who were beginning to retire for the night. My father was in the centre of the garden laughing cheerfully. His worries were over now. His daughter was married into a rich family.

My new husband was waving his hands about, entertaining guests with Jack by his side laughing supportively. He glanced my way before suddenly directing his attention to the Count whose smile quickly slipped.

Jack whispered something reassuring in his ear I assumed which made me angry. His mission would also be to ensure the past runs smoothly. If we were supposed to consummate the marriage, he was going to make sure it would happen. There was no cheat code with Jack. The

Count looked at Jack for a long, silent moment before taking a deep breath, swivelled to face me and began walking to me.

"Shall we retire for the night, husband?" I asked.

Please stab me. I hadn't nearly had enough to drink just yet. The count didn't say anything, just nodded stiffly and held out an arm to lead me into the house.

Before we turned past the door I turned my head, wide eyes searched for Jack before they finally settled on him, he nodded his head.

Asshole.

I tried my hardest to separate myself from the situation. The same technique as when I have to kill someone. You know... usual mundane things.

"I need to take care of something. Shall I send help for you to take off the dress?"

I shook my head wide-eyed. "I'll be fine."

He slipped out the room, closing the door behind me and for a moment I jumped to action, readying myself to grab the bedsheets and throw them off the balcony. But instead, I listened to the *oh-so-wise* words of Jack and tried to take off the dress.

I suddenly wished I had asked for help as I began to undo the corset and tried to wiggle my way out of the tight and itchy material. Once it dropped to the floor I lay it on the sofa, running my hands over the gold embroidery, watched as the tiny flowers gleamed at me. It was such a beautiful dress.

Fortunately, underwear in the 17th century felt like what a nun would wear and so I climbed on to the bed after I'd poured myself a drink and spread myself on the bed.

When he entered the room, he avoided eye contact. His hand brushed over the dress and he admired it.

I watched as he drank by the table - his back turned from me. I remembered the conversations I'd been having with Jack, the ones in which he told me what I did was wrong - that I could change. *Please… kill me, someone.*

Do the job Nova, you aren't getting paid and usually, you kill them afterwards but just do it.

I stood abruptly before I had the chance to chicken out. This was just like pleasing your fans in the future. You had to please the ones in power. I pulled the nightgown over my head, dropping it to the floor and standing there bare with all the confidence I had in me. Honestly, and I hate to admit. But it felt normal. Sex was a powerful weapon used to gain power, and as much as I hate and despise it, it was one of my most valuable weapons as a female. But it shouldn't be. Men were just so easy to manipulate in the past, and taking off your clothes was easier than killing people (unless you wore a corset).

It took a moment for him to realise I was behind him and when he did, he turned to me, not even looking down at my body as he spoke in the calmest voice. "There will be no need for that tonight."

I - what? My cheeks burnt.

Jesus, I was embarrassed. I'd just been completely rejected by a not even *that* good-looking man. How awful must he find me?

I nodded my head shocked, picked up the nightgown and quickly pulled it back on feeling more embarrassed than I'd ever felt. *That had not just happened.*

1661 was turning out to be a huge awakening call. First Jack and now the Count? Did Marion have a third ear that I wasn't aware of? Or a tail? What the hell was wrong with these people - how could they resist *me?*

I swallowed the lump in my throat when I felt the bed dip and he sighed next to my ear. He slivered in next to me and I held my breath, waiting for him to say something, to apologise and explain why we weren't consummating the marriage. Except nothing happened. We lay in silence for a few minutes before he finally spoke. "Could you blow out the candle?"

I sat up numbly and blew out the candle shocked. Well, that was easier said than done.

When it was finally morning I rose and walked around the bed tiredly, then opened the door to the balcony and let out a shriek as my foot made contact with a knee and Jack turned his head towards me. My heart picked up as he squinted through bleary eyes and ruffled his dark hair.

"Morning."

"What are you doing here?" I bent down.

"Watching out."

"For what?" I snapped, he raised an eyebrow and yawned.

"Nothing apparently."

My mouth dropped open. "You were watching me?" I hissed and he chuckled.

"No."

"I don't believe you."

He rolled his eyes. "I'm not a pervert. I came up here at like three in the morning because I was worried he would have... you should go back to sleep."

"What do you mean? What do you think he would have done?"

Jack sighed. "He uh, he's killed two of his wives before because they were persistent, they accused him of being gay."

I nodded my head as it suddenly dawned on me. I couldn't believe it had taken me so long to notice before. Thank god - it was just because he was gay. "That does make sense."

The blood drained from my face. *Killed* his wives?

"Woah, woah, hey, hey," he murmured, taking hold of my shoulders as my face turned pale. "I'm not going to let that happen."

I looked up at him, brown eyes reaching deep into me. "Even if its Fate's will?"

He didn't falter. "You have until you give birth to a stillborn at least. I don't know what happens after that... but I... I can't let my ride of this shithole die can I?"

I took a deep breath and blinked rapidly. "Great."

He rolled his eyes and climbed to his feet, stretching his arms and yawning. He then wrapped two arms around me and pulled me into his chest.

He was hugging me - Jack - the person I was sent here to kill. We were hugging.

I probably needed it.

I clenched the back of his shirt. "Can we please leave?"

"Trust me Nova, I'd love to."

CHAPTER 21

Time: 8th August 1661
Location: England, Montgomery Estate

Saying goodbye was surprisingly harder than I would have thought. This entire time I'd been trying to find a way out of this life - not caring to soak in the appearances of my friends and families faces.

Once upon a time (a really long time ago) I was Marion, my future hadn't been written yet and my timeline was very short. I had no idea when I died I wouldn't go to heaven like everybody had raised me to think. Instead, I would be reborn in the same flesh and skin with only experiences to shape my personality within that life.

The entire team of staff was lined up down the stairs and a sleek, grey carriage with gold trimmings waited patiently. Horses holding the Counts' own servants and soldiers shuffled from foot to foot restlessly.

One by one I thanked each servant for raising me up until now. I was glad I'd grown to know their names otherwise I would have felt incredibly guilty by the tears some of them wiped away.

Harold clapped my hands and kissed either side of my cheek solemnly. "Thank you for being my guard dog.

Great job," I whispered sarcastically under my breath, he chuckled.

"Everyone needs a little freedom," he replied.

Donald was a little more hesitant than Harold but still ended up wrapping his arms around me and squishing me into his belly. "I apologise for running away from you." I smiled, gaining a laugh from both my father's men.

Cecilia and Abigail stood at the end of the line, posted either side of my father and aunt. First, Cecilia hugged me tightly and I was conscious that she'd placed something in the pocket of my red skirt but I didn't risk showing any sign.

Abigail was by far the hardest to say goodbye to. She clung onto my shoulders shaking silently as she fought back tears. "Marion you better not forget us here. And don't let all that money get to your head. Alright, Countess?"

I rolled my eyes and muttered under my breath. "Please don't ever call me that again."

"You will always be a Montgomery," my Aunt interjected from the side, speaking under her breath but my Father caught it. If he'd heard he didn't show any sign of it though, just the rapid blinking of his eyes as he embraced me.

"Be careful."

"I know Father."

"I suspect you shall visit, and write to us?"

"Of course," I replied, kissing his cheek and backing away. My Aunt quickly took me into her arms and breathed me in.

"You were the daughter I never had," she whispered, her voice cracking slightly as she tilted the black hat back into place and poofed up the red feather. "Beautiful," she murmured, kissing my cheek one last time.

I took a last look at the estate's grey walls and somehow the early morning sun made it look a lot less grim of a place to be trapped in.

And here I was trading one prison for another. *Oh the irony.*

I was helped up into the carriage and sat opposite the Count who smiled brightly, clearly eager to leave this place behind.

Killed his wives? I'd clearly underestimated this man.

My aunt stood by the window, waving and dabbing her eyes with a handkerchief. Jack sat next to the Count whilst another man dressed in fine clothes sat next to me. This man was younger and had his nose turned up.

He seemed like a cheery character to make the journey go by fast (that was most definitely sarcasm).

Soon the carriage was on its way, circling the tree and flying out of the gates. I didn't look back. I didn't want to. I imagined Marion wouldn't have as well. I had a feeling that I'd have jumped out of this carriage if we did.

I avoided Jack's eye contact, for the most part, fearing the Count might see a look I couldn't depict on my own face. I didn't want to be killed - worse yet I didn't want Jack to die.

From what memory I did have before cars were invented, I could remember that carriages were uncomfortable. We were travelling down the bumpy gravel Tobias had carried me along and I was already beginning to feel a little travel sick. I'd made it quite a way when I escaped it seemed, it was only a shame I had run into Ace's doppelgänger.

I shifted my eyes from the window to Jack. His jaw was clenched and his dark hair was groomed back away from his face into a short ponytail. He continued to wear his hat and had strokes of dark hair artfully groomed on his top lip and chin and stylish sideburns. I wondered what he looked like in the future, whether he was younger or older. What was the use in thinking of the future or a future where I saw him? If we found a way back, this friendship or peace treaty or whatever we had here was to be dropped and he'd kill me.

He turned his head to face me, maintaining eye contact until we hit a bump on the road and I turned my head to look out the window.

"How long is the journey?"

"A day at the most," the Count replied. The snotty man was looking at me in a way that made me uncomfortable, tapping his cane on the floor of the carriage as it made it way closer to my ankle. *I swear to Jesus if he doesn't-*

Jack stretched his feet forward with a yawn, tapping the cane out the way so the man bent down to grab it.

"Oops." Jack yawned, stretching his arms for the full effect. The snotty man beside him scowled, turning his nose up even more than I thought possible and moving closer to the door, which was hard considering the size of the carriage. The Count barely even noticed the encounter, just watched Jack thoughtfully. And Jack had no idea.

I was starting to realise the extent of how much I liked Jack when he leant across to look out my side of the window, practically crawling onto mine and the snotty man's laps meanwhile crushing the man's hand which had found its way to my knee.

"My bad, I thought I saw a deer." He sat back in his seat and the snotty man's hand reluctantly returned to his lap.

After an hour of no conversation, we all began to drift off either into sleep or our own thoughts. I didn't blame Jack for falling asleep. He had after all been awake the whole night looking out for me. It was just incredibly unfortunate for me when the snotty man realised the other two were out of it, he finally looked my way whispering, "I simply cannot be the only one feeling... this passion between the two of us-"

"I need to take a whizz," Jack exclaimed suddenly causing us all to jump. I immediately pushed myself into the furthest corner of the carriage.

"What is a *whizz?*" the snotty dude uttered.

Jack and I shared a look and smiled. "I need to piss," Jack stated.

The Count sighed and watched Jack with a now blatant attraction. "Jack my boy you are like an absolute child."

Jack laughed - forced laughter I noticed. His genuine laugh was more relaxed and his eyes scrunched up and cheeks revealed dimples.

The carriage came to a halt and the doors were opened. I was offered a hand but I pushed past it, jumping down into the mud and walking as far away as possible.

I placed my hands on my knees taking deep breaths and jumped when I felt a hand rubbing my lower back.

"Are you feeling alright, wife?"

Ugh if you call me that again I will genuinely throw up.

"Travel sick." I stood up straight and turned to face the Count who was now awkwardly standing behind me. No doubt he had realised how it must look that he had been ignoring me.

"Can a man not have some privacy?" A voice called from behind us. Jack stuck his head out from behind a tree and hell I wanted to hug him - kiss him or anything. He was a lifesaver from awkward moments like this.

The Count's cheeks turned red as he continued to watch Jack. "Pardon us Jack we'll-"

The Count turned to guide me behind a clearing but Jack stepped away with a broad smile. "No worries I'm all finished now. We can head back."

The snotty man had decided to clamber onto a horse, opting to stay away from our group and by the look on his face, he expected Jack to follow his lead. "Don't you think the newlyweds would be better off alone? You'll get far more scenery riding."

"Nonsense. Jack is no intrusion whatsoever," the Count replied adamantly. The snotty man raised an eyebrow as if it had confirmed his suspicions.

I smiled to myself and leant my head against the carriage walls as it began moving once again. I watched the light through the trees and through the leaves and bushes I saw meadows of fresh green grass and sheep grazing.

I reached into my pocket where Cecilia had slipped in a letter, it was folded up and the edges were slightly ripped and brown with age.

Slowly and carefully I unfolded the paper, checking to see if the Count was watching but he was looking out the window bored.

It was a short letter with cursive writing and smudged ink that read: *To my Daughter, who is by now reading this. I am sorry I couldn't be there for your wedding day. I've dreamt of what you might have looked like dressed in white but I know I can't be there for you. I can feel you have a destiny greater than what I can give you, and I can't bear to see it happen to you. I'm sorry I love you. I do. I keep telling you I do. It's for this reason that I have to let go. I have to leave before I ruin you. I can't keep going. I can't keep fighting.*

It was a rambling mess - nonsense and madness. The sentences didn't make sense but it was something I'd never received. It explained what I had been told in all my lives. My mothers go crazy – they called it postpartum psychosis in the future. Here it was crazy. To me it was Fate. They were just vessels to introduce me into my next life – perhaps part of them knew it. Maybe they knew what I was and why some of them had attempted to kill me before they could kill themselves.

Perhaps they knew I was a monster.

We all had recurring themes that happened in our lives. This was mine.

But I'd never gotten a letter from a mother. Not a mother strong enough to fight the urge of killing me and spend their miserable time writing me a (somewhat) heartfelt letter. I know... talk about family issues.

This was what made me curious. It made me question why I was reincarnated if my mother's all wanted to kill me. And who were these mothers? Did a greater force randomly select them? *Was* there a greater force? Why and how could we Time Bend? Did we have a purpose? Who created us? Or *was* there a creator? Or were we just by chance reincarnated every now and then for no apparent reason?

It was too much.

The Count began to get restless after the third stop we had and said moodily, "how much longer?"

It was closing into the evening and we were still in the middle of what seemed like nowhere.

"Long, probably," Jack mumbled crunching loudly into an apple.

"Stop the carriage!" I cried catching a glimpse of a figure standing by the side of the road.

Jack and the Count watched me with their mouths open wide - like I was crazy. I didn't know what urged me to say it. My mouth had opened for me before I'd even noticed the person.

"Stop the carriage," Jack repeated, curiously watching me intently.

"I just need to - excuse me," I gasped for air.

As soon as the Count gave the order to stop the carriage I'd flung the door open and was looking left, right and centre for the person.

Jack climbed out behind me and stood by the carriage watching me. But it was gone. I didn't know what the hell it was but it was gone. The person I wanted to see was no longer here and I was left - a deer caught in the headlights.

"Are you alright?" The Count called from the carriage, I turned around and Jack caught my eye.

What is it? He mouthed.

"It can wait..." I trembled, feeling mad as I was helped back into the carriage.

"Perhaps we should stop at the nearest village, my Lord?" Jack suggested, watching me concerned. The Count seemed put off by the idea but looked over me worried and nodded his head with an uncertain yes.

Jack sent the order by knocking on the roof of the carriage and sticking his head out of the window. Then as the carriage jolted into motion he leant back watching me intently.

I was going crazy.

We went on until we came across a village not far from London and I was led in by Jack to a tavern when I felt the feeling again.

It was a weird feeling, a familiar feeling. Like someone who knew me was watching me. Or I knew them, and they weren't any ordinary citizen.

"Jack," I whispered, clutching onto his arm. "If I'm wrong then you can officially call me crazy and mock me for however long you want. But we need to go outside."

"What?" he muttered, sidestepping out of the way of a drunken man stumbling towards the exit. There were table's scattered around and loud laughter stopped abruptly once we stepped into the centre of the room. We must have been a sight: two guards, a Count, a silver-haired girl and… well Jack who actually looked pretty normal.

"Now," I hissed, pretending to fall into his side. The Count let out a shriek and pulled his arms into his chest as someone bashed into us.

"Nova needs some fresh air," Jack exclaimed, and the Count looked at him surprised.

"You mean Marion?"

"I said Marion," Jack said, walking backwards as I slumped into his side. He wrapped his arms around me as we were engulfed by the crowd and spewed out into the evening air. The sun had just about set and shadows shielded us from those making their way home or out.

"This way."

"Nova hold on." He grabbed me by the shoulders and turned me to face him.

"I can't explain it, Jack. We just have to go."

He searched my eyes for a moment and then nodded. Looking back on it, it must have been that moment he realised he trusted me. Foolish.

CHAPTER 22

Time: 8th August 1661
Location: In the woods behind an inn in the middle of nowhere

I took his hand in mine and followed whatever feeling was leading me towards this person, the feeling of familiarity.

We'd left a path and stepped into a forest when we both came to a stop, a feeling of ice-cold water trickled down my back and I clenched onto Jack's hand.

"Did you feel that?" he breathed. I nodded my head as we turned our backs on each other, feet apart and ready to take on whatever was coming our way.

And it was at that moment we realised the team we could make. Foolish.

Jack reached to his side and produced a beautiful sword. "Where did you get that?" I asked, not actually noticing it before.

"Shh," he hissed and I paused for a moment scanning the trees. Anyone could be here hiding behind one - or in the pile of leaves beside us.

And then Jack sprung into action, spinning and pointing the tip of his sword to somebody's neck. The person laughed, it was a girl, dark long hair and narrow face.

"Please no swords," she sighed, straightening her brown skirt and walking backward to sit on the stump of a tree.

"Who are you?" I asked. I knew her - somehow I knew her and I didn't know how or where I knew her but she was familiar.

"I go by the name of O in this life."

"Oh?" Jack questioned, taking a step towards her but lowering the sword.

"No, O."

"Oh..." He nodded his head, still puzzled.

"But who are you?" I asked, taking a step in front of Jack to catch a clearer glimpse of her face. She was deathly pale and her young eyes sparkled with a playful and somewhat wise glaze.

"I'm not a Time Bender like the two of you."

Jack stumbled back a little, shuffling his feet and regaining his posture. "So what are you?"

"I'm reincarnated into this life and another in the future. That's all I'm allowed to say."

"Allowed?" Jack questioned. "By who?" But she didn't answer.

"So why are you here?" I asked.

"I was hoping you'd tell me why. I've been called."

"Called by who?" I asked.

O looked at me softly and her head tilted to the side. "I can't say."

I took a step forward intimidatingly. "It felt a whole lot more like you were calling me instead of the other way around," she shrugged helplessly. "Well, you obviously have answers," I snapped.

Jack placed an arm in front of me and sent me a look. She knew about Time Bending, she'd been called by a what or a who to help us and I had a hell of a lot of questions.

"What is our purpose?" I decided to ask.

She took a deep breath. "There is no real purpose."

Helpful.

I grimaced. "So we're just a mistake that keeps happening?"

The girl played with her fingers and waited to respond. "I can't say."

What was the point in this bitch then?

"I swear to-" I took a step towards her aggressively but she only looked up into my eyes and sighed.

"Okay then..." Jack said, using his sword to drag me back by the skirt. If he weren't here I would have already lost my patience and I'd only been here for a minute talking to this girl.

I sighed, forcing myself to be more patient. "Okay. So why do you feel so familiar?"

She smiled, finally a question she could answer. "We are sisters in another life."

I'd only had a couple siblings throughout my lives, and especially not one who was also reincarnated. It made me

235

wonder how many more siblings of mine were also reincarnated. How hadn't I known?

"What year?"

"I was born in the year 2010. You died at the age of seventeen in 2019."

I remembered it was a car accident in Paris. I'd been back to that life before but I'd never stuck around long. It was always to deliver messages from my clients to ancestors telling them which companies to invest in and so on.

I didn't really know what to say, I couldn't remember everything from that life, only the select important bits.

"It's okay, I know you won't remember."

"Did you know you were reincarnated in that life?" Jack asked suddenly.

She nodded her head. "I keep all my memories from this life. It's complicated. There are others of us too."

"Others?" Jack asked curiously.

"Most Time Bender siblings are of course accidents if they come from the same parents. We're the less powerful versions of you guys - some would say."

"I have a sister in the present day."

O shook her head. "She is not one of us. Her mother must be different from yours. But you do have a brother reincarnation who appears sometimes."

"Brother?" Jack stumbled.

She smiled. "He has multiple reincarnations in different bodies and has other Time bender siblings as well. But most of the time he's a brother to you." She turned away from Jack. "You will meet him someday too, Nova."

So she could see the future, she knew about our lives and what would happen to us. Which would suggest they (whoever they were) had a way of watching us live. This was yet another thing she couldn't say.

"Well then I presume you do know why we're here?" I asked.

"I know why you're in this life and I know you're trapped. But I'm going to guess you've been called to me because you need help getting out."

She was good.

"Yep," Jack replied. "So can you do some magic poof and send us back to our bodies in the future?"

She rolled her eyes and stood up stretching. For a moment I felt surprised. I hadn't expected it to be that easy.

"I can't do that." My heart sunk. "But I can tell you how you can get back."

I grasped Jack's arm. This was it. This was exactly what we'd needed. For over a month I'd been trapped in this life and I was finally about to be told how to save myself.

"Well?"

"You go back the old fashioned way," she said it like it was a matter of fact and we were complete idiots for not knowing it.

"And what is the old fashioned way?" Jack asked.

"You go through a Time Portal."

"Like a time machine?" he asked and O shook her head chuckling. "It's a bridge - to the timeline."

"But what happens to these bodies...?" I asked.

"They will be stranded in the middle of nowhere, don't worry. They won't remember what's happened to them. It all gets cleaned up so there are no loose ends. They'll have no recollection of the last few months."

That was a lot of information to take in but OK.

"So where is the Time Portal?"

She smiled knowingly. "For the closest one, you have to head North. It's an old well in Scotland."

"Well do you have a map?"

She shook her head. "You won't need one, you'll feel it the closer you get. You know, hot and cold directions."

How helpful.

"What about our Totems?" Jack asked, clever. I'd completely forgotten about that part.

"Ah yes, now that's easy, you drop what your Totems are into the well."

Easier said than done except mine took the form of any kind of blue light. Hell if Ace was here, how was he supposed to drop in the moon?

I cringed. "What do I drop in?"

"It can be anything - a blue firefly that's how you got here in the first place."

I nodded my head thoughtfully. "It's as simple as that." O smiled and pulled the hood of her cloak over her head.

"Now if you'll excuse me-"

Shouts were heard from behind us. "Find her and lock her up!"

The hell?

Jack pulled me into him and placed the sword into my hands as we shielded the girl.

"Goodluck," she called, forcing her way between us and quickly hugging my side. "Nothing is written in stone – it's written in pencil," she whispered to me before she walked into the hands of a group of men holding fire torches.

"What?" I hissed, trying to grab her arm but the men had already spotted her as she slid down the slope and into the custody of the village.

"Witch!" The men cried, spitting and grabbing her arms, they cheered at their success. Jack had stuffed me into his chest as we tried to hide behind a tree. We didn't want to be seen with a witch and we didn't want to be burnt alive for it - especially now that we had a chance.

Their shouts continued as they walked back into town and I began to think, so this is how she died in this life? A young girl with not much of a life at all... but she had so much ahead of her and she knew it. There was something before she was born into this life, it was obvious and there would be something in between this and her next life with me. And yet there was no such thing as a purpose? Or were purpose and destiny different?

"Let's run," I said as the shouts faded away.

Jack looked at me for a moment and then at the bottom of the hill. "We can't. We wouldn't get far before we get exhausted, your illness takes over and I'll be forced to carry you."

"I can manage."

"Easy for you to say." He rolled his eyes. "You're not the one who will have to carry you."

I laughed, and god it felt good. I felt the tension leave my neck and I could smile, I could breathe and relax for a moment. I had hope again. It had been restored now we had a plan. We knew how to save ourselves and I would go through hell if I meant I could get back to where I belonged. Even if the future was worse than in the past.

Jack and I watched each other, smiles on our faces and yet something felt unsettled - something wasn't right about the moment. Something was missing.

But nothing happened.

He only looked at me, his brown eyes providing warmth the chilled evening air didn't. He never put his arm around my waist. We stopped ourselves from letting go and crashing into a world of possibilities.

We were just two young people in the year 1661 on a chilly August evening with so many questions about the past and the future staring at each other.

"Well, what happens when we do get back?" I asked.

Jack's shoulders stiffened and his eyes turned sharp enough to cut clean through me.

He swallowed tightly. "We go back to fighting, I guess."

The disappointment hit me with such force I had to clench on tightly to my emotions before they showed on my face. I'd wanted it to be different - any answer but that.

"Gee thanks." I tried to play it off, but my strangled voice betrayed me by hinting that I was disappointed.

He blinked, surprised by my response. "I suppose you just want everything to get back to normal." He spoke to the ground with his lip turned down and for a split second, I wondered if we both wanted the same thing. But that was foolish, I should have known from the beginning. In what story does the hero fall in love with the villain?

My breath caught in my throat. I blamed these thoughts on my loneliness. Jack was attractive and I missed sex - clearly.

"What do you think my normal is?" I nudged his side gently. Jack rolled his eyes and took a deep breath as if to list all the wonders of my life.

"Cocktails, parties, money, fame, cameras-"

"Okay, but you realise there's a little more to my existence right?" I said and he looked my way as though not believing it. I didn't believe it really. I just needed to defend myself somehow. He was completely right, that was the majority of my life now.

"Please elaborate."

"I train pretty much all day most days. And you've made my life a living hell in that regard - so thanks-"

"You're welcome."

"But there's more to it," I trailed on not really knowing how to persuade him I wasn't just a normal Prospect celebrity, there was more to me.

Now I realise he knew that. He knew I wasn't just Nova, a Prospect celebrity and he didn't hate me. He just hated the world I was a part of and what I did.

Nevertheless, he shook his head bewildered by my ignorance. I didn't blame him. "I try pretty hard to understand you Nova but it amazes me how you can be so blind-"

"I'm not blind," I interjected quickly, continuing before he had the chance to jump in. "I can see that I'm the bad guy in all of this, I'm the one who gets paid to go kill completely innocent and vulnerable people." He opened his mouth to speak but I quickly cut him off. "I'm the one who sips my fancy cocktail and laughs along with the rest of the city whilst waiting for my next client to tell me who to kill." I took a deep breath, watching his face for any kind of reaction. "And I'll do it. Hell the number of generations I've wiped out because of my-"

He snatched my fist and brought it to his chest, forcing me to level with him. "You have a chance." He pressed my palm against his chest and I felt the dull thud of his heart pick up when I looked up at him.

"It's a bit late for that."

"You can help us," he said, a moment of excitement appearing before he shut it down completely.

I began. "At the beginning of this. I thought you intended to wipe out the entire city of Prospect by changing the past. But now I realise that's the complete opposite." He leant forward, listening to my words eagerly as if I'd just figured it out. "But now I see you were only trying to stop me from doing that to your people. I'm a part of the evil dystopian hierarchy and you're the Robin Hood." His face broke out into a small smile. Those were some weird references that I was glad he understood.

"Sorry for calling you blind."

"I'm sorry for uh a lot." I took a breath. "You realise I'm a shallow bitch and I'm too scared to actually leave my life at Prospect, that means no more cocktails."

He let out streams of laughter. "We're going to have to get out of the past before you have that to worry about."

I watched him curiously. "Well now we know how to get back my only worry is waking up in Prospect with you miles away about to launch a bomb on me."

He smiled softly. "No bombs are coming your way."

"That's one less thing to worry about then."

CHAPTER 23

Time: 8th August 1661
Location: A Tavern somewhere

"Where have you been?" The Count moaned as the guards opened a bedroom door for us.

"She was very sick my lord." Jack bowed his head, and helped me into the room, continuing with my 'weak energy' act.

The Count flapped his hands for a moment and stood over me in the bed.

"How are you feeling?"

You tell me, Count. How did it look? Was I doing well? Was it Oscar worthy?

I grimaced and clutched my stomach. "Not great, the journey made me feel rather ill."

"We only have one room," he said, standing and looking around with plain disgust. It wasn't that bad of a room - clearly it was the nicest one the place had.

"Did you not tell them who you were?" Jack asked, to which the Count shook his head defiantly.

"If I had it would have been likely for them to throw me onto the street. I am not well-liked in these parts..." he said, standing in the centre of the room. He looked incredibly out of place - it was quite amusing.

"It's fine," Jack chirped, taking a blanket off of the bed and whooshing it into the air. "I'll just sleep on the floor."

"Don't worry Jack, the bed's big enough for us all," the Count suggested. Both our mouths dropped open and the look the Count gave us was one of incredulous horror and he stumbled for words.

"Take a joke will you?" The Count laughed nervously.

After ordering Jack to go downstairs in search of food I turned my back from him as my husband began to peel off his shoes quietly.

"We don't have to consummate the marriage if you don't wish to," I finally said after building up enough courage.

"Why would you think?" he snapped defensively.

"I was just saying," I replied quickly.

"No. We need to bear a child if we want to stop people from gossiping," he snapped. I nodded quietly, turning away again and struggling to remove the dress.

"Let me help," the Count sighed.

As soon as the red dress fell to the floor and I was left in a white underdress. I backed away and avoided looking at him as I brushed past and climbed into the bed. I stared at the ceiling as he turned and sat on the edge of the bed beside me.

Thankfully Jack threw open the door with a tray full of cheese and fruit. "Hello Jack." He finally smiled, standing from the bed and walking over to the table Jack now sat at.

They began talking about stuff I didn't care for but hearing Jack's voice brought me comfort.

He didn't give anything away and he was really good at doing that; hiding how he felt with a clenched jaw and straight lips. The only thing that showed me there was a sign of him in there was his eyes - alive and wild with adventure. They never changed.

I'd fallen asleep by the time Jack had grabbed his pillow and blanket, placed his hat over his eyes and lied down on the rug at the floor of my bed. When I felt a tug in my mind I allowed myself to be dragged in by Jack. We watched silently together, each unable to communicate with each other or see one another - we just watched this imaginary-like but real timeline.

I don't know why we did it. We were just lying here watching for no reason. We knew this wasn't the way - I think in our own way we just didn't want to let it go. This place we had created and watched for so long together no longer had a purpose. Nor did we.

It was like an idea of ours had died - it was a hopeless idea but it was an idea we'd had hoped would work once upon a time.

I was pulled out of the state by my husband snoring next to my ear, the air was being blown into my shoulder and I was now aware of the position he'd put me in whilst I'd been meditating with Jack, who seemed not to notice I'd left.

The Count was literally lying on top of me so how I wasn't already suffocated to death I didn't know.

"Jack," I whispered. I didn't really need to. There was no way the Count was going to wake up any time soon. There was a jolt of the bed and a startled groan as Jack hit his head on the bottom.

"What? What is it?" He sprung to his feet, sword in hand.

"I can't breath," I gasped, gesturing with my free hands to the pig lying between my legs.

Jack blinked blearily and scowled at the Count's back. "I could kill him. He's cruel to people… If you'd seen him do the things he's done - the things he'll do," he said, standing by my side of the bed and detaching the hand away from my thigh.

"But that would go against everything you stand for," I whispered, and froze when the Count mumbled.

"I would do it for you," Jack murmured, looking at me for a moment and bracing himself to roll the Count.

"As soon as I move him, I'll duck and roll. Got it?" he whispered.

I didn't respond, he had just... he'd just said he'd kill the Count for me... cue ovaries exploding.

Who was I turning into? I was becoming soft... I'd wanted to rely on Jack to save me this whole time and I liked it. I liked being the one rescued for once and not the one being relied on from the whole of society to kill the Raven.

I couldn't do it. I could not go back to the future and stand in front of Prospect saying the reason I was unable to kill the Raven was because I was... no.

Jack looked at me expectantly and I nodded, clearing the thoughts from my head. He pushed him off of me and onto his front and I quickly closed my eyes.

Jack ducked behind me as the Count blearily opened his eyes. I sighed, pretending to be asleep. The Count grumbled slightly slumping back on to the pillow asleep.

I was free again and once again because of Jack.

This was going to be a problem.

CHAPTER 24

Time: 9th August 1661
Location: A village North of Eldermore, London

By morning the Count was in higher spirits and we were only a short distance away from my new home.

I didn't know what our plan was, but I had little opportunity to ask Jack if he had any idea how we were going to get all the way to Scotland without getting caught.

The Count had helped me dress into a light blue dress in the morning. Thankfully my luggage was with our carriage and not with the servants who rode on through the evening.

"Are you excited?" the Count asked.

"Yes, very," I replied automatically, looking out of the carriage window as we weaved through the dirty cobbled streets.

"Jack?" The Count clasped his hands together awkwardly. I turned my head to the side, careful to avoid catching my hat on the ceiling.

Jack was staring at his lap, tapping his foot on the floor when he looked up and smiled tightly. "Yes my Lord, I'm eagerly awaiting our arrival."

My face turned red and Jack turned his head to face the window once again.

There was an air of difference surrounding us, I couldn't pinpoint what it exactly was other than I wanted to touch him more than I usually did - a hand on his forearm as I climbed into the carriage - a brush of our knees opposite each other.

"One new guest and a new household member. I know I am excited," the Count grinned.

I turned and smiled weakly, focusing my eyes on Jack's head and then his reflection in the window. His eyes were on me and they stayed that way until the Count began to speak to him.

I was ignored for the rest of the journey and only leant out of my corner as we began travelling up a long path.

A row of Cyprus trees led us down a muddy path into a garden with perfectly round bushes and neatly kept flowers.

Soldiers surrounded the estate and their eyes followed our carriage as we circled a large fountain and pulled to a stop outside a grand stair entrance. Jack was the first out and then the Count who helped me. I could feel their eyes on me, all of them straining to catch a glimpse of the new wife. More than likely there were going to be whispers of whether I would be successful. Rumours would shortly follow, circling the large bright walls of the estate.

It was huge and I'd definitely get lost here. Immediately looking around I began to feel like a fish out of water. The Count linked his arm through mine and we began our way up the staircase.

The servants had their eyes turned to the ground as we entered the large lobby-like area. The Count seemed to stare right through them as though they weren't there. I would have smiled but there was no use in smiling at the tops of bent heads.

"This is the main entrance," he explained.

Our shoes clipped against the tiled floors as we came to the end of the line of servants and one woman stepped forward. She was dressed far nicer than the other servants, which would suggest she was a little higher up in the staff ranking.

"Ms Brown, could you please show our new Countess to her living space and then guide her to breakfast as soon as possible." He waved his hand, and the woman stepped forward.

"Jack, you can come with me," the Count said and I turned to him and panicked. Jack's eyes were wide and he too looked out of place, more so than anyone else.

It dawned on me. Jack probably had never lived a high-quality life, sure he might remember events in this life but he probably didn't remember much of this rich lifestyle. Maybe not even in any of his future lives from this one. But then again, he was very quiet about any of his lives. For all I could have known he'd been a king.

"Ah, Lord Sanders!" I heard the Count's voice echo as the woman began leading me up the stairs. We came to a large landing overlooking the main entrance and she took me down another corridor.

I had to skip to keep up with her pace, whilst also casting my eyes over the large paintings that hung on the walls and the decorations that were scattered neatly throughout the corridor. We came to white double doors and she threw them open to reveal a large sitting space. There was a piano in one corner, a gigantic fireplace with sofas and an oak table in the centre. A large mirror hung above the fireplace accompanied by two bookcases either side, and a round table in one corner with a teapot and cups placed on a tray.

It was a lot to take in.

"Thank you..." I trailed off not knowing what to call her.

"Ms Brown," she replied. She was much older than me and her brown hair was tucked neatly into a bun. She didn't look nearly as comforting and nice as Abigail.

"There is a bedroom through these doors and a bathroom on the opposite side," she explained, opening the door to two male servants who carried my chest of belongings, which weren't much. I figured they'd look quite lost in a room this size.

"Now quickly, we don't want to keep the Count waiting," she ordered. I tapped the chest and rotated around the room awestruck. It was different from the modern walls of Prospect, it was just as grand but more... antique.

And for once this place felt familiar, cold and distant but nonetheless familiar. A long time ago, in a lifetime far,

far away I had been confined to these very walls. This was where I would have spent the majority of my life.

Soon Ms Brown was flying down the stairs and swiftly walking down a long corridor with tall thin windows. Our footsteps seemed to echo in every room adding to the feeling that something was missing.

There was an emptiness that filled the house, the place felt old: a void of something new, no children and no happiness. It was all very serious and sad. The place reeked of death and had no place for birth.

And it seemed it never would because I would never be successful in providing a child that stayed alive.

She showed me into a dining room with a long table and then closed the door behind me. The Count was sitting at the head of the table with Jack and the snobby man sat either side of him.

"Marion!" The Count exclaimed, his face brightening as he saw me. "Come, come! Sit."

I opted to sit next to Jack, whose plate was piled high with eggs, sausages, tomatoes and potatoes. Mine was also piled high and I desperately wanted to stuff my face with the greasy food.

As I flattened the napkin onto my lap the doors swung open and two more men walked in. Was this place always filled with people? My thoughts trailed off as I looked to the man who chose to stand behind a chair opposite me and I gasped and scraped my chair backwards.

Jack gripped my knee tightly and I looked at my plate shakily.

Was I really that surprised?

"Marion? Are you alright?" The Count asked. I looked up wearily nodding my head and then turned to face our guest.

At first, I hadn't recognised him. I'd never seen him with a beard and this time his black hair was tied neatly behind his neck and he was dressed less like a fugitive.

"I'd like to introduce you to Mr Tobias Smith and Lord Sanders."

The Lord bowed his head politely and then pulled out the chair beside me.

"Gentlemen, my wife."

"I believe we've met!" Tobias exclaimed, taking his seat and already taking a bite from an apple.

I nibbled on a buttered roll of bread and Jack squeezed my knee, stopping me from taking the butter knife and jamming it into Ace's throat.

"Really?" the Count asked, his mouth dropping open in surprise. Tobias nodded his head pointing his fork in my direction and chewing on his apple. Who held a fork whilst eating an apple?

"Don't you remember Mar? You were like 'Ah!' And I was like 'Oo!' - then you fainted and I escorted you home like the true gentlemen I am."

I clenched the bread until it turned into crumbs and a doughy mess. "I seem to remember the encounter quite

254

differently." I ran my tongue in front of my teeth. "Darling." I turned my eyes to face my husband and drew the words very carefully. "Were you aware Tobias is a wanted murderer?"

I was expecting the Count's face to drop in shock and he'd cry out for the guards but instead his face broke into a large grin. "I know! I ordered him to kill the man, the issue is resolved now thankfully."

You've got to be kidding me.

"How has it been resolved?" I asked.

Jack clenched my knee tightly and coughed. I looked around the table at the men's faces with eyebrows raised in shock.

"Are you questioning my authority?" The Count's voice was cold and less excited than usual. I'd embarrassed him, and it wasn't a woman's place to ask - let alone talk about business.

Get me the hell out of this place.

"I-"

"Leave," he ordered.

My face grew hot as I screeched the chair against the floor and handed Jack my napkin. He rose as well but the Count held a hand out for him to stop. I could faintly hear them talking as I turned my back from them and walked the embarrassing stretch out of the dining hall.

I was going to kill him. To hell with what Jack told me to not do. I would kill him when he least expected it and make my own way back with or without Jack.

Thankfully, there was only one servant standing outside the door and he didn't look my way when I began pacing outside. I couldn't just go in there and stab him - especially in broad daylight. I'd never make it out of here alive and I'd end up killing the others, which might wipe out a generation and that'd just be ugly.

No, I had to wait until we were alone at night. I'd take my opportunity that night if he planned on sleeping with me. I'd kill him and then work my way from there.

I was sure I'd figure out a plan the moment it was put in motion. It was how things usually worked for me.

Now I imagine you're thinking, 'what a spoilt brat, she gets embarrassed once in front of a few guys and she wants to kill him', but I think if you'd be spouted out into an unfamiliar life and forced to marry a cold-hearted murderer struggling with his sexuality, you'd probably feel a little indifferent about him.

I was going to get out of this hellhole one way or another. I swore it.

CHAPTER 25

Things hadn't worked out very well since then. I'd had zero opportunity to kill the Count because people constantly surrounded me.

Jack and I were no longer on talking terms after an awkward argument about my plan to kill the Count:

"I've got a plan, just don't kill him!" Jack hissed.

"What's the plan?" I snapped. He watched me for a moment before shaking his head.

"Well-"

"Jack. I'm actually trying to get this life on the same track as our timeline by trying to get this wrinkly old raisin to have sex with me."

His face went red and he clenched his jaw. "I thought you were used to that."

My mouth fell to my knees and it felt like a weight had just been dropped onto my chest.

All I saw was red. I slapped his head to the side, ignoring the fact a servant had just walked past our hidden corner of the estate.

"Shit- I can't believe I said that - I'm so sorry Nova." He reached toward me but I'd already pushed him out the

257

way. I understood him and I knew he didn't really mean it. We'd gotten to the stage of joking about how terrible Prospect really was and comparing it to old societies. He'd often pretend like I was this evil person (which I still kind of was) - like every other Prospect citizen. It was apparently a stereotype for people as high up in society as I was that we'd gotten there through sleeping with people.

Clearly, I was hated and judged by the Rebellion - even if I wanted to join and help him I'd never be accepted anyway so what was the point?

"Nova." He wrapped his hand around my forearm and pulled me into him, I struggled against his arms and glared up at him.

"I would kill him if I could. I would. You know that," he breathed into my hair. I froze, listening to his breathing and waiting for him to do something - to push me against the wall and kiss me passionately. Jack leant his forehead against mine, his brown eyes watching mine until I closed them, parted my lips and waited. But he tore himself away from me and snatched his hands into his chest with an instant look of regret.

He wanted me but he hated me.

The story of my oh so lonely life.

It had been a month. A whole month since I had arrived. Already I felt like I was trapped. The people here were polite, they did their job well - too well as a matter of fact.

It was lonely, nobody talked to me here, and I couldn't speak with Jack because he was constantly running errands for the Count. He was out of the estate more than he was in it and yet somehow he hadn't run away - he hadn't escaped to Scotland because he couldn't just leave me here. Apparently.

He was fighting an internal battle with liking me and hating me. He was just as confused as I was.

Or maybe he felt nothing toward me but hatred - maybe the reason he couldn't leave me here was because he didn't trust me enough.

I'd only been out of the estate twice. Once to go to this sporting game I didn't know the name of and once to somebody else's place - both were occasions to flaunt off the Counts new possession.

And Tobias, *Jesus Christ* he just would not leave. The other two Mr Snob and Lord Farquaad or whatever his name was had left but Tobias had clearly opted to annoy me for as long as possible. I was also 99% sure the Count and Tobias were having an affair (which was incredibly weird considering Tobias was the past version of Ace who had the largest crush on me in the future).

I could only hope Ace would check his life files, do some reading up for Christ's sake and remember me. It would save me a lot of pain from having to ride all the way to Scotland and fall down an unknown well. But then again he also didn't have a Totem.

The Count had decided on one particular day to take me on a walk - of course, we weren't alone because then I would have killed him. Instead, he decided to show me around the gardens, claiming I'd been cooped up inside for too long. When really *he* had kept me cooped up, he ignored me constantly.

I hadn't learnt anything about him other than that he was blatantly a closeted homosexual (obviously there were rumours).

I only wished that he knew he didn't have to be so cruel - killing people who judged him. I wish he knew I would be on his side if he weren't so horrible (this was, of course, all hypocritical because I was also a pretty cold-hearted murderer - I mean assassin).

Also, I was starting to worry about what I was supposed to do. Because we still hadn't had sex yet and I knew I was supposed to get pregnant but when was that? So I'd started to push it a little more, suggesting we sleep in the same room together (which he always denied).

"My Lord!" cried a familiar voice over the sound of hooves - it was Jack. He'd been away for a week and I was incredibly glad to see him. Turning in his direction I felt my shoulders relax immediately.

"Jack," the Count said excitedly. I was beginning to suspect by the excitement on the Counts' face by Jack's return that it wasn't the Count who was the one pushing him to go away on these long trips - but rather it was Jack.

"I'll meet you inside once I put the horse away," Jack said.

"Tonight my love." I gripped the Count's hand stopping him from following Jack eagerly. "The rumours are starting to arise, and you know I don't listen. But our reputation... and I wish to give you a son to carry your family name."

He watched me for a moment with a red face and for a moment I thought he would strike me, but instead, he nodded his head. "We do it my way though," he said coldly.

I nodded my head numbly, if that involved me being hurt it was okay, I had kept a knife under my pillow to kill him (which was my plan). It would also be likely that he'd order guards to a different part of the building.

The Count had arranged a feast for the two of us and some form of a bird sat in the centre of the table surrounded by colourful foods Marion had probably never seen before. I tried to act surprised as some of the more exotic foods arrived in front of me.

We didn't speak much. I was sure for Marion it would have been awkward as she tried to calm her nerves. However, I was blissfully chewing away thinking of possible ways to kill him.

So far the plan was to kill him whilst he was on top of me with a knife I'd prepared under my bed.

Once we sat back with our stomachs full he stood up and offered me his hand. I took it cautiously as he led me in the opposite direction of my room.

Uh what the hell?

"Why don't we go to my room?" I said, trying to not sound so unprepared as I was feeling.

"I said my way," he replied quietly. His hand was clammy with nerves and I tried not to look at him.

At the top of the stairs were two of his guards, who waited patiently as we came to the top. "Take the night off gentlemen."

They nodded their heads and made their way down the stairs - how lucky.

This was not the plan at all but I supposed I could work with it. I was the queen of improvisation after all.

The Count undid his top buttons and rolled up his sleeves. "Please take a seat." He gestured towards the sofa in the centre of the room, everything was coated gold in here including the teapot he'd carefully arranged by the table.

I sat still, searching around the room for any object I could kill him with. If worse came to worse I could kill him with my hands I supposed. He handed me the teacup and I gulped it down quickly, it was an odd-tasting tea no doubt something expensive and exotic he had just lying around.

Soon we became deathly quiet and my mind entered its eerily calm autopilot mood as he led me into the bedroom.

I made my way to the bed, lying fully dressed and propped against the cushions drowsily. This was my opportunity I decided as he unbuttoned my dress and lifted up the skirt, his hands were shaking as he undressed me and I reached under the pillow for the...

There was nothing there.

Of course, there was nothing there, what was wrong with me?

He took his time clearly nervous, taking off all my clothes until I was completely naked. But where was the knife? I hadn't intended for it to get this far. Hell, I hadn't actually expected to get naked at all seeing as he was as uninterested as a sloth.

He groaned as he backed away from the bed, leaving my legs spread open. Where were my legs? I shrieked in my head. I couldn't feel them - literally nothing and I couldn't move.

He sat on the edge of the bed for a moment with his back turned to me and then he stood and went to the corner of the room, holding onto the wall. It was then I realised he couldn't you know... I listened to the range of swear words he panted.

There was no knife, I couldn't move and I was naked. I began to panic but I couldn't quite use my voice to shout for help.

Why had he done this? He'd drugged me. How worse could this life get? My gay husband had drugged me so it wouldn't be as embarrassing for him. Jesus Christ. If only he knew how many women I'd slept with too. We were no different - except he was evil.

Well, I guess we weren't so different after all.

I watched him helplessly as he turned away from the wall and walked back over to me, settling himself between my thighs. I attempted to scream at him.

"Close your eyes," he snapped, though it sounded more like a plea. What good was being a badass assassin if you couldn't do anything?

I was once again the damsel in distress.

Holy shit was I about to be-

The Count arranged himself and sighed before crushing his lips against mine. "I can't do this. I'm sorry," he whispered. It was then I felt something wet against my cheeks and he removed himself from me - he was crying.

"I'm sorry," he said, reaching to his nightstand, pulling out a knife and wrapping his hands around it.

No, I was about to be killed instead.

He brought it above his head ready to plunge it into my chest when suddenly a figure stood over him. It gripped his arms and removed the knife from the Count who meekly removed his gaze from mine to face him.

"Jack?" The Count whimpered in betrayal.

"Why did you have to go and do *that?*" Jack said and suddenly I was looking at the Count's wide eyes and the blood that squirted from his mouth. I looked up and met the eyes of Jack - a sword in hand and determined face.

Life had been cruel to the Count, but he *had* just tried to kill me.

CHAPTER 26

The Count's body rolled off of mine and onto the floor. Quickly Jack moved into motion. First, he covered my body with a blanket and forced his fingers down my throat.

"We need to get it out of you."

It was a little late for that idiot.

So much was happening all at once, Jack was moving around the room quickly stuffing the body under the bed and wiping the floor with a blanket. His hands were surprisingly steady as he moved the Count's body.

I thought he wasn't going to kill the Count?

Had that been his first kill? He seemed remarkably calm. Realisation settled over me like a damp cloud as I caught a look at his wild eyes. This was most certainly his first kill and he was doing a good job at not showing the storm raging behind his face right now.

"Don't look at me like that," he hissed, moving around the bed to pick up my dress. I had no idea how I was looking at him although I reckoned I was drooling.

I tried to move my mouth to speak but all I could feel was numbness. Although eventually I could wiggle my toes and Jack had helped my floppy body up, putting the maroon dress back on my bare body.

He grumbled. "Let's get the hell out of this place."

Jack was wearing a hat with a feather hanging off (which I must admit suited him very well) and maroon cloak. We were leaving. Finally, thank the Timeline we were leaving. I was going home.

Well first I had to get out of here without being stopped, and then we had to make it to Scotland without being hunted and put on trial for our actions. And well - that'd probably take a couple of weeks.

Jack lifted me up over his shoulder and grabbed his sword from the floor. "You're going to have to walk once we get down the stairs and you might have to fight."

I groaned in response, giving a slight kick of my right knee and he was off. My own personal chariot flew down the stairs, keeping to the side of walls and checking corners. He trod on the floor lightly, one foot in front of the other, holding his balanced sword in front of us like a fencing expert.

"Holy – crap," I slurred as I was jolted when he jumped off some stairs.

"Shush!" he hissed. Blending into the shadows, he helped me off of his shoulder and onto solid ground, supporting me below the shoulders as I tried to stand on my legs. Jack looked from side to side and then pushed our backs against the wall as two maids giggled together and then turned a corner.

We paused for a moment. "Are you okay to walk?"

I leant on his shoulder and nodded my head. "You killed him," I slurred.

He didn't reply, he just looked at the ground and clenched his jaw.

"He was going to-" I started to say, but he stopped me from speaking with a look.

He didn't want to talk about it and nor did I. If he were a minute later then I would... The thought made me sick. I was only sad that I hadn't been the one to kill him.

Jack propped me up and we continued. Once we came to a long corridor we began to pick up our speed, until I stumbled into a chest of drawers and smashed a pot. Jack swivelled to face me with wide eyes and we froze for a moment looking to each end of the hallway panicked.

"Okay, I'm just going to carry you." He hoisted me over his shoulder so that I caught a mouthful of feather and then he picked up his sword again. He groaned. "How do you wear this dress? Jesus Christ, it puts one too many pounds on you." I weakly slapped his back and groaned as he came to an abrupt stop.

"Well, well, look what we have here." *Are you kidding? Couldn't we have just one break?*

I peered through Jack's legs and scowled - or whatever expression my face could do. I probably just looked droopy - especially when hanging upside down. You guessed it - my favourite person Tobias produced a sword from his side.

"Kidnapping the Countess?" He raised his eyebrows. Once I got back I was going to do a whole lot more than hit Ace for being such an asshole.

Jack sighed. "Nah we're just going for a stroll."

"She does not appear to be strolling," Tobias pointed out, bending to the ground and tilting his head to the side to see my face.

Jack sighed. "Ah well spank me and call me daddy. I suppose you caught me." *What did he just say?*

I wiggled my hand free and attempted to stick up a middle finger, which proved to be difficult and probably didn't look as cool as it had in my head.

"Ah! So she wants to be kidnapped?"

Jack adjusted me over his shoulder and stretched his arm a little. "Let's just get this over with, shall we?"

"Let me down!" I shrieked as Jack lunged into fighting with Tobias. I was dangling from left to right as they rotated around each other, the only sound being their scuffling feet, swords clashing together and their masculine grunts. *Men.*

I groaned as I felt something pressed into my side and when I reached for it I found a dagger hidden behind Jack's cloak. I wrapped my fist around it, flapped the cloak out of my face and when Jack turned to avoid Tobias's sword I threw it - not entirely knowing where it had landed but the yelp from Tobias would suggest I got him somewhere.

"Guards!" he screamed before Jack took the hilt of his sword and bashed him on the top of the head. I watched his body slump to the floor. Jack stepped over him cautiously and then began to sprint.

The sound of heavy footsteps seemed to echo from behind us and Jack was beginning to stumble by the time we'd made it to the main entrance where two guards began to rise from their game of cards.

"Okay Novs you're going to have to stand now," he panted, not waiting for a reply before he bent down and put me on the ground. He then forced Tobias' sword into my hands, clasping them around the hilt. My eyes widened as I noticed two guards over his shoulder. In an instant he'd turned to the two guards whose mouths were dropped open. The other lot hadn't caught up just yet, thankfully.

"Good day chaps, don't mind us." Jack had already sprung into action, jumping into the first one and jamming the sword into his gut. The other put up more of a fight and Jack expertly clashed their swords against each other. Once I'd finally snapped out of it Jack looked over the male's shoulder and raised his eyebrows.

"A little help Countess?"

The guard clearly didn't expect anything from me as he looked over and continued to fight against Jack so I stormed forward, turned, jumped and sliced my leg across his back.

He fell instantly and Jack bonked him on the head. He reached into the uniform and pulled out a pistol and then grabbed my hand.

"Were you just fooling with me?" He panted, as he unlocked the locks on the door and pushed them open,

"What do you mean?" I asked, following him as we ran down the large staircase and onto the path. Two guards were leant against the wall fast asleep and Jack scuttled past them and through the garden.

"Well you made me carry you throughout the house but then you just karate chopped that guys ass back to the Stone Age."

I watched him for a moment; the hat covered one side of his face, which only accentuated his jawline and the beard made him look like some kind of Zorro. His lips were parted as he breathed deeply and he then stopped in his tracks, turning to face me curiously.

"Jack," I breathed shakily, lunging towards him and wrapping my arms around his neck in a hug. His hand came up to stroke my hair as we both panted heavily into each other's necks.

There was the sound of a gunshot behind us and Jack suddenly dropped to the ground. For a moment I thought he'd been shot and my heart stuttered but quickly I realised he was just crouching below the bushes, scuffling around for something.

"What are you doing?" I hissed, also crouching down. He brought out a bag full of male clothes and then began crawling in the direction of a tree.

"Get down," he snapped, aiming from behind the tree and shooting. He was a perfect shot. Instantly taking one guy out in the leg, he was clearly not trying to kill them - just disable them. He shot them down one by one and I watched in amazement. Where in the hell had he learnt how to shoot like that? In his present life with the Rebellion? Or a former life?

Jesus Christ.

"Okay let's go." He shrugged, taking a hold of my hand and turning his back away from the moaning bodies. He led me a little away from the estate, all the time running until we came to a black horse agitated from the shooting and struggling against a tree.

"Where did you learn to fight like that?" I asked, starting to strip off my dress whilst he turned away and calmed the horse.

"I practice a lot back home but I've always been good at this. I probably got it from my next life from this, around 1720 to 1740 maybe? Some serious *Pirates of the Caribbean* shit, except in Spain."

"I was born in 1705 I think. Italy," I said surprised. That was the furthest I'd gone back for a life. It was surprising we had lives so close together. I stumbled, still drowsy from the tea as I finally got the dress off and tossed it into the bushes. "Although I wasn't quite a pirate."

Jack moved around busily behind me. "Nor was I - sort of, kind of - I didn't rape or steal," he tried to explain exasperated. He stuck his arm out and handed me some new clothes - all whilst not looking at me as I stood naked and bloody in the woods.

I forced a tired smile. "Were you Captain Jack Sparrow? What about the wooden peg? Eye patch? Parrot?"

"Jack Sparrow - clever." He rolled his eyes and began arranging the horse. "Except maybe instead of Sparrow it's Raven."

I smiled tiredly and reached down to get the clothes. Quickly I pulled the oversized shirt on then climbed into trousers and the pair of shoes. Jack tossed me a dark cloak from the horse's back and I put it around my shoulders. I quickly fastened my hair into a braid and Jack grabbed hold of my arm, hoisting me onto the horse behind him and then we were in motion.

CHAPTER 27

We rode for hours through the deserted streets and villages outside of London. The cobblestoned roads echoed the sound of horse hooves and we followed the light from the moon to guide us anywhere in the direction North. I was relying on Jack to get us out of the city before dusk.

Eventually we came to a stop when we exited a village and were a short distance away to where we'd stayed the night before we arrived at the estate - a neighbouring village to the one O was probably burned at.

I jumped off the horse first, my legs almost crumbling beneath me. Jack hopped down after me and started to direct the horse in the direction of a group of trees.

I followed, careful to cover our trails. Hell, these people were going to have fun trying to find two people from the future.

"Have we just ruined our past selves lives?" I asked, sitting on a log as Jack searched through whatever he'd packed.

"Yes. I was foolish to think we'd make it out of here without changing something though. Though I suppose it's not changing anything if it hasn't actually happened on this timeline," he said, thinking out loud.

I sat still, playing with a loose thread of the shirt and tightening the navy cloak around me to stay warm. I looked at the side of his face and the straight line of his mouth. I wanted to ask him if that had been his first kill - if he was okay. But I was worried he'd take it the wrong way and think I was making fun of him so I clamped my lips together.

Quietly I settled for easier words. "Thank you, Jack. I don't know what I would have done without you."

This would have been the moment he said something sarcastic and cocky to break the seriousness that was suffocating us. But he only nodded his head with a ghost of a tight smile. We couldn't smile yet - we weren't safe.

I tried not to think about what would happen. I tried not to think of the fact we had no direction as to where we were going only that it was North. I tried not to think about the stupid risk we'd just taken. If we got caught that would be it. We'd be hung or beheaded and we'd be reborn into new bodies - or we wouldn't. I didn't know what would happen to us. I tried not to even think about getting back to my present body - an older version of myself, taller and longer, straighter hair.

I didn't want to think of what Jack would think of me. I avoided imagining waking up after months in the White Room with Vix and the others crowded over me, waiting for me to tell them I'd killed the Raven when really I was falling - not falling in love with him. I tolerated him.

I didn't want things to change. I didn't want a Rebellion or any problems but I couldn't go on living the way I had been knowing Jack was in the Rebellion trying to find a way to bring us down. It would feel like a betrayal after how far we'd come together.

"I reckon it will take us twenty days-" he cut himself off whilst watching me and reached into his pocket for a handkerchief.

"Your nose," he said. I took it gratefully and dabbed at my bloody nose.

"Redcoats will be after us by morning, they'll be searching every end so we have to keep moving north." He was speaking fast, his hands moving nervously and feet tapping against the ground.

"We'll stop at dusk and find a village to sleep in. But after that we might be sleeping on the move - sorry Countess."

I stilled and then rasped. "Please don't call me that anymore."

"Right, sorry. I guess the joke kind of died once the Count died."

I raised an eyebrow, *insensitive much?* For Jack at least. I guess I was rubbing off on him. He blushed and turned his head to the ground awkwardly and helped me back onto the horse.

I cleared my throat and forced myself not to ask about him killing the Count. "Where to, Jack?"

"This is where I'd need Jack Sparrow's magic compass."

I rolled my eyes. "*You* are a broken compass." I pointed in the direction of North and we stood together, our break over and ready to continue the journey. Once settled on the horse, he kicked her into action so we began trotting through the trees. I was conscious about whatever sign we were leaving behind for them to catch so regularly checked behind us.

Jack was unfortunately quiet throughout the ride, keeping to his own thoughts and replying one-worded responses to me. After a while of trying, I gave up embarrassed. He didn't want to talk - that much was obvious. But I needed to talk about what had happened. I'd seen and lived some seriously bad moments and I'd almost relived another one with the Count.

I could feel his cold body covering mine, I could feel him above me and feel his hands grasping for me - I couldn't shake free of it. I could feel his blood spew onto my naked stomach and the blood from his mouth drip into my own and I wanted to forget. I wanted to forget this horrible, non-fairy-tale life and leave it as far back in the web of timelines as possible.

I tightened the cloak around my shoulders and pulled the hood over my tired eyes as Jack tied the horse up by a post and walked us into a building almost identical to the one we'd stayed at the night before we arrived at Eldermore.

A drunk was draped over the table, and a half-naked woman snored on the floor by his feet.

We managed to get a room after a lot of tired grumbling about how late it was but Jack insisted for us to get a few hours of sleep in a bed whilst we still could.

I stood over a water basin, soaking a cloth to wash the Count's dried blood off of me and numbly I began scrubbing my chest.

"How did you know I was there Jack?" I spoke quietly, not turning to face him but knowing he was lying on the single bed staring at the ceiling just as numb as I was feeling.

"I went to your room first and when you weren't there I went to the dining room but your food was being cleared, I figured you'd be in his room." He was silent for a moment. "I had to pick the locks - when I heard him - I thought I was too late."

"Any later and…" I didn't finish. I just put the shirt back over my head and turned to face him whilst leaning against the wall.

There was a long silence, as he kept his head turned away from me and his eyes screwed shut.

Then finally, his voice broke the unbearable quiet. "I wasn't even going to kill him," he croaked, his head turning to face me, brown eyes warming me. "Just seeing him over you... with the knife - it disgusted me."

I sat on the edge of the bed and slowly sank down next to him. "Was that-"

"I'll sleep on the floor," he said immediately, sitting up, but I grabbed his arm and forced it back down onto the bed.

He watched me for a moment, resting on his elbow as my fingers gently touched the hair on his chin and then smoothed out to cover his cheek. "Thank you," I whispered.

For a moment his eyes softened and fluttered shut as he sank into my hand but then his eyes opened and he sat up, repeating himself. "I'll sleep on the floor."

I watched him as he climbed off the bed and arranged himself on the floor until he finally stopped moving and stared up at the ceiling. "Goodnight," he said, before turning his back towards me with a sigh.

I watched his back for a moment with a stab of embarrassment in my chest before I finally turned over and blew out the candle. He was struggling - just like I was. He needed time. I thought back to my first kill and something in my chest clenched. I wouldn't have wanted to talk about it with anyone back then - especially not an assassin who'd killed countless people and no longer blinked at the sight of decapitated bodies.

I wasn't sure what to make of my disregard for life - although something had sunk its claws into my mind and I realised it scared me how death and murder unfazed me most of the time. I scared myself.

I slept well but I was painfully aware that Jack didn't. I could hear the rain pattering against the roof of the tavern and the dripping of it through a hole in the old building. I could also hear Jack tossing and turning on the creaky floor and each grumble sent a jolt of guilt up my spine - guilt that he was sleeping on the floor, guilt that he'd been the one to kill the Count when I should have taken that burden off of him.

And it worried me - it worried me that I'd been able to sleep peacefully after what had happened. Surely I should have been just as restless?

What part of my brain was so broken that I could easily switch off any kind of trauma? I blinked at my thoughts. I'd been trained that way - to switch it off. They'd told me I could fix my mind by switching it off but I'd just called it broken. Had they broken me?

I didn't like the thought of that. The realisation terrified me. So, like I'd been trained, I smothered the thoughts - delayed the self awakening and when the rain slowed and the sky lightened through the grey clouds, I cleaned myself up and got something for Jack to eat. I got the horse ready and then went to wake Jack up. At first, he didn't move but then he groaned and stretched, his back cracking as he sat up.

He looked around the room blearily and I lent him a hand. "I'd dreamt I was home."

"Soon," I replied through a mouthful of bread.

✕

We went on for the entire day. The weather was confusing - one moment it was pouring with rain and drenched right through our cloaks and the next it was sunny, immediately drying us. The only forms of entertainment were trees, trees and trees because Jack wasn't talking at all. I was starting to think he'd fallen asleep so I'd touched him on the shoulder and he jolted slightly, mumbling.

I didn't annoy him, but I used this time as an excuse to secure my arms around his waist as we climbed up a steep, muddy slope. I watched the brighter sky and wildlife - the shine the sun cast on lightly watered leaves filtered through my eyes and made everything around us sparkle. The air was rich with the scent of rain, mud and fresh earth and I gulped it down with each breath.

This was the longest I'd spent in a life, it wasn't everyday people got to relive a time long forgotten - where trees were real and birds still existed somewhere other than on screens.

We came to a halt sometime in the evening - the rain getting too heavy to navigate any longer. Now we were surrounded by trees in the middle of nowhere.

"We'll leave at the first sign of morning light," Jack said - the first words he'd spoken all day. I savoured them, listening to his soft voice and jumping off of the horse, holding on to a tree as I regained my balance.

"Jack?"

281

He didn't reply. He just walked over to a small cave covered in moss and damp earth. He ducked down and nodded his head. "This should shield us enough. I'll go collect some firewood. Stay with the horse."

I watched as he left the clearing, his broad shoulders moving as he bent to pick up wood, his head slick with rain. Since when did he tell me what to do? I walked the opposite direction, determined to do something useful.

Wet leaves crunched beneath my feet and the trees above me cast a protective canopy from rain. I trod carefully, feeling as though I was a huntress. I hadn't planned on actually hunting properly but when I saw a rabbit just sitting with it's back turned to me I skidded to a halt. *Thank you Fate. You were finally starting to hear me out.*

And this is where my training came in useful I thought to myself. I fought off my cold, shivering body as I took Jack's dagger from my belt and hurled it towards the rabbit. It was a perfect shot, almost too good to be true. Beginner's luck?

"Nova?" I heard a panicked shout echo through the woods, bouncing off the trees and into my ears. I crouched to the ground and picked up the rabbit feeling a sense of guilt. Here I was killing wildlife when in the future no such thing existed. I felt like I was the root cause of how the dystopian world I lived in came to be.

"Nova," Jack breathed, grabbing hold of my shoulder and pulling me to my feet. "Why did you run away?" he snapped, looking down at the dead rabbit only slightly impressed. *I just got you dinner and that's how you speak to me?*

"You don't speak to me for a day and now suddenly you're worried when I move twenty metres away from camp?" I growled.

"Excuse me?" he snapped.

"You clearly don't know the first thing about me," I snapped, grabbing hold of the animal and storming back in the direction I'd come in - not quite realising where that was. Heavy drops of water fell from leaves and landed on my forehead. I squinted through my wet eyelashes.

"I know very well who you are," Jack retorted, his voice cold and distant.

"You know only what you see," I growled, stopping urgently and spinning to face him angered. This wasn't even about the fact he'd ordered me to stay with the horse. It had turned into something else now.

"You know I wear pretty dresses, you know I work for important people, you know I go to parties and you know Prospect adores me because *that's* what you see!" I snapped. "You see that I'm the symbol of Prospect and you choose to take me down."

"We are enemies," he spat.

I threw my hands in the air annoyed. "So what are we doing? Why the hell haven't you killed me? Why haven't I killed you?"

He clenched his jaw for a moment and closed his eyes, curled his fists into balls and then stormed past me.

"Listen to me!" I growled, grabbing his shoulder and forcing him in front of me. He watched me, his chest moving up and down as he tried to calm himself.

"Kill me," I stated like it wasn't a big deal. But as I detached the wet dagger from the animal and forced it into Jack's grip my hands shook. He didn't look at the knife, he breathed deeply and clenched his teeth together whilst watching me.

"Kill me!" I repeated, directing his hand and pressing the tip of the dagger to my heart. "Kill me then," I breathed.

"Kill me - go home and win. I can't go back, not to who I am there. So kill me." My voice began to crack, as did what little determination I had left.

He swallowed tightly, his eyes flicking between the knife and my chest, his jaw clenched so tightly I thought it would break. "Kill me." I began to cry, begging him - not really conscious we were both fighting. He was straining against my hand that was trying to plunge the knife into my chest. With my trembling hands, I finally gave way and Jack pulled the knife away.

His eyes flitted to the side for one moment before finally falling shut and in one swift motion he'd dropped the knife, pulled me in by the waist and locked his mouth against mine. I was still for a moment before his other hand came up to cup my cheek. His mouth was wet against mine, and my breath caught in my throat. I stilled against him until finally my arms wound their way around his neck and I kissed him back.

"No," he mumbled against my lips. He brushed his thumb under my eyes and held either side of my face. He tilted his forehead against mine and I watched him with wide eyes. "No," he repeated again, kissing my lips softly.

There were a thousand unspoken words between us and yet this kiss - *this kiss* spoke more to me - it spoke more to me than the insults - the hatred that was between us.

"I am tired of fighting this - you," he said. His voice strained with the effort of keeping his emotions in check. But I didn't want him to keep them in check. I wrapped my arms around his neck, finding myself on my tiptoes as my lips hovered over his.

"Then don't."

He didn't allow me time to catch my breath before his lips landed on mine decisively and there was nothing sweet and slow about this kiss. It was burning with leftover hatred, it scolded my tongue and evoked a feeling deep from my chest that left me aching for more. When he finally tore his mouth from mine our faces wet from the rain and pink with emotion.

"I - I wasn't ignoring you because I was struggling - well I was struggling because of what happened with the Count. But it wasn't just that." He blinked furiously, shifting on his feet as he held me tightly at my waist; his hand came up to cup my cheek as he took a deep breath. "I was struggling with - with us." He swallowed tightly.

I stilled and held my breath so tightly my lungs felt like they might burst into fire.

"Things have changed and - I don't care." His shoulders sagged in what might seem like defeat but I knew him - *I knew him now* - it was relief. "I am tired of fighting you, fighting whatever this is between us."

My lips twitched as I lightly brushed them over his, running my hand through the silk strands of his dark hair as it hung loose. "I don't hate you anymore either," I told him quietly.

And he exhaled a short, breathless word: "Good," and then he was kissing me and there was nothing and everything at once. He destroyed me and rebuilt me. He tore me down my defences and strode right up to my dark, bleak, hopeless heart and offered me a slice of the good in him. He'd given me a beautiful, wonderful chance of redemption. He'd given *us* a chance.

I didn't know then, but redemption was a long wordy contract with a fine print I wasn't willing to pay.

CHAPTER 28

The rabbit tasted good if you were wondering - cooked to perfection, moist and juicy - a tad chewy but still amazing.

And Jack... Jack was also amazing – no, no I didn't eat him. I just meant, in general, he was pretty cool, and not in some weird sexual tasting way. We were doing well with the journey and we hadn't come to any trouble yet although the threat of being found was overhanging.

I used the time we were travelling wisely, teaching him everything I knew about Time Bending. The most important discussion was of course his ability to prevent Time Bending whenever he travelled into a past life.

"Say it again," he groaned, shaking his head as if to clear his brain of its cobwebs.

"When you go into the darkness, your Totem takes you back to the Timeline correct?"

He nodded his head slowly as I continued. "But your Totem is taking you from the different timeline in the past you've just visited – it's apart of you now - so when you follow your Totem back to your original Timeline, you need to cut the tie with the timeline you just visited."

287

"How do I do that?"

I pursed my lips. "It takes a lot more concentration. You need to go further into the web of timelines and find our Timeline that way."

"So basically - Time Bending is the shortcut home - and then whatever this is - is the long way home."

I grimaced and shrugged. "Sure - if it helps you to picture it that way yes."

"And that will leave that timeline alone to progress with whatever change has happened - but not directly change anything where we come from?"

I nodded my head. "They'll be two completely different timelines - unless you accidentally visit that timeline again and bend it again. It's why you need to be so careful that you're always using timelines you've never visited before."

He nodded his head slowly. "Simples."

"Well not really - it takes a lot to organise all the timelines so we know what we're doing-"

"I suppose I've shifted some stuff around then?" Jack interrupted.

I pursed my lips. "I'm just curious to know how you knew which timeline you'd be able to find me in 1944. How did you know what my Totem was?"

Jack titled his head to the side and winked at me. "You should really be careful about what you put in your records."

I narrowed my eyes and scowled at him. "I don't even know the rest of my friend's Totems, how do you?"

"I could tell you theirs." He grinned mischievously. "It was also fun to know that we'd figured out how to follow Totem's before you did. Not so high and mighty now are you?"

I fought back the urge to scoff. "You didn't even know what the word Totem actually meant – so no."

"Guide and Totem are basically the same thing!" he exclaimed. "I didn't pay attention to any of your fancy names for stuff – just what it was."

I glared at the back of his head. "How much have you actually read about us?"

"Nothing - my sister in law does all the heavy lifting to be fair. I'll let her take all the credit – I'm just her little lab rat."

Sounds familiar. I thought of Vix and all the theories and work he did for us surrounding Time Bending.

"I suppose she's the one I'll have to thank when you give me that delicious cure for helping you?" I smiled sweetly.

"Yup." He popped the word and then groaned. "Can we talk about something more fun now? I'm getting a headache."

I rolled my eyes and thought to myself for a moment before tightening my arms around him "Favourite life? Go."

He breathed in sharply and turned his head to look ahead. "My favourite life for sure was in 1870 - I was a cowboy." I could hear in his voice he was grinning. "I go back to it all the time."

"You're weird." I rolled my eyes.

"I'm mostly a fan of ancient history. Everything before I was a cowboy was pretty awesome. Hell even ancient Rome was pretty sick."

"Of course you like ancient history," I replied, rolling my eyes and looking at our surroundings.

"There was one where I was really rich, I don't remember when... probably sometime around the Tudors but in France, or was it Rome?"

"A merchant or something?"

He laughed loudly. "No... like a historic family kind of wealthy."

I choked. "Oh wow... well that sounds great."

"What? Surprised?"

I stumbled over my words. "No. I just thought since you're... you know in the future, and have been a pirate, a cowboy and a... servant of sorts in this life - I thought the rest of your lives were you know..."

"Nah, my wealth is pretty inconsistent."

"I'm always..."

"No shit," he laughed when I didn't finish my sentence. "Actually, the only thing that's consistent in most of my lives is me," he said and I placed a head on his shoulder laughing.

"Oh really?"

"Not like that... I mean I come close to death a lot."

"Hence the Raven? I always assumed you'd just lost a lot of people," I said quietly. He turned his head to the side and gave a crooked smile. "Nah, I'm always very sickly – if I'm not killed then I die from an illness. I've never lived above forty."

"Maybe we can prevent that now we have so many more cures," I suggested hopefully. "Besides you don't want to see yourself get old. I reached 70 once and it was terrifying going back."

Jack laughed loudly. "I couldn't imagine you being any less beautiful than you are now."

I slapped his arm "Ouch, thanks a lot." He turned to the side confused before realisation dawned on his face and he scrambled for words. "No! I just meant – I – you know what I meant."

"I'm not sure I do," I replied, clutching my heart wounded.

He released an exasperated sigh. "You know you're beautiful – I also know you're... beautiful." He released a long breath.

I chuckled softly, then reached over his shoulder and kissed his cheek. "Thank you," I mumbled.

"Do you think we could do it?" I asked after a moment of silence.

"Do what?" Jack asked, turning his head to the side to see me better.

"Change the future. Do what you were trying to stop us from doing and what we were afraid of what you were doing."

He contemplated this for a moment and turned back to face the horizon. "I think it would be a start if we both knew how Prospect came into making. None of you had lives that suggested how? That could change it?"

I held on for a moment as we moved along a bumpy path. "My last life was fifty years before I was born into my present one. I know it pretty well, I'm always there for clients since it has the most impact," I explained. Jack stayed quiet for a moment clearly disapproving but not wanting to say anything.

"Mine was forty-five years from the present and everything was mostly normal. The only issue was climate change still. I looked into it once, Prospect was being built, completely detached from the rest of the world. That's why most of the world is still relatively normal."

I stilled at his last words. "Wait. What do you mean relatively normal? I thought everywhere was like Prospect."

I could feel Jack stiffen, and he turned his head to the side. "Not really. The old world still exists. You've just given it the name 'Rebellion'. Yeah, sure it's small. Cities like Prospect that are corrupt pretty much dominate us. But there are others like us. I thought you knew that?"

"Yeah... I always thought it was more like urban versus countryside though." My cheeks burnt red as embarrassment crept up my spine. "I thought the Rebellion was a break off from Prospect, not part of the - uh outside."

Jack sighed irritated. "You realise how that sounds? The outside? You're trapped in the walls of Prospect. You didn't even know what was outside those walls."

I pursed my lips and looked at the side of his face. "I always knew they were keeping us from something outside. But there was never a need to leave... there is now."

Jack raised an eyebrow with a faint smile, I rolled my eyes and smiled.

Jack's smile grew even larger. "Are you turning away from the dark side?"

"Alright Sparrow let's avoid that topic," I sighed and rolled my eyes at him.

"Raven," he corrected me.

"Okay *Raven*," I emphasised the words sighing and looked over his shoulder. We were travelling through fields now.

"So what about the other Time Benders?" he asked. "Would they know anything from their lives that would suggest how to change it all?"

"Ah now look at you, wanting to join the dark side? Change the future?" I teased.

He rolled his eyes. "I'd be changing it so save thousands from a life of misery."

I stayed quiet for a moment because I couldn't tell if he was talking about the rest of the world living in misery or if he thought I lived in misery. I disagreed, but I wasn't going to start an argument. "The others have lives way before then. I think we're running out of juice, you know?"

"I don't know," he replied bluntly.

"Well, early on our lives came one after the other - well they did for Fynn, Ace and I." He turned his head back around to watch me. "But now the years between them are stretching out much longer before we come back."

"Now that you say it yeah... mine are becoming longer."

"So how many lives do you think you have?" I asked nonchalantly, secretly competitive of whatever his answer is.

"Ah I don't know, two hundred maybe? I remember a few of them, anything before this life is a blur."

I smirked, unable to help myself.

"Do you ever miss them?" I asked, jolting slightly.

"Not really. How did this whole Time Bending thing get discovered?"

"Landon mostly, he and Vix were friends and did some experimenting and research. At that point, all they knew was that Landon had appeared in a photo a hundred years ago and he could remember it. He also had dreams about memories he didn't have in this life. Anyway, they searched for others and my face kept popping up in historic photos. So they brought me in and Vix began trying stuff. I was the first to go back when I was just ten. Of course, it wasn't revealed to the public - only my clients knew. Then the other five popped up over the years and we were formed."

My heart had clenched slightly at the thought of Landon. I wondered if they'd pulled the plug on him yet. I wondered if they were about to pull the plug on me... I clenched my jaw - these thoughts did nothing and were useless.

"Where were you before you were discovered?" he asked finally.

That was definitely not a question I was comfortable answering.

I clenched my jaw. "I don't remember much before I was ten, I was in an accident and suffered from memory loss."

Jack's eyebrows raised. Either out of surprise that I didn't remember much before I was ten or the fact I was ten when it began. Ten was young to be doing this. And I'd been going into the past regularly for years - it was bound to have an effect on my health.

After all, it broke nature - changing things from the past. I was a loophole in existence.

Who knew? O did. Every full sibling I'd ever had knew who I was. Maybe it was just an accident we found out we could go back into our lives? But how did they know how to? And how many reincarnated siblings were there? Jack has had a brother in a bunch of lives and O mentioned me meeting him, but had I already met him? Or *would* I meet him? In a new life that had already been written - just waiting to start as time rolled closer?

Life was confusing - time was confusing.

Jack hadn't pushed me to decide whom I would stand with once we got back - maybe he was scared of my answer. We didn't want to be enemies but it wasn't so easy for me to just switch sides overnight.

"How did you discover you could bend time?" I asked.

"It was a mistake, I just kind of... fell into a past life. The rest of our information came from books published on it and of course-" he winked, "-from hacking your files."

"How the hell did they hack us?" I asked genuinely puzzled, we had the strongest system. We had to in order to stop the public from finding out all our dirty secrets and hating us from wiping out generations from existence.

I never said we were the good guys.

"Don't ask me."

"So you've got access to all the things we've changed - all our research and yet you still didn't know what a Totem was? Let alone how *not* to bend the timelines?" I laughed and he shoved his elbow backwards to catch me in the stomach.

He grunted. "Surely by now, you'd know I don't listen very well - besides, lab rat remember? I don't need to know *everything*."

I rolled my eyes. "And here I was thinking you were smart enough to trap me in the past."

CHAPTER 29

Time: 14th September 1661
Location: Headed North

I rested my forehead on the back of Jack's shoulder, avoiding the feather that tickled my cheek and the fact a strong wind was trying to blow my own hat off.

"Nova?" Jack shifted slightly and my head fell forward as I almost slumped off the horse. I'd fallen asleep.

"We need to get to a village - there's a storm coming." I nodded my head and looked up to the sky through a canopy of pine trees. Dark foreboding clouds rolled overhead and drops of rain trickled from leaf to branch and settled down the back of my neck.

We rode quickly, even though our horse was beginning to get tired and restless. Magically a village wasn't that far from us which was surprising because we had been avoiding any kind of path for the last few days in fear of being tracked - if it were possible for them to work that fast.

It was pouring with rain by the time Jack had secured the horse in the stables. I was dripping and shivering as he led me toward a building with a puzzled look.

Jack paused and looked at his surroundings. "Something feels..." He shrugged and continued walking.

"Thomas?" A voice cried from a doorway behind us. Jack continued to walk but I swivelled to face the person. It was a middle-aged man with barely any teeth and a head full of wild white hair. He stumbled down the wooden staircase shocked.

"My boy!" he cried once Jack turned to face him.

"Oh *shit*," Jack hissed under his breath, wide-eyed as he looked at the man.

He cleared his throat and forced a fake smile. "Ja... Jim... Jamie?"

"No! It's Jeremy! Jamie's inside. What - how - please come inside before you soak to the bone." He waved us forward with a dirty-toothed smile.

We stood in the mud for a moment before Jack took my arm and led me up the stairs. Jeremy swung open the door to reveal loud laughter that stopped once Jack entered the room. We were in some kind of tavern surrounded by the whole village it seemed.

"Thomas?" A group of men came forward all different sizes and then they grasped onto Jack, crowding around and clapping him - firing questions his way in a loud blur of deep voices.

Jack looked at me panicked and I shrugged. Whilst he tried to answer questions wondering where he'd been I stood outside the bubble waiting for it to be over.

"Who's he?" A man with a large stomach and red beard pointed to me. Jack broke through to answer but a smaller man stood on the table behind and ripped the hat off.

"It's a girl!" he shouted. The others exploded into laughter and shifted their attention away from Jack towards me. Then, when everyone seemed to notice my features the room went silent. I didn't exactly look normal for these parts - silver hair, pixie features and the way I held myself made me stick out a lot.

"Someone give the poor girl a cloth," a woman with grey hair snapped.

"I'll keep her warm," a man chimed in to which Jack slammed his foot down on his toe.

"Jamie," he said to the man who'd spoken before finally breaking into a large grin. He remembered Jamie and that's all apparently.

Jack's smile faltered as he seemed to realise another detail. *That* detail, sure enough, made her presence known when she shoved her way through the crowd of males and ripped Jack's hat off his head - throwing it in my direction.

She looked like a prostitute, makeup smudged and lipstick smeared down her face from getting too cosy with another man somewhere. Besides, I had every right to judge her when she leapt onto him and smooched his face. I raised my eyebrows as Jack attempted to push her away.

"Tommy!" she cried gasping and pushing him onto the table where she sat on his lap. He looked my way, pale with lipstick smeared across his lips. The men were cheering and clapping his back proud. I watched amused.

"Beatrice." He turned his lip up into an awkward smile. "Looking as... charming as ever."

"I've waited." She pouted. "I thought we was gon' get married."

"Who told you that?" Jack grimaced and placed a finger on each of her shoulders and pushed her away from his face.

She giggled feverishly. "Tom's been playing!" cried the men, clapping him on the back. The small man jumped from the table behind me and pushed me into the circle.

"What?" Beatrice stood up, stumbling drunk to face me. "Tommy, who's this?" she gasped, looking me up and down.

"Umm," Jack stuttered at a loss for words.

"Hi there." I smiled sweetly. This was going to be fun. "Sorry you're a bit late. He's already married."

"To who?" Her face dropped into an ugly scowl. I held up my left hand where my wedding sapphire ring still sparkled and pouted apologetically. OK maybe it was a little mean, but she seemed like trash and she most certainly had not been waiting for Jack whilst she was selling her body to the poor paralysed man in the corner who couldn't do anything to stop her. So sad.

"Tommy is this true?" She turned to face him shocked.

Jack looked at me and then at the woman. "You married this - this girl thing?" She gasped.

Jack looked at me with wide eyes and then turned to face her again. "I suppose so?"

"You suppose?" She gasped.

"Yes," he said, a little more confident this time. He stood from the table he'd been pushed on by her and scowled. "Jealousy makes you even uglier."

She chewed on the inside of her cheek as if she were about to cry and looked at the two of us. "Consider this a wedding gift," she said as she slapped Jack's face to the side. Beatrice turned to face me and raised her hand to slap me but I caught it, watching her face contract into pain as I tightened my grip. Then I grabbed a bottle of rum on the table and smashed it against her head.

"Likewise," I smirked.

For a moment everything was silent and everyone looked at the passed out girl on the floor with greasy strands of matted blonde hair and smashed glass. Alcohol dripped onto the floor and the room held its breath - before the small man let out a cheer and everyone threw their hands into the air echoing his cries.

The problem with saying Jack and I were married was now they expected us to act like we were. Mr Red-Beard was blatantly asking Jack if I was any good in bed to which he shrugged shyly. And across the table, Jamie was looking me up and down sussing me out curiously. He knew something was up.

Avoid him.

After more drinks and food were forced down our throats we were finally allowed to go to a room after we'd said goodnight to the woman with grey hair and Jeremy who stood at the bottom of the stairs smiling.

"Ah, sorry we haven't gotten much time to catch up Uncle Jeremy."

He shrugged, wrapping Jack into a hug. "We'll catch up in the morning right Thomas?"

Jack smiled crookedly. "Yeah we'll stay for a bit in the morning."

"A bit?" the woman asked, upset.

"We-" Jack sighed and looked at me for a moment. "It's probably best not to tell you for your own safety. Just know that we have to leave."

"You'll be back though right?" Jeremy grinned, showing his gums.

We pursed our lips and nodded guiltily. *No, we'd be hung for our crimes and if they found out you hid us here then you'd also be hung.*

We were too selfish not to leave though.

"That was interesting," I said, leaning against the bedpost. Jack stood by the window, peering through the curtains cautiously. You could never be too safe. But it was hard to see anything past the rain pattered windows. A steady, calm rhythm of rain enveloped the room and the distant rumble of thunder made me grateful for the heat of the fire.

"Sorry, I didn't remember that part of this life. We should have carried on as soon as I felt the slightest sense of familiarity."

"You didn't know," I replied, shrugging off the cloak and hanging it by the fireplace that crackled and snapped at us.

I crossed my arms in front of my chest, conscious the shirt was incredibly see-through when wet and plopped myself down by the fire.

When I opened my eyes, feeling my face grow hot from the heat I turned and faced Jack, almost letting my mouth drop open when I noticed he'd taken off his shirt, leaving it in a wet pile with his shoes and sword. I cleared my throat and turned my attention back to the fire, focusing on the glowing flames and resisting the temptation to turn and face him. I wouldn't be able to draw my eyes away from the smooth, hard muscles of his slightly tanned body - and they looked so good with the fire shining against the wet muscle.

"Ah! Here," Jack exclaimed. I snapped out of my daze and took a deep breath before facing him. I watched the muscles of his back contract as he sifted through drawers of clothes before grabbing an old white nightgown with three-quarter sleeves and silk bows. It was a size too small but I turned away from Jack and pulled it over my head anyway.

"Do you need help with the buttons?" Jack asked, his back facing the wall. I walked over to him, finding my hands were trembling slightly and turned around so he could help me.

"I think this was my mother's," he said lowly.

"She was tiny."

"She usually is," he replied, his hands were rough and calloused in this life as he clumsily fiddled with the tiny buttons on my back. Cold fingers brushed against my neck and my body jolted slightly - a flood of heat and goosebumps scattering across my body.

"Who were they in this life?" I rasped.

"I can't remember. They both died when I was born," he said quietly. I turned to face him our chests only millimetres away from each other.

"I understand." I placed my hands on his chest.

He frowned. "Sorry. Here I am complaining about not having parents when you-"

"You read my files I'm guessing?" I smiled. He nodded his head with a grimace. "It's okay. My recurring theme just happens to be that my mother's go crazy and try to kill me. Yours is that you die a lot. Shit happens." I smiled again and looked down so I could tie the string at the front of the nightgown but then Jack grabbed my hand.

Jack gulped and parted his lips, looking down at me even when I tilted my head back up. "Nova," he breathed, closing his eyes and connecting our foreheads. His hand slipped between the fabric of the nightgown and lightly traced the skin along my collarbone. My head tipped back slowly as his cool fingers began working their way further down, his head lowered as his stubble grazed my neck. I swallowed my moan and opened my eyes.

My hand came up between us and rested lightly on his chest and then I closed what little distance there was between us and kissed him until we were completely absorbed in each other.

Absolute darkness, a safe haven to the world outside: Just the two of us connected by our pasts that were bent together to form something beautiful - something unexplainable.

I didn't know why we did it. Even whilst we knew it wouldn't work in getting us home. We did it because we could and because we found comfort in each other. Two people, who had met intending to kill one another - now sought comfort in one another.

Once we tore ourselves from the darkness we were both panting. I tried to grasp my surroundings for a moment before realising we were completely wrapped in each other. I hadn't tied the front of the nightgown so our bare chests were pressed against each other - warm skin still glistening from the rain - hearts beating together in unison.

I gulped savouring this moment before he would pull away and we would keep our distance like every night. I closed my eyes, swallowing my whimper and pulling away first before I had to endure him being the one to do it.

But then his eyes flitted open as he came back down to reality and he pulled me back to his chest, his hands wrapped around my waist.

I was surprised when he lowered his head and pressed his lips against mine and was even more shocked when the kiss turned heated and his tongue began to graze my lips. Somehow he'd backed me onto the bed, lowering me onto the mattress so I was sprawled out in front of him. He paused, taking me in for a moment and I winced as cool air brushed my skin, but it didn't take long before he'd closed the distance between us again and was kissing a trail of hot kisses down my neck.

"We can't," I gasped as he pulled my inner thigh behind his back so it wrapped around him. My actions completely contradicted my words though and they fell on empty ears when I used my leg to tug him closer to me and *god* the sound that came out his mouth made every part of me turn red.

He sank into me for a moment, his head tucked between my shoulder and my neck as he breathed deeply. Then reluctantly he rolled onto his side, tugging my leg with him though. "You're right," he groaned.

Dammit no. I wasn't right. I was wrong, keep kissing me.

But there was still that voice in the back of my head that told me it would be too far. Kissing was already too far for two people still supposed to kill each other. We hadn't crossed that line. There was just an unspoken truce right now. What stayed in 1661 stayed in 1661.

Well, at least that's what we told ourselves.

No more words were spoken between us, just the sound of our breathing as it calmed down. Jack pulled me even closer to him - if that were possible - and wrapped his arms around me, resting his chin on my head until I fell asleep.

I slept well - if it weren't for the awakening surprise in the morning I probably would have slept longer.

A light was flashing in my eyes. As soon as I opened them and they adjusted I realised a flame was floating in front of me. I jumped, rolling into Jack's bare chest and looking up at Beatrice's makeup stained face.

I shrieked, grabbing the dagger from Jack's side of the bed and holding it out to hit her but Jack had grabbed my arm tightly and forced it down between our bodies.

"*Bitch*," Beatrice hissed. The door swung open to reveal Jamie and Mr Red-Beard.

"Found her!" they shouted and Jamie stormed in. "Beatrice," he snapped. "Go home." The woman glared at me one last time and whipped her hair to the side, stumbling out of the room.

"Apologies." Mr Red-Beard grinned cheekily. "Get back to it." He winked, closing the door shut.

"Did she just hold a candle in your face?" Jack grumbled, his voice raw from sleep.

"Mhm," I replied shell-shocked. He grumbled and grabbed my waist pulling me back into him, then his leg slipped between my thigh and I tried to catch my breath at the sudden heat between us. I closed my eyes, willing my heart to slow down and listened to his breathing as he fell back asleep - leaving me to try to avoid the conflicting feelings of wanting to stay with Jack but wanting to leave this hellhole.

CHAPTER 30

Time: 15th September 1661
Location: Unknown Village somewhere near Scotland. Still.

We slept for a long time, savouring the comfort of the soft sheets, the warmth of each other and the rich earthy scent of 1661.

When we were finally up, we got dressed in our clothes and Jack scowled as he searched under the bed.

"Where's my hat?"

"Beatrice threw it somewhere downstairs. It's probably ruined Jack."

He groaned, hoisting himself up and grabbing hold of his maroon cloak satisfied with how dry it was now, mine was still damp.

"I'll buy you a new one." I fought off my smile.

He didn't reply, just took my nightgown and folded it gently. "What about this?" I asked, bringing out a piece of grey cloth and using it to cover part of his hair. "That's better, now you look more like a pirate."

He watched me for a moment, his eyes softened and he smiled gratefully. "Let's go."

Downstairs was surprisingly quiet and Jack led us over to a table with his aunt and uncle, Jamie, the small man and Red-Beard.

"You've been up there a while!" Mr Red-Beard winked at us and we both laughed awkwardly and sat down as Jack's aunt brought us some food.

"When are ye leaving?" someone grumbled, watching us eat at the same time as juggling different questions fired at us. Jack looked at me and then around the room.

"Now."

"And when will you be back?" Jamie asked brightly, I looked at Jack.

"One day." Jack shrugged.

And then we were off, back on the road galloping through the scenery - leaving the village Jack lived in once upon a time in the distance.

"So Thomas," I said after a while of listening to the horse's hooves splash in the newly wet mud. There was a faint fog in the air just starting to clear up. "Why did you leave?" He turned his head to the side. "Was it, Beatrice?"

He shook his head. "No, I can't remember what it was exactly. I was running from something."

"And you met the Count whilst on the road?"

Jack nodded his head. "He'd been stopped by a group of bandits and I saved the day... as usual. That's where I appeared in this life."

"As usual?" I raised an eyebrow. "We'll see about that Raven. We still haven't found the well."

"Ah but we're close," he leant forward as the horse picked up its pace. The fog had cleared now and the ground was a little harder.

311

"Can you feel it too?" I asked, referring to the sensation in my chest - a feeling that picked up every now and then, barely noticeable but there. I could tell it was the feeling of being close, and the feeling would only grow and spread to your whole body the closer you got to it.

"It's like heartburn," Jack grumbled irritably.

"How many days do you reckon?" I asked.

"Only a few," he replied. "If you're feeling alright we'll carry on to the next town - it's a while away from here though."

I let him know I would be okay and we carried on for the rest of the day. Riding a horse was not the most pleasant feeling but sacrifices had to be made - especially when they relied on a whole bunch of people from the future.

I tried to block out thoughts of the future as much as possible and for the last month every time I fell asleep I wondered if the next time I opened my eyes I would be in a new life far into the future because my friends pulled the cord.

In fact, a small part of me was starting to want to go home less desperately. I was actually enjoying the 17th century - although the lack of flushing toilets, Wi-Fi and electricity was a bit of a let-down. Something was refreshing about being outside in non-polluted and contaminated landscapes. Everything was so different here and I'd been a part of it once.

A long time ago I had pictured what the future might look like - never imagining it would be as insane as it was now. Mind you in 1661 I wouldn't have been able to comprehend a camera let alone a holographic screen, virtual reality and a pristine white city named Prospect.

Once I had imagined that after I died I would go to heaven as everyone told me I would - I would pray, abide by the Bible and live my life knowing I would either go to heaven or hell. Never had I thought it possible to be reborn again and grow the same way I did every life - with the same hair, same nose, same chin and the same body.

But maybe that still happened. Maybe there was a heaven and hell, maybe there was a God to everyone else. Maybe I had this power for a reason. Maybe we all had a purpose and everyone else was just there to add to its effect.

I didn't know. I didn't like to think of it, I just liked to live my life as it came.

But I did want to know what would happen if I had another life. Would it be different now I knew I had past lives? I wondered if this whole Rebellion thing wouldn't have happened. Would I have carried on with my life and died, then been reborn and sought after by the government - everyone I knew in my current life, Gina, Vix - all old or dead.

What happened now?

✗

We were avoiding town after town as Jack had spotted posters of our faces a few days ago. We were desperately trying to seem as less English as possible knowing the history between the Scots and English and we didn't want to draw attention to ourselves.

We'd started to be more cautious than ever, knowing Redcoats could be anywhere and so we avoided the direction of Edinburgh like the plague and tried to follow the sensation as much as possible, sticking to the woods. We were well into Scotland by now and we began enjoying the landscape of the Scottish highlands.

We had been travelling for six hours across empty hills at night when I heard a familiar sound, a consistent engine and the sound of planes getting closer. I clutched onto Jack and looked up into the sky, shrieking as three German warplanes soared overhead. The sound of machine guns echoed over the hills and the whooshing of the planes that circled the air in a uniformed structure began shooting as our own air force chased after them. I screamed as the wailing sound of sirens flooded the hills and searchlights scanned the sky. Then I felt an urge pull me from the disaster surrounding me.

"My baby!" I began shrieking, jumping to the floor and stumbling through the streets of rubble, an explosion from the local corner shop shook me from my feet and my fingers grasped at the broken glass of a door. "My baby!" I screamed hoarsely as someone grabbed hold of my shoulders, lifting me into the air in the opposite direction of my baby. I screamed - kicked and screamed until my throat was raw. I was left sobbing, rocking back and forth with my eyes clenched tightly shut and my hands covering my ears from the loud sounds. "My baby," I sobbed.

It continued around me. The collapsing of buildings - the utter emptiness and shattering sounds - the whine of sirens and heavy gunfire - the sound of a falling bomb and the silence that followed before the bang.

I screamed - unable to move, paralysed.

I lost track of time completely.

CHAPTER 31

"Nova!" Jack shouted into my ear, peeling my hands away from my eyes and wiping floods of tears away from my cheeks. I opened them cautiously, checking the sky was no longer filed with white light, fire and bombs. Now there were thousands of stars - a cloudless night and Jack's tanned face. I held my hands out in front of me touching his face, the dark hair above his lip and froze.

"It was a hallucination. I'm fine." I cleared my throat. I stood up from his lap and wobbled uneasily.

"Are you okay?" Jack's eyes were wide with surprise and I looked away before my face betrayed me.

"I'm fine," I snapped, running a shaky hand through my hair.

"You aren't fine," he grumbled and followed me towards the horse. "Why do you have to act so tough all the time? You're dying, you're allowed to want to cry and feel sorry for yourself once in a while. You've been dragged through hell – stuck in a life you don't remember. Then you were… you were drugged and almost assaulted." His voice cracked.

I stilled immediately, feeling the warmth of the Count's blood on my naked body - of the fear, relief and embarrassment of seeing Jack over me. But worse than all of that: being completely out of control of my own body. I hated that the most. I hated that my body had not belonged to me for that amount of time.

I supposed that made me a hypocrite – since this wasn't my real body and I'd locked Marion out of it.

Jack took a moment before continuing. "It's not unusual that you'd feel upset. It's more unusual that you're able to compose yourself after everything you've been through."

"Is it? You're the one who thinks I'm a cold-hearted bitch who deserves to die!" I fired back without really thinking and it was a stupid thing to say because he didn't think that anymore. "Sorry," I said quietly, gulping and looking over his face for any kind of reaction.

He looked at me tired and sighed. "It's okay. Look, how about we set camp now and get some rest?"

I nodded my head in silence and looked away embarrassed. We moved around each other, unloading the horse and collecting firewood. Then when we were done we slumped down next to each other.

I watched the fire numbly, playing with the thread of a wool blanket and grasping the leather satchel of water. Jack handed me some of the food we'd been carrying for the last couple days but I refused. He didn't push me to eat - just set it between us and moved closer to me. I pulled the blanket more around me and turned my head away from him, feeling my chest swarm with emotion and my throat burn with tears.

"What was her name?" he asked softly before quickly adding, "you don't have to talk about it if you don't want to."

I didn't really want to talk about anything but something told me it might make me feel better.

"Adelaide," I said. I'd never had to relive that moment before. My Totem always took me to before she was born or after when I became a spy in the war. There was probably a good reason why our Totem's never took us to timeline's with presents that had our children in them.

"She didn't survive." My voice cracked and I coughed quickly, he nodded his head - he understood. It was impossible for any of us to have children that lived long. In most lives, I could never have a child and the ones where I did none had ever lived to their first birthday. I didn't know about the other Time Bender's - we tried to avoid the topic.

Fynn was the only person who had a girl in the present time - like a ticking bomb Fynn couldn't prevent. Time Bending was a gift and a curse in so many ways. Further pointing to the fact we were freaks of nature.

He hadn't asked me to continue, but I'd never spoken about one of my children. "She was just ten months old." He took a deep breath, probably trying to tell me it was okay but I carried on.

"She would crawl everywhere, she used to hang on to the bannister and she looked exactly like me." My voice cracked and I spluttered out a sob, Jack wrapped an arm around me. "I had to run out for an errand and so I left her with the babysitter... when I heard the sirens, I watched the bomb fall on my neighbourhood."

"Nova," he rasped.

"We found her in the early morning crushed to death." I shook horrifically, my whole body tightening as I tried to keep in the tears. "Ten months."

Jack engulfed me in a hug, stroking my hair and crushing me to his chest tightly. Finally, when I felt the weight come off my chest and I felt ten times lighter, I imagined her - every other child of a Time Bender in a better place. Wherever that was. If there was a place where regular people went when they died, whether they were faeries or whether they were just dead - in a dusty box surrounded by mud and insects.

"I had a boy in the year 2025... his mother ditched us when he was just a month old, he made it to two years old. Spitting image of me," his voice strained.

I looked at the fire, trying to imagine a boy with dark curly locks and the warmest brown eyes.

"I hate that we can't remember them," Jack continued, also watching the fires flames jump and crackle.

"It's probably best our Totems never take us to the moment in the timeline when they're alive - even if we're pleading for that time. It's like they know we'd try to change it," I replied quietly, fiddling with the loose thread of the blanket, pulling it and stroking the material under my hands.

From the corner of my eye, I watched Jack turn to face me. "Unless we waited for them."

"It would never allow us."

"It allows us to change things. It allowed us to kill the Count," he pointed out.

I shook my head. "That's different. Even I couldn't do that. I couldn't change the fate of my children - it would have changed everything for other timelines." There was a pause of silence before I spoke again. "I never asked for this. All I want is a normal life."

He pulled me closer against his chest and I closed my eyes. "What kind of normal life?"

I smiled a little. "I don't know. I quite like the internet so maybe the 2000s."

I felt his lips on the back of my head and he laughed lowly. "Not early 2000s right?"

"Oh god no. I'm talking about the Vine era and onwards, I could lose myself in YouTube videos."

Jack sucked in a breath. "Damn, YouTube. Whatever happened to it? Not to mention Tik Tok."

I raised an eyebrow. "I think I died before *Tik Tok*..." I pronounced the words carefully and Jack's lips twitched.

"Finally something I know that you don't."

I scowled and rolled my eyes. "Do you even have social media in the Rebellion?"

Jack laughed. "We use your social media - we don't have our own."

I smirked. "Do you follow me?"

He threw his head back and laughed loudly. "No - it's only looked at so we know what's happening in Prospect."

I sighed. "Social media in Prospect isn't like before. It's like a crappy sequel." We both laughed and already the hallucination was slipping further and further into the back of my mind.

Jack batted his head against mine softly. "Okay, I'll agree with you. The 2010s were pretty sweet, we'd have a normal life and only have to worry about global warming and 2020."

I suppressed a shudder - I hadn't had a life during that period but the history books were definitely packed on the year.

"We can handle that." I felt my lips twitch. "Two Time Benders against a global pandemic? We'd easily cheat the system."

"Bulk buy toilet paper?" he joked and I cocked my head to the side in confusion.

"What?"

He pursed his lips and laughed silently. "Don't worry - you weren't there. You wouldn't understand." He sighed dramatically and I shoved my elbow into his side. He laughed and pulled me closer. "What about global warming? That could be an issue."

"We *still* have to worry about global warming." I rolled my eyes at him.

"The aftermath of mass extinction... I mean can it really get worse than it already is?" Jack added and I felt myself smile that we were discussing a serious topic about the present and it didn't involve arguing.

"Okay. So we'd go back to the 2000s and save the world from global warming and 2020 before it was too late." I tilted my head back and smiled at him, warm brown eyes greeted me.

"Not just that." He tucked a strand of hair behind my ear and smiled. "We'd live a normal life. We'd go to high school together. You'd probably be some preppy cheerleader and I'd be on the football team."

"No you would not." I threw my head back and laughed loudly.

"Okay true. Football kind of sucks but for the sake of our cliché normal life let's just pretend," he replied and sighed wistfully.

"Keep going," I whispered after a moment of silence. I started to close my eyes and tried to imagine this life.

He took a moment and tightened his arms around me. "I'd take you on a date to go see a movie in a really old pickup truck."

"What movie?" I asked dreamily.

"Hmm, I don't know, an Avengers film of something?"

"Damn, that's old," I laughed quietly. "Still, I'd watch it but secretly I wouldn't be paying attention to the movie."

He chuckled. "Why's that?"

"Because the entire time I'd be hoping you'd hold my hand."

He kissed my head. "Okay, I'll remember that for when it happens."

"Someday," I sighed, coming back to reality and looking at the green hills and trees surrounding us but then Jack turned me to face him and kissed me with such force I forgot where we were and could pretend to be in our imaginary world.

We would be at the end of a perfect date. I wouldn't smell like mud and dirt - I'd smell of some flowery perfume and Jack would be wearing an aftershave that drove me insane with butterflies. We'd be kissing outside my house, still in his car, hiding away from the peeping eyes of my parents. I'd have a mother who would want to know everything about the date over hot chocolate late at night. I'd tell her how he held my hand during the movie and took me to get ice cream afterwards even though it was winter. I'd tell her how I'd met him in some boring math's lesson and not that I'd met him with the intentions of killing him.

"Someday," Jack promised, his hands were soft against my cheeks and he stroked my bottom lip with a gentleness that shattered me.

It was a pointless word, with no meaning other than a glimpse of hope we had. We hoped for change - we hoped that someday things would be new and different for us even though they never would be. But maybe - just maybe we could entertain ourselves with the word *someday*.

CHAPTER 32

We were back on the road. It was risky but we couldn't ignore the pull from the well. I was making my way through trees for a toilet break - which was the worst part of the 17th century might I add... especially for us ladies.

After making my way through the weeds I stopped at the path I'd left Jack and the horse on, finding both were gone. I sighed irritated, turning my head either side of the path and finding nothing. I stomped my foot. "Jack!" I yelled crossing my arms irritated.

"Jack!" I repeated, waiting for him to come out of the trees with the horse laughing his dumb ass off.

"You can think again if you think I'm going to go searching for you!" I shouted. I stubbornly sat on the floor despite the mud that was only just starting to dry up and crossed my legs together. I sat waiting for longer than I'd like to admit - I was stubborn I know.

I only froze when my eyes began looking at the ground, where more than one horse's hoof prints were marked in the mud. I scrambled to my feet and studied the floor. A little while back there were a lot of footprints scattered around and a few that looked as though there'd been a struggle.

Oh for god's sake.

What had you gotten into Jack?

I pulled the hood of the cloak over my hat and began striding angrily in the direction the horses and footprints were heading. They couldn't be too far ahead of me.

"Idiot," I hissed. "Actual idiot!" I stopped in my tracks and splashed in a puddle on the side of the path and jumped up and down irritated. "*Idiot!*" I shouted.

I felt the pull in my chest wanting me to turn in a direction and I paused for a moment, contemplating leaving him. I got as far as walking ten steps in the right direction before stopping and turning back around to follow the tracks muttering angrily under my breath.

If he got us both killed and screwed everything up, I swore I would force myself to get reborn and find him in my next life to kill him again.

Was it Redcoats? Surely not, the footprints would be the same and there'd be a lot more of them. These were locals and they had something against Jack - or Thomas. Maybe Thomas got in some trouble and that's the reason he ran and met the Count. It wouldn't be completely out of the question.

The road gradually led to a town surrounded by a strong brick wall and upon entering I was instantly hit by the smell of shit and death. I had to fight to keep my rising sick from spewing onto the street and instead covered my mouth with the cloak. *What kind of shit hole had you gotten yourself into Jack? Literally.*

Something was going on. There was nobody by the entrance of the village, houses were deserted and as I walked further into the village, winding my way through the streets of manure I began to hear crowds shouting.

Where there was a crowd shouting, "die!" there would be Jack - likely in the centre of all the commotion.

I skidded to a halt as I saw wanted signs nailed to walls and doors. Jack's face looked at me slightly cocky, his nose portrayed a lot bigger and less straight than it was in person. He was depicted with devil horns and a pitchfork - so he was known around here for being trouble I guessed.

I panicked even more when I saw my own *'wanted'* poster trampled on the mud - I looked slightly better looking and my reward price was a lot higher than Jacks which had been gradually marked down several times. I smirked to myself and pulled the hood over my face, making my way into the crowd. Now all I had to do was find Jack.

People piled out of the doors of a building where there was a large amount of shouting. I wiggled my way through the crowd of sweaty people with rotting teeth and Scottish accents but gave up when I only got shoved back out of the crowd.

So there was some kind of trial I was guessing?

I didn't really know what my plan of action was. There were a lot of people that needed to get out of the way.

But then I didn't have time to come up with a plan. People had parted from the doors and were scrambling to the floor. I stood in the back watching curiously as people inside the building began shouting and then Jack was shoved out of the building.

He'd been sentenced... *death?*

He stood up, his head tilted back with no remorse. "Idiot," I hissed, watching the two men shove him forward whilst others piled out to keep the crowd from going mental. I realised the reason they were all on the floor before he came out was that they were collecting stones to throw at him.

I saw Jack speak to the guards panicked, dodging stones as they soared through the air past his face.

I imagined he was requesting to be taken away and shot or something but the guard looked at him with his eyebrows high. Nice try Jack.

The crowd began moving, some people began hissing and spitting from their houses and Jack was forced down the street. We came to a square next to where he'd been on trial.

Jack was forced on to a stage where an average man with a black mask sat on a stool sharpening an axe. Jack looked at the crowd wildly and then at the smooth wood they were waiting for him to put his head on. He turned to face the executioner and they spoke amongst themselves.

I looked around the square for anything when I spotted carts upon carts of grain and food that clearly supplied the village.

I smirked.

Bull's-eye.

I made my way towards the carts loaded with all sorts. Starting with one cart full of hay. The audience was focused on Jack as I quickly lit it and instantly the fire began to grow. *Thank you Fate.*

I checked to look for Jack whose face had turned white as he placed his head on the wood. The executioner brought out the axe and the crowd fell quiet. Now was my chance.

"Fire!" I screamed, grabbing the shoulders of people and pointing to the carts where flames began to gradually pick up - eating up the grain.

Technically it didn't go against any rules because I didn't blow anything up. But I had just sentenced an entire village to a very hungry winter.

My eyes lit up like a child watching fireworks for the first time.

I watched the flames rise and people scrambling around for water to put the fire out. Then the fire caught on a thatched roof, which instantly went up in flames and I smiled like an evil demon child.

Once I finally tore my eyes away from the fire and was satisfied the crowd and executioner were distracted I realised Jack was running away from the crowd, waddling as fast as he could with shackles that kept his feet together. Everyone was too busy running around in a frenzy to notice him gone.

"Idiot," I snapped, running through the chaos of people screaming. I swore if I was hallucinating again I'd be really annoyed.

I chased after him - not taking long before I snatched the back of his torn cloak and forced him into an open doorway. He growled, turning to fight whoever had caught him but paused when he saw me.

"Nova?"

"You're welcome." I grinned, looking around the room for anything. We were in some kind of carpenter workshop and thankfully there was a range of tools lined up on the wall. I grabbed for the axe.

"Did you see that?" I asked excitedly.

"Was that you?" Jack panted, watching as I took a few swings in the air feeling it's balance.

"Yeah, did you see it?" I grinned.

He looked at me like I'd gone mad. "Of course I saw it! The British *fucking army* probably saw it!" he hissed. Bell's were being rung urgently outside the shop.

"It was quick thinking," I reasoned watching him grow red with anger.

"You practically killed them all. What happened to wanting to change Nova? Hell you could have changed so much-"

"Will you relax? It was just a fire and it's not winter just yet," I snapped, gripping the axe tightly.

"Winter is coming," he snarled.

I raised my eyebrows, settling the axe down for a moment. "Please tell me that was a *Game of Thrones* reference."

He blinked at me horrified that I could even joke at a moment like this. "What? No-" He paused for a moment and then tilted his head to the side as an amused smile graced his face. "It makes sense. Daenerys went mad you know? The similarities between you are pretty creepy... Silver hair - you just burnt an entire village-"

"Dracaras, bitch," I interrupted with a huge grin and took a last practise swing of the axe before turning to face him.

"Do you know how to use that?" Jack asked, flinching when I forced the chain onto the edge of a table.

"Nope," I said, bringing the axe above my head.

Jack let out a cry just as I was about to drop it down. "Keep your eyes open!" he yelled.

Oh yeah, that would have been a good idea.

Two successful breaking of chains later and stealing a saw for the cuffs we covered our faces and were just about to leave when an elderly man stood in the doorway.

"What - what are ye doin'?" he cried, stumbling into the room and clutching onto a hammer.

I held the pistol up and directed it at his head but faltered when I looked down and saw a young girl clutching the man's legs. She was pale and thin, brown-haired and clutching on to a ragged old teddy bear. They'd seen us. He was old and I had permission to kill him. Shoot him.

Pull the trigger.

Shoot the man. Leave the girl.

Shoot him.

God damn it Nova shoot him.

"Nova," Jack snapped, forcing my arm down.

I swallowed the lump in my throat. "Get off me!" I screamed, forcing the gun to face them again, the man shakily put his hands in the air.

"Please spare her, spare young Ange."

I looked down at the girl as she stared right through me - eerily calm grey eyes connected with my own and I gulped. The calm before the storm.

"Hide under the bed poppet," he said shaking. The girl watched me with young innocent eyes. I recoiled, feeling as though she was peeling the layers of me apart - searching for something lost.

"How old is she?" I rasped.

The man hesitated. "She... she's nine."

I stumbled into Jack's side and held the gun in his direction. He peeled my hands off of it and watched my wide eyes in shock.

"Terribly sorry." Jack forced a tight smile and patted the axe I'd used to cut his chains with and then we backed out the doorway. Jack flung it shut and blocked it with a metal prod to buy us some time

"Are you okay?" Jack grasped for my hand as we ran through the crowd of people and tried to navigate our way out of the town.

"Headache," I replied at the same time I stumbled on my feet.

"Sorry – it's my fault entirely."

"No shit," I muttered and watched a flood of Redcoats swarm in through the gates I'd entered through.

"Damnit," Jack mumbled, directing us to the side of the road and into the shadows. Instantly his body pressed my body against the wall and his dirty hands held onto my face as he kissed me hard.

I released a shaky breath and placed my hands on his shoulders, flattening the material of his cloak shakily. "I thought you were going to die."

"You saved me," he replied, searching my face with his eyes. "I thought I was going to die."

"You can't die now. You aren't allowed to." I pursed my lips together, blinking to avoid the tears and then planted my forehead on his chest breathing him in: sweat, the smell of rich earth, leaves and leather mixed with rain and smoke.

"It's okay," he mumbled into my hair.

"What did you even do?" I asked, pulling away and looking at him.

He smiled cheekily and took my hand and kissed it gently. "I'll save that for once we're back on the road."

We looked back at the gates that were being forced shut by a group of Redcoats who were running around searching houses. Jack squeezed my hand and we fled down an alleyway with no sense of direction and no plan.

"Now I remember how I escaped this shit hole the first time," Jack explained, weaving through houses and slowing down every time we caught a glimpse of a red uniform. I couldn't stop myself from smiling.

Jack led me behind a building, squeezing through the small gap. I managed to get through, though I probably wouldn't have if I were still wearing all the large dresses I'd been wearing for the past few months.

Months.

Had it really been months since I was sat being interviewed in front of the entire city? Since I'd been trying to find some asshole called the Raven - who I was now holding hands with, escaping through a burrow hidden behind the back of a building that led to the other side of the wall. *Yes, yes I was.*

I sighed, slithering under whilst Jack covered my back. When I climbed out and saw two Redcoats sitting together on a log with their backs to us arguing childishly. I bent down to look at Jack through the hole.

"Ugh, I think I've eaten too much since last time I got through here," he groaned, wiggling on his elbows.

"Shh," I hissed. "There are two soldiers here."

Jack made it through and stood up, dusting himself off and watching the soldiers cautiously as one slapped the others hand as they made a grab for another apple.

"You're putting on too much weight!" The other snapped, swiping for the apple.

"What do we do?" I asked Jack, staring at them.

Jack shrugged, also watching and then flicking his eyes over to where one of their horses was.

"Should we?" Jack said, already starting to shuffle his way over to the horse grazing behind them.

"I'm not sure..." I replied, taking cautious steps forward whilst keeping my eyes firmly focused on the two men in a heated argument.

We walked slowly, one foot in time with each other as though we were walking on a beam. Once we got to the horse Jack hoisted me up before jumping on himself.

The horse began to move behind the men and we held our breath, keeping our eyes fixated on the men who were beginning to shove and hit one another. Jack reached behind him and tightened the knot on his head, securing the bandana again. I held on to his waist and he gripped the reins, kicking the horse until we bolted out of there.

When we were a fair distance away, I turned around to see the two men look behind them for the horse, searching behind the tree and then standing in the middle of the path where they saw the pile of dust into the air as we sped up. I smiled and turned to look over Jack's shoulder, feeling the satisfying pull that informed us we were going in the right direction.

"So Jack, are you going to tell me why between the time it took me to pee and get back to the horse, you weren't there?"

I could feel Jack trying to fight a smile. "I ran into some old friends."

"It really looked like it," I commented, turning back to face the stone walls in the distance and the cloud of smoke rising steadily.

Jack took a deep breath. "So remember when I told you I didn't remember why I ran away?" I nodded my head at him. "Well, I remember now."

"And?" I cocked my head to the side amused.

"And turns out I *did* run away to escape that Beatrice girl who - I think we can both agree - is a psycho."

"Yep, I can definitely agree."

"But originally I ran North, in a moment of a spontaneous need for adventure and found this shit hole of a town. I got into a little trouble as you might have imagined - especially with these two guys Harold and Harry. One of them was this big shiny bald boulder kind of dude and the other in this skinny hairy guy-"

"Okay Jack I get it. And they were the ones who found you on the horse?"

"Yep - they were pretty proud of it. The whole village seems to hate me."

336

I rolled my eyes. "I couldn't tell... they were throwing rocks at you."

"Oh trust me. I would have preferred that than getting beheaded - losing your head is a lot more painful - honestly."

"Have you been beheaded before?" I was intrigued.

He turned his head to me. "Twice. But that's beside the point. I tried to bargain with the executioner - see if I could get stoned instead - but he said getting the crowd engaged had already happened that morning. Whoever that was, was clearly the opening act."

My mouth dropped open and I stared at the back of Jack's head. "Are you high?" I slapped his shoulder. "You would have *died*. Probably for good and here you are joking about getting beheaded like-"

"But you saved me."

I huffed angrily, not bothering to argue with him. I was the one who took death so lightly. He was the one who valued life.

"I trust you, I knew you would have come."

"Don't get used to it." I sighed and placed my head on his shoulder as we began climbing a steep slope. I watched the mountains surrounding us with the steep jagged edges of stones.

The highlands. This place was seriously far.

"Thank you," Jack said after an hour. I didn't reply, I just breathed in the cool air and squeezed his waist with my arms. Back on the road, I sighed.

CHAPTER 33

Time: 22nd September 1661
Location: Scotland, Highlands

We'd been travelling for what seemed like forever when really it had been a couple days since Jack got kidnapped and almost beheaded.

We were following the strange sensation in our chest that was beginning to feel suffocating with the amount of pressure spreading through our body - igniting every cell with a dull thud that made our ears ring for an entire hour. Jack and I couldn't speak to each other, just clenched our mouths tightly and rode closer to it.

Then in a split moment, everything stopped. We were at the base of a large sloped hill with long grass that tickled our ankles and small trees that were scattered around the surface of the hill. It was here. We'd travelled across the country for however many days, almost gotten killed numerous amounts of times - for us to then climb this bloody hill.

And we had to climb. We had no horse after it flipped out on us, kicking its front legs into the air and dropping half our stuff on the ground as it bolted away from the hill.

It was magical in a way - not in the rainbow over the hill and pixies holding hands as a pot of gold sat waiting to be collected way. No, it was a kind of magic that warned people away. Dark clouds surrounding us for miles overhead and the shudder of thunder we felt in our chests.

"It's like we just stepped into a fantasy film."

"Lord of the Rings," I replied, watching the top of the hill. "It's just up there," I said. We didn't move. We just continued to watch the top and the clouds and rain that surrounded it. Honestly, it wasn't the same kind of feeling we thought we'd get. We weren't running to the top as if we'd just found treasure. We just stood silently, watching it not quite wanting to leave so urgently now we knew we could.

"Want something to eat?" Jack suggested taking his eyes off the sudden clouds and turning to face me hopeful.

I nodded my head because this would be it. Our last meal together before we jumped down into a dark well that was hopefully at the top of the hill.

Who was I kidding? Hopefully? The place was surrounded by a dark cloud that swirled and shot lightning at a single tree repeatedly whilst at the bottom of the hill it was just a normal day, albeit pretty miserable too. But still, it was almost comical how fantasy-like it was.

Jack was slow and deliberate in choosing a place for us to set up camp for however long we intended to stall. There was a large oak tree with roots sticking out that Jack decided to place his stuff between. I stood watching him move, the muscles of his back contracting as he collected some of the dry leaves and sticks sheltered under the roots and piled them together. He struggled to set light to it for a moment and once it did he blew gently and added dry leaves, then built the flames higher with sticks.

We moved silently around each other, occasionally holding eye contact for a moment before we finally sat down, our backs against the tree and our legs pressed together as we faced the hill. It would be dark soon and we had a lot to do before then.

Still, we ate the last of our bread and took slow gulps of the water we'd collected from streams as slowly as possible.

I was digging my heels into the dirt and tore bits of leaves off with my hands when my eyes caught sight of a feather, I reached between the roots and picked it up, it was slightly old but it would do.

"Is this a Raven feather?"

Jack looked at me and plucked the feather from my fingers with a sharp intake. He replied, "definitely."

I looked at him as he turned the feather over with his fingers, his eyes examining every part of the black feather and stroking it fascinated.

"Ravens signify death," I pointed out and he turned to me with a smile.

"Thanks for the light-hearted remark," he chuckled. "I know, my lives clearly have a lot of death in them." He smiled with his mouth closed sadly.

I leant my head on his shoulder and watched the hill. "I have no idea where I'm going to find a blue light."

He turned his head and I looked up finding him with wide eyes. "Seriously? You've been carrying it this entire time." I looked at him expectantly and he returned my look dumbfounded. "Oh my God Nova," he said, taking my left hand and pulling off my wedding ring.

He was right, I wouldn't have known because I never paid any attention to it. He held the wedding ring up in the light and the blue sapphire caught what little light there was left from the day.

"Oh."

"Yes, oh," he laughed, taking my hand and slipping it back onto my finger. When he tried to take his hand back I pulled it softly forward, interlinking our fingers and gazing up at him.

"What is the first thing you're going to do once you get back?" he asked, brushing his thumb against the back of my hand. It was covered in dirt and rough to my skin but I didn't complain, I didn't want him to stop.

"Have a shower."

He let out a loud laugh. "Ugh, a warm shower." We both moaned and laughed under our breaths. Under the leaves of an old tree that no longer remained, two people who could change the future, go back into lives they lived hundreds of years ago were spending these last moments in each other's company. Two people who had intended to kill one another but now couldn't bring themselves to do it.

"We should get a move on if you're ready," Jack mumbled, watching as the dark grey clouds grew in size and the trickle of rain pattering onto the top of leaves sped up. It fell beneath the branches and landed with a heavy splash on the top of our heads. I nodded numbly, accepting the hand he held out for me and was hauled to my feet.

Jack stomped the small fire out with his feet whilst I tightened my belt and put my hat back on. Jack pulled his things together, taking his sword and attaching it to his side.

"Ready?" he asked. I nodded and led the way to the hill.

CHAPTER 34

Time: 22nd September 1661
Location: Two minutes away from getting home

"It's so typical," Jack panted once we'd gotten a quarter of the way up. I turned to face him as he was a few paces behind me and raised my eyebrows at him.

"What do you mean?"

"Well, of course, it has to be at the top of a hill surrounded by thunder and lightning. Pathetic fallacy much?"

"What a big boy you are, using big words Jacky-boy," I teased, laughing when he scowled at me.

"Might I remind you that you aren't the one carrying all this crap?"

"Let it go, we won't need it once we get to the top."

He stopped in his tracks and looked at me incredulously. "That's true," he said, dropping most of the stuff including his tattered maroon cloak under a tiny shrub of a tree. "Goodbye old friend," he said.

Jack picked up his pace, climbing the hill alongside me. The rain was falling in heavy but refreshing drops and I welcomed it as it trickled down the back of my cloak and through the shirt.

I twisted the ring on my finger, running my thumb over the sapphire, willing my Totem back, drawing it to me instead of being drawn towards it. *Show me what I desire most, take me there.*

Soon I would be home, back in my body alive and real - my mind, my own life where I could live freely. *Well as free as it gets.* I was going to be in a lot of trouble once I got home. I breathed in the air - air that was hundreds of years old. I felt the rain that hadn't yet been contaminated. I lived my final moments of 1661 and enjoyed it - relished in the forgotten but renewed memory of it all.

This would probably be one of my last times in a past life. I couldn't keep doing it. And I could never go this far back again, not with the risks.

I would never from this moment accept money to go and change the future for some corrupted assholes in the future - to worsen the lives of others and gain from peoples misery. I would not erase another thing from history.

I was done.

Jack held out a hand as we reached the top of the hill and he pulled me up onto the rocky slope. It was windy and larger than I would have thought from the bottom. But there it was, a circular well just big enough for a person to fall through. All that remained was the circular wall, everything else had long rotted away. The tree you could see from the bottom of the hill was behind it, scorched black from being struck by lightning. I could only hope it wouldn't get struck whilst we were here.

Jack was the first to stand over the well, pulling back weeds and greenery and dropping them to the floor. I stood in my place, not wanting to go near it.

"Do I just drop it in?" Jack shouted over the howling wind. He didn't wait for a reply before throwing the feather into the well, he turned expecting me to be behind him but I stayed a little away.

"You ready?" he asked, peering over the broken stones. Jack placed both hands over the well until a rock crumbled, he moved around it until he found a way to get in. I felt a rush of panic as I saw him take a step forward.

"Jack!" I cried.

I ran forward, scared he was going to leave already. He met me in the middle and caught me in surprise, clutching onto my body as I held him tightly. We took a moment to separate ourselves from each other and when we did Jack looked at me and took a step back with a smile. I grabbed his arm, in one fluid motion he wrapped his arms around my waist, drawing me back into him so our lips collided against each other. His lips moved gently against mine and I savoured the feeling of his warm mouth against mine and the feel of his hands on my waist.

It would be the last time we kissed for a good six or seven hundred years. I relished the feeling of his lips on mine - the way the rain fell down both our faces as we kissed with open mouths, drinking the rain and each other's lips. I memorised the feeling of every curve and dip in his face, the feeling of his facial hair as his lips moved against mine - the warmth his body provided flushed against mine even as we were drenched.

Our noses rubbed against each other as he brought one hand up to cup my cheek. Quietly, I asked. "What do I do once I get back?"

He pulled his head away from mine and held on to my face. "What do you want to do once you get back?"

I contemplated it for a moment, wondering if this is what I really wanted. "I want to help you."

He watched me with wide brown eyes and soaked black hair attached to his neck and then nodded. "Follow the Raven." He smiled, quickly kissing my wet forehead. "Keep a close eye on the sky."

He pulled away sharply and turned to face the well, when he stopped suddenly. I put one foot out to join him on our travels back to the future when I noticed what he was looking at.

A group of Redcoats had surrounded us from either side of the hill, even more at the base of the hill waiting. We were trapped.

"Jump!" I screamed to Jack who was closer to the well than I was but he didn't. Instead, he drew his sword and turned to the person in charge.

The Redcoats parted to reveal an officer. Tobias.

I didn't know how and I didn't care to find out if he'd always been so high up in the ranking or whether he was just playing dress-up. I'd met him as Redcoats were chasing him and now he was suddenly one of them?

346

"Marion Countess Of Eldermore, and Jack... whatever your name might be, you are sentenced to death for the crime of murder. We have you surrounded so hand over your weapons."

Dramatic much. I had a strange sense of déja vu that Redcoats had surrounded me before and honestly I wouldn't be surprised.

Jack stepped forward confidently. "She's not guilty. It's me you want."

Tobias raised an eyebrow and stepped forward. "Fine then, Ms Marion will be hung for witchery."

"What?" I shrieked, scanning my eyes over the soldiers surrounding us, they looked at one another concerned, muttering amongst themselves and instantly praying.

"And why the hell is that?" Jack shouted, looking between us frustrated. *For god's sake, Jack, just jump in the goddamn well. Stop trying to save the day.*

"She bewitched the Count, I saw it with my very eyes, and now you." He puffed out his chest, clasping his hands together before continuing. "Gentlemen," he caught the attention of his soldiers. "I believe she was intending to tempt him into the well, sending him to his death for what he did to her husband. Or better yet - she cast a spell on him to kill the Count."

The hell?

The soldiers adjusted themselves nervously and then looked at me with glares, spitting on the floor and hissing.

They believed this lunatic?

"Do not worry. We will bring her to justice for all her devilry and she will be sent to the depths of a fiery pit." They let out cheers as Tobias stepped towards me, his hands behind his back thoughtfully.

"Tobias. Please." I turned to him begging. He cocked his head to the side and spoke to me quietly.

"I must admit Marion, you haven't changed much. Constantly running away it seems, always into the hands of another man." His eyes flashed with dark amusement. "You ran away from home to run into me, you ran away from me to end up back where you started, and then you ran away from the Count with him." He turned his lip up. "Only to end up here... again... with me."

"Go to hell," I spat.

He raised his eyebrows. "Well the whole *please Tobias* didn't last long."

I hate you so much right now Ace. You have no idea. I am so going to send you to the 'fiery pits of hell', you hopeless good for nothing asshole.

"Arrest them."

Well if that's how it was going to go. I faced Jack, much to my relief he already held his pistol. So much for my *new start - new me.*

I aimed the only pistol I had at the man closest to me and instantly guns were raised. "I'll shoot him," I threatened, watching Tobias carefully.

He looked at the soldier and then me. "Go for it. I don't know him."

The soldier whimpered and the men looked at each other carefully not doing anything. Tobias may not have known him but these men were clearly all friends.

Jack angled one of his pistols in one fluid motion to face Tobias and suddenly guns were redirected. Tobias had one gun facing me, I had one facing the soldier.

"Alright lads," Jack sighed, and then pulled the trigger.

Nothing happened.

All confused, we began pulling the triggers, the men began clicking their guns and staring in dismay at the wet gunpowder.

"For fu-" Jack started to say but a grumble of thunder covered his words. The man I was aiming at released a cry as he brought out a sword and raised it above his head

I grasped the sword from my belt, swivelling to stab him instantly. Then I turned to the two men who were running for me and jumped onto the shoulder of the one who dropped to his knees. I flew through the air and pierced the sword through the man who had snuck up behind him.

Jack and I fought side by side, using our swords and each other to turn and kill like we were a part of a dance routine - trading positions by going through each other's arms.

We were fast, trained fighters from the future with the huge advantage of poor weather. The Redcoats were better at shooting than sword fighting apparently; clearly the storm troopers to the grand finale except they no longer had their guns.

Who didn't love a good fight?

At some point, Jack and I were forced apart and we turned to each other panicked but determined.

As I rolled away from fighting one soldier I saw another charge at me with his sword poking out like a needle. I simply sidestepped and watched as the man slipped and plunged his sword into his comrade. When he stared shocked I kicked him and pushed my own sword into his stomach.

A man who'd somehow lost his fancy hat stormed forward and knocked the sword from my hand. It skidded a little away from where Jack was fighting with a soldier. I glared at the man and swung my arm out. He caught it with perfect timing a millimetre away from his face and used his other hand to catch me in my stomach. I gasped as all the air was forced out of my lungs, and brought my knee up, forcing his head with my hands to clash with my knee. He groaned, falling to the floor unconscious.

"Nova!" Jack called turning away from the few standing soldiers and threw me my sword.

I grinned at him, taking his hand as we turned into one another, letting go as we defended each other's backs. I clashed my sword against one man whose face I didn't see but ended up forcing to the ground. I didn't manage to kill him before someone came from behind me, slashing my wrist. I dropped the sword in pain and turned to face whoever had cut me, another red coat that smiled triumphantly.

I kicked his knees sending him to the floor and grabbed his head forcing my thumb into his eyes and listening to his screams. I grinned as blood splattered to my face. I guess you couldn't get rid of bad habits too easily.

Karma soon caught up with me when I felt the cool metal of a blade rest on my throat and the barrel of a gun tipped my hood back.

My arms were forced to my side and when someone squeezed the gushing wound on my wrist I screamed in response.

Jack halted and turned in my direction. By his feet were a group of wounded or dead Redcoats and Tobias who stepped out from behind him.

"Jack!" I warned him, but Jack had already moved to turn to face Tobias who clashed their swords together. I watched intently, seeing Jack handle the sword, perfectly slicing it through the air to clash against Tobias', but his feet were getting sloppy. Their swords met in the middle and they pushed against each other teeth bared and growling.

"Its her or you Jack!" Tobias screamed over the wind and a surge of rain pelted us from the side. Jack was weakened and I watched him fall against the well. I willed him to fall in, to just tip over instead of slumping onto the floor. He panted, trying to pull himself up with the rubble of stones surrounding him. When his hand reached out for the sword Tobias stepped on his fingers, crushing them with his boot.

Jack's face contorted in pain and he turned his head towards me, I struggled from the two men behind me, flicking wet hair from my eyes as I watched him only a few metres away. The blade was pushed further against my throat, drawing blood. I whimpered.

"Her or you Jack?" Tobias repeated, I shook my head *don't you dare you goddamn idiot.* They wouldn't kill me here and you knew it but they would kill you, so tell them to kill me. *Pick your goddamn self back up and throw yourself into the well.*

Tobias pressed the sword to Jack's heart waiting. Jack faced me breathing deeply. The rain had soaked him through and he shivered slightly. I struggled against them and managed to rip my arms free from my cloak. I was out of their grasp. I skidded towards Jack but halted when Jack grabbed the blade of the sword and plunged it into his own chest.

I skidded to a halt as a gush of air left my lungs. There was a sword protruding out of his heart like a flag.

There was a sword in Jack's heart.

I let out a strangled scream and watched as Tobias clenched the hilt of the sword and twisted the blade further into Jack's chest. Jack's body shuddered and he gasped for air. A splatter of blood erupted from his mouth and I screamed, tearing my way through soldiers and falling next to his body.

I brought my shaky hands in front of me, clasping for his face moving dark strands of hair away from his cheeks and gasping for air.

Looking back on it I noticed details I wished I'd relished more. I wished I could draw the memory because there was something so eerily beautiful in the way he had died. The way his features looked so dark - so perfectly rugged and boyish all the same.

"No!" I shrieked, my hands fumbling over his chest as blood started to seep through his shirt. He looked up at me blankly. His eyes started to fade and I clenched his hand in mine. "Stay with me, Jack." I stroked his face wiping the rain from his eyes. "Stay with me," I repeated and a sob caught in my throat - I made an inhuman sound. Something had snapped inside of me: an emotion of pure horror.

"Help!" I screamed, turning away from his face and at the soldiers who stood around blankly. More had arrived and injured or dead were being carried away. No one would help me. I turned back to Jack where his eyes watched me.

With his lips stained red and trickle of the dark blood at the side of his mouth, he smiled in a grimace sort of way and lifted his arm, his fingers lightly brushed beneath my eyes. Tears mixed with the blood on his hand and for a moment we just stared at each other - trapped in time. *Time.*

I closed my eyes, willing him to do it, to take us there where our minds were at peace and we'd be nowhere for once - trapped between space and time but *together*. Nothing happened, the persistent rain fell on top of us like bullets and the wind ripped my hair from its braid until it flapped around my face, wet and bloodied.

When I opened my eyes, I stared into his; a void of all the adventure and determination there had been before.

"Jack," I breathed, shaking his face gently. His fingers that had wiped my tears away now lay limp on my lap. "Jack!" I cried and my entire body shook with sobs and shuddered as I grasped for his face.

Arms came around my shoulders and tried to pull me up but I dragged my knees against the ground tearing the trousers as I tried to scramble my way toward him. I screamed, tearing my chest right down the middle as I let loose crying and calling his name until I was physically lifted into the air.

"I won't leave you!" I let out a blood-curdling scream as I kicked and tried to fight my way off of the two men. "Let go of me!" I yelled whilst thrashing.

A sob rose to my throat but I smothered it with another scream as I was passed from one man to the other. I clawed my way over the shoulder of the soldier towards Jack. Tobias stood over his body looking down at the swaggering sword in the wind before finally taking it out. I groaned trying to break free from them but we were already walking down the hill and now the well was out of sight.

The men were quiet, they didn't cheer out of triumph and victory. They skidded down the hill and avoided eye contact with me and once we got to the bottom they sat me on the back of a carriage with a thick door with bars and chained my hands together. One of them pushed me further into the carriage, prodding me with his gun and then two more jumped in.

They climbed past me and sat awkwardly in the back watching me cautiously, ready to defend themselves if I made a move because surely - I would... surely I would fight back - to get revenge. But only a dark emptiness suffocated me - left me thoughtless and cold.

Jack was dead.

CHAPTER 35

Dead. Jack was dead.

I realised the two men who sat with me in the carriage were the ones who had been arguing with each other whilst Jack and I stole the horse and they watched me carefully, disturbed as I sat uncomfortably silent. I was rocking back and forth with the carriage whilst I cried softly, clinging to the bars of the door and rattling my chains. I looked up at the hill and jumped when a flash of lightning hit the tree, a rumble of thunder shortly followed and soon we'd turned a corner and the hill was out of sight. I hunched over my bent knees and shook quietly, running a shaky hand through my hair.

Dead. Jack was dead.

I couldn't stop thinking about how he should have had last words that I could cling onto and repeat in my head, haunting myself with his voice. But there were none. He hadn't had any last words to say to me - he'd simply touched my cheek and was gone.

Dead.

Already that lingering ghostly touch was absent from my cheek - I could no longer feel the warmth of his hand and wet of his blood. I could feel *nothing*, hear *nothing*.

After a long moment of silence and nothing I suddenly came a little further down to the earth. I could see it again, like a tiny dot beneath me as I hurtled to the ground. But I could hear and see again.

The two men were whispering under their breaths at each other angrily before the slightly smaller one turned to me. "I- uh. You won't feed our souls to the devil if we give you something warmer to wear?"

I turned my head to the side and glared. "I am not a witch," I spat, my voice hoarse.

"But uh- say yous was. You wouldn't hate us if we gave it to you?"

"Why even risk looking at me if you thought I was a witch?" I croaked. "I'd be able to curse you easier."

The small man pulled away, folding the cloak and leaning to his friend. "Is that true?"

"I don't know." He turned to me. "Is that true?"

Were they serious? I looked through my wet strands of hair and watched their knees bounce up and down as they shuffled back and forth nervously in their seats. The man snatched the material from the smaller man's hands and pushed it across the bench towards me. "Just in case," he whispered to the man and then they forced their eyes to the ground.

I pressed the palms of my hands to my eyes and took a deep breath. I'd be able to kill them, quite easily. But what was the point now? And so I took the material from them and placed it numbly around my shoulders, once I caught a glimpse of the embroidery of the coat my fingers froze and I examined it closely. It was Jacks - the tattered maroon cloak I'd told him to leave under a tree on our way up to the hill. I clenched it tightly, closing my eyes and breathing it in.

Moisture squeezed past my tightly clenched eyes and trickled down my cheeks. I told myself it was blood - not tears and quickly wiped it away with the cloak. If I gave into crying now I would never stop. I had nine whole years of tears building in the back of my throat.

We rode through the night and then through the day, only taking brief minute stops before continuing. I didn't sleep much throughout the journey. I just looked at my hands and twisted the ring uncomfortably.

He was gone. We were so goddamn close to being home, he could be back in his body now, hugging his sister telling the Rebellion of this nightmare adventure he'd had. However he wasn't, instead, his body was cold and lifeless because I'd stopped him from leaving - because I was too selfish.

Finally, we arrived at a fortress. Where that was I had no idea but I didn't care. There was no point left in anything. It felt like all the life had been sucked out of me. I gave up. I was tired and I was ready to accept whatever would happen to me. I was done with being alive, done with being recycled like a piece of plastic.

I wanted peace. I wanted Jack.

I was led to a cell. Usually, I would have looked at my surroundings, found some kind of way to escape but this time I didn't. I sat in a cell, cold and shivering, crying and feeling sorry for myself. There was no need to hold in the tears now - not when death was so close I could almost touch it with my fingertips.

I was as close to death as I had been to home. It had been a grasp away. We should have climbed the hill as soon as we got there - not sat down for a tea party.

Jack's cloak had been ripped away from me despite my screaming and crying for it - but a torn part of the fabric was clenched tightly in the ball of my hand. I stroked the dark maroon material, holding it to my lips as I lay curled on the floor of my cell.

Maybe he was home though. Maybe he died and woke up in his present body instead of being dead and reborn in a few years. And if he wasn't... then it was only a few years until I'd see him again, providing I also got reborn.

But I wouldn't remember him. Even if I was told of all my adventures and remembered some, would I remember this? Even memories from past lives were starting to blur into one confusing mess.

And what if because I'd done so much Time Bending I would die before I even got the chance to get executed. Would I even be reborn?

Even if I did everyone else would be dead. Maybe everything would be gone - Prospect and the Rebellion having destroyed one another.

There was something worse about knowing when you die you'd come back but everyone you knew from your old life would be dead. They would have grieved you already - moved on and forgotten.

"Nova?" a surprised voice exclaimed from the cell next to mine. There was some scrambling and then a familiar man's face appeared through the bars. Jamie smiled at me cheekily, his bruised fists clutching onto the bars as he looked me up and down.

"You've looked better," he continued talking. "This place is so deathly I'm surprised I didn't realise you were here."

I saw him adjust himself into a seating position as his chains clanked together. "I got myself into a little trouble once you two left and then I wound up here. In these." He waved his chains in the air with a grin.

I looked through the greasy strands of my cluttered hair and he frowned. "Don't worry girl, my men are coming. They'll get us out of here. Anything for Tom's girl." He grinned. "Where is Thomas?" he asked suddenly, his face pale.

"He's dead," I replied blankly, turning my head away and staring at the wet stoned floor, stroking the fabric between my thumb and forefinger. Both Thomas and Jack were gone.

It was silent for a moment and then there was the sound of splashing as he stumbled against the stonewall.

"He's not supposed to- how?" he asked breathing deeply. I curled up tighter, bringing my knees to my chest and swallowing the lump in my throat.

"He did it to save me from being killed. A bullet to the head, no pain," I lied. I didn't know why I lied, but if I had a cousin who'd just died I'd want to know it was quick and painless - not that he forced a sword into his heart in a final act of foolish heroism.

Jamie let out a long breath and then sniffled trying to contain a sob, he cried for a moment. He didn't let himself cry long though before speaking again.

"I don't understand."

For a moment I truly considered telling him the truth. That his cousin wasn't really his cousin but it was his cousin from the future. To hell with it. I wasn't going anywhere, there was no reason for me to lie.

"You don't have to understand. It's hard to understand, I don't even understand." I took a shaky breath. "Thomas wasn't really Thomas, he was... in a way possessed by Jack, who once a very long time ago was Thomas." I stuttered on my words so awfully that I imagined he wouldn't understand what I was talking about anyway.

I didn't bother caring, what was the use? I'd always wanted to tell someone. Especially when their loved one wasn't really dead. Except Jack was - for now at least.

It poured out of me in a messy tangle of words and snot. "And we were trying to give his life back, and I was trying to give my person's life back. But we got captured and Jack died to save me, killing Thomas with him-"

"I know Nova. I know what you are." Jamie held onto the bars of the cell and looked at me frantically. I blinked at him, my breath stuck in my throat. "Don't ever reveal that to anyone again. It's just it's against the rules for me to say anything when you're travelling unless you're in trouble, but I just-"

"You're a Reincarnation," I realised. He looked at me from his cell and nodded numbly. "Twenty-three lives with Tom - Jack. And now two with you."

I shook my head and wiped my eyes. "Is he dead in the future?"

"I can't say if he's dead or alive," he replied sympathetically. "But hell to the rules. You'll see him again, but in the past."

I watched him momentarily. "What year?"

"It will be before this life, and I'll be there." He smiled sadly. "I'll never get over the complicatedness of the past still having more to be done to it. The past is unfinished."

"What does that mean?"

He shook his head. "You will see... Mary." He held my face lightly and smiled sadly.

Mary? I'd been called Mary in a few lives, it was a common name but I couldn't remember any specific life he might be talking about.

"Let's not let Tom's death be in vain," he said finally.

I didn't respond. We sat quietly each lost in our own thoughts of Jack. The only difference being I couldn't remove his lifeless brown eyes and the sword sticking out of his heart. However, I imagined Jamie was thinking of a whole lot more than that, he was thinking of life from years ago.

CHAPTER 36

Time: 25ᵗʰ September 1661
Location: Unknown Prison

I'd fallen asleep with my fist clenched around the material of Jack's cloak. I was curled up on the wet floor shivering and listening to another man's series of coughs echo down the halls. But I awoke with a start when there was a crank of metal. The door swung open and a Redcoat clutched at a fire torch. He held it in front of me and I welcomed the heat, turning my head towards it and sitting up on my elbows.

How long had I been asleep?

How much time had passed?

The man said something about me going somewhere but I didn't catch the whole thing. *Time to die* I thought to myself, crawling onto my knees and pressing my hands to the ground to push my feet up. Before I stood I quickly placed the fabric in my shoe - I wanted it to be with me when I died - a part of Jack with me.

Jamie rushed to the bars and watched as the soldier took me by the elbow and shoved me out of the cell. *Calm it, buddy, I was going. No need to be so rough.*

I turned to face Jamie wondering why he wasn't being taken before the soldier forced me up a spiral staircase and

Jamie was out of sight. We went down an empty stone corridor that I couldn't see the end of. There were no windows but I assumed it was night-time from the lack of soldiers patrolling the corridors.

My theory was proved to be right when he led me up another staircase and I passed the ground floor where moonlight lit the halls. I thought I would be taken out and hung but instead, he walked me up to a room at the top of the fort and knocked on the door. Another soldier opened it and made way for me to enter.

The door closed behind me and the soldier moved to the far end of the room. He picked up a dress, placed it on the back of a dining chair and walked over to me.

I was in a fair-sized room, surrounded by bookcases and a large fireplace between them. In the centre was a long dining table with a plate either side stacked high with food.

I wondered if this was some kind of torture technique they didn't mention in history books.

"He requests that you wear this dress," the soldier said, not meeting my eyes as he twisted a key into my shackles and let them drop to the floor. He swooped them up and left me standing next to the dress puzzled.

I rubbed my wrists, poking them, running my fingers over the pink-blistered skin and looked around the room. What was I supposed to do? I was too high up to escape through the window and besides what was the point anyway?

My plan was to die.

I was in a secure enough position for that wish to be happily granted.

I decided the most comfortable option for now was to climb into the deep red dress and out of the cold and disgusting clothes I'd worn for almost an entire month.

It felt strange putting such a beautiful dress on such a disgustingly dirty version of myself. My skin was coated in a thick layer of filth and my hair was wet and matted, my face was stained with blood from nosebleeds... and blood that wasn't my own.

Once done I looked at myself in a long mirror, my skin was deathly pale and the dress only made me look ten times whiter than I already was. The three quarter length sleeves and bows on the dress itched against my skin and I squirmed uncomfortably. Basically, I looked like a zombie bride.

I took it upon myself to use my old shirt as a cloth and the jug of water to clean my face - not caring about whoever would drink this later. When I looked back in the mirror and saw all parts of skin that were showing a little cleaner I felt a lot better about myself, more presentable: who I was presentable for, I didn't know.

That was of course until the door opened and Tobias stepped in. I wasn't surprised, but that didn't stop the uncomfortable flip in my stomach when the face of Ace smiled at me: the face of the man who killed Jack. He took off his hat, threw his jacket onto the back of a chair at the far end of the table, sat down and picked up the cutlery.

He paused and waited for me expectantly. "Please, take a seat, Marion. You look beautiful, the dress compliments your body marvellously."

I didn't move, I held his eyes and wished I really were a witch so I could make him spontaneously combust. "I'm sure you're hungry," he stated.

I walked slowly to the other end of the table, dragging the chair out with care and sitting myself down calmly whilst inside every nerve of mine was screaming.

He began cutting his meat, chewing large mouthfuls and taking large sips of wine. I watched him cautiously.

"Eat," he ordered through a mouthful. I looked at the food and back at him.

"How do I know it's not poisoned?" I held my head up high, only faltering when he pulled out his chair after a moment of thought and walked to my end of the table. I froze, holding my breath and staring forward as he leant in on my right. He picked up the knife and fork either side of me, his arm brushed against my chest and he began cutting the chicken slowly. He held it to his mouth and began to eat. Once he'd demonstrated that with half the food on my plate he pulled away and put the knife and fork on the plate.

"Eat," he repeated, walking back to the other end of the table. His boots were heavy on the floor and with every thump my heart sped up.

I began to eat despite my pride. I didn't care that fatty grease was running down my chin or the gravy smudged against my cheeks and when he offered the wine I gulped it quickly, afraid it would all be taken away from me.

"Do you remember when we first met?" Tobias asked pleasantly. I looked up from the food and wiped my mouth with the napkin. I nodded my head slowly.

"You were running away from Redcoats. And yet here you are," I replied.

He smiled tightly. "You called me Ace?"

I wished so badly for Ace to appear in Tobias' mind and see me sat at the end of the table. He'd sigh with relief and have to convince me it was really him and he was going to help me get out of here, he'd take me to the well and then meet me home.

But that's not how these things worked. Sometimes you wouldn't be rescued by a knight in shining armour because they were already dead or hundreds of years into the future. Sometimes you had to be your own hero. But I was no hero - and I was not supposed to have a happy ending.

"How did you get here?" I responded, ignoring his question.

He looked agitated. "Tell me, Marion do you believe in fate? Is that something witches believe in? Do you believe in destiny?"

"That's a rather deep question." I narrowed my eyes because I actually liked that question. Surely I had some destiny? Surely it was Fate that had awoken Time Benders in the present now of all times. Surely we weren't all a mistake? It would be a colossal mistake if so. But I could change fate apparently... Or maybe it was all Fate's will that I was able to change the past.

Nothing is written in stone – it's written in pencil O had told me.

I cleared my jumbled up thoughts and looked him in the eyes. "I believe our destinies are written in pencil - not stone."

Ace's eyes grew wide with a curiosity that didn't fit the cruel sneer of Tobias' face and I felt my shoulders relax as the surroundings of the past faded away and I was back on the balcony in the future with Ace, sharing our totems.

"I feel like I'm chasing after my fate, trying to keep up with it." He leant forward in his chair with wide eyes. "Do you ever feel like that? Do you feel like you're chasing the truth? Your destiny?"

My breath caught in my throat. "What?" I rasped.

"I feel like I'm being locked out of the truth," Tobias replied hesitantly.

Did all of us from the past feel that way? I'd never heard one of us say that - feel that at all.

Was that how Marion was feeling now? Locked out of her own body? Hidden away from the truth? But Tobias hadn't even been interfered with by Ace. I wish he had been.

"Why are you telling me this?" I asked.

"I want you to tell me the truth, I want you to tell me my destiny." He smiled and I grimaced.

"I don't know your destiny," I replied, hardening my gaze on him. *Liar.* You know his destiny. You know everything about that boy because you had a stupid crush on him. Not anymore.

Tobias' face turned into a sneer. "Tell me or you'll be executed tomorrow."

Boohoo. Die again? Bitch, please. I wasn't scared of death; we were well acquainted. We sent each other Christmas cards.

"Fine, tell me more about yourself." I cleared my throat and sat forward. "I can't exactly tell you your future without knowing your past. How did you end up here?"

Yes tell me more about yourself, then maybe I could figure out your recurring theme. Maybe then I could figure out why you felt so lost. Heck if I was lucky maybe I could find out why you were an absolute sociopath in this life.

He narrowed his eyes. "I don't know what brought me here. I needed to follow you for answers."

"That's not what I asked," I snapped.

"You have answers and I need to know them." He gripped the table.

"Yeah well, you have answers I need to know too," I fired back. "Like how comes you have so much power?"

Tobias smiled. "Money is power, and I have money because of your husband... and the additional help from your father."

"Why would they help you? A murderer." I sat forward on my chair waiting for a reply.

"Well, you already know the answer to the Count. I suppose your father just wanted an ally. He knew I worked for your husband you see. Now, give me answers. Why did you call me Ace?"

"I was out of my mind. How did you end up so high in the ranking?"

"That would be telling. Why are you lying? You thought I was someone else."

I slammed my fists on the table. "Why am I lying?" I repeated. "You handed me over to my father after drugging me. I wouldn't be surprised if it was your idea to get the Count to drug me and you just killed Jack!" I snapped.

He finished his mouthful and wiped the corners of his mouth thoughtfully before standing.

"Jack is a puzzling one. I never understood why the Count admired him so much and you could never have imagined my surprise when I saw you draped over his back trying to escape." He sipped his wine. "And then to find the Count's body stuffed under his bed, naked and bloody. Yes, that was a tad bit of a surprise."

He walked over to a cabinet beside me and I avoided turning and looking at him as he unlocked a top drawer.

After a moment he asked in a dark voice. "Did you love him?"

"The Count?"

"Jack. Did you love him?"

I didn't reply. The fabric of his cloak throbbed against the ball of my foot, tucked in the straggled shoe that was concealed by the length of the deep red dress.

I put the napkin on the table, sliding a knife between the folds of my dress and pushed the chair out from beneath me as I stood. I turned suddenly to leave but Tobias walked into me. I swallowed tightly and stared as his chest moved up and down. "I'd like to be returned to my cell now."

His hand came out from behind him and he placed a parcel of something on the table.

"Did you love him?" he asked slowly.

I looked at the folded up cloth feeling the air catch in my throat. "What do you want me to say?" I gasped for air.

Tobias placed two hands on my shoulders. "I want you to answer my question."

"Yes okay, I loved him," I snapped, closing my eyes tightly and flinching when he slammed his fist to the table. I felt him breathe deeply against the back of my chair before he suddenly continued.

"I thought it would have been excellent to serve it on your plate but that would be too cruel even for me."

My eyes focused on the package on the table and I didn't flinch as Tobias' hand came up and tucked a strand of my hair behind my ear. It moved down my neck like a trail of fire and rested on top of my chest, slipping between the folds of my dress and still my eyes didn't move from what was on the table.

He was disgustingly cruel.

"Sit down." I couldn't move. He had to physically push me back onto my chair, sliding it under the table as my eyes fixated back on the package.

The truth was I didn't know what love was. I did not know if I loved Jack, if it were possible to love your enemy - your prey. But I wanted to believe I was capable of such a thing, even if he hadn't felt the same way for me. Whatever it was - it was strong and it consumed me.

But this - this emotion whilst looking at the package on the table, it overwhelmed what I might call *love*. It was a whole new emotion so fierce that hatred burnt at the back of my throat. Tobias moved around me, before finally settling behind my chair, his hand coming round either side and stroking my hair, and yet still I couldn't move.

I hated him.

His lips moved up the side of my neck pressing cold kisses before finally pressing against my ear as he whispered, "open it."

I didn't dare move closer towards it and so Tobias stretched across me, making sure to slide his head in between my neck and shoulder as he began to unwrap the cloth. I turned my head away and clenched my eyes shut, only being forced to open them when he grasped my chin and turned my head sharply to the side.

Jack's lifeless heart sat in the middle of my plate and it was enough to completely send me over the edge.

I scraped my chair against the hardwood floor, bashing Tobias in the stomach. Quickly, with what adrenaline I had from seeing his heart sat lifeless in front of me, I stabbed the knife into Tobias' neck.

Fuck the future. Fuck whatever life Ace might have had after this moment. Fuck the rules because *God* did it feel good to watch blood squirt from his neck and his mouth open in shock.

He'd underestimated me massively.

Even as soldiers threw open the door by the sound of his gurgled cry I snarled triumphantly as he dropped to his knees and then onto his back.

"I'm your destiny, asshole."

I was held by my shoulders and my wrists were clamped together with iron cuffs - not that I needed holding back or restraints - I walked back to my cell willingly.

Once we arrived back in the dungeons there were soldiers already running around frantically crying about an escape. It was only then I realised a bell was being rung and the heavy sound of boots echoed above us.

When I got pushed into the cell I turned to my left expecting to see Jamie when really there was a hole in the stonewall that had been blasted by a canon. Jamie had been rescued, and I wouldn't be. The gap between the blown-out wall and where the metal cell ended wasn't large enough for me to climb through and so I'd been left here to die.

Perhaps Jamie hadn't saved me because I was supposed to die here. So much for not letting Jack die in vain. But he hadn't now. I'd killed the person who sent him to his death and gotten his revenge.

Despite telling myself this, it didn't stop the floods of tears that cascaded down my cheeks as I sat alone in a puddle of prisoner's piss and water. I held onto the dress tightly wanting to rip it to shreds. Then, when my hysteria faded I began stroking the torn fabric of Jack's cloak I'd taken out of my shoe. I closed my eyes as I tried to imagine a time before everything took a terrible turn.

I imagined the summer days at the Montgomery estate, the evenings I'd spent with Jack trying to find a way out of this life - when now I would die in it. I pictured the feeling of his torso and the horse as we climbed steep hills and the night we spent sleeping soundly in each other's arms - safe in his family's home.

I slept well, dreaming for once of the future - not the present but the future. I dreamt that for once the world would be at peace - that there was hope for humanity yet and none of it would rest on my shoulders. I would no longer be the risk to humanity everyone thought I was.

Someday. Jack's voice echoed in my head. Someday, I would see him again.

Someday...

CHAPTER 37

Time: 26th September 1661
Location: Unknown Prison

It was a good day to die, I'd decided before I even knew it was sunny outside. I was eerily calm - ready for my next death or maybe even the possibility that I'd wake up back in my body. But that wasn't possible. I'd checked the ring too many times to count to know.

I was forced into a line of prisoners, all of them were gaunt and skinny. Some watched me curiously, whispering and praying to themselves.

I could hear male prisoners behind me spitting and hissing at me and I rolled my eyes at their superstitions. Little did they know I could Time Bend and travel to previous lives. I suppose in that regard I sounded even more like a witch.

I'd changed my mind about the day the instant I stepped out from the shade into a patch of sunlight and hadn't moved for five minutes. The dress was painfully heavy and hot.

You'd think the weather would have been cool and rainy - being near Scotland and all - but I supposed 1661 was going through a heatwave or something.

The line was moving slowly, probably to the relief of many of the prisoners behind me but I wanted it to get a move on. I clenched the fabric in my hand tightly, it was covered in sweat, dirt and blood but so was I.

Only one person was hung at a time and that included a whole speech about whatever their crime was and then the time it took for them to die. In most cases it was instant but there were a few stragglers. Then they had to untie the body from the noose and move them to a cart whilst the next person stepped up.

I leant forward to the woman in front of me. She was fair-skinned and crying. "Can I skip in front?"

Her eyes lit up and she gestured me forward welcomingly. "May God be with you."

The man behind her clanked his shackles together and whispered to her I was accused of being a witch and she gasped. A soldier appeared from the side, bashing her head with his gun. "Back in front." He forced her in front of me and I watched helplessly as she was pushed up the stairs.

Her crime was theft but I imagined she was wrongly accused. You could see the goodness in her - the only similarities she shared with the other prisoners was fear of death and poor hygiene.

She struggled longer than the others, gasping and trying to save herself when the fall didn't break her neck instantly. *Just let it go you silly girl, you're going to die anyway.* Nevertheless, she was a fighter.

I practically jogged up the stairs, which was hard to do when you were wearing a dress that swept the ground and your feet were chained together. I faced the view of the rest of the criminals and there weren't many left. It was spring-cleaning here in fort-wherever-we-were and they were throwing out all their prisoners.

The wood was creaky and the executioner stood with his arm bent over the stick, sweating uncomfortably. Although he perked up when he saw me. He adjusted himself and came forward with the noose.

I stepped onto the trap door, lightly bouncing on it curious to see how much strength it could hold. Not much it seemed - it was probably the reason they starved their prisoners before sending them on to get hung.

It seemed my luck just kept getting worse when the executioner became aroused at the sight of me. He took his time, pressing himself against my ass ignoring the awkward shuffles of soldiers as they tried not to look like they were enjoying the show.

You have got to be kidding me.

I balled my fists in their chains tightly, the fabric squeezed in my grip. I closed my eyes, and soaked in my final moments.

"Marion, former Countess of Eldermore-" It wasn't as long as a list I knew I really had. I'd killed a total of... how many people? Some not born and quite a few that I'd killed in this life. I was accused of using witchcraft on another man and the murder of English soldiers. I didn't know if I'd killed Tobias but one could hope.

I opened my eyes and scanned the crowd of soldiers carefully taking my time to pick out if Tobias was here or if I'd been successful. But perhaps he was watching from a window in bed unable to speak – but also unable to miss the opportunity of seeing me die.

The executioner swept my hair to one side breathing in deeply and groaning. I didn't imagine I smelt good enough to be wanted in bed but hey - this man spent day after day hanging rotting prisoners.

Even worse, the executioner took his time tightening the noose around my neck, sweeping his gloved hand against my cheek and then tightening the rope. "I'll be seeing you later," he growled in my ear, taking strides to his lever.

Did he just?

"What the f-" I began to say but he'd pulled the lever forward until there was a loud thump and the ground fell beneath me as I fell.

Death wasn't up to my standards honestly.

It wasn't as special as I thought it would have been - probably because I landed with a thud into a pile of mud. I lay on the ground for a moment staring up through the gap and wondering why I wasn't hanging.

Everything seemed to freeze for a moment, none of the soldiers moved. They just stood still, as did the prisoners as they watched in amazement

"She really is a witch! She's doomed us all!" cried one prisoner, dropping to his knees and pointing at me. The rest cried in horror whilst the soldiers suddenly came to it, stepping forward to grab me. They tried to run forward until one by one they were shot down.

I sat up, the air having been forced from my chest as I realised the rope hadn't just snapped - somebody (very talented) had shot it.

By the time I'd managed to crawl myself up, there was chaos surrounding me. It was only when I saw a familiar face that it dawned on me what was happening. He gave me a slight smile and held out a hand, then hauled me to my feet and cut me free from my chains.

"You aren't supposed to die just yet." He winked.

Jamie handed me a sword and dagger and jumped back into the action. I followed along slightly dazed as I watched men bash soldier's heads. There was the small guy from Jamie's family and the red-bearded man. But it wasn't just those two butchering their way through soldier upon soldier, clumsily missing bullets - there were more men with them.

So Jamie was part of a... group on bandits or something? Jack failed to mention that slither of detail, although I imagine he hadn't remembered.

There was a thud behind me and I swivelled to face the executioner. In one hand he was swinging rope and in the other was an axe.

I narrowed my eyes. "You're a disgusting-" What was the word again? "Necrophiliac."

He cocked his head to the side, taking a step forward to fight but before he could take another I threw the dagger into his chest and he looked down shocked. He was a beast of a man so I didn't really know what I'd been expecting when he pulled it out and staggered his way towards me with a growl.

I froze momentarily, watching as he charged towards me before I tightened my grip on the sword and brought it up to defend my head as he took a swing with the axe. He snarled through his mask trying to break against my force and before he put in all his strength I turned to the side.

It was just like fighting Cedrix really but a weaker version. This man was slow and clumsy - he was used to killing people in chains, not actual combat. So I used this to my advantage, swivelling around him with my speed and stabbing him from behind.

At first, he fell to his knees and then onto his front. But just as I thought he was dead he managed to climb up on his elbows and caught the rope underneath my feet.

Oh fu-

I fell to the floor caught in the rope as he hauled me towards him, grabbing my legs and then using the rope to tie it around my neck. I wheezed, trying to tear the rope from around my neck when suddenly it went limp and the executioner landed on me with a thud.

I looked up and met eyes with Red-Beard who held his hand out for me, which I took gratefully.

"We need to leave now," he said and I nodded enthusiastically. *Get me the hell out of here.* Most of the Redcoats were crawling on the ground and the prisoners had now joined in on the fun, taking fallen weapons and running around like mad people. The bell was being rung and the sound of heavy footsteps echoed from inside. More were coming.

Jamie was beckoning from a doorway and we ran quickly to it. He led the way around the corridors avoiding any trace of Redcoats appearing.

However, when was I ever lucky? What a surprise that the one person who *did* storm down a corner and skid to a halt was Tobias. His neck was wrapped in thick bandages and his eyes widened when he saw me and his lip turned up into a scowl.

"Are you kidding me?" I threw my hands up into the air as if I were talking to a higher power. Then my eyes settled on Tobias with a grimace. "How many times do I have to try and kill you?"

He didn't reply - maybe he couldn't now. Hopefully, he couldn't. If I had to hear one more cocky word come out of his mouth I'd stab him... again. Instead, he drew out a sword to fight - not a pistol. Clearly, he wanted this to be fun.

I wasn't up for dramatics though. I held my hand out for a pistol and Jamie cautiously handed me one.

Tobias raised an eyebrow with a smirk, putting his sword back and reaching for his pistol. But like I said - I wasn't up for dramatics. He'd forced Jack to kill himself and then ripped out his heart with the intentions of serving it to me for dinner. Just two of the things he'd done to ruin literally everything about this life. Hell - even from the beginning. If I hadn't met him I might have found Jack within the time and would have made it home with my Totem still present unless Jack killed me first. Even if that meant I couldn't have spent time with Jack and developed feelings for him - Tobias was *still* and always would *be* - an *asshat*.

I didn't think twice about shooting a bullet into his chest, sending him to the floor. The shot seemed to echo down the corridors and the others shuffled restlessly.

"One second," I replied, hastily moving towards Tobias on the floor motionless. I glanced over his black hair, stupid uniform and the wrinkles surrounding his eyes. *Thanks for being a former asshole Ace.* I pressed the pistol to Tobias' head and shot again.

I didn't look back as I strode toward the others with a smirk. I imagined Tobias thought his destiny was more epic than that and maybe it would have been in this life but he didn't deserve epic.

"What was that for?" one of the men asked.

"A double-tap."

Just in case Fate had other plans.

I squeezed the material in my hands and felt my shoulders relax slightly. Even so, I held my breath as we came to a thick oak door on a level below us. Jamie heaved it open to reveal a small passage below the hill and quickly climbed a slope.

Red-Beard and two other men followed behind me and Jamie held out a hand for me to grab as he lifted me up the slope. The other two followed as we kept close to the wall. Our backs pressed right against it as we looked up cautiously at the Redcoats that ran around panicked, turning canons in the direction of the courtyard to shoot at the prisoners.

Whilst the soldiers focused their attention on the prison riots we were able to slip away without being noticed. Which I supposed was lucky.

The small man and a few others had a group of horses, which we all climbed on to eager to get out of this place.

"Where are the others?" a blonde man asked. Red-Beard shook his head and climbed onto the back of his horse. Meanwhile, Jamie held a hand out for me and helped me up behind him. Almost as soon as the last person had got on their horse we stormed down the hill, quickly heading for North.

"What did you tell them?" I asked Jamie a little way into the journey. He glanced behind at the handful of men that were following us.

"That you needed to get home."

"And they're willing to ride a few days north from here just to accompany me home?" I replied dumbfounded, wiping my nose with a handkerchief and feeling my eyes drop tired.

"They would do anything to help Tom's girl out."

"I'm not *Tom's girl*," I replied, feeling my chest tighten with the sensation that told me we were heading to the well. I held my breath until I got used to its familiar feeling.

"Ah right."

I narrowed my eyes. "I'm not Jack's girl either. We were supposed to kill each other, and then he got us stuck here." My throat tightened and I stroked the fabric. It felt good to talk about him - even making fun of him and shedding light on the fact I was stuck in the past. But it left a painful jolt in my chest.

"I thought you had to have the same parents as a Time Bender, to be a reincarnation?" I asked.

"Jack and I are usually brothers, but for this life, I had another Time Bender brother - he died. He only has three more lives after this before he stops being reborn."

I nodded quietly, wishing for more answers.

Jamie adjusted his position on the horse and looked back at the men before speaking. "They think you're an angel."

"An Angel?" I exclaimed with a laugh - *the irony*. I was even *Satan's* worst nightmare. "I'm far from anything angelic."

"They don't ask questions, and if you are an angel then they think it's their duty to help you get home."

"Do angels exist? Does God exist?" I asked. Jamie tilted his head to the side and smiled.

"People will believe what they want to believe. I don't believe in angels. For us there is no God, the only thing that exists is Time. It is our creator. But in terms of religion, I guess reincarnations are some kind of angel and Time is some kind of God."

Even when reincarnation was proven - we still needed something else to believe in. More answers. Humanity - or Time Benders - or Time's Bitches, (if we're being all inclusive now that Reincarnations exist) would always need more.

"I thought you couldn't say - why can't you say? Is Time stopping you from saying? Is Time a person?"

He chuckled. "You have a lot of questions. The only thing stopping us is nature and the rules we created. I do not know if Time is a person. All I know is that it exists."

Clearly.

"But... how don't you know that when you know everything that is going to happen?"

He shrugged. "All time does is tick, and you have the power to change it. You don't need a purpose for that. Nature stops you from remembering but really there is no beginning or end. Does a circle have a beginning or an end? No. Clocks are circles, aren't they? So where does time begin? Does it have an end?"

It sounded crazy, ambiguous and full of clues I couldn't figure out but for some reason I trusted him. Even though he had completely avoided my question.

"If time is like a circle why is the timeline I see made of lines?" I was confused.

"You need to look at the full picture."

"That'd be great if I could see the picture."

Jamie continued with a small smile. "You're more powerful than you believe." I thought I already believed I was pretty awesome. "You can change time, so perhaps you are angels of some sort." He winked.

The more he spoke the more confused I was becoming. "But O said we were mistakes."

He sighed. "That girl thinks she knows everything being ancient and all." I blinked in surprise but he moved on quickly. "Yes. You are essentially mistakes, but so are we. But then maybe it was Fate's plan all along."

"So now fate is a real thing?" I exclaimed loudly. Fate or fate? Was fate a Fate now - a *thing*? Was this confirmation? I looked up and realised heads were turned from their horses and towards us and I blushed. *Nothing to see here, lads.*

"There is a lot you don't know but I hope you find your answers," Jamie replied.

Seriously?

"Or you could give them to me!"

"No. I can't. We don't know every answer. Did you listen to a word I just said?" he laughed breathlessly. "We just believe in this stuff. Just as these men believe you're an angel as a way of explaining things hard to understand. We believe in Fate to explain why we exist and what we know about the future."

Oh. I suppose that kind of made sense. But still! There was something that told me he knew more, but it was clear his lips were sealed. Besides, I think the 'I hope you find your answers' part was a hint that I would eventually find out. So I just had to trust him - trust Fate.

CHAPTER 38

Time: 30th September 1661
Location: Bottom of the hill

Overall the men were lovely, they weren't your average evil group of bandits. They were more of the Robin Hood kind of guys stealing from the rich to give to the poor. Well, that's what I assumed they did, I had no idea what kind of business they were all in. Either way, I knew it was against the law. Clearly.

My health was deteriorating faster than it had been over the past few months. Thankfully before I started to believe in my hallucinations, the men surrounding me helped me realise I wasn't stuck in WW2 - I wasn't in a 1920s bar and I *definitely* wasn't at a Britney Spears concert.

However, it had dawned on me that I had no cure. Unless Vix could help in record time - Jack wasn't there to give me the cure he'd promised he could get his people to give.

I was wondering how the Rebellion even knew how to make a cure? How they did it and why?

It all added to the long list of answers I didn't have. But the simple answer was that Jack had lied or had been told lies. I didn't care about either answer because I'd finally accepted I was probably going to go insane once I got home anyway and I'd be taken in like Ace. At this rate, I was only going home because nothing was preventing me anymore and because I was in desperate need of a warm shower and brushing my teeth.

That made me think of Ace and all the cursing I'd done towards him in this life. Maybe he did remember a strange girl named Marion in a former life but he couldn't get to me because he didn't have his Totem back. Either way, I was going to slap him once I got home.

For the past hour, I'd been hunched over in extreme pain. It had taken us longer to get back to where it all went down than it had when I left with the Redcoats.

When it finally stopped and the horses began to get spooked I cried for them to stop and climbed down. We were at it from a different angle but there it was; a dark hill surrounded by dark clouds and rain. Time to go home.

This time I didn't sit around and wait at the bottom of the hill. I didn't stall at all. I turned to the men with a smile. "Give me a shout if any Redcoats give us a surprise attack."

However, by the time I'd turned to face them fully they were already down. The small group of men were down on one knee with their heads bowed.

I faltered, looking at them shocked and wishing they would just get up.

"We'll wait till nightfall and we'll leave." Red-Beard smiled at me. I returned it with wide eyes as they all rose. The small man whose name I'd learned to be James came forward bending on his tiptoes and turning his head to the side, I kissed it laughing. The other men: Joseph, Fred, Hans and Jacob all beamed at me.

They really believed I was an angel. I smothered my scoff. At least I looked like one.

"You guys realise I'll be back. I won't remember you, but I'm coming back down this hill. Not me specifically - but it will also... be me..."

They looked at me puzzled, dusting their knees off and grinning goofily. They didn't understand but they didn't care to understand, they just believed.

I hugged each of them before turning to Jamie. He extended his arm. "The rope gentlemen?"

Red-Beard chucked it to him and followed Jamie and me up the hill. I was assuming once I fell down the well Marion would wake up down there. She wouldn't just disappear into oblivion. Well, I hoped she didn't. She deserved a better life after I'd gotten so involved in it.

The rain wasn't as heavy but it was colder than when Jack and I climbed the hill. I shivered in the dress, climbing with what little energy I had left and once we got to the top I released a tired sigh of relief.

"How does this work?" Red-Beard asked. Both hands were on his knees and he was taking deep breaths. His arm was shielding his eyes from the wind and rain but he was already soaked to the core. Jamie also looked faintly like a drowned rat.

"Well," I replied, looking around at the top of the hill. It felt different being here, like an old place I never thought I'd see again. I'd kissed Jack in this spot. I hadn't wanted to leave just yet and so ultimately I was the one who sent him to his death.

He was dead because I didn't want him to leave. He was dead because I was too scared of missing him.

Red-Beard called me. "Marion?"

I jolted slightly, I'd lost track of time. How the hell was I going to have the energy to get myself back to the present time even with my Totem?

Well, let's hope the well worked first. I didn't just want to jump into a ton of water, sink to the bottom and get nowhere. That would be humiliating.

"You just drop it in and dive in," Jamie instructed me.

I took my eyes off of the well and the scorched tree above it and faced the two men, holding up my hand where the blue sapphire glistened.

"When you hear me start splashing, throw the rope and say you're here to help. I'm guessing she won't remember anything so you'll have to come up with some excuse. Introduce yourselves and ask for her name. Tell her she's on the run and has amnesia – if people know what that is yet." I grimaced. "Then do me a favour and help her."

"Shall we take you - her home?" Red-Beard asked. I shook my head.

"Stay away from the south, get her as far North as you can. Or at least point her in the right direction."

Jamie nodded determined. "Of course."

"And, if it's me who comes back out, then let's forget it ever happened," I laughed nervously.

"It works." Jamie grinned, clasping my shoulders and shaking them lightly, he reminded me a lot of Jack but there was a clear divide between them. Jamie was more free-spirited whereas Jack was more serious - although he certainly knew how to have fun.

I looked down at the torn part of Jack's beloved maroon cloak - it was frayed at the edges and covered in dirt and blood but I still brought it to my face and clenched it tightly, my fingers trembling as I turned to Jamie and held it for him.

"It was-"

"Take it with you," he said softly.

I shook my head. "But-" I stopped my words, noticing something in his eyes - a look that told me to trust him. Hesitantly I retreated my hand and kept the fabric in my grip with a thousand questions floating in my head.

I had so much to ask Jamie - so much I wanted to know about Time Bending and Reincarnations. But there wasn't time.

It was time to fall down the rabbit hole and into wonderland.

I stood over the well cautiously before slipping off the wedding ring.

"Wait!" Red-Beard finally called, stepping forward. "Sorry. I uh, sorry for thinking you were a boy."

I smiled. "It's fine."

"I'll see you soon," Jamie called with a grin.

I sighed, wishing he'd be able to tell me more and echoed Jack's words. "Someday."

I dropped the ring into the water, hearing its plop accompany the dribble of rain. I wondered if Jack's feather was somewhere down there too, waiting for him to fall into.

There wasn't much point in it but I took the dress off anyway so Marion or me would have something warm to wear once we climbed out.

"Adios gentlemen." I saluted them, shedding a little light on the situation. Red-Beard looked at me puzzled whilst trying to avoid looking down at my body with rosy cheeks. I climbed over a pile of rocks to the opening of the well.

So I was supposed to just jump in?

I looked down into a dark abyss. I couldn't see the water but the rain splashing and echoing up the walls of the well assured me I wouldn't jump to my death.

I let go of the side of the well, holding my breath as I stepped forward, the fabric of Jack's cloak tight in my grip as I fell.

I didn't know how to describe the feeling. At first, it felt like I was falling forever. My mind went blank as I fell through nothing. It almost felt as though there was a lack of gravity and my hair was floating but I was still falling. With a gasp, I was being dragged under by a swarm of hands and as soon as I hit the water it felt as though my veins were on fire. I sank lower, paralysed with pain until I hit the bottom of the well. All at once, I was dragged from my body - forcibly split from Marion and I fell through the bottom layer of the well. Still, my fist was wrapped tightly around the fabric, protecting it.

Then I was no longer cold. I was dry and could breathe and when I opened my eyes, instead of darkness there was light. Blue light everywhere, surrounding me and warming my veins until the light became hot - it consumed me, splitting my chest right down the middle and I screamed in agony.

All at once, the pain was gone and gradually the light became smaller until it was just a ball of blue tendrils in front of me. She was back. As I moved my body towards it I felt the smooth strands of darkness slip over my body and I searched - finding the timeline.

I was overwhelmed with emotion, so much so that I didn't think I'd have the energy to get out of the timeline and go all the way to present time without bending the timeline with my own. My Totem thankfully did the hard work for me - seeming to know the dangers of bending. It taunted me - dragging me through a web of sparkling, bright timelines until I saw my timeline.

I was almost undone with emotion and relief. I was exhausted but I was here. I was home. My Totem finally stopped and beckoned me closer, wrapping itself around me until I became the blue light, it pulled me back into my body and for a moment I felt myself slip from the darkness before I was pulled back by a muffled frantic voice moving around me.

I gasped as hot electricity shot through my body and I jolted like a pulsating heart. My eyes opened to bright blue everywhere and a dull thud spread throughout my body.

I awoke.

CHAPTER 39

Time: Present
Location: Prospect

I was floating in a large tank of blue, gel-like liquid and I was naked. As I looked out the window I saw Vix staring at me through the glass before another person came forward and there was the muffled sound of a loud smash.

I slumped forward, instantly hit by a blast of cold air. I curled into myself, the goo enveloping me. I felt as though I'd been reborn - exited the womb of my mother and now everything was cold and loud. I gasped for breath and the cocoon of goo finally broke around my mouth. I gulped in air - choking on it.

"Quick! Damn, get her out of it. Be careful not to step in it," I heard Vix exclaim.

There were loud footsteps around me. "That's quite impossible!" I heard someone shout before two arms scooped my naked body up. I began shivering instantly as I was placed on a white table. I dripped all over it and slowly I felt my body be stretched out on the table and a towel rub me down. The voices all seemed to fade out as I began to feel my body being prodded in different areas. I struggled to move my hands and my legs but eventually, I could tilt my head either side.

Vix was the one attaching wires to me and frantically jabbing things into my body. Halo stood by the door both hands on her mouth and one hand on a slightly raised stomach... pregnant? I gasped when I felt a needle go into my arm.

Aeron was standing behind Vix's shoulder slightly pale and dodging out the way every time Vix started moving frantically. Fynn was standing by a monitor that had just been attached to me, his brown eyes reading the screen urgently before flicking back to meet mine concerned.

The door slid open and Cedrix stepped in with wide eyes. "I heard the scream."

Halo latched onto his arm and he looked over me from a distance. I wish I could smile. I wish I could do anything.

I let out a moan of discomfort as Vix pulled on my leg. A soothing voice came from behind me, someone stroked my gooey mess of hair and I looked up curious. Only to meet with very bright blue eyes, dark hair and slim face - a lack of wrinkles and facial hair.

Panic raced through my body like a bird trying to break free and the heart monitor began beeping wildly. My body jolted free of its cage and I let out a hoarse scream. I sat up boldly with what little adrenaline I had and Ace let go of me panicked. I scrambled in a slippery mess and ripped free of the cords and propelled my hands to his throat.

A wicked smirk and red uniform met my gaze as his lips parted. His eyes narrowed and both his hands grasped my wrist with a snarl - Tobias.

399

Instantly someone tore my hands away and I let go weakly. Tobias stepped backwards. Fynn grasped my chin and forced me to face him. I struggled, snarling like a rabid dog and Fynn held my cheeks, keeping his eyes firmly on mine.

"Time: 2143, Location: Prospect," his voice cracked. "You're Nova and you're home." He repeated this sentence eleven times before I grew limp and began nodding my head, repeating it to myself. It had been a year since I'd left.

Fynn took his eyes away from me and faced Ace who was no longer Tobias. I curled into myself, realising I was completely naked and my friends stood around pale and terrified of me.

"Get her some clothes," Fynn mumbled, taking hold of a fresh towel and wiping my face free of the blue jelly. Halo stood still for a moment before stepping forward and holding out a dressing gown.

Ace forced his way in front of me and I flinched away with a glare. His eyebrows pulled together and he faced Vix with determination. "What's wrong? Is there another way we can help her?"

"Just give it to her," Aeron sighed from behind Vix.

"We can't be sure we can trust him," Vix replied, slowly gathering the cords I'd ripped away from me.

"Did you not just see that? What do we have to lose?" Aeron reasoned. Ace snapped his head towards Aeron and glared. I couldn't bring myself to even look at him. Halo wrapped a towel around my shoulders and helped me down onto the floor, which had been coated in a layer of blue slime.

Slowly we began to make our way out of the room but I managed to catch a part of their conversation. Fynn was arguing alongside Ace against Aeron. "This could just be another way of them trying to kill her..."

Vix sighed. "Let's just find out what she knows. We need to know everything that happened."

And then the door slid shut.

We moved slowly down pristine white corridors, everything felt unfamiliar. Everything was too white, too bright and too clean and an eerie silence filled my ears.

Was this real? Was I back?

"Are you pregnant?" I managed to ask - my voice was low from not having used it in so long. But it wasn't as bad as I thought it would have been - perhaps the blue goo had something to do with it.

Halo looked at the ground. "I didn't want to keep it. It's just pointless and will only cause me pain. But they wouldn't let me."

I nodded my head. I didn't really know what to say. I understood why she wouldn't want to keep the baby and I understood that Vix and the others would never allow her to abort a child of ours that could be researched and possibly answer questions we didn't know the answers to.

They liked to make us think we had free will when really we didn't. I was surprised by this thought - it hadn't ever occurred to me before.

Halo and I stood inside the pod and I inhaled sharply as I felt it suddenly move. I clutched at the glass walls as we began to descend even lower into the ground. Halo held onto my arm, leading me into the training room. Instant white light flooded me and I clenched my eyes shut as a headache began to form. I wasn't used to this. The change from past to present had been too much and I was still ill.

What was the point in me coming back? I was going to die either way. I might as well have saved myself the pain of waking up in a bright, noisy world.

But a shower...

Halo helped me over to the showers in the back of the training room. She waited for me whilst I stood in the shower, cleaning every crevice of my body and soaking my hair in soap. What had happened in a year? We were clearly still alive so it couldn't mean the Rebellion had done anything.

I stepped out of the shower - wrinkled and clean. I'd been waiting for that moment for months, to feel hot water jet onto my head and soothe my aching muscles but somehow I didn't feel it. I couldn't relish in it because I was still numb all over.

I climbed into tracksuit bottoms and a loose t-shirt. I was wearing clothes from the present time. It felt weird to be out of a tight fitted 17th-century dress and into loose fitted Pj's. I stood in front of the mirror for a moment and took myself in. My body was different too. I was taller and my hair was longer and straighter. I looked stronger than Marion - well I was. I'd been training since I was ten.

Still, the change in height caused me to trip a few times over my strange long legs.

Halo was brushing her hands against a rack of weapons with a forlorn look. I appreciated her waiting. She understood this was a lot for me to take in.

"What was that blue tank you had to break me out of?" I asked quietly.

Halo replied after a moment. "It's new technology another city developed. It's supposed to help preserve your body for long periods of time - feeding your body the same way a baby is fed in a womb."

A giant blue - fish tank womb. Great.

"We have pods similar to it - adapted to show our Totem's the best," Halo continued.

I nodded my head, full of questions but too tired and weak to ask any of them. Halo could probably kill me with a single punch in that moment, seeing as I'd said such terrible things to her in the past. But she didn't. She probably pitied me - and I hated that - I hated the thought of anyone pitying me.

One look at her scowling face and I relaxed - Halo most certainly did not pity me.

We made it back up to the room where the floors had been cleaned and the others stood around.

Aeron stepped forward first, engulfing me in a hug. For once he had nothing stupid to say, just clutched the back of my head and soaked me in.

Cedrix hugged me from the side and Vix smiled at me tightly whilst Fynn pulled me into his chest and kissed the top of my head. "I missed you," his voice cracked.

Tears welled in my eyes but I blinked them away quickly, hiding my face in Fynn's shirt as I held onto him tightly. I'd missed him too - missed him the most. In fact, being here in my best friend's arms I finally felt at home. The surrounding walls and the pod hadn't felt anything like it - but here with him, I could finally feel my body relax. Home.

Ace was the last to stand up from his chair, he walked to me cautiously but I stopped him urgently by holding out a hand and shaking my head. He backed away confused.

"Please take a seat Nova and we'll grab you a log," Vix said, wheeling on his chair and opening a draw from his desk.

"No," I said adamantly. "There's no point in logs, it's a waste of time," I continued.

The others looked me up and down cautiously. I walked over to one of the chairs, sitting on the end of it and looking around the room. My eyes stilled and my heart began thumping wildly in my chest as I looked at the dark, wet fabric on Vix's desk.

"What is that?" I rasped, standing to my feet and wobbling.

I stumbled forward, lurching towards his desk and grabbing onto the sides. Several hands reached to help me but I stepped forward quickly, gently plucking the fabric that was covered in goo from his desk.

"It was on the floor with the goo," Fynn said softly. "Why?" he asked cautiously.

"I... the well," I gasped. "It came with me." My eyes welled up and I bought the material close to my chest, staring at it with wide eyes.

This was not possible.

It couldn't be possible - because... because Time Bending was the travel between minds - there was no physical swap over. It shouldn't be possible - and yet here it was with me.

Vix spoke first. "Okay... how is that possible?" he asked.

I looked at him and shook my head dumbfounded.

"How did you get back?"

I blinked dazed. "A well... it was a sort of portal."

Vix opened his mouth to continue asking questions but Fynn stepped forward and looked at him sternly. "Let's take a moment. She needs to process - start with an easier question." Fynn stood in front of me and lowered himself so he was eye level with me. "Which life you were in? Did you see the Raven?"

I swallowed tightly and flicked my gaze back down at the material - clenching it like it might be taken from me.

"Jack," I breathed and blinked the tears away from my eyes rapidly.

Ace sighed irritated. "She clearly doesn't want to talk about it. Either give her the cure or leave her alone," Ace snapped as Vix began to pull out more equipment.

I snapped my head to the side and sneered at Ace. "1661."

He looked at me lost. He had no idea. He couldn't remember, he didn't know.

I stilled. Of course, he wouldn't remember - I hadn't bent the timeline.

But he was - he was once that person on this timeline too. It was still *him*.

"What? I was there? What happened?" Ace began to ask, stepping forward but I glared at him.

Hot panic shot up my spine and I jumped back. "Stay the hell away from me or I'll kill you again."

Fynn grabbed hold of Ace's shoulder and forced him backwards but Ace lashed out, pushing against Fynn's shoulder and working his way back to me. Two hands were placed on my shoulders and I slapped him across the face.

It was silent for a moment. Then Ace's head turned to face me and he backed away pale.

Please no more hallucinations.

"Landon?" I asked with realisation. I'd been searching the room for anything different before I finally had the feeling of something missing.

No one replied. They looked at the ground and then at each other before Halo finally broke and spoke in a monotone voice.

"We prolonged it as much as possible but eventually we were forced to pull the cord." I looked at the ground processing the information and repressing the burn in my chest.

"I did some tests. The main factors causing this were his age and the number of times he's gone into the past. It was always bound to have physiological and physical effects on your health," Vix explained, clasping his hands together.

"Why didn't you pull it on me? The entire time I was worried my mind would become unplugged and that would be it."

"I hope you understand why we couldn't find you. But we did try - until we all started to show signs of fatigue." Fynn held on to my hand and I nodded numbly wondering why he hadn't answered the real question.

"There's a cure," I stated and they nodded their heads. They meant they had a way to cure me. I didn't know how. Jack had told me only the Rebellion had created a cure and I didn't know how they'd have created a cure too... so many unanswered questions.

"We were privately contacted... well rather bribed into saving you or losing you. The Rebellion."

"Why would they do that? They wanted Jack to kill me."

"Well... we aren't entirely sure it was the Rebellion. This is why we need to know," Vix began.

"What happened? You lost your Totem we guessed, but how did you get back? What happened with the Raven?"

"Jack," I corrected Vix, clenching the material tightly in my hands.

"The Raven is really called Jack?" Ace questioned. I nodded my head, hating the sound of Jack's name on his tongue - his accent was different from Tobias' but watching his mouth move made my stomach turn.

"He's the one who gave it to us. He said we could either save your life or the Rebellion would make it their best interest to take you. We didn't understand why they needed you," Fynn said.

"I... I don't understand." I shook my head, staring at my fingers that numbly picked at the fabric.

"It's kind of obvious don't you think?" Aeron piped in, staring at the room in shock. "They were there together for god knows how long, both had lost their Totems and had no way back. Why would they have wanted to kill their only way out of there?" He looked at Ace and Fynn. "They clearly... you know... bonded? And now he wants to save her from what happened to Landon. He's probably convinced the Rebellion they could use her as a symbol against Prospect and when we refused he gave us the cure as proof." He smiled proud of himself.

"You don't understand," I replied quietly. "Jack is dead. I watched him die and he didn't have his Totem - there was no way he could have gotten back."

"He's not dead Nova." Aeron stopped in front of me with a wide smile, purple hair slightly faded and the mole above his lip twinkling at me.

"It's *impossible*," I emphasised.

"How did you get back?" Vix asked suddenly, swivelling his chair past Aeron and in front of me.

"A well in Scotland, we had to throw our Totems in and then jump in ourselves... a woman told us - you know what, it's a long story that can wait."

Vix continued. "Do you not suppose he threw his Totem in - a Raven before he died. When he did die he could have followed his Totem back?"

My eyes grew wide. I needed to be sure. But of course... He'd almost jumped in after throwing in the feather but I stopped him. Really the well would have brought his Totem back like it did mine and then he could have followed it back before his mind died with his body.

"I trust that you'll tell me everything you... you've experienced - time portals and all." Vix scratched the back of his neck. "But perhaps if... this fabric being here is possible-" His eyes lit up as he stared at the fabric between my fingertips. "Then the possibility of Jack being alive is not so far fetched after all."

Vix's words processed in my mind and I sat up straight. "Did you see him?" I asked urgently. "Is there a way I can talk to him?"

Vix's eyes grew wide as he looked at me and then reached into his pocket, handing me a tissue and pressing my hand to my nose.

"Can we trust him? Yes or no?" Vix asked urgently.

I pulled the tissue away and stared at my blood, red, alive. I nodded my head quickly. "Of course we can." I felt myself begin to shake with excitement.

Jack. He made it.

He survived the sword of Tobias, he survived his heart being ripped free from his chest and he'd flown from his cage like a Raven. Alive. He was alive.

"Well, it's this or nothing," he said wiping my arm clean and taking out a long needle.

CHAPTER 40

Time: Present
Location: Prospect

"We can't be sure - what if it was someone from the Rebellion posing as the Raven," Ace exclaimed.

Fynn rocked back on his heels, shaking his head. "Vix, we can't risk it."

I shrugged. "Sure we can. Just the other morning I planned on dying because I thought Jack was dead. If this kills me then it means Jack is really dead and someone pretended to be him, but if this cures me then he's alive and I'm going to find him."

Ace's eyes widened and he watched hurt as Vix flattened my arm against the table top beside me. I kept the material in my hand, watching it with my heart almost leaping out of my chest.

Fynn glowered at me and exclaimed. "This isn't some Romeo and Juliet crap Nova. This is serious!"

Ace stepped forward quickly. "You're the first person who will have been injected with this. They won't even know if it would work-"

Vix paused for a moment, holding the syringe at my arm. "There's a first time for everything," I replied, nodding my head at Vix to continue.

He closed his eyes, looked away and began speaking. "This won't be the first injection, you'll have to go through more before you're completely really cured. That's what I was told. We'll have to find a way to replicate this though for more. I've already taken samples-"

I nodded my head. I didn't care. "Vix, it's okay," I assured him, smiling. I'd always been his lab rat. Today would be no different, just that my life was on the line either way. He nodded his head and plunged the needle into my arm before Fynn or Ace could object.

The room seemed to fold in on itself as everyone leant forward eagerly waiting. I took my arm back, crossed my legs together and sat back.

There was a beep from Vix's monitor and he swivelled around to answer it. I watched curiously as his face turned pale and he sent an urgent look at Fynn and Cedrix. They moved to the door and began speaking under their breaths.

I raised an eyebrow. "So whilst we wait for me to die, does anyone want to tell me what's got them so panicked?" I pointed to the door.

No one spoke at first. They shared concerned looks before Halo finally stepped up to the task of telling me. Her voice was bold. "We bombed West Prospect."

They what?

"We?" I growled.

"Not technically us-" Aeron started to explain before cutting himself off exasperated. He took a deep breath and

412

continued. "Prospect leaders. Clients, the President ordering Guards to bomb-"

"What the hell? Why?"

"For one it was to break up violence-"

"Violence?"

"There's a civil war," Ace replied in a sombre voice. My eyebrows pulled together and I placed a hand on my mouth. "They framed the bombs as the property of the Rebellion - to cause fear against them."

It was silent for a moment. I processed the information by myself quietly. "And so how are we safe?"

Halo answered. "We're with Elite Power now. We work for them and in return, we're protected from the Alliance."

"What? Take it back. The Elite Power? Alliance?"

Fynn held a hand out for me and pulled me to my feet, then walked with me out the door and into the pod whilst explaining. "The Elites are the guards, the President and us. All those fighting against the Rebellion."

I nodded my head slowly. *So I was still a bad guy. Would I always be a bad guy?*

"The Alliance are more sided with the Rebellion, they fight with the other half of the city who side with the Elites," Ace explained. So it really was a civil war.

"And we're stuck with the Elites? The bad guys. We're always the bad guys."

Vix looked at me shocked, as did Fynn. "You should be more grateful," Vix said. Cedrix nodded his head in

413

agreement. Halo seemed to be somewhere in the middle unsure of where she sided so I was left to face Ace and Aeron with my mouth open in protest.

They shared a looked between them - a knowing look. A look I now saw in myself.

Whose side were they on?

"The reason we didn't pull the cord on you was partly because of the President forbidding us to. You're too important to the Elites," Aeron explained briefly, I nodded my head. For once I didn't want to be important.

"Where are we going?" I asked as Vix slid the pod doors shut and a bright light filled the glass structure as we came to the outside of the building.

But it wasn't as bright as one might have thought. I turned to face the city shocked. Grey smoke filled the air and in the distance was a view of broken-down buildings, fires and suffering. And beyond that, just in the horizon, you could finally see the white wall, which was usually covered up by white buildings.

Now it was black with ash and crumbling, it stood undefeated but damaged.

But that wasn't the worst part. The worst part was the streets below us. We were in an untouched part of the city, but that didn't mean it was fine.

Below us were crowds of people running. Guards dressed in white uniforms turned grey were forcing them away from our building and fights were breaking out from either side of us.

"What is this?" I croaked.

The doors slid open and we entered the meeting room. Except it was no longer ours. Various people were moving around, a cup in hand and screens in the other as they moved around each other.

Guards were occupying *our* screens, *our* holograms and *our* files and by the skyline window, a woman dressed in white swivelled to face me: the President.

"We're under their control now," Aeron growled under his breath and Ace stood on my other side despite me trying to stand as far away from him as possible. I hated the thought of having to tell him what he did and why I couldn't stand even breathing the same air as him.

"Assholes," Ace snapped as someone brushed past his shoulder.

Vix and Fynn led us to the President who waited patiently for us to arrive beside her.

The other 5 - no longer 6 stood back with Vix watching bored as I stood to face the President.

"Ma'am." I nodded my head politely.

"It's good to see you back on your feet. The Raven?"

A test? Did she know about the cure he'd somehow given my friends or had they kept it quiet? I placed my hand over my pocket, the fabric beating against my thigh still shocked and confused about how it was possible. I turned and faced Vix who nodded his head discreetly. "The Raven will no longer be a problem."

She narrowed her eyes and then released a long breath smiling with relief. "Good. Then we can move on to our next movement, our last, hopefully."

I clasped my hands together and looked back at my friends. Ace and Aeron stood together with their heads focused on the tragedy outside.

"Take out the Rebellion. Cut them down, go back and erase everything."

My head snapped round to face her in shock. "What?" I found it came out more of a yell than a question. "No," I growled more quietly.

"I think you'll find you'll do as I say," she said under her breath, I shook my head again.

"That is too high of a risk - we'd be erasing thousands. Changing everything."

"No?" The President laughed. "The Rebellion has been around for hundreds of years. They developed from a discreet group of people. But we never cut down their roots," she sneered. "They are a weed that needs to be destroyed. An evil cult that has caused panic and destruction."

"*You've* caused panic and destruction," I snapped. She sounded insane and I briefly remembered Jack telling me that the rebellion was part of the old world. I didn't know what to believe. *Definitely not this whack job.*

She raised her eyebrows with a glare and turned to face the window, examining the terror she'd caused.

"Do you want to survive this?"

"I don't understand," I replied. It wasn't the Rebellion causing all this; it was her. Why was she so determined to erase a small group of people and completely change the entire world?

"You wouldn't even know what's happened. I could wipe out the entire city from existence if I don't even know how it began. How did this shitty Dystopian-"

"We've done the hard work. You won't be erasing enough to change anything too drastic," she laughed. "Look around. I have a team of incredibly clever and devoted people. We have worked out every possible outcome over the last year. And the Rebellion no longer has a Raven to stop us from killing the ones who matter the most."

"How many exactly?"

"Only seven. Spread out through time." *Only seven.*

"And how will people in the past have any kind of effect on the Rebellion?"

She glared at me. "That won't concern you. You can trust me though. If I were to give you any drastic task I'd put everything I have at risk and I can assure you I love my job," she continued. "And now we know you can spend longer in the past, you'll have time to find our individuals and do as we say."

"I can't stay more than two days though... I lose my Totem." *Did she know anything?* She certainly didn't care for my health like she let on.

"Then we'll fix it," she replied brightly.

I nodded my head numbly. "I suppose I don't have a choice."

"I'm trusting that you'll be able to do this. A final task with a grand sum of money."

"Final?"

"We'll release you with enough money for a lifetime." I wondered if there would be a life for me to go back to after this. "It's come to my understanding that Time Bending has had drastic effects on your health. We wouldn't like to risk losing our most prized possession."

I felt hot rage surge through my veins and I plastered a smile. "Thank you." *Possession*, it's all I'd ever been.

"We'll have a team of specialists working on some form of treatment in the meantime," she continued. I nodded my head as she turned to face me with an innocent smile.

"Right well, we'll send you the details." She said it as though we weren't living in the same building. Our home had been taken over by her workers, her friends - my clients. The Elites.

I bowed my head and backed away from her before swivelling to face my friends. My jaw clenched and my fists balled together tightly as I fought every nerve telling me to turn and kill her with my bare hands.

Fynn smiled, wrapping an arm around my shoulders. "We're almost done with this life, don't you see?"

No I didn't.

I was ashamed - so ashamed. I'd spent months in the past only for me to come out the same person I'd been. It was a part of my identity. But it didn't have to be.

"How did this happen?" I breathed. Aeron came from behind me and tilted his mouth to my ear.

"Someone - one of us from the future told her."

"Who?" I snapped.

"I don't know. I can't imagine any of us doing it."

It seemed an awful lot like something I would do if I were being honest. Still, I shook that feeling from me, not wanting to even *risk* planting the seed of thought in my mind.

I caught Ace's eye and clenched my jaw as Aeron held him back from cutting through the stream of people working and making his way towards me. They didn't want this, I realised.

I didn't know how or when they'd realised what we were doing was wrong and I was surprised that out of all of us, the two people who loved Prospect life the most, no longer wanted it. You could see it written all over their faces.

But they wouldn't see it on mine.

I would do as she told me. I'd plaster a smile and find a way to show change without actually doing anything.

I clutched the fabric. I'd find Jack. If he was alive then it meant we'd still be connected somehow. I would find him. I knew I would because Jamie told me so.

I didn't have to be cold and uncaring, materialistic and evil. I could be who I wanted to be: I could be all of my lives. I could be selfless like Marion, free like Daisy, moral like Lucy, intelligent like Nicki and I would save the world instead of ruin it for once. I was going to be one *badass* Nova (minus the bad part). Even if it meant taking down an entire city...

Which seemed like a pretty solid option.

THE STUFF AT THE BACK OF THE BOOK

Right, buckle up for some shameless self-promo and a large thank you to everyone who finished reading NOVA. Nova and the whole concept of Time Bending has consumed me for years now so I'm beyond curious to hear your thoughts: who was your favourite character? What parts did you like - even better, what parts did you laugh at?

Follow me on Instagram @bellesxbooks for updates on Book 2 of the Time Bender Series and DM me! I want to chat! Or if that isn't your thing but you enjoyed the book and made it this far please leave a review! I love feedback and it would help massively if you recommended it to someone you know. Let's build a fandom!

WHERE YOU CAN FIND ME:

https://www.instagram.com/bellesxbooks/
https://twitter.com/IsabelleChampi7

If you still need more I've also created some Spotify playlists on Isabelle_ with songs that remind me of the series:

https://open.spotify.com/user/m7pt4bk0mkrs8mxopnui65j
dq?si=paJIN0HTQCC_li7fncYVjw

Now all the begging for you to follow me is over I want to thank you for reading and everyone who has supported me thus far through the series! You'll see more of Nova very soon! In fact... you'll see her in the next page of the first chapter of RAVEN.

Is it really that easy to change over night?

The answer is no.

FIND OUT MORE IN THE SECOND BOOK OF THE TIME BENDER SERIES:

RAVEN

COMING SOON

(But until then, here's Chapter 1)

CHAPTER 1

Time: 13th January 2018
Location: Paris, France.

Right.

How long did you think that would last? *Oh! I'm Nova! I'm going to change! I'll save the world instead of ruin it!* Christ - I mean have you ever heard more dramatic bull crap in your life? If you really thought this was going to be some kind of beautiful character arc about the journey of me growing to be a better human, then I think I'm not the only one who made a mistake.

I mean - I went *backwards*. And that's saying a lot because I've done some seriously screwed up stuff. So the whole '*Let's save the world and find Jack!*' attitude died pretty quick - so quick it'd give you whiplash.

Speaking of whiplash… How about I take you back to before shit hit the fan (the first time) and I was getting my ass handed to me by a bin lorry.

In my defence, the streets of Paris in 2018 were a little bit of a shock to the old system.

"Jesus Nova! Are you trying to get yourself killed?" Halo shrieked, accidentally slipping into English as she pulled me away from the speeding lorry.

My head flew backwards and I stumbled back onto the wet pavement. This was too much for someone who hadn't even stepped out of her room in the future. I hadn't been outside since 1661 and trust me - this was incredibly different.

For one the air smelt of cigarettes, petrol and wet pavements; the clouds were grey and there was the distant sound of sirens that echoed in my head.

"You need your head focused on the mission," Halo continued and I stared at my trainers embarrassed. *Yes, think of the mission - the mission you plan on stopping. Focus on making sure the mission fails - shouldn't be hard.*

You see, after being stuck in the past for 4 months with a handsome rebel from the future I'd learnt a lot. For example, crapping in bushes 5 feet away from the said handsome stranger was incredibly uncomfortable. Not to mention peeing in the wild is much harder for girls - what's up with that? Oh and I suppose I'd learnt a lot about what not to do that would change the future. For example: maybe don't set an entire village's winter supplies on fire. Oh and whilst you're at it, try to refrain from causing a prisoner uprising.

Likewise, think twice before eating any kind of wild mushrooms or berries (I learnt that the hard way... or good way).

But hey that's not all I'd learnt on 'Summer Camp: 1661 edition'. I suppose I'd learnt some pretty valuable lessons on Time Bending as well. I'd discovered we weren't the only ones with this... gift of travelling into past lives and bending time to change the future. There were others - Reincarnations who were brothers and sisters of ours who seemed to know everything.

Speaking of which: my reincarnated sister O was also my sister in this life. But on my way to meeting Halo I hadn't come across her, which was disappointing. I was hoping for some answers about Jack. How would I find him? Why couldn't I see his Totem? Was he even alive? Perhaps more importantly - how was it possible that the fabric of his cloak followed me to the future? I didn't want to think about that though - not if I wanted to keep the target alive.

They'd taken it from me - to study it.

I clenched my fists, standing still and breathing heavily.

"What the hell is wrong with you?" Halo hissed, grabbing my arm and pulling me further down the street. I shrugged her off and glared at her. Halo's dark wild hair was hanging freely over her shoulders and she was decked out in black. Standing next to her I looked like a child, well technically I was. I was only sixteen in this life and she looked like she was in her mid-thirties.

"There's a list of things wrong with me at the moment," I grumbled, shaking my head and stumbling after her.

I was taken aback when her gaze softened slightly but then she scowled at me again. "He should be sitting at his

427

desk by 8:30. I've already booked an appointment in advance."

"You'll make it fine right?" I asked.

"We have two days. I've only been here since last night. Stop acting so paranoid." Halo rolled her eyes and strutted her way down the street.

I clenched my teeth together and refrained from tripping her up. "I'm surprised you're even allowed on this mission, wouldn't Time Bending affect the baby?"

"Yeah, can't say I'm not surprised that the President dragged me out of constant examinations on it to make me go on a mission that her favourite Time Bender could have done alone-" she turned her head towards me. "Oh wait. Never mind, you need me here to save you from getting run over."

Not true. The mission would be easy if I wanted to complete it - but I didn't. And Vix probably sensed it so convinced the President to allow Halo to come. I wasn't going to say that though - even if I suspected Halo had her own doubts about the mission.

If you don't remember what I'm talking about: this was one of seven missions the President had instructed us to complete to wipe out the rebellion. I know, it was insane - wiping out an entire society of people with just seven people randomly spread through time? And trust me they were random. 2018 was miles away from the present time - heck I think they wanted me to go to the 1800s at some point.

It didn't make sense (well yet at least but I'm not about to hand out spoilers for free).

How did the President know that these were the exact people who needed to be taken out - you might ask? Well someone from the future told her.

Anyway, enough about all that. I'll keep the interruptions to a minimum. Sound fair?

Insert dreamlike sounds and ripple of the picture back to 2018:

"So when's the baby due?" I attempted to make conversation as we carried on walking through the crowded Paris streets of tourists arriving at their hotels early in the morning with bleary eyes and suitcases and other people on their way to work.

Halo didn't turn her head to me when she answered. "Does it matter? The baby's going to die as usual and then shit will hit the fan for me..." Her voice trailed off and her breath got stuck in her throat as she realised she'd let one slip.

But not really. I already knew what secret she'd let slip and it wasn't about the fact all Time Bender's children die.

You see, I was a nosy bitch and one day read all her logs trying to find some dirt to bully Halo with (this was a long time ago).

I found out her recurring theme in all her lives and it wasn't pretty. Whereas all my mothers tried to kill me - Halo's recurring theme was that she went insane -

specifically after giving birth to a faulty half human half Time Bender.

Our reoccurring themes were something we never spoke about and only Vix studied in private. No one knew why they were always random and no one knew why they kept happening. Just like no one knew why we existed.

I turned away from Halo and pretended I hadn't heard the last part. Yeah, it was definitely bullying worth material, hello? Think of all the psycho, insane jokes I could make up for her. But still, something had stopped me in the past from teasing her, and I wasn't going to now.

Instead, I took a completely unnatural Nova approach and made an attempt to comfort her. "Maybe it will be different between two Time Benders, we don't know-"

"Jesus Nova stop talking," she snapped, crossing the road suddenly and stopping on the pavement.

Why did I bother?

Despite her being years older than me in this life I still towered over her. "What the hell happened to you? You never spoke to me unless it was to tell me I was doing something wrong, or to call me a slut. But now you suddenly want to become buddies?"

She flicked her hair over her shoulder and began walking again but I snapped a hold of her wrist and lowered my face to hers. "I might have gained some morals. - but not enough to stop me from killing you."

I tried?

We walked the rest of the way in a tense silence that only grew stronger when Halo practically shoved me through a glass door and we stepped into a tight, air-conditioned building with marble floors and barred windows. Cosy. Halo made her way over to the desk where a woman sat tapping away at a keyboard with red fingernails. Halo leant over the desk and smiled warmly. "I have an appointment with Mr Holmes."

The woman looked up from her computer and glanced at me as Halo continued, "this is my daughter."

"She'll have to stay here."

I scowled at Halo who turned to me smugly. "Go sit over there, darling."

I looked at an old man holding a magazine and sat next to him tapping my feet anxiously as Halo began filling out a form. When she finally walked through double doors and up a white staircase I grew anxious.

What was I supposed to do? I was meant to *not* complete the mission and Halo was in the way.

Soon enough my question was answered when the fire alarm began ringing and the woman at the desk rose to her feet with a tired sigh and strutted out of the building, barely sending us a glance. I couldn't stop the smile that crawled its way to my face. I bet Halo hadn't accounted for the man pulling the fire alarm. She was probably panicking like a headless chicken right now.

I made my way over to the double doors Halo had gone through and spared a glance at the old man who appeared as though he hadn't even heard the blaring alarm but then he stood with a sigh and made his way out the front turning his head to face me and raising a bushy grey eyebrow. I shrugged helplessly and gestured to the doors my 'mother' had gone through.

As soon as I saw the glass door close behind him I crashed through the doors Halo had gone through and into a long stretched hallway. Holy crap it was loud. My head began to feel dizzy from the blaring alarm - I was still extremely sensitive to loud noises after spending time in the peaceful countryside of England in 1661. Or perhaps it was because of the constant injections Vix had been giving me, you know, so travelling into 200 and however many past lives didn't kill me - mundane things really.

There was a crash in the room to my left and when I flung the door open two startled faces met my own and looked down at the table on the floor. Halo had a gun pointed to a man's chest whilst he had a gun pointed at her. He wasn't very old and appeared quite dad-like actually.

"Who the hell are you?" he spoke in English.

"Nova," Halo snapped to me looking down at a small handgun by my feet.

"No time for this kiddos," I breathed. "Police are downstairs," I lied but hey ho it worked temporarily. We skedaddled out of there by jumping out the window onto a metal ladder. "No bending okay? It was like this never happened?" I snapped.

Halo looked like she wanted to say something else but I split ways with her before she could say anything, quickly following my Totem and forcing myself to drift away from that timeline - not taking it with me as I found my own timeline.

You see, there was a difference between travelling to a past life and then Time Bending. How about we just do a small recap on what it is. Everybody, no talking, hands on the table and listen to me carefully.

When I went to 2018, I had to go to a different timeline, understand? Remember that thing about there being parallel timelines all with different presents – and there were millions – a timeline for each second of the universe let's say.

I can visit these beautiful timelines, choosing whichever timeline suits my needs – providing I had a life there and my Totem was there.

But if I wanted to change my own timeline (the timeline of my present) I'd have to make the changes on another timeline and intertwine it with my own by bending them together. This happens naturally. To get back to my own timeline (or own present) I have to cross the timelines over, essentially bending them together.

And that's Time Bending.

But for special instances, it is possible to go against this universal rule and not bend the timelines. For example, although it took a lot of energy to resist in 1661 – I did not bend that timeline with my own.

Because think about it? All those conversations with strangers... the British army chasing me, Tobias, the Count – I'd done so much in that timeline.

So why had I cared so much about preserving that life, why didn't I just break all the rules? Well, just because it's not my timeline – doesn't mean it's not someone else's. Us Time Benders like to keep every timeline neat and simple – we don't need to screw things up for anyone else. I mean, could you imagine if we exposed ourselves before our own timeline? What if one of us from that timeline bent their timeline with ours – I didn't even want to think about it.

Sorry, I'm getting off track.

In simplified terms: I'm able to not change my own timeline with this mistake.

Whilst it took more energy after 1661, this time it didn't take a lot of energy since my Time Bender abilities or 'power' had grown stronger. I put it down to the antidote the mystery person claiming to be Jack had given us. Now my Totem practically blinded me with its blue light.

The worst part about the new way of coming back was the electrical impulses that hit my body in waves of blue goo. Thankfully Vix had found a way of getting me out safely without smashing the glass and had fixed a door above the tank that displayed me as if I were some naked goldfish. I didn't see why that was necessary especially now that the Presidents workers had invaded the room and my privacy. I'm no prude but there are some limits.

Don't ask me why they were here or what the purpose of putting me in a fish tank and electrocuting me was because I had no idea. Not to mention the fact I had no way of breathing for hours - sometimes days that I was gone. Magic.

Science was magic or was it magic that was science?

Either way lying down and closing my eyes with a blindfold always seemed to work for me.

But then again, that way had also almost killed me.

I was still new to this.

Well - we all were.

The numbness gradually left and I realised I was back in my body when my eyes opened. Through the blue jelly I could see people with their heads down at computers and others moving busily around.

Before I knew it two hands had grabbed my shoulders and pulled me out of the goo as if I were nothing but a rag doll. I lay on the cool metal above the tank taking long breaths and wiping the blue goo away from my eyes.

When I could finally breathe and felt my legs go back to normal I knelt on my knees and stared at the two guards looking down at me as though they'd never seen a naked woman before - and they hadn't because for guards it was forbidden.

"Take a picture, it'll last longer," I panted, cringing at how overused the line was despite how relevant it was.

Then I raised my head to look at the two men who turned their heads to each other puzzled. "That was a joke, asswipe."

Vix's voice flooded my senses. "You were gone a while, don't worry Halo already told us everything."

Ah crap, what had she said? Vix climbed up a set of metal stairs behind a door in his room that had been invaded. He wrapped a towel around me and I clambered to my feet with the support of his arm.

"Is the blue crap necessary? The others don't have to have it, I just look like a Smurf." I sneered at the blue gunk.

"It's more effective in helping you back. The others have their own pods that help us get them back." *Ugh not this again.* The first time I'd asked why I was in a tub and why I was able to survive Vix had launched into this whole scientific explanation that I hadn't understood a word of.

I yawned as Vix continued, "-this is by far the most effective method especially as it enables us to look into your mind."

My body froze and I stopped on a step, Vix turned to face me by the door expectantly. "Not literally." He rolled his eyes. "It's new technology friends from a different city told us."

"City? I thought most cities left were either less developed or destroyed?" I asked, catching up to him and wrapping the towel further around me.

"Here." He led me into a narrow corridor behind the lab and to a white shower cubicle lit up by blue strip lights. As I showered he gave a brief explanation to his words.

"No, we're currently second in development, Pleeno city used to be named uh... what was it? Seoul I think – formerly part of South Korea."

I raised an eyebrow. "Is Korea still divided?"

"Well, they no longer address it as North and South now," he explained. "So I suppose they didn't last – I think there was a war and the South won." But like everything else – no one here knew what had entirely happened with the rest of the world – let alone our own city.

"But the city only addresses itself as Pleeno."

What did a name matter? The place had a history that couldn't be removed - the name only kept the past alive which didn't really matter when there were Time Benders. Vix had a lot to say about *that*. Apparently, more Time Benders had been found. The new Seoul - *Pleeno* had 7 Time Benders and we were down by a Landon.

I stepped out of the shower and accepted the clothes and clean towel Vix handed towards me with his eyes cast to the floor. "There's more," he said – his voice was tight.

"About Pleeno?"

"We made a trade whilst you were away."

I hated the use of 'we'. He must have hated how people were taking over his equipment, working in his space - taking over his job and yet it had become 'we'. As if he had a say in any of the decisions made here now.

"How long was I?" I lowered my eyebrows and quickly dried off back in the cubicle, I put the t-shirt on the hook and pulled on some undies and jeans. It was weird to be in jeans again, part of me missed the long princess dresses despite how impractical they were.

"Only about two days."

"Well, what was the trade?" I asked nonchalantly.

"We traded for another Time Bender with a life in the correct period and location the Prospect leaders wanted."

An ice-cold hand felt as though it crept up my back and I held my breath fearing the worst. Hot anger crept through my veins and I slid the door open in just jeans and my bra.

"What did you trade, Vix?" I spoke slowly, as though I was talking to a child who'd just done something they shouldn't have.

"Cedrix."

Printed in Great Britain
by Amazon